Chapter 1: A Sli

The sun hung low in the sky, casting a warm golden glow through the small window, illuminating the chaos that was my kitchen. Flour dust danced like tiny fairies in the light, swirling around mixing bowls and cake pans that had seen better days. I could almost hear my mother's laughter, a melodic sound that used to fill this very space, as I poured batter into a pan, its rich aroma mixing with the sweetness of the vanilla. Baking had always been our sanctuary, a place where time paused, allowing us to lose ourselves in creativity and frosting. Now, it felt like the battleground of my insecurities.

I pulled out my notebook, pages filled with sketches and scribbles that represented not just cakes, but dreams and aspirations—each doodle a slice of my heart. The latest design I was working on was a three-tiered masterpiece adorned with delicate sugar flowers, each petal crafted with painstaking detail. I had spent countless hours perfecting the recipe, hoping to transform my vision into something that would make brides swoon. Yet, as I stared at the notes, a wave of doubt washed over me. What if Elara hated it? What if my effort crumbled like a poorly baked soufflé?

The doorbell rang, echoing through the quiet moments of my thoughts, and I jolted upright, spilling flour across the counter. "Well, that's one way to make an impression," I muttered to myself, brushing my hands against my apron as I wiped the remnants of my earlier stress off my brow.

I opened the door to reveal Elara, her presence both intimidating and dazzling. She stood there with her hair cascading down her back like a waterfall, a perfectly tailored blazer accentuating her frame. She had an air about her, a mix of authority and artistry that instantly demanded respect. I could see why she was revered in the wedding planning world. Her eyes sparkled with excitement, as if she were on the cusp of unveiling a grand secret, yet I could also detect a sharpness in her gaze that suggested she wouldn't hesitate to cut through any nonsense.

"Hello, darling! You must be the cake artist I've heard so much about," she exclaimed, her voice smooth like velvet. The compliment washed over me, but beneath it lurked an undercurrent of expectation.

"Uh, yes! That would be me," I replied, stumbling slightly over my words. "Welcome to my humble abode." I gestured to the kitchen, the flour-covered surfaces an unfortunate testament to my nervous energy. "It's a bit... chaotic right now."

"Chaos is the creative process," she replied with a dismissive wave of her hand. "Let's see what magic you can conjure for my clients."

We settled at my small kitchen table, strewn with sketches and inspiration boards. As I laid out my ideas, I could feel the tension thickening the air, like the humidity before a summer storm. With every design I presented, I watched her reactions closely. The way her eyebrows furrowed or her lips curled into a smile felt like a litmus test for my talent.

"Okay, this one," she said, pointing to a sketch of a cascading floral arrangement. "This could work, but I'm thinking more drama. We want something that will leave guests breathless, like the first view of the ocean after a long flight."

"Right, more drama," I echoed, scribbling notes furiously. I could sense the wheels turning in her mind, but I also felt the weight of the challenge settling on my shoulders. "I could add gold accents—maybe a drip effect with a chocolate ganache?"

"Perfect! But let's skip the gold. It's been done to death. What about a deep blue instead? Something unexpected?"

Her suggestion struck a chord in me, igniting a spark of inspiration. Deep blue, paired with white blooms that looked like they were kissed by frost, could be exquisite. I felt the pulse of creativity rush through me, and my confidence began to surge. "That could be stunning! I can see it now—a midnight sky on a cake."

"Exactly! I want this cake to tell a story—your story, not just another Pinterest replica."

I nodded, buoyed by her enthusiasm, but I also felt a wave of pressure crash down. This cake was not just for any bride; it would be a piece of art, a reflection of their love story. I couldn't shake the thought of my mother standing beside me, her soft voice whispering encouragement in moments like this. She had always believed in the power of storytelling through food, how each bite could evoke memories and emotions.

"So, when do you think you could have a prototype ready?" Elara asked, her eyes narrowing slightly as if assessing my capacity for brilliance.

I took a deep breath, the air thick with anticipation. "I can have a sample ready in two weeks. That should give me time to perfect it, and we can schedule a tasting."

"Two weeks it is. I'll be counting on you, and I promise I won't go easy on you," she replied with a sly grin that made me wonder just how many aspiring bakers had faltered under her watch.

As she left, I felt a mix of exhilaration and anxiety. The clock was ticking, and this was my chance to prove myself, not just to Elara, but to the ghosts of my past who lingered in the corners of my kitchen, pushing me to be better. I turned back to my sketches, the shadows of doubt starting to lift. Maybe this time, I would rise to the occasion, just like my cakes in the oven, slowly but surely becoming something extraordinary.

The kitchen was a battleground of flour and frosting, but today it buzzed with an energy that pushed the anxiety to the background, if only for a moment. After Elara's departure, my mind raced with ideas, each one blooming like the sugar flowers I practiced daily. I pulled out my mixer, the familiar hum soothing my frayed nerves.

With each ingredient I measured, I envisioned the cake taking shape—a cascade of layers crowned with those deep blue petals glistening like raindrops under the sun.

"Focus, focus," I chanted softly to myself, stirring the batter with fervor. "No more disasters. Just perfection."

The mixer whirred to life, drowning out my thoughts, and I let myself get lost in the rhythmic motion. The world outside faded as the smell of baking began to wrap around me, a comforting embrace in this whirlwind of expectations. I imagined the cake as a conversation piece, the centerpiece at a wedding where laughter filled the air, and love stories were celebrated in every bite. My heart quickened at the thought, a warmth blooming in my chest that pushed away the shadows of doubt.

After the batter was perfectly mixed, I poured it into the prepared pans, smoothing the top like I was tucking a child into bed. "You're going to be beautiful," I whispered, patting the sides affectionately. I slid them into the oven, and as the heat enveloped them, I felt a sense of anticipation begin to swirl, almost tangible in the air.

A knock at the door interrupted my thoughts, startling me. My heart raced, half-expecting Elara to have returned, ready to critique my every move. Instead, it was Sam, my neighbor and an old friend who had seen me through countless baking trials and tribulations. He leaned against the doorframe, a lazy smile gracing his lips as he took in the floury scene.

"Baking again, I see. Are you expecting another wedding invite, or just practicing to impress the next unsuspecting guest?"

"Ha-ha. Very funny," I shot back, wiping my hands on my apron. "I have a meeting with a wedding planner later. This cake is going to be the talk of the town."

His brow raised in mock disbelief. "Isn't that what you said about the last one? The one that collapsed under the weight of its own ambition?"

I groaned, the memory still fresh. It had been a beautiful cake, layered with the best intentions, but gravity had no sympathy for a baker's dreams. "That was a fluke! This time, I'm determined to make it work."

"Determination is great and all, but I'm here for quality control." He stepped inside, his playful demeanor replacing my anxious thoughts. "So, what's the flavor profile? I assume it's not just another vanilla-almond snooze fest?"

"It's actually a rich chocolate cake with a hint of espresso, layered with a raspberry cream filling," I explained, a smile creeping onto my face as I described my creation.

"Now that sounds decadent. But let me guess, you're planning to decorate it with flowers that probably cost more than my rent?"

"Please, that's the kind of negativity I can't afford right now," I shot back, rolling my eyes. "These flowers are hand-crafted sugar petals! They're like edible jewels. And besides, you should know by now that good cake requires a little extravagance."

"True, true," he conceded with a laugh. "But I still think we should incorporate some chaos—maybe some wild sprinkles or edible glitter? You know, really spice things up!"

"Sprinkles? This isn't a five-year-old's birthday party," I countered, the laughter bubbling up between us. "I'm aiming for elegance, not a carnival."

"Elegance can be fun too, you know." He leaned against the counter, eyeing the mixing bowls with a hint of mischief. "But if you want to keep your sanity, you need to stop setting the bar so high. You're not a one-woman bakery empire, despite what you might think."

"Tell that to my ambition," I retorted, crossing my arms defiantly. "It's like a needy toddler—always demanding more attention."

"Alright, wise baker. Just remember, no cake is worth losing your mind over." His tone softened, a genuine concern hiding behind the humor. "You know I'm always here to help. You've got this."

As I nodded, the warmth of his support seeped into my heart, easing some of the tightness that had settled there. We continued to chat about everything and nothing, the conversation flowing like a favorite recipe, adding spices of laughter and camaraderie.

When the timer on the oven chimed, the sweet sound filled the kitchen, signaling the moment of truth. I rushed to the oven, opening it to a wave of warm air infused with chocolate, the scent wrapping around me like a hug. The cakes had risen perfectly, golden-brown tops promising moist layers underneath.

"Look at that! You're a miracle worker!" Sam exclaimed, peering over my shoulder.

"It's just the beginning," I replied, trying to keep my excitement in check. "The real test comes with the frosting and the decorations."

"I'll take your word for it. But first, how about we celebrate this victory with a slice of that?" He pointed eagerly at the cooling cake, his eyes lighting up like a child at a candy store.

I chuckled, shaking my head. "You realize that I'm not slicing this until it's a finished masterpiece, right? It's not a free-for-all!"

"Fine, fine, but when you win awards for this beauty, remember who was here to support you through the chaos," he said, raising his hands in mock surrender.

"Deal. But you'll have to pay with taste tests for the next month."

As we both laughed, I felt an unfamiliar sense of clarity settling over me. Maybe I could balance ambition with a touch of levity. Perhaps in the pursuit of my dreams, I could invite laughter and joy rather than drowning in pressure. With the sun setting outside, casting a soft glow over the countertops, I found renewed energy in the kitchen, determined to transform this cake into something not just beautiful, but memorable. Just like every great love story, it was all about embracing the journey, sprinkles and all.

The cake cooled on the counter, its presence a silent affirmation of my progress. I glanced at Sam, who was rummaging through my pantry like a raccoon searching for a midnight snack. "You know, not everything in here is edible, right?" I quipped, watching him pull out a jar of sprinkles.

"Hey, I have to ensure that your pantry is up to snuff. A chef's tools are only as good as what's in their toolbox!" He popped a handful of colorful sprinkles into his mouth, his expression turning into one of delight. "Okay, maybe some of this is acceptable for a touch of whimsy. You should consider it—an unexpected twist!"

"Twists are for stories, not cakes," I replied, trying to keep my voice serious despite the laugh bubbling up. "But who knows, maybe you've inspired a new trend: edible confetti for weddings."

"Now you're talking!" He leaned against the counter, his eyes dancing with mischief. "Just think of the marketing campaign: 'Make every day a celebration—one sprinkle at a time!'"

"Sam, you would be the one to turn cake into a sales pitch." I shook my head, grinning. "But in all seriousness, I think I want this to feel like an intimate moment rather than a party. I want people to savor it, not just toss sprinkles on it and call it a day."

"Intimate and elegant, huh? That's you to a T." He leaned in closer, lowering his voice as if sharing a secret. "But you know what will really add that touch of intimacy? A signature flavor. Something that tells a story. Like a childhood memory or a romantic night under the stars."

The way he looked at me made my heart skip a beat, as if he were seeing through to my very soul. I pondered for a moment, reflecting on flavors that spoke to my heart. "What about a hint of lavender?"

I suggested. "My mother loved lavender-infused desserts. It always reminded me of spring."

Sam's eyes lit up. "Lavender! Now that's unexpected. It's like a secret whisper in a loud room."

We continued brainstorming flavors and designs, throwing ideas back and forth like a playful game of catch. The energy between us buzzed, and as we talked, the weight of my worries seemed to lighten. It was as if, in this chaotic kitchen, we were creating something bigger than just a cake; we were weaving a tapestry of shared moments and hopes.

As the sun dipped below the horizon, painting the sky in hues of pink and orange, I moved to start prepping my frosting. Buttercream was my canvas, and I intended to make it as rich and decadent as the chocolate cake it would adorn. The soft clinking of utensils filled the room as I measured sugar and butter, each scoop accompanied by Sam's jovial banter, which transformed the otherwise mundane task into a lively dance of creativity.

But just as I reached for the vanilla extract, a loud thud reverberated from outside, shaking me from my thoughts. I paused, exchanging a look with Sam, who had gone still, his playful demeanor vanishing in an instant.

"What was that?" I asked, my heart racing.

"Not sure. Probably just the wind," he replied, although his voice had taken on a cautious edge.

I turned back toward the window, peering out into the dusky twilight. The street was empty, the evening air heavy with a creeping sense of unease. I shook my head, trying to brush it off. "It's probably nothing," I insisted, attempting to convince myself as much as him.

"Maybe we should check it out," Sam suggested, his tone now more serious. "Just to be sure."

"Check what out? It's probably just a stray cat or—"

Another loud crash interrupted me, this time followed by the unmistakable sound of shattering glass. "Okay, that was definitely not a cat," I said, my heart pounding like a drum.

"Stay here," Sam commanded, his protective instincts kicking in as he moved toward the door.

"Like hell! I'm not sitting here while something is going on out there. If something's broken, I want to know what it is!"

With a shared look that conveyed our mutual determination, we stepped out into the cool evening air. The world around us felt different, charged with an unspoken tension. The shadows deepened, stretching across the yard, as if waiting for something to happen.

We rounded the corner of the house, and there it was—a large trash can had toppled over in the wind, its contents strewn across the sidewalk, but that wasn't what had caught my attention. No, it was the figure standing in the shadows at the end of the street, a silhouette barely discernible against the fading light. My breath hitched, my heart racing as I squinted to get a better look.

"Sam, do you see that?" I whispered, pointing.

"Yeah, I do," he replied, his tone low and steady, yet there was a flicker of worry in his eyes. "What do you think they want?"

Before I could respond, the figure stepped forward, illuminated by the faint glow of the streetlight. My heart dropped. It was Elara, but there was something unsettling about her demeanor. She stood rigid, her eyes locked onto mine, an intensity behind them that felt almost predatory.

"I need to talk to you," she said, her voice steady yet laced with urgency.

"What's going on?" I asked, trying to maintain my composure.

Elara took a step closer, her gaze darting to Sam before settling back on me. "It's about the cake. There's something you need to know."

And just like that, my entire world shifted on its axis, the delicious sweetness of my cake dreams threatened by an unknown force lurking in the shadows. What could possibly be so important that it demanded her presence at my doorstep? The night had transformed from whimsical to menacing in an instant, leaving me hanging on the precipice of a revelation I wasn't sure I was ready to face.

Chapter 2: The Unexpected Encounter

Elara's laughter echoed through the sunlit room, a vibrant melody that danced alongside the soft strains of classical music playing in the background. Her fiery red hair caught the light, creating an aura around her that made her look almost ethereal. She leaned forward, her eyes sparkling with excitement as she shared her vision of a wedding that was as much a fairytale as it was a celebration. Each detail she painted—a lush garden adorned with twinkling lights, the scent of fresh peonies wafting through the air, a cake that towered like a castle—made my heart flutter with delight. She had this infectious way of making every moment feel significant, as if the very act of planning a wedding was akin to crafting magic.

I sat across from her, fingers fidgeting with the edge of my notepad, where I had sketched out my ideas for her floral arrangements. As much as I thrived in my role as a florist, I couldn't help but feel a pang of envy mixed with admiration. Elara embodied everything I had ever wanted—a whirlwind of ambition and joy, unfazed by the pressures of life. In contrast, my own journey as a solo business owner often felt like I was trudging through a dense fog, each day an uphill battle where I grappled with the weight of uncertainty. But in this moment, with Elara's enthusiasm washing over me, I felt a flicker of hope igniting within me.

"And what about you?" she asked, tilting her head slightly, her red curls cascading like a waterfall. "What's your dream?"

The question hung in the air, charged with vulnerability. I hesitated, unsure of how much to reveal. "Honestly? I want my floral business to flourish," I replied, my voice quieter than I intended. "But I often feel like I'm fighting an uphill battle. It's hard to break through the noise, you know?"

Elara's expression shifted from joy to understanding, her smile softening as if she could sense the weight behind my words. "I get that," she said, leaning back in her chair. "But you have to believe in your vision. I mean, look at me! I'm determined to have my wedding reflect who I am, not just some cookie-cutter idea. You can do the same with your business."

Her words resonated deeply, igniting a spark of determination I hadn't felt in a long time. But just as I was about to share my grandest idea for a new floral line, a loud crash shattered the moment. The sound reverberated from the adjoining room, startling both of us into silence. Elara's eyes widened in surprise, a mixture of amusement and concern flickering across her face.

"What was that?" she asked, biting back a giggle.

Before I could respond, the door swung open, and a tall man stepped into the room. He had tousled dark hair that seemed to defy gravity and a sheepish grin that instantly softened his rugged features. He was a striking contrast to Elara—where she radiated warmth, he exuded a cool confidence, as if he had just stepped off a magazine cover.

"Sorry about that," he said, his voice deep and warm, the kind that could wrap around you like a cozy blanket. "I thought I could carry the boxes in one trip." He gestured to a pile of boxes teetering precariously in his arms, one threatening to tumble at any moment.

Elara burst into laughter, her joy infectious. "Max! You know better than to try and carry everything at once!"

Max shrugged, a playful glint in his eyes as he carefully set the boxes down. "What can I say? I live for the thrill of nearly breaking my neck." He turned to me then, his gaze sharp and assessing. "And who's this?"

"This is my florist, who's helping with my wedding," Elara replied, her voice bubbling with excitement. "Her name is Lily, and she's incredible."

I could feel my cheeks heating under Max's scrutiny, an unexpected thrill zipping through me. "Nice to meet you, Max," I said, trying to sound casual despite the fluttering in my stomach.

"Nice to meet you too, Lily." He stepped closer, a teasing smile playing on his lips. "So, how's the wedding planning going? I hope my sister isn't driving you insane yet."

I chuckled, feeling an instant rapport. "Insane? Not at all. Just trying to keep up with her whirlwind of ideas."

"Good luck with that," he said, his tone light yet sincere. "I think she's aiming for a wedding that would make even Disney jealous."

Elara shot him a playful glare. "Hey! I have standards."

Max raised his hands in mock surrender, laughter dancing in his eyes. "I'm just saying, you're not exactly aiming for a backyard BBQ here."

The playful banter flowed effortlessly between us, igniting a spark that felt both thrilling and alarming. As we exchanged teasing remarks, the air around us buzzed with an unexpected tension, one that hinted at something more profound lurking beneath the surface. I couldn't quite place it, but the connection felt palpable, charged with potential and possibility.

"You should come help us with the wedding prep," Elara suggested, her enthusiasm undeterred by the sudden shift in the atmosphere. "I could use another pair of hands—especially one that knows their way around flowers."

Max looked at me, his expression thoughtful. "Only if you're okay with that, Lily. I mean, weddings are chaotic, and I'm not sure how much help I'll be."

The invitation hung between us, heavy with implications. I could feel the weight of my own hesitations battling against the thrill of possibility. Helping with the wedding would mean more time with Max, more opportunities to discover the spark that had ignited between us. But it would also mean stepping into a world filled with pressure and expectation.

"Why not?" I said, surprising even myself. "I'm all about tackling chaos head-on."

Elara clapped her hands together, her excitement radiating off her in waves. "Perfect! It's settled then! Welcome to the team, Max."

As laughter filled the room once more, I felt a tangle of anticipation and anxiety weave through me. This unexpected encounter had opened a door I hadn't anticipated, leading me into a vibrant world where dreams mingled with chaos, and connections were forged in the most unexpected of ways.

Elara flitted about the room like a butterfly, her energy illuminating even the dimmest corners as we dove into the details of her wedding plans. I found myself swept up in her enthusiasm, painting mental pictures of blooming peonies and fluttering ribbons. The more we talked, the more my confidence blossomed, as if her joy were contagious and somehow tethered to my own aspirations. I felt myself sharing more than just floral ideas; I spoke of my dreams of a shop filled with the scent of fresh blooms and the laughter of customers delighted by their arrangements.

"Your floral designs are going to steal the show," Elara said, her voice melodic, laced with sincerity. "I can already see it. Imagine the guests' reactions when they step into a garden full of your creations!"

I grinned, warmth blooming in my chest at her praise. "I'll try not to steal the spotlight entirely. After all, it is your big day."

"Spotlight? Ha! The way I see it, we're both creating something beautiful here. Your flowers will be the art, and I'll just be the charming frame." Her smile was like a beacon, and for a moment, all my worries melted away.

Then, just as I was about to suggest a unique centerpiece idea involving cascading greenery and twinkling fairy lights, the door swung open again. Max returned, this time sans boxes, his tousled hair more of a delightful mess, and his grin broader than before. "Lily, I think I've just discovered the secret to wedding planning," he announced dramatically, hands on his hips as if he were some kind of sage. "Bribery! My sister has promised to give me a lifetime supply of cupcakes if I help her through this ordeal."

Elara laughed, shaking her head. "You know that promise isn't binding, right? I was just trying to coax you into helping, not making a legally binding agreement."

"Who says I won't hold you to it?" Max shot back, a playful glint in his eyes. "I have a feeling this wedding will require a lot of snacks. You know, to deal with the stress of watching you run around like a headless chicken."

"Oh, please! I run like a gazelle!" she retorted, hands on her hips, but there was a twinkle in her eye that revealed her enjoyment of their banter.

Watching them felt like glimpsing a performance that had been rehearsed for years—light-hearted teasing layered with the kind of affection that comes only from shared experiences. It was an intimate glimpse into their sibling dynamic, one I found myself envious of in that moment.

"Can I be your cupcake manager?" I asked, half-joking but half-serious, as I fumbled with the petals of a peony. "I can make sure you have a delicious stash on hand to keep you both energized."

Max's eyes lit up, and he nodded eagerly. "Count me in! But I have a proposal: for every cupcake you bring, you have to teach me a new flower arrangement technique."

"Deal!" I said, the thrill of collaboration surging through me. There was something refreshing about their light-heartedness, a contrast to the usual gravity that enveloped my work as I hustled to keep my business afloat.

As the conversation flowed, I found myself reveling in the easy banter with Max. His wit was sharp, cutting through the air like the clinking of glasses at a toast. I found myself laughing more than I had in a long time, drawn into a world where my worries seemed distant, overshadowed by the potential of new beginnings.

"Okay, let's get back to the important stuff," Elara said, leaning closer, her voice dropping to a conspiratorial whisper. "What do you think about incorporating some herbs into the arrangements? I want everything to smell as amazing as it looks."

"Oh, absolutely! Fresh rosemary, perhaps?" I suggested, excitement bubbling in my chest. "It adds a rustic charm and a lovely aroma. Plus, guests can even take a sprig home as a keepsake."

"Perfect! You're a genius, Lily." Elara beamed, and the sincerity in her compliment made my heart swell. I could see her envisioning it all, and for the first time in what felt like forever, I allowed myself to imagine my own future blooming with the same vibrancy.

As we continued to hash out ideas, I noticed Max's gaze lingering on me more than once, his dark eyes filled with a mixture of curiosity and amusement. The spark that had ignited between us was still there, crackling beneath the surface like a well-tended fire waiting for the right moment to blaze. It was both exhilarating and disconcerting; I had no room in my life for distractions, not when I was on the cusp of chasing my dreams.

Elara suddenly interjected, pulling me from my thoughts. "You know, you two would make quite the team. It's like a rom-com waiting to happen." She wiggled her eyebrows dramatically, her expression playful, but beneath the surface, I sensed a deeper intent.

Max chuckled, leaning back in his chair with an exaggerated sigh. "Let's not jump to conclusions. I mean, I do have a reputation to maintain." He shot me a wink, and my heart did a little somersault.

"What reputation?" Elara teased, her eyes dancing with mischief. "The one where you almost toppled over while trying to impress Lily with your box-carrying skills?"

I laughed along with them, my cheeks warming at the thought of being included in their playful sibling banter. But I couldn't shake off the nagging feeling in the back of my mind, a whisper reminding me that this was all just a pleasant distraction from my reality. Max was charming, but I didn't need the complication of a romantic entanglement.

"Maybe I should focus on my flower arranging skills instead of my acting skills," I interjected, eager to steer the conversation back to safer waters. "Let's talk about how we can make Elara's vision come to life."

"Wise choice," Max agreed, his voice low and teasing. "Less drama, more flowers. But if you ever change your mind about the rom-com, I might just audition for the lead role."

"Keep dreaming, Max." Elara smirked, but there was warmth in her tone that made me feel even more at home in this burgeoning friendship. As we delved deeper into the plans, the laughter and lightness wrapped around me, a comforting cocoon that made me forget, even if just for a moment, the trials of my own journey.

The room pulsed with ideas and creativity, the three of us building an atmosphere that thrummed with potential. As the sun dipped lower, casting golden rays through the windows, I couldn't shake the feeling that this unexpected encounter might lead me down a path I hadn't even considered. The tangled web of friendships and connections was starting to weave itself, creating something intricate and beautiful that promised to evolve in ways I was only beginning to comprehend.

As the sun dipped lower in the sky, casting a warm golden hue over Elara's living room, our conversation unfolded like the petals of a blooming flower. The air was thick with the heady scent of blooming gardenias, a fitting backdrop for the vibrant discussion swirling around us. Max leaned back in his chair, arms crossed behind his head, a playful smirk dancing on his lips as he chimed in, "Just think, Lily. You could have your own 'Wedding Whisperer' franchise if you keep this up. It could be a hit reality show: 'Crazy Couples and Their Floral Fantasies.'"

"Oh, please," Elara scoffed, rolling her eyes dramatically. "More like 'Floral Disasters and Family Drama.'"

Max feigned shock, placing a hand over his heart. "You wound me! I thought we were aiming for wholesome, family-friendly content here. Can't we at least throw in some puppies for good measure?"

I chuckled, feeling the warmth of their camaraderie seep into my bones. "Maybe a garden full of puppies—cuteness overload while keeping the guests distracted from any wedding mishaps?"

Elara leaned forward, eyes sparkling. "See? That's the kind of creativity I need on my team! You might be the secret weapon I didn't know I was missing."

"Or the one who'll make your wedding turn into a three-ring circus," Max chimed in, his dark eyes glinting mischievously. "But hey, a circus theme could be fun! Imagine the popcorn and cotton candy."

"Okay, we need to rein it in before we actually start planning a circus wedding," I replied, laughing at the absurdity of it all. The playful banter filled the room with a lightness that made my heart feel a little less heavy.

As we tossed around more ideas, I couldn't help but feel like I was being swept up into their world—a world where dreams were big and laughter flowed freely. Every time I caught Max's gaze, there was a flicker of connection, a silent communication that sent my heart racing, reminding me that distractions were a dangerous game I shouldn't be playing.

Elara's phone buzzed on the table, snapping me from my reverie. She glanced down at it, her smile faltering for a brief moment as she read the screen. "Ugh, my mom wants to know if we've decided on the table settings yet," she groaned, rolling her eyes. "It's like she thinks I'm not capable of managing my own wedding."

"Just tell her you're going for the 'mystery box' approach—each table is a surprise!" Max teased, but I could see the worry etched on Elara's face.

"Not a bad idea, actually," I said, trying to lighten the mood. "Mystery can be enchanting. Imagine the guests' excitement when they discover what flowers are hiding under each table setting."

Elara laughed, but the tension in her shoulders didn't dissipate. "If only she could be as open-minded as you," she replied, her tone light, but the hint of frustration lingered.

Max reached across the table, placing a reassuring hand on Elara's. "Hey, you've got this. You're the one getting married, and you know what you want. Let's make it happen."

The moment hung in the air, filled with unspoken promises and the kind of understanding that only close siblings could share. My heart twisted, wishing I could bottle that support and share it with my own family. Instead, I was here, part of a new dynamic, reveling in the warmth of their connection.

As we returned to our brainstorming, I felt the buzz of my phone vibrate in my pocket. I hesitated, the name on the screen pulling at my attention. It was the supplier I'd been waiting to hear from about my latest order. I swiped it away, choosing to immerse myself in the moment instead.

Max's voice cut through my thoughts. "So, Lily, what do you do for fun when you're not juggling flowers and wedding plans?"

I pondered for a moment, trying to remember the last time I truly let go and enjoyed myself. "Well, I suppose I have a penchant for gardening. There's something incredibly soothing about digging in the dirt and watching things grow. It feels like a little piece of magic, you know?"

"Absolutely!" Elara exclaimed. "What else? There must be more than just dirt and petals in your life."

I felt a flutter of shyness at the question, my insecurities surfacing. "I do like to read—especially romance novels. The ones that whisk you away to another world, where everything is beautiful and perfectly tied up by the end."

Max leaned forward, curiosity sparkling in his eyes. "Ah, so you're a hopeless romantic? I can already picture you with a cozy blanket, a cup of tea, and a good book. Sounds dreamy."

"It can be. But the reality is a bit messier, isn't it?" I replied, my voice softening. "Sometimes I feel like I'm living in a world where the plot twists never stop coming. You know, the kind where you're just waiting for that moment when everything comes crashing down."

Elara leaned back, an expression of deep understanding crossing her features. "You mean like when you're on a roller coaster and the thrilling highs are suddenly followed by the terrifying lows?"

"Exactly!" I laughed, grateful for her analogy. "But I'm not sure I want to be strapped in for the ride anymore."

"Maybe you need to take a break from the wild rides," Max suggested, a serious note creeping into his tone. "Find something that grounds you instead. Have you thought about taking a trip? Just you, away from work and stress?"

The idea hung in the air, tantalizing and terrifying all at once. I had dreamed of taking a spontaneous trip, but the fear of abandoning my business held me captive.

"Maybe," I said slowly, weighing the thought. "But... where would I go?"

Elara clapped her hands together, her eyes lighting up. "What about that little coastal town everyone raves about? I hear it's picturesque, with charming shops and plenty of beaches."

Max nodded enthusiastically. "Yes! You could immerse yourself in the scenery, relax, and maybe even come back with some new floral inspirations."

The idea sent a thrill of excitement coursing through me. It was tempting—a chance to escape, to breathe, and to refocus. But could I really leave my responsibilities behind, even for a few days?

The moment stretched, the three of us lost in our thoughts when suddenly, my phone buzzed again, this time with a notification that sliced through the moment like a bolt of lightning. I pulled it out, and my heart sank as I read the message from my supplier: "I'm afraid your order has been delayed. We'll have to push your timeline back."

"What's wrong?" Elara asked, noticing the change in my expression.

"Just—" I hesitated, feeling the weight of disappointment settle in my chest. "It's my order for the wedding flowers. They've been delayed."

Max's expression shifted to concern. "That's frustrating. But hey, we can work around it. Let's brainstorm some alternatives."

"Yeah," I murmured, forcing a smile, but my mind was already racing with the implications. The wedding was just a few weeks away. Delays meant scrambling, and scrambling meant more stress than I could handle.

"I have to take this," I said, trying to keep my voice steady as I excused myself to step outside. The air was cooler, a refreshing contrast to the warmth of the room, but it couldn't quite quell the rising tide of anxiety in my chest.

As I dialed the supplier's number, the world around me faded, each ring echoing in my mind like a countdown. I needed answers, solutions—anything to avoid letting Elara down. But just as someone picked up on the other end, a sudden crash echoed from within the house, followed by a sharp shout.

I froze, heart racing, a knot of dread tightening in my stomach. "What was that?" I muttered to myself, my heart pounding as I rushed back inside.

The sight that greeted me was chaos. Elara stood wide-eyed, Max crouched by the table, an overturned chair beside him, and a shattered vase lay in a million sparkling pieces on the floor. "What happened?" I gasped, stepping over the debris.

"Just a minor mishap," Max said, his voice strained as he rubbed the back of his neck, laughter struggling to break through the tension. "But on the bright side, I've now got a good excuse to eat a lot of cupcakes."

But I wasn't focused on the humor in his words. My heart raced as I noticed the look on Elara's face—her expression was a mix of fear and disbelief, and my instincts kicked in. Something was wrong, deeper than broken china and spilled flowers.

Before I could ask what was really going on, Max shot me a look filled with urgency. "You need to get out of here," he said, voice low. "Now."

I opened my mouth to protest, but the look in his eyes told me this was serious. The tension thickened in the air as I caught Elara's gaze, a silent communication passing between us, and just like that, I realized I was standing on the precipice of something much larger than just a wedding.

Chapter 3: Cake and Confrontation

The kitchen hummed with the familiar sounds of whisking and mixing, the soft thud of flour meeting the counter, and the soothing rhythm of my thoughts blending into the aroma of vanilla and butter. I stood there, lost in the swirl of it all, a delicate dance between memory and creation. Elara's request lingered in the air, wrapping around me like a thick fog. A cake that embodied love and loss. It was an audacious challenge, one that tugged at the corners of my heart. With each sift of flour, I felt the weight of those words, the gravity of my own experiences pulling me under.

My mother had loved baking as much as I did, her laughter ringing like a melodic bell in the kitchen, mixing seamlessly with the rich scents of baking bread and cookies. I closed my eyes, allowing her spirit to wash over me, filling me with warmth and a bittersweet ache. The memory was a double-edged sword—an inspiration that brought comfort but also a pang of longing. I reached for the sugar paste, rolling it into thin sheets, cutting intricate petals shaped like her favorite blossoms. Each flower was a tribute, delicate yet resilient, a reflection of the love she had poured into my life.

The process was cathartic. I lost track of time, the world outside fading into insignificance as I lost myself in the artistry of baking. The cake layers stacked higher, perfectly aligned, adorned with a lavish cascade of white and soft pink sugar flowers. With every stroke of the icing spatula, I poured out my emotions, layer upon layer, creating a masterpiece that spoke of joy and sorrow intertwined. I could almost hear my mother's voice, encouraging me to let my heart guide my hands, to create something not just for the eyes but for the soul.

Just as I placed the final sugar flower atop the cake, the bell above the door jingled, snapping me back to reality. I turned, a slight frown creasing my forehead as I noticed Max stepping into the shop, his presence a bolt of unexpected energy. His expression shifted from casual curiosity to awe as he took in the sight before him. "Wow," he breathed, stepping closer, his hands tucked into the pockets of his jacket. "That's... something else."

"Thanks," I replied, trying to shake off the flutter of nerves in my stomach. "I'm working on a special order. It's a bit different from what I usually do."

He leaned in, examining the sugar flowers with a keen eye, as if searching for a hidden secret within their delicate curves. "Different how?"

I paused, searching for the right words. "Elara wanted something that captured love and loss. It's... a challenge."

His brows knitted together, and for a moment, I thought I saw a flicker of understanding in his gaze. "Love and loss. That's heavy for a wedding cake, isn't it?"

"Yeah, well, it's not exactly a straightforward request." I took a breath, willing myself to be open. "But it's also kind of liberating. You have to dig deep, you know? Get into the heart of what it means to celebrate—what it means to remember."

Max's expression shifted, a moment of vulnerability flashing across his face before he masked it with a smile. "Sounds like you're doing more than just baking. You're crafting memories."

"Something like that," I said, feeling a connection forming between us, threads of understanding weaving through the air. "What about you? What's brought you here?"

His gaze drifted to the window, where the sun began its descent, casting a golden hue over the street outside. "Just wandering, really. Trying to figure out what I want, what I'm supposed to do."

"Big questions," I mused, mixing a small bowl of frosting absentmindedly. "What's the answer so far?"

He chuckled softly, a sound that echoed against the backdrop of my kitchen, warming the space between us. "I wish I knew. Family expectations, you know? It's like they've drawn this path for me, but I'm not sure it's one I want to walk."

His honesty resonated with me, a mirror reflecting my own struggles. "I get that. My mom had plans for me too. Expectations that felt more like chains than dreams."

"Is that why you throw yourself into baking?"

"Partly," I admitted, shrugging slightly. "It's like therapy. Each cake tells a story, helps me reclaim pieces of myself."

"I like that," he said, stepping closer. "You make the sweet things in life, even when they're tied to something bittersweet."

A moment passed, thick with unspoken words. The weight of our confessions hung in the air, a fragile connection binding us together in this little shop filled with flour and sugar. I looked up, meeting his gaze, the corners of my mouth twitching into a smile. "And what about you? What do you make?"

He tilted his head, considering my question, and I could see the wheels turning behind his eyes. "I guess I'm still trying to figure that out. But I want to create something genuine, something that resonates."

As the warmth of his words settled in, a flicker of hope ignited within me. Maybe, just maybe, we were both on the brink of something new—a connection formed not just through shared experiences, but through the realization that we were not alone in our struggles. Just as I began to feel the moment's significance, the sharp clang of the shop's door caught my attention, pulling me out of my reverie.

Elara swept in, her presence commanding the room. "I hope I'm not interrupting," she said, her voice a mix of cheer and authority. Her eyes landed on the cake, and I could see her approval light up her face. "Oh my, that's beautiful! You've outdone yourself."

"Thanks," I replied, my heart racing as the shift in energy enveloped the room. I exchanged a glance with Max, silently acknowledging the conversation we had just shared.

"Well, it's almost time for our meeting, and I want to see how this beauty fits into the vision," Elara declared, her excitement palpable.

I nodded, the thrill of our earlier connection mingling with the flutter of nerves. As we began to discuss the details, the warmth that had blossomed between Max and me lingered in the air, a promise of what might come next amidst the whirlwind of sugar and frosting.

Elara's presence infused the air with an urgency that felt almost electric. She paced the small space, her fingers twitching with excitement as she studied the cake, its layers gleaming under the overhead lights like a polished gemstone. "This is exquisite," she declared, her voice brightening the room. "But we need to ensure it tells the story we've envisioned. The love, the loss... it all has to resonate."

I nodded, feeling the familiar pressure of creativity and expectation swirling within me. "I get that. But how do I visually represent something so complex? Love is vibrant and bold, while loss is often quiet, subdued."

"Exactly," Elara said, clapping her hands together like a conductor rallying an orchestra. "We want the cake to evoke emotion, to be a conversation piece. It shouldn't just look good; it should feel profound."

As she spoke, I stole a glance at Max, who had leaned against the counter, arms crossed, a bemused smile dancing on his lips. "Sounds like you're in a bit of a pickle," he chimed in, teasingly raising an eyebrow. "You've got a love story mixed with a tragedy. What are you going to do? Bake a cake that sings?"

I couldn't help but chuckle, the tension in my shoulders loosening. "If only it were that easy. Maybe I should add a little speaker in the bottom tier for some dramatic effect."

Elara grinned, but her enthusiasm quickly morphed into focus. "Well, why not? Let's brainstorm! What if we incorporate colors that symbolize the journey? Soft pinks for love, deep blues for loss—"

"Maybe a touch of gray?" Max suggested, his eyes glinting with mischief. "You know, to remind everyone that this is a wedding cake, not a funeral cake."

I snorted, caught off guard by his humor. "Right, because nothing says 'I do' like a healthy dose of melancholy."

Elara rolled her eyes but couldn't suppress a laugh. "Touché. Okay, let's steer clear of that. But I do like the idea of contrasting colors. They could weave together, representing how intertwined love and loss can be."

As we debated ideas, the atmosphere thickened with possibility. I felt myself stepping into a creative flow, buoyed by the exchange of thoughts, the way they bounced between us like ping pong balls in a game. Each suggestion held the weight of our experiences, layered with laughter and the sharp pang of vulnerability.

But as we pushed deeper into the creative process, a sense of unease began to creep in. With each idea we tossed around, I felt the shadows of my past looming closer, the bittersweet taste of memories mixing in with the frosting I envisioned. It was one thing to talk about loss, to represent it in a cake; it was another to confront it directly.

"Okay," I said, feeling the need to anchor myself amidst the rising tide of emotions. "Let's keep it real. What does love and loss mean for each of us?"

Elara paused, her expression shifting to one of contemplation. "For me, love is my parents' commitment to each other, the way they've always been there through thick and thin. Loss, on the other hand, is the time I lost with them when I was chasing my dreams elsewhere."

Max shifted, the casual demeanor slipping momentarily from his shoulders. "For me, love is watching my sister build her life, and loss... well, it's the expectation that I should follow a path that feels more like a cage than a road."

"Wow," I whispered, feeling the weight of their words settle over me like a warm blanket. "That's powerful."

I knew my turn was next, the spotlight of introspection flickering my way. I hesitated, the words lodged in my throat. "For me, love is baking, the way it feels like a warm hug when I mix ingredients together. And loss..." My voice wavered, the familiar ache rising. "Loss is my mother. She poured so much into me, into every cake we made together. She should be here now, helping me with this."

A silence followed, heavy yet soothing, wrapping around us like the rich scent of vanilla that filled the air. Max's eyes softened, and he stepped closer, a genuine understanding lighting up his expression. "I'm sorry for your loss. I can't imagine how hard it must be to keep that alive while creating something new."

I managed a small smile, grateful for his sensitivity. "Thanks. It's a balancing act, really. But I want to honor her memory, not be shackled by it. It's all part of this journey."

Elara leaned in, her expression earnest. "You've got this. The cake will be a reflection of your love, your memories, and a celebration of everything you are now. You're not just baking; you're sharing a part of yourself."

"Okay, enough of the mushy stuff," Max interjected, a playful grin breaking the seriousness. "Let's make sure we have some fun in this process. You're creating a wedding cake, not a therapy session."

"Speak for yourself," I shot back, grinning. "I might just need a therapist by the end of this."

"Maybe we should schedule an appointment after the wedding," he quipped, leaning back against the counter with a relaxed demeanor that contrasted sharply with the serious tones we'd been exploring.

Elara laughed, breaking the tension. "Deal. But only if I get a piece of that cake as payment."

"Then consider it a contractual obligation," I replied, my heart lighter, the earlier heaviness lifted by the banter we shared. "Now, let's talk about flavors. We need to make this a cake worth talking about—not just for its emotional depth, but for its taste."

The discussion veered into a flurry of suggestions—zesty lemon, rich chocolate, the occasional hint of raspberry. The more we tossed ideas around, the more I felt the creative energy rekindling. With each suggestion, the cake transformed in my mind from a solemn tribute to a vibrant celebration of life and love, beautifully interwoven with the reality of loss.

As we debated frosting options and design elements, I caught glimpses of the connection forming between Max and me—a playful spark igniting beneath the layers of our pasts. It was invigorating, exhilarating even, to share this journey with someone who understood the complexities of both joy and sorrow. The afternoon drifted on, the light outside fading into a warm glow, and for the first time in a long while, I felt like I was exactly where I was meant to be.

With the cake design blossoming into a vibrant tapestry of colors and flavors, the atmosphere in the shop shifted from tense reflection to playful creativity. The soft afternoon light spilled through the window, casting a warm glow that enveloped us like a comforting blanket. As we debated the merits of raspberry ganache versus a classic buttercream, I couldn't help but revel in the camaraderie blossoming around the cake stand.

"Raspberry ganache is definitely the way to go," I insisted, twirling a spatula in my hand like a wand. "It adds a tangy twist that perfectly balances the sweetness of the cake. Plus, it's like a little surprise with every bite!"

Max leaned back, a teasing smile tugging at his lips. "A surprise? You make it sound like a game show prize. 'Congratulations! You've just won a mouthful of fruity goodness!'"

Elara chimed in, her laughter ringing through the shop. "And for our next contestant, we have the delightful baker who's about to serve up a slice of emotional complexity!"

"I think I'd prefer a slice of the cake instead of being the contestant," I quipped, my heart buoyed by the lightness of our banter. "But hey, if it gets me on TV, I might consider it."

Max feigned shock, placing a hand over his heart. "How could you do that to your loyal patrons? I thought this was a sacred space, a cake sanctuary."

"Cake sanctuary? Now that's a brand I could get behind," I mused, leaning into the banter. "I can see the tagline: 'Where layers of love and frosting come together in harmony.'"

Elara clapped her hands together, excitement dancing in her eyes. "I love it! But let's not forget the serious stuff. We still need to ensure this cake encapsulates Elara's vision of love and loss."

"Right," I said, feeling the creative gears click into place once more. "So, if we're going with raspberry ganache, I think we should layer it between some moist vanilla cake and finish it with a light lemon buttercream. The lemon adds brightness, a celebration of new beginnings amidst the bittersweet."

"Now that's poetic," Max remarked, leaning closer, his interest piqued. "You've got a way with words. I can see the story coming to life already."

I felt my cheeks warm at his compliment, but before I could respond, the shop door swung open, and the bell jingled cheerily. A gust of cool autumn air swept in, along with a couple of customers who strolled in, momentarily disrupting our creative bubble. They exchanged quick glances at the cake before approaching the counter.

"Wow, that looks incredible!" one of them exclaimed, pointing at the masterpiece before us. "Are you taking orders for that one?"

"Yes!" I replied, my voice brimming with enthusiasm. "This cake is a special commission, but I can definitely whip up something similar for you."

While I took their order, I felt Max's presence lingering just behind me, a warm energy that made the task feel lighter. It was fascinating how he seemed to pull me out of my shell, encouraging me to embrace the moment, the customers, the conversation. I could hear Elara whispering to him, probably making her own observations about the cake, its layers, its story.

As I finalized their order and ushered them out with promises of a delightful treat in a few days, I turned back to find Max and Elara deep in conversation. I caught snippets about wedding details and floral arrangements, their excitement palpable as they plotted and planned.

"Okay, we should probably get back to brainstorming," I said, stepping closer. "What if we sketched out the final design? It might help me visualize how the cake will come together."

"Great idea," Elara said, her eyes sparkling with determination. "Let's make this cake something truly unforgettable."

We gathered around the small table in the corner, a smattering of colored pencils and paper scattered about like fallen leaves. As I sketched, Max leaned over my shoulder, his breath warm against my skin. "You know, your cake designs could probably win awards. You've got an artistic eye."

I suppressed a shiver at the proximity, focusing on the paper before me. "Thanks. I just want each cake to be more than just a dessert; I want it to tell a story."

"Like a literary cake?" Max mused, tapping his chin thoughtfully. "What's the plot twist? Someone sneaks a bite and suddenly realizes their life choices are all wrong?"

"Maybe the main character realizes she's been baking her feelings instead of facing them," I shot back, my wit flaring in a playful jab. "And she just has to take a bite to see the light."

Elara laughed, the sound echoing in the small space, while Max smirked, his eyes dancing with mischief. "Well, I hope this cake has a happy ending, because the last thing we need is for a wedding cake to be filled with existential dread."

As the laughter faded, a moment of seriousness swept over us. The design began to take shape, each line and flourish reflecting the emotional journey we had embarked upon together. It was both exhilarating and intimidating to blend our thoughts into something tangible.

But just as I felt a surge of confidence in the design, the door swung open again, and a figure stepped inside, casting a shadow that disrupted the cozy atmosphere. I turned, ready to greet the newcomer, only to find my heart plunging at the sight of my father standing there, a frown etched deeply into his features.

"What are you doing here?" I asked, the warmth of the shop suddenly feeling cold.

Max straightened, and Elara glanced between us, confusion flickering in her eyes. My father's presence loomed over the joyful scene, a stark reminder of all that had been left unsaid, a ghost from the past come to haunt my present.

"I came to talk," he said, his voice steady but heavy, like the first hint of a storm brewing on the horizon. "We need to discuss your plans—your future."

A chill ran down my spine, the air thick with unspoken words. I could feel Max's gaze on me, a silent question hanging in the balance. Would I allow my past to dictate my future, or could I carve out my own path amidst the layers of family expectations and heartache? The cake before me, a symbol of love and loss, seemed to echo that very struggle.

And as my father took a step closer, the tension in the room crackled with uncertainty, the promise of unresolved feelings hanging like a ripe fruit, ready to drop at any moment.

Chapter 4: Sweet Distractions

Flour dust danced in the golden light filtering through my kitchen window, creating a soft, ethereal glow that surrounded Max as he leaned against the counter, arms crossed, a playful smirk tugging at his lips. The chaos of our shared culinary adventure lay strewn about: bowls tipped over, colorful sprinkles spilling like tiny jewels, and the faint scent of vanilla intertwined with a hint of burnt sugar. We had embarked on a quest to perfect my latest creation, a lemon lavender cake, and as usual, it had devolved into delightful chaos.

"What kind of cake were you going for again?" Max asked, feigning an innocent tone while expertly balancing a spoonful of frosting just out of reach of my hand. His blue eyes sparkled with mischief, drawing me in like a moth to flame. I felt the warmth of my cheeks blush under his gaze, a sensation both familiar and terrifying.

"Uh, that would be the kind that doesn't resemble a pancake," I shot back, trying to maintain my composure while snatching the spoon from his hand. A swirl of frosting landed on his cheek, and I couldn't help but laugh, the sound echoing in the cozy kitchen. "See? Now it's a cake with character."

"Oh, it's got character all right," he replied, wiping the frosting away with the back of his hand, his expression shifting into something more serious as he focused on me. "It could use a little more sugar, though."

The air crackled between us, charged with something that felt much deeper than mere friendship, but I shook it off. This was just Max being Max—charming, infuriating, and entirely too distracting. I had learned to be cautious around him, aware that each lingering glance was a step toward a cliff I wasn't sure I wanted to leap off. My heart beat in sync with the swirling flour as I forced a smile, trying to brush aside the tendrils of attraction weaving their way through my thoughts.

"Perhaps you're just a little too sweet for my taste," I teased, yet I couldn't help but relish the back-and-forth we shared. The way he challenged me was refreshing, and every laugh echoed in my heart like a sweet melody I wanted to replay.

"Me? Too sweet?" he exclaimed, placing a hand dramatically over his chest as if I had dealt a grievous blow. "I'll have you know, I've been told I'm as bitter as dark chocolate."

"Right, because you're just a little ray of sunshine," I said, rolling my eyes playfully. Yet, there was a truth to his jest. Beneath that easygoing charm lay a man shaped by shadows, someone who carried scars invisible to most. I had caught glimpses of them in the way his smile sometimes faded or how he became distant in thought, lost to whatever battles he fought in silence.

We fell into a comfortable rhythm, measuring ingredients and stealing bites from each other's creations until I felt the pull of a deeper connection. The kitchen became our world, a bubble where nothing else mattered except the laughter and the warmth of the moment. It was hard to ignore the way his presence filled the air, how he had seamlessly woven himself into my daily routine, a sweet distraction that threatened to unravel the carefully tied ribbons of my heart.

Then there was that moment—one I had anticipated yet dreaded. We were both elbow-deep in frosting, laughter bubbling over like the batter we had over-mixed, when the atmosphere shifted, becoming thick with unspoken tension. I could feel the magnetic pull, a gravity drawing us closer. Our gazes locked, a charged silence enveloping us as he took a step closer. I could see every detail of his face, the freckles that danced across his nose, the way his hair fell slightly over his forehead. The world outside faded, and all I could think about was the intoxicating idea of being lost in him.

But just as our lips were about to meet, a sudden shrill ping from my phone shattered the moment. My heart sank as I pulled away, reaching for the device. Elara's name lit up the screen, a reminder of the stakes I was balancing precariously on the edge of my heart.

"Work?" Max asked, his voice tinged with disappointment as I glanced at the text. It was a reminder of the fundraiser we had planned for the community center, a crucial event that felt like a lifeline to the world I had built around myself.

"Yeah, it's Elara," I replied, forcing a smile as I read her enthusiastic messages about last-minute preparations. "We need to finalize the cake design. You know, the one I was supposed to make for the bake sale."

"Right, because baking for the community is way more important than possibly kissing me," he said, sarcasm dripping from his words, but there was an underlying current of sincerity that made my heart twist.

"Don't be like that," I protested, though I could feel the heaviness of his gaze as I turned back to my phone, fingers tapping away. "This event means a lot to me. We're raising funds for kids who need after-school programs. It's important."

"Of course it is," he replied, though his tone was a touch sharper than before. "Just... don't forget to take care of yourself while you're at it."

His words hung in the air, a gentle reminder that even amidst the chaos of frosting and laughter, there was a part of me I had been neglecting. The sweet distraction he represented was both a temptation and a threat. My heart wrestled with itself—should I allow myself to be swept away in this moment, or was it time to anchor myself back to the responsibilities I had sworn to uphold?

I sighed, torn between two worlds: one filled with the joy of flour-dusted laughter and the other heavy with obligation. Yet, in that very moment, I understood that perhaps it was possible to navigate both—to blend sweetness and purpose into a single, delicious recipe for my life.

Elara's text glowed like a neon sign, demanding attention with an urgency that felt almost sinister in its timing. "Don't forget the fundraiser!" it read, and with it came the weight of responsibility crashing back into my thoughts, the chaotic reverie of frosting and flirtation instantly shattered. I turned away from Max, the warmth of his gaze still tingling on my skin, but the reality of the moment pushed its way back in, relentless and unwavering.

"Right," I said, forcing the word out with a cheery inflection, though my heart was still a dissonant chord away from the harmony we had just shared. I tried to focus on the screen, but the tension in the air was palpable, like the final seconds before a roller coaster descends, all thrill and fear blended into one. "The community center needs those cakes for the bake sale. Every penny counts, you know?"

"Of course," he replied, though the edge in his voice hinted at his reluctance. "But just so you know, I was kind of enjoying our little cake escapade before the universe decided to meddle."

I caught a glimpse of that trademark smirk of his, but it felt different now, shadowed by an undercurrent of something deeper—frustration, perhaps. Or maybe longing. It was hard to pinpoint with all the swirling emotions bouncing around like flour in the air. I busied myself with a new bowl, mixing the batter with an exaggerated ferocity, trying to dispel the tension that lingered.

"You're not the only one with distractions," I quipped, daring to look up. "I'm practically drowning in them. Between the cake orders, the fundraiser, and now your charming presence, it's a wonder I haven't turned into a walking cupcake."

Max chuckled, a rich sound that wrapped around me like a comforting blanket. "A walking cupcake would be a delightful distraction," he replied, eyes glinting with playful mischief. "But you might want to rethink your frosting flavor. Maybe something less... chaotic?"

I shot him a mock glare, unable to suppress a grin. "I'd take chaotic over bland any day. Speaking of which, how about we focus on perfecting the lemon lavender instead of getting sidetracked by my supposed cupcake persona?"

"Fine, lead the way, oh master of the baking arts," he said with a theatrical bow, and I found myself rolling my eyes, but the smile on my face betrayed my amusement.

We plunged back into the frenzy of mixing and measuring, the kitchen alive with laughter and chatter, each moment a sweet reminder of the friendship we had built amid the sugar and flour. As we created our cake masterpiece, I stole glances at Max, who had a way of making even the most mundane tasks feel like an adventure. His passion was infectious, the way he could transform a simple cake into a shared experience, one laden with layers of laughter and easy camaraderie.

But as the day wore on, I sensed an underlying tension simmering beneath our playful banter, a flicker of something unacknowledged lingering between us like the final hint of sweetness in a dessert. I watched him carefully, noting how his gaze shifted when he thought I wasn't looking—how it lingered just a moment too long on my lips or how his fingers brushed against mine when reaching for a spatula. Each accidental touch sent a spark dancing through my veins, igniting all the fears I had carefully tucked away in the recesses of my heart.

"Okay, maybe we can add a little more lavender," I suggested, shaking off the spiraling thoughts that threatened to pull me under. The lemon zest was bright and invigorating, but it was the lavender that brought a sense of calm to the cake. It felt oddly symbolic, a small rebellion against the chaotic swirl of emotions that had taken root in me since Max first stepped through my door.

"More lavender it is," he replied, pouring in the delicate petals with an exaggerated flourish, a playful grin dancing across his lips.

"A little sweetness, a little chaos. That's the secret ingredient to life, right?"

"Sure," I shot back, trying to keep my tone light. "Unless you add too much chaos and end up with a cake that could double as a doorstop."

The way he laughed made my heart skip. It was the kind of laughter that could brighten the dreariest of days, and I felt the corners of my mouth tugging upward in response. "What's life without a bit of risk?" he countered, eyes sparkling with challenge. "And besides, I've tasted some of your 'doorstop' cakes, and I'd take one any day."

The flirtation hung between us like the lingering scent of vanilla, sweet yet dangerous. I glanced at the clock, the hands ticking away, each second a reminder of my looming commitments. The fundraiser wasn't just about the cakes; it was about the community that depended on our efforts. I couldn't afford to get swept away in the current of feelings that threatened to carry me off course.

"Max," I began, struggling to find the right words to bridge the widening gap between us, "I don't want you to think—"

But before I could finish, the doorbell rang, shattering the moment like fragile glass. I jumped, the spell between us broken, and a rush of relief flooded through me, though I couldn't help but feel a twinge of disappointment.

"I'll get it," I said, taking a moment to compose myself as I wiped my hands on a flour-dusted towel. The brief reprieve from our conversation offered a necessary distraction. Stepping away from the warmth of the kitchen, I moved toward the front door, but the feeling of his gaze lingered like the sweetest scent of lavender.

Opening the door, I was greeted by Elara, her enthusiastic energy spilling into my home like a ray of sunshine. "I hope I'm not interrupting anything too scandalous!" she exclaimed, eyes sparkling as she caught sight of Max in the kitchen.

"Just a friendly baking session," I replied, attempting to sound nonchalant. "Nothing scandalous at all."

"Baking is only scandalous if there are secret ingredients," she quipped, stepping inside, her keen gaze darting between us. "And judging by the flour storm I see brewing, I can't help but wonder what you two are concocting."

"Just a little lemon lavender cake," Max said, flashing his boyish charm in her direction. "Your friend here is trying to turn me into a cake connoisseur."

Elara laughed, a melodic sound that echoed through the kitchen. "That's the spirit! But don't let her trick you into tasting something too chaotic. She can be sneaky like that."

Max raised an eyebrow, an amused smile dancing on his lips. "Sneaky? I thought we were being adventurous."

Their playful banter flowed effortlessly, and as I leaned against the doorframe, I felt a mix of gratitude and frustration simmering beneath the surface. Max and Elara together were a force of nature, a blend of wit and warmth that wrapped around me like a cozy blanket. But as the laughter echoed through my home, I felt the familiar ache of uncertainty—what if this light-hearted distraction had the potential to lead to something deeper, something that could once again leave me vulnerable?

Elara's entrance felt like a whirlwind, pulling me back into the realm of responsibilities I had tried to momentarily escape. "So, what's the plan?" she chirped, her enthusiasm infectious as she plopped her tote bag onto the kitchen counter, displacing a cloud of flour that danced in the golden light. "I brought more lavender! You can never have too much lavender, right?"

Max shot me a look, a mixture of amusement and exasperation, and I couldn't help but feel a slight pang of annoyance. This was our moment, one that had been sidetracked by a simple doorbell. I should have known better than to think I could steal a few intimate seconds alone without life rushing in like an unexpected tide.

"Right. The lavender," I said, forcing myself to smile as Elara rummaged through her bag, pulling out the delicate blossoms like a magician unveiling their next trick. "We were just about to make some very artistic decisions on the cake."

"Artistic decisions?" Elara raised an eyebrow, a sly smile spreading across her face. "Is that code for 'Max and I were almost about to kiss'?"

"More like 'we were about to agree on frosting preferences,'" I replied, my cheeks heating as I shot Max a glare. "I think we need to focus on the task at hand, ladies and gentlemen."

Max leaned against the counter, crossing his arms with a devil-may-care attitude. "Oh, but the frosting is crucial," he said, his tone mock-serious. "What's the point of creating a masterpiece if we can't admire its aesthetic? I say we should spend at least another twenty minutes debating the merits of lavender frosting versus lemon drizzle."

"See? He's trying to distract us from our work!" I exclaimed, half-laughing, half-annoyed.

"You're right," Elara chimed in, a conspiratorial grin creeping onto her lips. "I think we need to get Max on board with the chaos. It's more fun that way!"

Max feigned a gasp, clutching his heart as though scandalized. "Chaos? Me? I would never dream of such a thing!"

I chuckled, the tension from earlier slowly dissipating like the lingering scent of vanilla in the air. The three of us dove into the process, the kitchen alive with laughter and the sounds of clattering bowls. It was as if the universe had conspired to keep us grounded in the moment, even while the echoes of my unresolved feelings swirled just beneath the surface.

The conversation flowed effortlessly, punctuated by friendly jabs and shared stories. Elara regaled us with tales from her recent adventures, her vibrant descriptions painting vivid images that filled the room with warmth. I found myself increasingly drawn to the laughter, the joy of being surrounded by friends who felt like family.

But as the frosting began to take shape, I caught Max stealing glances my way, his expression shifting as if grappling with thoughts he dared not voice aloud. Each time our eyes met, I felt a magnetic pull, a silent communication that transcended words. The fleeting moments of intimacy we had shared loomed large in my mind, challenging the walls I had erected around my heart.

"I really think this lavender cake is going to be a hit," I said, breaking the silence that had settled around us as we prepped the pans. "But we need to get the flavors just right."

"Right," Max agreed, stepping closer, his arm brushing against mine as we leaned over the mixing bowl. "It's like life, you know? Balance is key. Too much lemon and you'll end up with something too tart to enjoy. But too much lavender? It could taste like soap."

"Ah, soap. The enemy of all bakers," Elara chimed in, her eyes sparkling with mischief. "I would pay good money to see someone try to sell a cake that tastes like soap."

Max laughed, the sound warm and inviting. "Let's avoid that, shall we? I don't think it would fly at the fundraiser."

Just then, the kitchen phone rang, slicing through our banter like a knife through frosting. I frowned at the sudden disruption. "I'll get it," I said, my heart racing as I moved toward the phone, hoping it wasn't another reminder of the mounting pressures waiting for me outside the warmth of this kitchen.

"Probably another order," Elara said, her voice casual. But as I lifted the receiver, an uneasy feeling slithered through me.

"Hello?" I said, my heart pounding as I prepared for yet another cake-related conversation. But the voice on the other end sent a chill racing down my spine.

"Is this Ava?" the voice asked, low and unfamiliar.

"Yes, this is Ava," I replied, my pulse quickening. "Who is this?"

There was a brief pause, and my skin prickled with unease. "I need you to listen carefully. There's something you need to know about the fundraiser."

"What do you mean? Is there a problem?" I demanded, anxiety curling in my stomach.

"I can't explain over the phone. Meet me at the park, by the fountain, in thirty minutes," the voice instructed, urgency lacing every word. "Trust me. It's important."

Before I could respond, the line went dead, the dial tone echoing ominously in my ear. I stood frozen, the weight of the conversation crashing over me like a wave, the playful energy of the kitchen draining away as the reality of the unknown settled into my bones.

"What was that about?" Max's voice cut through my haze, and I turned to face him, trying to mask my growing anxiety.

"It was just a—" I started, but I caught the look on his face, a blend of concern and curiosity. "I need to go," I finished, the urgency of the situation clear as the words tumbled out. "There's something I need to check on."

"Wait, Ava—" Elara began, but I shook my head, the need to leave pressing down on me like a heavy fog.

"Stay here, finish the cake," I instructed, trying to sound authoritative, though my heart raced with uncertainty. "I'll be back as soon as I can."

I didn't wait for their response. I grabbed my coat, the fabric feeling heavier than usual, as I stepped out into the crisp evening air. The park was just a short walk away, but each step felt laden with foreboding. The words of the mysterious caller replayed in my mind like a broken record—"There's something you need to know."

As I approached the park, shadows flickered beneath the streetlights, the faint sounds of laughter and life echoing around me, yet my heart thudded loudly in my chest, drowning out everything else.

Reaching the fountain, I scanned the area, every instinct on high alert. The wind whipped through the trees, carrying with it the faint scent of lavender from my earlier escapade. I felt a shiver of apprehension, but I couldn't shake the feeling that whatever was waiting for me was going to change everything.

A figure emerged from the shadows, their face obscured, and my breath caught in my throat. "You came," they said, voice low and steady. "Good. We don't have much time."

I opened my mouth to question who they were, but the words died on my lips as the figure stepped closer, and the truth unfolded before me, sending shockwaves through my heart, leaving me teetering on the edge of uncertainty, caught between the sweet distractions of my life and the unexpected storm threatening to engulf everything I held dear.

Chapter 5: The Wedding Rush

The air buzzed with a heady mixture of jasmine and fresh-cut grass, the kind of fragrant bouquet that made you feel a little light-headed, like love could just float right off the ground. I had meticulously crafted Elara's wedding cake, a towering confection adorned with delicate sugar flowers that mirrored the floral arrangements draped across the venue. The soft, buttery smell of the vanilla sponge lingered around me like a warm hug, each tier a testament to my passion and dedication. Today was supposed to be magical, a dream stitched together with whispers of love, laughter, and promises for the future. Yet, with each mile I drove toward the venue, a gnawing anxiety twisted in my stomach, heavier than the cake in the backseat.

The morning sun spilled golden light onto the road, and I clutched the steering wheel as if it were my lifeline. Each turn felt like a pendulum swinging toward an uncertain fate. What if the cake toppled? What if I miscalculated the number of guests? What if Elara hated it? As I parked, I took a deep breath, allowing the sweet aroma of vanilla to calm my nerves. My hands shook as I reached for the cake box, the cardboard feeling flimsy against the weight of my worries. The cake, after all, was not just a dessert; it was a symbol of Elara's dreams, an edible centerpiece of her happiness.

Stepping into the venue felt like crossing a threshold into a realm where love was tangible and artful. The décor was a riot of colors: blush pinks and muted golds danced together under the soft glow of fairy lights. Guests swirled like a lively watercolor painting, their laughter echoing like joyous chimes. I couldn't help but smile, even as my heart raced. The chatter and clinking of glasses created a symphony of celebration, yet an undercurrent of tension pulled at me, tugging the edges of my euphoria.

Then I spotted her—Elara. She glided through the crowd in a wedding gown that cascaded like liquid silk, the fabric catching the light in a way that made her look like she had stepped out of a fairytale. My breath hitched at the sight of her, radiant and glowing. I felt an overwhelming sense of pride swell within me; my cake was part of her day.

But just as I maneuvered through the throngs of guests to reach her, I heard it—a heated conversation, sharp enough to cut through the joyful chaos. It was Elara and her fiancé, Jake. Their voices, once sweet whispers of love, now crackled with tension. I felt the air shift, the festive atmosphere evaporating around me like mist in the morning sun.

"Jake, this is not what I envisioned," Elara's voice rose, each word laced with frustration. "We can't just ignore the things that matter to us because we're trying to appease everyone else."

I hesitated, caught between the desire to support my friend and the instinct to melt back into the crowd. Peeking around the corner of the lavish floral arrangements, I caught sight of Jake, his brow furrowed, hands shoved deep into the pockets of his tuxedo. "I'm trying to make this work, Elara," he retorted, the tension in his voice rising. "But it's like you're not even considering my feelings anymore."

My heart sank, heavy like the cake I was carrying. I had witnessed love before, seen it blossom and flourish, but here was a stark reminder that even the most beautiful stories could fray at the edges. I thought of the countless hours Elara and I had spent dreaming up the details of her perfect day, the way she had lit up at the mention of floral centerpieces and cascading ribbons. Yet here she stood, her dreams teetering on the brink of unraveling.

"Maybe we should take a step back," she said, her voice softening but still firm. "This day isn't just about the wedding. It's about us, and I refuse to lose sight of that."

I wanted to intervene, to pull her aside and reassure her that everything would be okay, that she was allowed to prioritize her happiness above all else. But the moment felt fragile, and I didn't want to intrude. Instead, I set the cake down carefully, taking a moment to breathe in the aromas wafting from the kitchen, filling my lungs with the scents of sugar and frosting.

"Wow, that cake looks amazing!" a voice piped up, breaking the tension and bringing me back into the present. A woman, presumably a bridesmaid with sparkling eyes and a wide grin, was gazing at the confection in awe. "Is that from your bakery? You're a magician!"

"Thank you," I replied, the corners of my mouth lifting despite the storm brewing between Elara and Jake. "It's a labor of love, just like today."

"I can't wait to see Elara's face when she sees it!" she exclaimed, and her excitement reminded me of why I had poured so much of myself into this cake. It wasn't just a dessert; it was a celebration of love, a canvas for memories yet to be made.

As I worked to set up the cake, the tension lingered like a storm cloud threatening to burst. I couldn't shake the feeling that the day held more surprises than just the anticipated vows and cake cutting. It was as if the universe was testing the bonds of love under the guise of celebration, and I was here, the observer caught in the crossfire.

But just as I slid the final tier into place, a soft, resolute voice broke through my thoughts. "We need to talk," Elara said, stepping away from Jake, her expression determined yet vulnerable. I couldn't help but root for her as she approached me, a mix of hope and uncertainty flickering in her eyes.

"Can you help me with this?" she asked, glancing back at Jake, who looked on, conflicted.

In that moment, the cake became more than just flour and sugar; it became a vessel of strength, a beacon of the love that had brought us all together. I nodded, ready to step into the fray, to wield frosting and fondant like armor against the chaos of love's expectations. As

Elara and I began to decorate the cake together, I felt a sense of purpose wash over me. This was about so much more than just a wedding; it was about crafting a moment that would echo through the years, a reminder that love, in all its messy glory, was worth fighting for.

The air around me buzzed with a mixture of excitement and tension, a strange cocktail that made my heart race in tandem with the bustling crowd. As Elara and I began decorating the cake, our hands moved instinctively, draping silk ribbons and positioning delicate sugar flowers with precision. Each flourish felt like an unspoken promise, a commitment to the love and joy this day was meant to encapsulate. I caught a glimpse of Elara's expression, her initial frustration melting into determination as she focused on the cake.

"Maybe we should add more flowers here," I suggested, carefully tucking a delicate bloom into place, wanting to distract her from the earlier confrontation.

"Yeah, that'll do it," she said, a flicker of that radiant smile returning. "It's like a tiny garden on a cake. Who wouldn't love that?"

Just then, Jake approached, his brow still furrowed, but there was a hint of uncertainty in his posture. "Elara," he said, his voice steady yet edged with concern. "Can we talk? Please?"

I exchanged a quick glance with Elara, and her eyes held a blend of hope and trepidation. The moment felt fragile, teetering on the edge of something significant. "Maybe you should," I urged gently, gesturing toward a quieter corner of the venue, where a few scattered tables sat, adorned with vibrant floral arrangements that seemed to echo the chaotic beauty of the day.

She hesitated, biting her lip as if weighing the gravity of the conversation against the joy that surrounded us. "Okay, but you stay here, right? I need to come back and finish this cake."

"Absolutely," I replied, trying to infuse a sense of calm into the whirlwind around us. As they stepped away, I resumed my work, although my heart thrummed with curiosity.

Time stretched in that liminal space, filled with the rhythmic clinking of glasses and distant laughter that somehow felt both celebratory and ominous. I found myself eavesdropping, catching snippets of their conversation. "It's just a wedding, Elara," Jake's voice was low but intense. "Why can't you see that we can simplify things?"

"Because it's not just about the wedding!" Elara shot back, her voice rising just enough for me to catch the underlying frustration. "It's about us. It's about starting our life together, and if we can't even manage this, how are we going to face the future?"

The ache in her voice tugged at my heart. I knew that weddings were a crucible of emotions, but the weight of their expectations was pressing down harder than I had anticipated. It was easy to forget the underlying currents of stress that could tarnish even the most beautiful of days. I busied myself with the final touches on the cake, hoping my distraction would ease the tightening knot in my stomach.

Minutes stretched like taffy until Elara returned, her face flushed with a mix of resolve and vulnerability. "We're okay," she declared, her voice stronger than before, but the sparkle in her eyes had dimmed a little. "We just... needed to clear the air."

"That's good," I replied, though I could sense the tension still coiling around her. "Want to keep decorating? We're almost done."

As we resumed our task, the cake transformed under our fingers, each layer becoming a monument to their love and a testament to the trials they had already faced. I looked over at Elara, her brow furrowed in concentration, and couldn't help but admire her spirit. She had always been the kind of person who fought for what she wanted, who believed in the power of love to transcend even the most daunting obstacles.

"Do you ever think about how weddings are basically a test?" I quipped, attempting to lighten the mood. "I mean, if you can survive planning a wedding, you can survive anything. It's like a boot camp for marriage."

Elara chuckled, a soft sound that brought a smile to my face. "Oh, definitely. If we can tackle this, I'm pretty sure we can handle anything. Like... house cleaning."

"Or picking paint colors," I added, my voice laced with mock seriousness. "The ultimate battle of wills."

We both laughed, the sound a bright note in the otherwise tense atmosphere. It felt good, reassuring. But just as the laughter faded, a figure loomed behind us, darkening the vibrant space with an unsettling presence. It was Jake again, but this time his face was etched with uncertainty, and he was wringing his hands like he was about to deliver devastating news.

"Can I, um, talk to you both?" he asked, his voice shaky, drawing my attention away from the delicate floral arrangements we had been arranging.

Elara looked at me, and I sensed her apprehension, as if a storm was brewing beneath the surface. "Sure, what's up?" she replied, her voice steady despite the tension radiating from her.

"I just... I don't want to do this without you," Jake began, his gaze darting between Elara and the cake, then back to her. "I realize now that I've been so caught up in logistics and expectations that I lost sight of what really matters."

Elara's expression shifted, the hope rising like the warmth of the sun breaking through clouds. "What do you mean?" she asked, her voice barely above a whisper.

"I mean," he took a deep breath, "I want us to make this day truly ours. Not just a checklist of things to do or traditions to uphold. I want to celebrate our love, not just the wedding."

A wave of relief washed over me, lifting the heavy atmosphere as Elara's face lit up with the spark I had been longing to see. "You mean it? You really want to do this together?"

"Absolutely. Let's create something beautiful, just like you've done with that cake. It doesn't have to be perfect; it just has to be us."

As he spoke, I felt an electric charge in the air, a transformative moment where love asserted itself against the backdrop of chaos. The wedding, once a point of contention, had become a canvas for their shared vision, a partnership grounded in understanding and love.

Elara stepped closer to him, and I couldn't help but feel like an intruder witnessing something profoundly intimate. Their fingers intertwined, and in that simple gesture, the world outside fell away. "Okay," she said, her voice steady, "let's do this together. But first, cake!"

And just like that, laughter filled the air again, echoing through the venue, mingling with the scent of vanilla and sugar. It felt like a promise—a pact forged in the heart of a whirlwind day, and I found myself swept along in the current of their love story, ready to celebrate whatever unexpected turns awaited us next.

The atmosphere shifted as Jake and Elara shared a moment that felt like a fragile truce, their laughter mingling with the background music, but beneath it lay an undercurrent of unresolved tension. I busied myself with the last touches on the cake, applying an elegant border of royal icing that mirrored the lace of Elara's gown, hoping to weave a bit of calm back into the whirlwind of emotions surrounding us. Just as I finished, I caught sight of Elara's mother approaching, her expression a mixture of pride and concern that sent a ripple of anxiety through me.

"Everything looks stunning," she said, her eyes lingering on the cake before drifting toward her daughter. "But we need to finalize the seating arrangements. Have you seen your father?"

"Mom, I'm a little busy right now," Elara replied, a hint of frustration seeping into her tone.

"I understand, dear, but we're running out of time," her mother pressed, her voice a sharp contrast to the gentle chaos of the wedding preparations.

The crackle of tension returned, but before Elara could respond, a sudden shout from the entrance caught our attention. "What do you mean the flowers aren't here yet?" It was the florist, waving her arms in dramatic fashion, as if she were directing an orchestra gone awry.

"Of course they're not here! The order was confirmed!" she continued, and the wave of anxiety seemed to rise, swallowing the happiness that had been flourishing just moments before.

"Does she even know it's a wedding today?" I murmured under my breath to Elara, who let out a surprised laugh, the tension easing just a little.

"Honestly, it feels like the universe is conspiring against us," she replied, shaking her head. "But we'll figure it out. We have cake, after all."

"Yes, cake—always the centerpiece of any drama," I teased, my heart lightening at her resilience.

Just as I felt a flicker of hope that the day might right itself, the venue doors swung open, and in burst a group of women wearing matching pastel dresses, all chattering and giggling like they had just arrived from a magical realm. "Where's the bride?" one of them shouted, her eyes darting around as if Elara's wedding gown would shine like a beacon.

Elara's expression shifted from amusement to alarm. "Oh no, the bridesmaids!" she gasped, glancing at me, her voice tense. "I thought they were coming earlier!"

I could almost hear the collective sigh of relief as the group surrounded Elara, showering her with compliments and excitement. "You look incredible!" one of them squealed, while another pulled her into a hug so tight I was sure Elara's corset would snap.

Amid the joyful chaos, I watched as Elara tried to keep her composure, her smile teetering between genuine delight and the looming specter of stress. "Okay, ladies, let's get you organized," she said, her voice firm. "I need you all to focus! I don't want to end up with someone's great aunt sitting next to my ex!"

Laughter erupted from the bridesmaids, a sound that felt like sunlight breaking through a cloudy sky. But I could sense Elara's simmering anxiety beneath the surface, and it made my heart ache.

"Are we ready to cut the cake?" I asked, trying to divert her attention from the tumult of preparations. "I think we should have a cake cutting ceremony—what do you say?"

The idea seemed to catch her off guard. "Right now?" she replied, blinking as if the world had momentarily stopped spinning.

"Why not? It can be a fun distraction," I suggested, my mind racing to defuse the brewing storm of emotions. "Plus, it'll give everyone something to focus on besides the chaotic seating chart."

"Okay, let's do it!" Elara's eyes brightened, and for a moment, the weight of the day seemed to lift just a little. I turned to the bridesmaids, raising my voice slightly. "Gather around, everyone! Cake cutting time!"

The crowd responded with enthusiastic cheers, and I felt a surge of relief wash over me. As Elara and Jake approached the cake, I stepped back to allow the moment to unfold. The tiers stood proudly, adorned with blooms that seemed to dance in the soft lighting, a sugary monument to their love.

Elara and Jake exchanged glances filled with unspoken vows, and as they held the ceremonial knife together, I caught a glimpse of the love that had, against all odds, survived the day's many trials. "On three?" Jake suggested, a playful grin on his face.

"Absolutely," Elara replied, her voice steady, embodying the poise I had come to admire. "One, two—"

The blade sliced through the top tier, and cheers erupted around us. But just as the first piece was lifted, an urgent voice cut through the celebration. "Wait! Hold on!"

All heads turned, and I felt a cold chill run down my spine as a tall figure strode through the crowd, a flash of familiar green eyes piercing the joyful atmosphere. It was Mara, Elara's estranged sister, clad in a sleek black dress that screamed sophistication but felt utterly out of place among the pastel hues of the wedding.

"Mara?" Elara gasped, her voice almost a whisper, and the air thickened with tension as the moment froze. "What are you doing here?"

"I had to come," Mara declared, her voice clear and unwavering. "You can't just start a new chapter without me in it."

The room shifted, a palpable weight descending, and I could see Elara's expression harden, her happiness teetering on the brink of something fragile. "You didn't even RSVP!" she shot back, her earlier composure slipping away.

"Because I knew you didn't want me here. But guess what? I'm family, and I'm not about to let you make this day about anyone else but us."

The crowd stood in stunned silence, the tension spiraling like smoke around us. I exchanged anxious glances with the bridesmaids, each one looking as bewildered as I felt. The weight of unresolved issues hung heavy in the air, and I could see Elara's carefully constructed world begin to unravel at the edges.

"Maybe we should step outside for a moment," I whispered, trying to keep my voice steady, but it was clear that the wedding I had hoped would be filled with joy was now poised on the brink of disaster. Elara hesitated, her eyes darting between Jake and Mara, and I knew this was a moment that could alter everything.

As the first drops of rain began to patter against the windows, a feeling of impending storm settled in the room. The fragile balance of love, expectations, and family secrets hung precariously, and I could feel my heart racing. What would Elara choose? And would love be enough to withstand the tempest that was about to unfold?

Chapter 6: Crumbling Foundations

The sun hung low in the sky, casting a warm, golden hue over the sprawling gardens of Thornfield Manor, where laughter mingled with the gentle rustle of leaves in the evening breeze. The scent of blooming jasmine clung to the air, sweet yet bittersweet, like a lingering note of happiness edged with a hint of something darker. Guests, adorned in their finest, floated around the manicured lawns, their laughter bright yet echoing with a certain unease. I clutched my glass of sparkling rosé, its bubbles fizzing like the thoughts racing in my mind.

Elara, radiant in her lace gown that seemed to shimmer with every step, was the center of attention—her smile dazzling enough to light up the most shadowed corners of the estate. Yet, despite her ethereal beauty, there was an undeniable tension in her posture, an almost imperceptible tremor in her hands as she clutched the bouquet of white peonies. They had been her mother's favorite, but even the scent of nostalgia couldn't mask the undercurrent of uncertainty rippling through the gathering.

I stood slightly apart, watching the spectacle unfold like a play where I was merely a spectator, hoping for a happy ending that seemed increasingly out of reach. Whispers threaded through the air, each word sharp enough to cut. "Did you see the way he looked at her?" "Is it true they've been having problems?" Each murmur weighed heavily on my chest, knotting my stomach. How could they, of all people, question her happiness? I longed to sweep Elara away from the prying eyes, to reassure her that love didn't always fit neatly into the boxes society prepared for it.

As the sun dipped lower, painting the sky in shades of fiery orange and soft pink, I found a quiet corner behind a tall hedge, seeking solace amidst the swirling chaos. The quiet hum of distant laughter faded into the background, allowing my racing thoughts a moment of clarity. Just then, Max appeared, his tall frame cutting through the shadows, eyes bright with concern. "Hey," he said, his voice a low rumble that stirred something deep within me.

"Hey," I replied, forcing a smile that didn't quite reach my eyes. He stepped closer, the air between us crackling with unspoken words and lingering tension. Max's presence was both a comfort and a complication. I knew the way he made me feel was dangerous, yet here we were, together in this moment of vulnerability, our worlds intertwined like the vines climbing the ancient stone walls around us.

"Is she okay?" he asked, glancing toward the gathering, his brow furrowing as he caught sight of Elara, now surrounded by guests, though the smile on her face looked more like a mask than a reflection of her true feelings. My heart sank as I nodded, though the gesture felt hollow. "She's trying, I think. But it's hard. People are talking."

Max shifted closer, his shoulder brushing against mine, sending a shiver racing through me. "What do you think?" he asked softly, his eyes searching mine. "Do you think she'll make it?"

I sighed, the weight of my thoughts spilling over. "Love shouldn't feel like a performance," I whispered, recalling the way Elara's eyes darted to her husband as if gauging his reaction, constantly assessing the mood of the crowd. "But I'm not sure how much longer she can hold it together."

A moment of silence stretched between us, thick with unspoken fears and the reality of our situation. Then, as if drawn by some invisible force, we leaned closer, our breaths mingling, anticipation crackling in the air. The world around us blurred, and for a heartbeat, nothing else mattered. I could feel his warmth, the intensity of his gaze, and just as our lips brushed against each other, the moment shattered.

"Elara!" Her voice rang out, sharp and urgent, cutting through the intimacy like a knife. My heart raced as I pulled away, guilt flooding my system. There she stood, her face pale, eyes brimming with tears that seemed to shimmer like shattered glass in the fading light.

"Can we talk?" she asked, her voice trembling, barely above a whisper. The laughter and music faded into a muted backdrop, leaving only her desperate plea hanging in the air. My heart sank, torn between the instinct to comfort her and the undeniable pull I felt towards Max.

I glanced back at him, his expression caught between concern for Elara and the frustration of being interrupted. "Of course," I said quickly, stepping away from the protective warmth of Max's presence. The world shifted around us as I crossed the distance to Elara, each step heavier than the last.

"What's wrong?" I asked, concern tightening my throat. She shook her head, wiping her tears with trembling fingers, her carefully curated facade crumbling like the petals of her bouquet scattering in the wind.

"I don't think I can do this," she admitted, her voice thick with emotion. "Not like this. Not with everyone watching."

The weight of her words pressed against me, a stark reminder that beneath the glittering surface of our lives, deep fissures could threaten to swallow us whole. I reached for her hand, feeling her pulse race beneath my fingers, a mirror of my own chaos. "You don't have to," I assured her, desperately trying to convey strength in that moment. "We can figure this out together."

The shadows deepened around us, engulfing the garden as night began to fall. The laughter, the clinking of glasses, and the music faded into a distant echo. Here, beneath the stars slowly emerging in the twilight, we stood on the edge of something monumental—both vulnerable and strong, poised between love and uncertainty. And

I could only hope that whatever lay ahead, we would find a way through it.

The air was thick with unspoken words as Elara's delicate fingers trembled in mine, her knuckles ghostly white against the contrast of her vibrant gown. I could feel the pulse of her anxiety vibrating through our joined hands, each throb echoing a silent plea for reassurance. "I can't keep pretending," she whispered, her voice a fragile thread that could easily snap under the weight of expectation. The garden, with its twinkling fairy lights and cheerful chatter, felt like a world apart, a beautiful lie I was suddenly desperate to escape.

"Then don't," I urged, my heart aching for her. "You deserve to be happy, not stuck in a performance." My words hung in the air, a fragile lifeline cast into the turbulent waters of her despair. She blinked, her lashes glistening with unshed tears, and for a moment, I wondered if I'd misread the depths of her struggle. Maybe she really did want this, whatever "this" was—perhaps even more than I wanted her to let go.

Elara released a shaky breath, her eyes darting toward the crowd, searching for something I couldn't identify. "What if I make the wrong choice?" The vulnerability in her gaze pierced me. "What if everyone knows?"

The thought of everyone knowing made me recoil. There was a rawness to her fear, a truth I had almost forgotten while immersed in my own swirling feelings for Max. "Then let them know," I replied, the words tumbling out before I could catch them. "Your happiness is more important than their opinions. If you need to—"

"I can't!" She cut me off, voice rising. "I can't just walk away from a wedding day. It's a fairy tale! And look at me—I'm the princess!" Her laughter was hollow, a brittle sound that echoed through the fading light.

A pang of empathy surged through me as I watched her struggle against her own dreams. The princess of this story was about to discover that every fairy tale hides a darker reality beneath its shimmering surface. I stepped closer, letting go of her hand for just a moment to wrap my arms around her, hoping the embrace would lend her some strength. "You can be the heroine of your own story. Just don't forget that being a princess doesn't mean being a puppet."

She melted against me for a brief moment, her body quaking with silent sobs before she pulled away, a newfound resolve flickering in her eyes. "You're right. I need to talk to him."

The finality in her tone sent a wave of unease washing over me. "What if he doesn't understand? What if he pushes you away?"

She squared her shoulders, shaking her head as if my words were mere clouds she could scatter with determination. "I have to try. For myself."

As she walked away, the shadows in her wake seemed darker, deeper, and I felt a sense of foreboding settle in my chest. I turned back to Max, who stood a few paces away, his expression unreadable. The air around him was thick with unsaid things, a potent mixture of longing and anxiety.

"Is she okay?" he asked, his brow furrowed, clearly having witnessed Elara's turmoil.

"Not really," I admitted, feeling a weight settle in my gut. "She's struggling, Max. She's caught between the life everyone expects her to have and the one she really wants."

He nodded, his eyes darkening. "It's a tough position to be in. I wish..." He trailed off, the unspoken wish hanging like a specter between us. I didn't need him to finish; we both knew what he wanted to say.

"Yeah, me too," I replied softly. The silence stretched, filled with the electric energy of what might be between us, the spark of something profound yet dangerously unformed.

Just then, a loud burst of laughter erupted nearby, a group of guests celebrating with overzealous enthusiasm. "Why is it that laughter always seems so hollow at moments like this?" I remarked, trying to lighten the mood, but the attempt fell flat.

"Maybe because we all know it can be a mask," Max replied, a hint of cynicism sharpening his tone. "People hide behind smiles and jokes as a way to deflect from what's really going on."

His words struck a chord, resonating with the truth I'd sensed in Elara's struggle. "You're right. And the last thing she needs is to feel like she's a character in someone else's story."

Max moved closer, a flicker of determination lighting his eyes. "Then let's make sure she knows we're here for her, no matter what. Even if that means..." His voice trailed off, and I could see the struggle in his features, the unspoken questions flitting behind his gaze.

"Even if it means what?" I urged, stepping closer, our breaths mingling, caught in the delicate balance of friendship and something more.

"Even if it means being just friends." The words hung in the air, heavy with finality, the longing between us palpable yet painfully restrained. I could almost hear the clock ticking, each second drawing us closer to a decision that would change everything.

"Just friends," I echoed, tasting the bitterness of that label. "But what if—"

Before I could finish, a familiar figure appeared at the edge of our private world, drawing my attention. It was Elara again, her expression now resolute, and for a moment, I held my breath, hoping for a glimmer of hope.

"I need to talk to you both," she declared, her voice steady despite the storm brewing in her eyes. My heart sank at the urgency laced in her words.

Max and I exchanged a glance, a shared understanding that whatever Elara had to say would either bind us together or unravel everything we'd been building. "What's wrong?" I asked, stepping forward, ready to support her, my pulse quickening with a mix of dread and curiosity.

"I... I told him," she stammered, her breath hitching. "I told him everything."

The weight of her confession fell like a stone between us, the air suddenly thick with tension. I glanced at Max, whose face had turned ashen, and in that fleeting moment, I realized this was just the beginning of a journey that could fracture or fortify our bonds.

Elara's words hung in the air like a thick fog, the weight of her confession creating a palpable tension. I could hardly comprehend the storm brewing behind her eyes, the fear mixed with a hint of liberation. "I told him everything," she repeated, her voice firmer this time, each syllable resonating with an urgency that sent a shiver down my spine.

"What do you mean everything?" I asked, trying to grasp the enormity of what she was saying. My heart raced, caught between concern for Elara and an unsettling curiosity about her husband's reaction. "Did you tell him about how you feel?"

She nodded, her lips pressing together as if summoning the strength to say what she needed. "I told him that I can't marry him, that I can't go through with this if it means sacrificing who I am."

Max shifted beside me, the color draining from his face. "And what did he say?"

Elara took a deep breath, the tremor in her hands betraying the strength in her voice. "He didn't take it well." The admission hung there, heavy and foreboding, echoing the concerns I had tried to suppress earlier.

"Does he—does he want to talk to us?" I asked, though deep down, I feared the answer.

"No, he's with his parents." The words slipped from her lips like lead weights. "I don't think he wants to see anyone right now."

A silence fell over us, the air thickening with unspoken thoughts. I could see the conflict etching lines on Elara's face, the very embodiment of a woman torn between two worlds. "What are you going to do?" I finally ventured, my voice almost a whisper.

"I don't know." She blinked, and I could see the tears brimming in her eyes again, threatening to spill over. "I feel like I've stepped off a cliff into the unknown. I can't go back now, but forward is just as terrifying."

Max reached out, a comforting hand on Elara's shoulder. "You're not alone in this. We're here for you, whatever you decide." The warmth of his words hung in the air, an anchor in the tumultuous sea of emotions swirling around us.

Elara's gaze shifted between us, and I could sense the turmoil within her. "I know you both care about me, and I appreciate it. But I can't ask you to be my support system when I'm so unsure about everything."

"Then don't ask," I said, a hint of determination rising in my chest. "Let us be here, no strings attached. You don't have to shoulder this burden alone."

"Right," Max chimed in, "we're your friends. It's our job to stand by you even when the world feels like it's collapsing."

Elara smiled faintly, but it was tinged with something darker. "I've built my entire life around this moment, and now..." She let the thought dangle, unfinished.

"I get that," I said, stepping closer, allowing my own vulnerability to break through. "I've spent so much time convincing myself that life goes as planned, that every step leads to some happy ending. But what if we're meant to redefine what happiness looks like?"

Her brow furrowed, and she seemed to ponder my words. Just then, a sudden raucous burst of laughter from the guests shattered the moment, a cruel reminder of the joyous façade we were all expected to maintain.

"Shall we head inside?" I suggested, glancing at Max. "Maybe a change of scenery will help us figure this out."

Elara nodded, her shoulders dropping slightly as if the act of making a decision had lifted a small part of her burden. As we stepped away from the soft glow of the garden lights and into the cool interior of the manor, the atmosphere shifted. The soft strains of a string quartet filled the air, mingling with the clinking of glasses and the murmur of conversation, creating a soundtrack of celebration that felt alien against the backdrop of our turmoil.

Inside, the hall was adorned with golden drapes and twinkling chandeliers, casting an ethereal glow on the polished floor. Guests danced, their faces alight with joy, unaware of the storm brewing just a few feet away. I felt as if we were all actors in a play, our true emotions hidden behind elaborate costumes and smiles that didn't quite reach our eyes.

"Let's find somewhere private," Max suggested, his voice low and steady, cutting through the noise. We navigated through clusters of guests, Elara trailing behind, her demeanor shifting between resolute and fragile.

We finally slipped into a small alcove, dimly lit and decorated with lush greenery that framed us like a living portrait. The muffled sounds of laughter faded as we settled into the sanctuary of our shared bubble, the weight of the world outside temporarily lifting.

"I don't want to drag you both into my mess," Elara admitted, her voice softer now, the fierce determination wavering under the pressure of her heartache.

"You're not dragging us anywhere," Max said firmly, leaning closer. "You're our friend, and we care about you. We can help you figure this out."

A moment passed where I could feel the three of us forming an unspoken pact, the bond of friendship intertwining around the uncertainty like vines creeping up a trellis, strong yet delicate.

"Okay," Elara said, the resolve returning to her voice. "But I can't promise to have it all figured out tonight."

"Who does?" I quipped, my lips curling into a half-smile. "Life's not a math problem. We're just here to find the answers together, one step at a time."

As Elara nodded, a flicker of something—hope? Fear?—crossed her face. Just then, the door swung open, and in strode Caleb, her fiancé, his expression a mixture of frustration and determination. The laughter and joy from outside seemed to retreat as he stepped into our private space, an unwelcome reminder of the life Elara had been trying to escape.

"Elara," he called, voice low but commanding, drawing all our attention. "We need to talk. Now."

The tension in the air shifted abruptly, charged with an electric current that sent a ripple of fear through me. Max instinctively moved closer to Elara, his body a protective barrier between her and the oncoming storm. "This isn't a good time," he said, his tone flat but resolute.

"Is it ever a good time?" Caleb shot back, eyes narrowing, the hurt in his expression morphing into something sharper, something dangerous. "I want to know what's going on."

Elara stood frozen, a deer caught in the headlights of an approaching vehicle, and for a moment, the world around us faded. It was just the four of us, teetering on the brink of a cliff with no safety net below, each heartbeat echoing with unasked questions and unspoken fears.

"Whatever you think you heard," I began, ready to step in and protect Elara, but she raised her hand to silence me.

"I need to say it," she said, her voice trembling but fierce, like a candle flickering against the dark.

As she took a step forward, her heart on her sleeve, I realized we were all standing at the edge of an unseen precipice, one word away from unraveling everything we thought we knew. And in that fragile moment, with Caleb's presence looming over us like a thundercloud, I understood that this confrontation would change everything.

Chapter 7: A Recipe for Heartbreak

The scent of freshly baked bread filled the air, mingling with the earthy aroma of rosemary and garlic, creating an olfactory tapestry that was both comforting and stimulating. I stood in my sun-drenched kitchen, a place where I often lost myself in the alchemy of ingredients, letting my hands knead the dough with an almost reverent care. My countertop was a canvas of flour, and my apron had seen better days, speckled with remnants of culinary experiments gone awry. Cooking was my refuge, a balm for the chaos that had taken root in my heart after Elara's wedding.

The golden hue of the late afternoon sun streamed through the window, casting a warm glow over everything, almost as if the world outside had paused to respect the quiet storm brewing within me. With each fold of the dough, I poured my thoughts and fears into the mixture, my hands instinctively working the gluten as if to mold the very fabric of my discontent into something beautiful. Each movement was a distraction, a way to channel the tumult of emotions swirling inside me, from the elation of the wedding to the crushing weight of Elara's impending divorce.

Just then, my phone buzzed insistently on the countertop, shattering my momentary peace. I glanced at the screen—Elara. My heart raced; I hadn't heard from her since the wedding. She had always been a whirlwind of laughter and light, her voice like honey dripping from a spoon, soothing and sweet. But that day, as I answered the call, I could hear the storm brewing on the other end.

"Lana," she began, her voice shaky, "I... I don't know how to say this." A tremor of vulnerability laced her words, and I felt a knot of dread settle in my stomach.

"Elara, take a breath," I urged gently, gripping the edge of the counter for support. The dough felt foreign under my fingers, as if it had absorbed the tension in the air. "What's going on?"

"It's David," she said, her voice cracking. "He's not the man I thought he was. We're getting a divorce."

The words landed heavily in the air, a suffocating cloud of realization. Elara and David had always seemed like the perfect couple, their chemistry palpable, each laughter-filled moment a testament to their love. But here was the shattering truth, raw and jagged, cutting through my heart like a dull knife. "Oh, Elara..."

"I thought we could work through it, you know? But every time I try to talk to him, it's like he's a stranger. I just feel so lost." Her pain echoed within me, a mirrored reflection of the doubts that had begun to creep into my own life. I took a deep breath, steeling myself against the swell of emotions threatening to spill over.

"Can I come over?" I asked, my voice steady despite the tumult within. "We can talk about it."

"Yes, please," she whispered, the relief palpable even through the phone. "I really need you."

I grabbed my keys and dashed out of the house, leaving behind the half-kneaded dough and the warmth of my kitchen. The drive to her apartment was a blur, a patchwork of red lights and mundane traffic, each moment an exercise in anticipation. The city outside was alive, unaware of the heartache that pulsed through my veins, but all I could think of was how Elara needed me.

When I finally reached her building, I found her sitting on the steps, a shadow of her former self. Her usually vibrant hair was pulled back in a messy bun, and the smudges beneath her eyes told stories of sleepless nights and endless worry. I rushed up the steps and enveloped her in a hug, feeling the fragile weight of her sadness against me. "Hey," I whispered, "I'm here."

As we settled into her cozy living room, the familiar surroundings became a sanctuary for our shared sorrows. We sipped herbal tea, the warmth wrapping around us like a protective blanket as I listened to Elara spill her heart. She spoke of dreams shattered, plans discarded, and the stark realization that love, once so vibrant, had faded into something unrecognizable. I wanted to take her pain and make it mine, to lift the burden off her shoulders, but all I could offer was my presence.

"Do you remember when we used to dream about our futures?" she asked, her voice soft but filled with longing. "We thought we'd conquer the world, hand in hand with our perfect partners."

I nodded, the bittersweet memories flooding back. We had envisioned lives filled with adventure, love stories that would rival the most romantic novels. But here we were, faced with the stark reality that life rarely follows the scripts we write in our heads.

"I feel like I'm starting over," Elara confessed, her voice trembling. "I don't even know who I am without him."

The gravity of her words hit me, a deep pang resonating within. I understood all too well the weight of self-discovery, of navigating a world that often felt more like a maze than a map. And yet, as I looked at her, I saw resilience flickering in her eyes. The woman who once twirled through life with abandon was still there, buried beneath layers of hurt.

"Then let's figure it out together," I said, determination igniting within me. "We'll discover who we are now—individually, and maybe even together."

Elara's eyes glistened with gratitude, and for the first time that evening, a spark of hope flickered in her gaze. We shared stories and laughter, piecing together the fragments of our lives, and for a moment, the heaviness began to lift. It was a small victory, but a victory nonetheless.

As the night wore on, I felt the bond between us strengthen, a thread woven through shared experiences and the promise of new beginnings. The pain of her heartache remained, but so did the possibility of transformation. Little did I know that my own heart was not far from its own reckoning, with Max lingering in the back of my mind like an unfinished melody.

A week slipped by, each day a careful blend of routine and quiet reflection. My mornings began with the rhythm of the coffee grinder, the rich scent of freshly brewed beans mingling with the crisp autumn air wafting through the window. I reveled in the solitude of my kitchen, where the world outside felt like a distant memory, and the only voices I heard were those of my thoughts, sometimes cheerful, sometimes haunting. Elara's face lingered in my mind, framed by the glow of her laughter, a stark contrast to the somber reality of her call.

I found myself buried in my work, designing floral arrangements for a local gallery's upcoming event, my creativity flaring to life in the midst of my emotional turmoil. Bright yellows and deep burgundies filled my workspace, colors dancing together like old friends reunited after a long absence. The flowers, each petal and stem, became my silent confidants, soaking in my feelings as I crafted intricate designs. In moments of doubt, I let the blooms guide me, their beauty a reminder that even in darkness, there was light waiting to burst forth.

Then came the invitation I never saw coming. It arrived in the form of a group text from Max, the flurry of messages igniting a spark of excitement that swiftly morphed into apprehension. "Let's do a friends' night out," he typed, a simple suggestion laden with unspoken tension. "Dinner at Bella Luna? Bring Elara if she's up for it!"

The thought of seeing him stirred a whirlpool of emotions within me—anticipation mixed with a tinge of anxiety. Would our conversations circle around the void left by Elara's heartbreak, or would we be able to navigate our own uncharted waters? My heart raced, wrestling with the implications of spending the evening with both Max and Elara, the juxtaposition of joy and sorrow swirling like the wine in my glass.

The night unfolded under a blanket of twinkling stars, the air crisp with the promise of autumn. Bella Luna was alive with laughter and the enticing aroma of Italian cuisine wafting through the air, enveloping us like a warm embrace. I arrived early, a swirl of emotions washing over me as I caught sight of Max across the restaurant. He looked effortlessly charming in a navy shirt that accentuated his warm brown eyes, laughter dancing at the corners of his lips as he spoke with the hostess. The sight sent a familiar jolt through me, igniting feelings I had tried so hard to contain.

Elara arrived shortly after, her usual effervescence slightly dulled, though she tried to mask it with a smile. "You two look like you just walked off the cover of a magazine," she quipped, her voice light, yet I could see the cracks beneath her facade. "Or at least a very stylish catalog."

"We aim to please," Max replied, flashing a grin that made my heart do a little dance. "Though I think we might need your expert touch to truly achieve that level of glam."

As we settled into a cozy booth, the conversations flowed like the wine, sometimes bubbling over into fits of laughter and other times dipping into more somber notes. I watched as Elara's mood oscillated, her laughter mingling with moments of pensive silence, and I couldn't help but feel the weight of the tension in the air, thick enough to slice with a knife.

"So, what's on your mind?" I asked her, leaning in slightly, my concern genuine. "You seem a little distant."

Elara picked at the edge of her napkin, her eyes downcast for a moment before meeting mine. "Just... life, I guess," she said, her voice barely above a whisper. "It's strange to feel so lost when everything seems normal around me."

Max chimed in, a hint of sincerity in his tone. "You know, it's okay to feel that way. It's a part of figuring things out. Just look at the pasta here—perfectly twisted and tangled, yet somehow still delicious."

Elara chuckled softly, the sound like music breaking through a heavy silence. "Is that your way of saying I'm a mess?"

"Only if we're calling delicious things messy," he shot back, his teasing laced with warmth, and for a moment, the shadows that clung to Elara seemed to lift.

As the night wore on, we shared stories, laughter echoing around our table like a soothing balm. But even amidst the lighthearted banter, I felt the tension simmering beneath the surface, each glance between Max and me crackling with unspoken words.

"Do you ever think about how our lives are so intertwined?" Max suddenly asked, his gaze lingering on mine. "Like we're all threads in the same tapestry, and each twist and turn pulls us closer together or pushes us apart?"

I blinked, the profundity of his words sinking in. "Yeah, it's like we're all characters in a story we didn't write," I replied, my heart thudding as I considered the complexity of our relationships. "Sometimes it's beautiful, and sometimes it's just a messy plot twist."

Elara looked between us, her brow furrowing slightly as if she sensed the deeper currents beneath our playful dialogue. "Well, I'm all for messy plots. They tend to make the best stories, right?"

"Right," Max and I replied in unison, our eyes catching in a moment that felt almost electric.

As the evening drew to a close, we stood outside the restaurant, the crisp night air alive with the rustling of leaves, the scent of impending rain lingering. Elara pulled us into a quick embrace, her smile brightening her features despite the underlying sadness. "Thanks for tonight, you two. I needed this more than you know."

"Anytime," I replied, my heart aching for her yet buoyed by the flicker of hope I'd seen in her eyes.

After she headed home, the atmosphere shifted, leaving just Max and me standing under the faint glow of streetlights. The silence that enveloped us was thick, charged with everything we hadn't said, the unsaid words hanging heavy in the air like an unfinished symphony.

"About earlier..." he began, his voice low, but I could see the uncertainty etched on his face.

"Yeah?" I prompted, my heart racing in anticipation.

He took a deep breath, the weight of our unspoken connection hanging between us. "I've been thinking... maybe we need to stop pretending that what's between us isn't real. It's there, and I can't ignore it."

My breath caught, the world around us fading into a distant echo as his words washed over me. What had started as friendship felt like it was blossoming into something more, something that could easily tip into chaos. But for the first time, I felt the glimmer of possibility, a flicker of what could be—a twist in our tangled lives that might just lead to a beautiful new chapter.

The chill of autumn had settled in, casting a golden hue over the city and wrapping it in a crisp embrace. As the leaves turned to a kaleidoscope of red, orange, and gold, I found myself in my kitchen once more, not just cooking but trying to conjure a sense of normalcy amidst the chaos that had invaded my heart. Tonight, I was determined to make something special—something to share with Elara that might lift her spirits. The familiar rhythm of chopping vegetables and stirring fragrant spices became my anchor, a grounding force against the tumult of my thoughts.

In the midst of my culinary endeavor, the sound of a knock on my door broke through the soothing cadence. I wiped my hands on a towel, surprised to see Max standing there, his hair tousled and eyes bright with an energy that both thrilled and unsettled me. "What are you doing here?" I asked, attempting to hide my surprise behind a teasing smile. "Did you come to steal my secret recipe for emotional healing?"

He grinned, his expression somehow mischievous and earnest all at once. "I might be here for a taste test. Or, you know, just to rescue you from your culinary isolation."

I stepped aside, allowing him to enter. "Welcome to my sanctuary of carbs and chaos. Hope you're hungry!"

He laughed, an easy sound that made my stomach flip. "I always am, especially when carbs are involved. What are you making?"

"Something that sounds more ambitious than it is—stuffed butternut squash with quinoa and cranberries. Fancy, right?"

"Fancy and fall-ish. I like it. Can I help?"

I handed him a knife, an impromptu partnership forming as we sliced and diced, our movements gradually syncing to an unspoken rhythm. With every laugh and shared glance, the tension between us softened, dissolving the weight of unspoken feelings like sugar in warm water. "You know," he said, his tone casual but with an undercurrent of something more serious, "I've been thinking about what I said the other night."

I paused, my heart racing. "About what?"

"About us." He turned, leaning against the counter, his expression earnest. "I meant it. There's something real here, and I don't want to pretend it doesn't exist anymore."

I bit my lip, a rush of emotions flooding through me. "Max, this is... complicated. Elara's going through so much right now."

"I get that," he replied, his voice low and steady. "But life is complicated, and waiting around isn't going to make it any easier. I care about you, and I think you feel the same. So why are we still dancing around it?"

I turned back to the stove, my hands trembling slightly as I stirred the mixture in the pan, the heat from the flame a distraction

THE TASTE OF AMBITION

from the whirlwind inside my head. I could feel the weight of his gaze on me, waiting for an answer. "It's just... everything feels so tangled. Elara needs me, and I don't want to add to her pain."

Max moved closer, the warmth radiating from him like a comforting blanket. "You're not adding to her pain by being honest about how you feel. It's not a competition, and you deserve to be happy too."

His words hung in the air, and for a moment, the kitchen felt like a world away from the realities outside. The scent of cinnamon and nutmeg swirled around us, enveloping us in a cocoon of possibility. But just as I began to lean into that warmth, the phone rang, piercing the fragile bubble we had created. It was Elara.

"Hey," I said, my voice shifting from warmth to concern in an instant. "Is everything okay?"

"I'm at home," she replied, her voice trembling slightly. "Can you come over? I... I need to talk."

"Of course. I'll be there in a few minutes," I assured her, my heart racing. I glanced at Max, whose expression had shifted from playful to serious.

"Do you want me to come with you?" he offered, concern etched on his face.

"No, I think it's better if it's just me. I need to be there for her."

As I grabbed my coat, the weight of Max's presence pressed against my back, an invisible tether that threatened to pull me in two directions. I turned to him, our eyes locking in a moment heavy with unspoken words and lingering tension. "I'll call you later?"

"Yeah. Please do." He hesitated, his eyes searching mine as if looking for a promise.

I stepped out into the crisp night air, the cool breeze biting at my cheeks as I made my way to Elara's apartment. The streets, illuminated by the soft glow of streetlights, felt eerily quiet, my footsteps echoing in the stillness. My mind raced with worry, trying to decipher what could have compelled her to call me so late, a sense of foreboding tightening in my chest.

When I arrived, the door swung open almost instantly, revealing Elara with tear-streaked cheeks and eyes that shimmered with both fear and determination. "Lana," she breathed, pulling me into a tight embrace. "I'm so glad you're here."

"What's going on?" I asked, stepping back to study her face. "You look like you've seen a ghost."

"I might as well have," she replied, a shaky laugh escaping her lips. "I've been doing a lot of thinking, and I finally had a conversation with David."

My heart sank at the mention of his name, the memories of their once-perfect relationship crashing back like waves against the shore. "And? What happened?"

Elara took a deep breath, her hands trembling as she ran them through her hair. "He's moving out. He wants to start fresh, and he says he needs to figure out who he is without me."

"That sounds... rough," I said carefully, my heart aching for her. "But maybe it's a step toward healing?"

Her gaze turned hard, a flash of anger flickering through her tears. "You don't understand. He's not just leaving me; he's leaving our life behind. And that's not all—he's seeing someone else."

The words struck me like a physical blow, the weight of betrayal settling heavily between us. "What? Elara, are you sure?"

"I caught him texting her." Her voice cracked, and I felt her pain as if it were my own. "I wanted to believe he was still the man I married, but now..."

We sat down on her couch, the air thick with sorrow and disbelief. I reached for her hand, offering whatever comfort I could but the reality hung between us like a chasm, one we couldn't ign

"I'm so sorry," I whispered, feeling helpless. "You deserve much more than this."

Her gaze shifted to the window, where the moonlight poured in like silver silk. "You know, maybe I've been too focused on what I lost instead of what I still have. I have you, and I need to remember that."

Just as the weight of her words began to settle in, the phone buzzed violently on the coffee table, its sound jarring us both. I glanced at the screen and my stomach dropped—it was a message from Max.

"We need to talk. Urgent."

Elara looked up, her brow furrowed with concern. "What is it?"

"I don't know," I replied, my heart pounding in my chest as I felt a sense of dread creeping in. "But it doesn't feel good."

"Go," she urged, her eyes searching mine. "I can handle this. We can handle this together."

As I stood to leave, an unexpected wave of uncertainty washed over me, pulling at my heartstrings. With a final glance back at Elara, I whispered, "Call me if you need anything, okay?"

I stepped into the night, my thoughts racing. Max's urgency sent adrenaline coursing through my veins, but as I moved through the shadowy streets, I couldn't shake the feeling that I was standing at a crossroads, torn between two worlds, two hearts, and a decision that could shatter everything.

Just as I reached my car, my phone buzzed again. I fumbled to check the message, my breath catching in my throat at what I read. "I found something you need to see. It's about Elara."

My heart raced, and I looked up just in time to see a shadow moving toward me, someone emerging from the dark, a face illuminated by the flickering streetlight. I froze, every instinct screaming at me to run, but curiosity pinned me in place. The figure stepped forward, and with a jolt of recognition, I realized who it was.

"David?" My voice trembled as the reality of the situation crashed over me. "What are you doing here?"

His expression was unreadable, a storm brewing behind his eyes. "We need to talk. It's about Elara... and everything you think you know."

A chill ran down my spine as the night held its breath, and I braced myself for whatever revelation was about to unfold, the tension coiling tighter with every passing second.

Chapter 8: Tides of Change

The sun dipped below the horizon, painting the sky in hues of lavender and gold as I measured flour into a bowl, the comforting scent of vanilla wafting through the kitchen like a warm embrace. It was one of those evenings when everything felt charged with possibility, yet the shadow of Elara's heartbreak lingered in the corners, darkening the edges of my newfound joy. I glanced over at Max, his presence a steady beacon against the chaotic tides of life swirling around us. He stood by the counter, meticulously slicing ripe strawberries, their ruby red flesh glistening like tiny jewels under the kitchen light.

"You know," he said, his voice rich and warm, laced with a teasing undertone that made my heart flutter, "if we keep this up, we might just make the best dessert on the planet. I'm not saying we should go for the Nobel Prize in Baking, but we'd definitely get a solid mention."

I chuckled, the sound brightening the dimness that occasionally threatened to envelop us. "Only if you promise not to burn it like last time. I still can't believe you thought adding extra sugar would save those charcoal cookies."

Max feigned offense, holding a strawberry to his chest as if it were a shield. "Hey, I was just trying to bring some creativity to the table! Who doesn't love a bit of surprise in their dessert?"

"Surprise? More like a culinary horror show. We're lucky I have a forgiving palate."

"Forgiving?" He arched an eyebrow, a smirk dancing on his lips. "You mean tolerant. That's different."

We shared a laugh, the sound echoing through the kitchen and momentarily drowning out the thoughts swirling in my mind. I had never intended for my baking sessions to become a retreat, a sacred space where we could explore the depth of our connection, yet here we were, creating something beautiful amidst the chaos.

Elara's pain was a constant reminder of what was at stake, a dark undertone to the symphony of our growing affection. As I rolled out the dough, I could feel the weight of her heartbreak pressing down on me. It wasn't just her tears I was carrying; they were intertwined with the grief I had tucked away since my mother's death, the specter of loss always lurking in the shadows. The thought of losing Max, of watching him crumble under the weight of his own struggles, made my heart ache with an intensity I had never known.

Max caught me staring off into space, his brow furrowing with concern. "Hey," he said softly, his voice slicing through the fog in my mind. "What's going on in that head of yours? You look like you're about to take a trip to Sadsville."

I shrugged, pretending to be engrossed in my task of shaping the dough into heart-shaped cookies. "Just thinking about Elara. She's having a rough time, you know? I want to help her, but it feels like I'm being pulled in two different directions. Supporting her while trying to figure out what we are... it's complicated."

He stepped closer, his warmth wrapping around me like a comforting blanket. "It is complicated, but you can't pour from an empty cup. You have to take care of yourself, too. I'm here for you. We can find a balance."

"I know, but what if I let her down? What if I focus too much on us and she feels abandoned? I can't do that to her."

Max took the dough from my hands, his grip firm yet gentle as he rolled it out on the countertop. "Elara will be okay. You're not abandoning her; you're living your life. Besides, sometimes, people need to see others happy to realize they can be happy too."

His insight made me pause, the truth of his words sinking in deeper than I expected. I wanted to believe that my happiness could somehow illuminate Elara's path, but the guilt gnawed at me. The juxtaposition of our laughter against the backdrop of her grief felt like a betrayal, a dance on the line of right and wrong.

"What if we fail?" I asked, the question hanging between us like a fragile glass ornament on the verge of shattering.

"We won't," he replied, his tone fierce and unwavering. "We're already building something together. That's what matters. Life is about risk and reward, right? If you don't leap, you'll never know how far you can fly."

I looked into his eyes, deep pools of determination and kindness. The very essence of him filled the room, the way his laughter danced with my own, how his fingers brushed against mine as we worked. In that moment, the tension coiling in my chest eased, if only slightly.

"Okay," I said, feeling a flicker of resolve igniting within me. "Let's make these cookies the best they can be, for both of us."

Max grinned, his eyes sparkling with mischief. "Now you're talking! A challenge it is! But, as the official cookie decorator, I must insist on adding sprinkles. It's a matter of life and deliciousness."

"Sprinkles?" I gasped, feigning shock. "What's next, chocolate chips in our shortbread?"

"Absolutely. And don't you dare try to talk me out of it. This isn't just baking; this is an adventure."

As we dove into the chaotic whirlwind of flour, sugar, and sprinkles, the air thick with laughter and flour dust, I realized that maybe, just maybe, love didn't have to be a choice between one person's happiness and another's. Perhaps it could be a shared journey, a tapestry woven from the joys and sorrows of our lives.

The night was heavy with the scent of baked goods, the air thick and sweet like a warm embrace. We had turned the kitchen into our makeshift sanctuary, flour dusting the countertops like soft snowflakes, a testament to our culinary war. Max and I were in the zone, our laughter echoing off the walls as we concocted a new recipe—a reckless blend of chocolate and pistachios that could either be a masterpiece or an utter disaster.

"Did you know that chocolate is basically the superhero of desserts?" Max declared, wielding a whisk like a sword, his eyes bright with passion. "It's rich, it's complex, and it can save even the most mundane cookie from the depths of despair."

"Ah, yes, the chocolate crusader. I suppose that makes you its faithful sidekick, forever trying to save the world, one cookie at a time." I grinned, stirring the batter while pretending to fend off his whisk with my spatula.

"Exactly! But I have to be careful. Last time I got too ambitious, I ended up with a batch of brownies that could double as doorstops."

"Maybe we should establish a 'No Epic Failures' rule for tonight," I suggested, my laughter bubbling up as I imagined our disaster from last week. "But where's the fun in that? I think we should aim for epic failure tonight!"

"Ah, the sweet sound of rebellion!" he exclaimed, throwing his hands up dramatically. "We shall forge ahead into the realm of culinary chaos. But first, we must test the ingredients—quality control and all."

He picked up a piece of dark chocolate and held it to his lips, his expression one of exaggerated contemplation. "Should I risk it? This could make or break our entire endeavor."

"Go for it! We need to ensure our chocolate is up to superhero standards."

With a flourish, he broke off a piece and tossed it into his mouth. "The chocolate is good. I can taste the potential for greatness," he declared, nodding sagely as if he were a wise oracle imparting life lessons. "What about the pistachios? Should I try one?"

"Only if you're ready for the revelation that they might change your life," I said, trying to sound serious while stifling my giggles.

He popped one in his mouth and raised his eyebrows in mock seriousness. "Life-changing indeed! And now, we must combine forces." He motioned grandly to the mixing bowl, where I could see the batter bubbling with anticipation.

We poured the chopped chocolate and pistachios into the bowl, and as I stirred, I could feel the chaos of the world beyond our little bubble drifting away. Each blend of ingredients was like a heartbeat, synchronizing us in our shared rhythm of laughter, love, and light-hearted rebellion against the mundane.

However, just as the batter began to take shape, the shrill sound of my phone cut through the laughter. I glanced at the screen and felt a twist in my gut. It was Elara. My heart raced, torn between the delightful chaos we had created and the reality that waited outside our kitchen sanctuary.

"Do you want me to get it?" Max asked, his brow furrowed as he noticed the change in my demeanor.

"No, let me just see what she needs," I replied, trying to keep my voice light. I stepped away from our makeshift culinary haven, my heart heavy with a mix of concern and the dread that came from knowing Elara's pain all too well.

"Hey, Elara," I said, forcing brightness into my tone, though I could already sense the gravity in her voice.

"Hey. I... I'm sorry to bother you, but can we talk?" Her voice trembled slightly, and it sent a ripple of anxiety through me.

"Of course. What's going on?" I said, glancing back at Max, who was pouring the remaining pistachios into the bowl, his expression a mixture of curiosity and concern.

"I just got off the phone with Mark," she said, her voice breaking slightly. "He wants to meet."

My heart sank, the weight of her divorce pressing down on me like a heavy fog. "And how do you feel about that?" I asked gently, my thoughts racing through potential outcomes.

"I don't know. I thought I was ready to move on, but now..." She took a shaky breath. "I just feel so lost. I'm scared."

"Listen," I said, my voice steady as I attempted to be her anchor. "You're not alone in this. You have me, and we can figure it out together."

"Can you come over? I really need your support right now."

"Of course," I assured her. "I'll be there soon."

I hung up, my heart heavy. The vibrant kitchen, once bursting with energy, now felt muted, as though the laughter had faded into the walls. I turned back to Max, whose expression had shifted from playful to serious, his worry palpable.

"Everything okay?" he asked, stepping closer.

"Elara needs me," I said, my voice barely above a whisper. "She's having a tough time with Mark."

Max nodded, understanding the weight of my words. "I can help. Let's wrap this up quickly, and we can head over together."

I shook my head, a mix of gratitude and guilt swirling inside me. "No, it's better if I go alone this time. She needs someone who can just be there for her without distractions."

"Okay, but promise me you'll call if you need anything," he said, his brow furrowing in concern. "You don't have to go through this alone, either."

"I know," I said, feeling the warmth of his sincerity. "I appreciate it. You're amazing."

He reached out, brushing his fingers against mine, his touch igniting a spark that made my heart race. "Just remember, you're stronger than you think. You've got this."

I smiled at him, my heart torn. "I'll be okay. I'll call you later, I promise."

As I grabbed my bag, the weight of uncertainty settled around me, but I felt a flicker of hope in Max's words. With one last glance back at the kitchen, filled with the remnants of our joyful chaos, I stepped out into the evening, ready to face whatever awaited me. The shadows were closing in, but I clung to the light of our laughter, knowing it would guide me through the darkness.

The moment I stepped into Elara's apartment, the weight of her distress enveloped me like a thick fog. The familiar scent of sandalwood and lavender was subdued, the air heavy with tension and unspoken fears. She sat curled up on her couch, a fortress of blankets cocooning her, with a mug of something steaming cradled in her hands, the remnants of her defenses clearly visible in the shadows beneath her eyes.

"Hey," I said softly, approaching her like a cautious deer stepping into a clearing. "I came as soon as I could."

She looked up, her expression a fragile mask of gratitude tinged with pain. "Thanks for coming. I really needed someone to talk to."

I settled beside her, the cushions sinking slightly under my weight. "Always. What's going on? You mentioned Mark wanted to meet. Is that happening soon?"

Her gaze drifted towards the window, where the last vestiges of twilight struggled against the encroaching night. "He called this afternoon. He wants to talk about... everything. I'm terrified, though. What if he tries to convince me to come back?"

I could feel the tremor in her voice, the way the words hung between us like an unwanted guest. "Elara, it's okay to be scared. You're going through a huge transition, and it's normal to feel overwhelmed. But remember, you have a choice now."

"I know, but what if I make the wrong one?" she whispered, tears glistening in her eyes. "What if I regret it?"

"Regret is a tricky beast. Sometimes you just have to trust yourself. You've fought so hard to get to this point," I replied, trying to infuse my words with the strength I wished to impart. "What did you tell him?"

She sighed, a weary sound that echoed in the quiet room. "I didn't say much. Just that I needed some time to think. But now he's going to think he has a chance to win me back. I can't go back to that life. I just can't."

"I get it. You've come so far, and you deserve to be happy. Don't let him pull you back into the shadows."

"I wish it were that easy. Sometimes I think it might be easier to just go back, to pretend everything is fine," she said, rubbing her temples as if the weight of her thoughts could be massaged away.

"Easy isn't always better. You know that. You need to fight for the life you want, not the life he wants for you."

Elara looked at me, her gaze piercing through the fog of despair. "You make it sound so simple."

"Simple doesn't mean easy. It takes guts to walk away, but you have those guts. Remember, you're not alone in this. I'm here."

As we sat together, the conversation slowly began to mend the frayed edges of her spirit, but the shadow of doubt still loomed large in the room. I could sense her wrestling with the ghosts of her past, each memory pulling her deeper into an abyss she desperately wanted to escape.

A few moments of silence passed, broken only by the distant sounds of the city outside—a muffled siren, the faint echo of laughter from a nearby bar. I leaned back against the cushions, searching for the right words to ease her mind when a sudden crash jolted me upright. The sound came from the kitchen, sharp and dissonant, like a knife against glass.

"What was that?" Elara's eyes widened in alarm.

"I don't know," I replied, the hairs on the back of my neck standing up. "Stay here."

I moved cautiously toward the kitchen, my heart pounding in my chest. The light overhead flickered ominously as I crept closer, every creak of the floorboards amplifying the tension. The sight that met my eyes stopped me in my tracks. The window was shattered, glass glittering across the floor like fallen stars, and a shadow darted outside.

"Call the police!" I shouted back to Elara, my voice sharp and urgent.

She rushed to her phone as I stepped closer to the broken glass, feeling a surge of adrenaline. "What happened?" she asked, her voice quivering.

"I don't know, but someone was here. We need to make sure you're safe." I scanned the room, looking for any signs of a break-in or anything out of place.

Elara was still on the phone, her eyes wide with panic. "Yes, I need help! Someone broke into my apartment!"

I turned my attention back to the window, my mind racing with possibilities. Who would do this? And why? Just then, a flicker of movement caught my eye—a figure slipped into the shadows of the alley below, barely visible but undeniably present.

"Elara," I called, urgency rising in my voice. "Did you see anyone? A person?"

She shook her head, her expression frozen in disbelief. "No, I just heard the crash."

"Someone's outside! Stay behind me." My instincts kicked in, and I positioned myself between her and the window, adrenaline coursing through my veins. The last thing I wanted was for her to feel any more threatened than she already did.

Moments later, I heard the unmistakable sound of sirens approaching, the wail growing louder. Relief washed over me, but as I turned to reassure Elara, the door burst open, and two uniformed officers rushed in, their faces set with determination.

"Police! Everyone okay?" one of them shouted, scanning the room with sharp eyes.

"We heard a crash—someone broke in!" I replied, pointing toward the window. "The glass is shattered. We need to check outside."

The officers moved swiftly, one heading to the window, while the other knelt beside the shards of glass, examining the scene. Elara clung to her phone, her face pale, the fear in her eyes still present.

As I stepped closer to the window, my pulse racing, I suddenly felt an eerie sensation that chilled my skin. Something was off, a presence in the air that didn't sit right. I glanced back at the officer, who was now examining the area outside, and then back at Elara, whose gaze was glued to her phone, a mix of fear and confusion clouding her features.

Then, in that moment of stillness, something unexpected happened. My phone buzzed violently in my pocket, and when I pulled it out, my breath caught in my throat. The message was simple, the words twisting in my stomach like a knot: I know what you're doing. And I won't let you forget.

The officer looked at me, concern etched on his face. "Everything okay, ma'am?"

Before I could respond, the lights outside flickered, plunging us into darkness, the oppressive silence broken only by the sound of shattering glass. I exchanged a glance with Elara, her eyes wide with fear, and suddenly, the weight of the night felt heavier than ever.

Chapter 9: Frosting and Fears

The soft hum of the mixer accompanied the comforting scent of vanilla wafting through the air as I meticulously piped frosting onto a batch of cupcakes, each swirl a testament to my resolve. The bakery was alive once more, its warm hues of cream and brown wrapping around me like a favorite quilt. A hand-painted sign hung above the counter, declaring in whimsical letters: "Happiness Served Daily." I wanted to believe that was true, but a gnawing feeling settled in my stomach, souring the sweetness that should have enveloped me.

Max's presence was like a warm ray of sunshine, casting playful shadows across the kitchen. He was in his element, expertly rolling dough for a batch of croissants, his deft hands moving with the kind of grace I could only dream of achieving. I watched him, an artist lost in his work, and I couldn't help but smile, even as the unease curled around my heart like a vine. The chaos of Elara's life loomed over me, filling every crevice of my thoughts. We had been through so much together, yet her constant turmoil was a weight I felt increasingly unable to bear.

As Max turned to me, his eyes bright with mischief, he tossed a dusting of flour my way, sending a small cloud puffing through the air. "Careful there, you might end up looking like a cupcake yourself," he teased, his smile a beacon of warmth. I chuckled, the sound momentarily cutting through the tension. The playful banter was our lifeline, a thread we clung to while the world outside swirled with uncertainty. Yet, beneath the laughter, I sensed a gulf widening between us, an invisible chasm filled with unspoken fears and the weight of our burgeoning relationship.

"Maybe I should start a new trend," I replied, wiping a flour-covered hand on my apron. "Flour-dusted chic. Very avant-garde." Max laughed, the sound rich and melodic, but the moment felt fragile, like spun sugar ready to dissolve at the slightest touch.

Our laughter faded into silence, a heavy pause settling between us as I turned back to my cupcakes. I could almost hear the clock ticking, marking time as the charity event loomed ahead. Each cupcake I decorated was like a tiny triumph, yet I couldn't shake the feeling that I was standing on the precipice of something monumental. The charity was supposed to be a celebration, a chance to give back, but the specter of Elara's troubles lingered like a stubborn shadow.

As the sun dipped below the horizon, casting a golden glow through the bakery windows, I felt the urge to reach out to Max, to share the swirling storm within me. But the words caught in my throat, choked by a fear that had taken root deep in my heart. What if opening up meant losing him? What if he couldn't handle the mess that was my life? My thoughts spiraled, wrapping tighter and tighter around my heart, suffocating the very connection I craved.

Just as I thought I might finally speak, my phone buzzed against the counter, shattering the fragile atmosphere. I glanced at the screen, my breath hitching. Elara's name glared back at me, and I felt a rush of dread. She never called unless something was wrong. With a quick glance at Max, who was now kneading dough with a furrowed brow, I stepped away, my heart pounding like a drum in my chest.

"Elara? What's wrong?" I answered, trying to keep my voice steady, but it trembled with concern.

"Cleo, I need your help. It's bad. I don't know what to do." Her voice was raw, laced with panic, and I could picture her, hands shaking, a world of chaos swirling around her.

"What happened? Where are you?" I moved to the back of the bakery, away from Max's curious gaze, my heart racing.

"I... I'm at home, but there are people here. They won't leave me alone. I just need you to come."

"Okay, I'm on my way. Just stay inside and lock the doors." I hung up, a rush of urgency igniting my veins. Elara had always been the stormy one, but this felt different, darker. I took a deep breath, steeling myself against the torrent of worry that threatened to engulf me.

As I returned to the front of the bakery, Max's concerned eyes met mine, searching for answers I wasn't ready to share. "Everything okay?" he asked, a hint of worry creasing his brow.

"Yeah, just... something came up. I need to go," I replied, trying to sound casual, but my heart sank at the look on his face.

"Is it Elara again?" he asked, his voice dropping, the understanding in his eyes piercing through my defenses.

I nodded, feeling the weight of the world settle back onto my shoulders. "She's in trouble. I have to help her."

"Cleo, you can't keep saving her if it's hurting you," he said gently, but the truth in his words felt like a slap.

"I know, but she's my best friend. I can't just abandon her."

The silence hung heavy between us, filled with the echoes of unspoken truths and the tension of our shared moment. I wanted to lean into him, to draw strength from his warmth, but I felt the walls closing in, the sweet frosting of our connection turning bittersweet once more. Just as I stepped toward him, yearning for solace, my phone buzzed again. It was a message from Elara, and the fear creeping into my chest twisted painfully.

I could feel the world tilt beneath me, the chaos of her life crashing into my own. I needed to help her, yet in that moment, I could almost hear the whispers of my heart urging me to stay. To choose Max. To choose love. But love, as it turned out, was a double-edged sword, and the cut was deep.

I drove through the quiet streets, the fading daylight painting the world in shades of gold and indigo, and I felt as though I were in a different universe entirely. The bakery, with its comforting scent of sugar and butter, had become my sanctuary, yet here I was, racing away from it like it was a ship sinking into the waves. I couldn't shake the anxious knot in my stomach, the fear gnawing at me as I thought of Elara and the unknown trouble that awaited. The radio murmured softly, but I found no comfort in the melodies, only a stark reminder of the world I was leaving behind.

Pulling up to Elara's apartment, I could see her silhouette behind the sheer curtains, moving with a frantic energy that sent my heart into a tailspin. I stepped out of the car and sprinted to the door, my pulse quickening with every step. The familiar scent of her favorite candles wafted through the door, a hint of vanilla and cedar that always made her home feel warm and inviting. But today, there was no solace in that fragrance; it felt foreboding, like a prelude to a storm.

I knocked, my fist connecting with the wood harder than necessary. "Elara! It's me!" My voice rang out, laced with urgency.

Moments stretched into eternity before I heard the click of the lock. The door swung open, and there she was, her hair a wild halo around her face, eyes wide and panicked. "Cleo! Thank God you're here!" She pulled me inside, her grip fierce, as if she feared I would vanish into thin air.

"What's going on? Are you okay?" I scanned the room, half-expecting to see a band of thieves lurking in the corners, but everything appeared normal—too normal, given the tension radiating off her.

"Can we talk?" she whispered, dragging me toward the living room. The walls were lined with photos of us, laughing and celebrating life, now feeling like a gallery of ghosts taunting me with happier times.

"Of course. What happened?" I sank onto the couch, instinctively reaching for her hand.

"It's about Chris," she said, the name hanging in the air like a bad omen. "He's been... different lately. Aggressive." Her voice trembled, and I could see her fighting to hold it together.

"Different how?" I asked, trying to mask my concern. Chris was the charming man Elara had been dating for a few months—a whirlwind romance that had left all of us in awe. But charm could be a mask for something darker, and as I looked at my best friend, I feared that was exactly the case.

"He yelled at me last night," she confessed, her voice barely above a whisper. "I thought it was a one-time thing, you know? But then he showed up at work today, unannounced, and when I tried to tell him I needed space, he... he lost it. Cleo, he said I was being dramatic, that I was just trying to push him away." Her eyes filled with tears, and I felt a rush of anger bubble up inside me.

"Why didn't you call me earlier?" I asked, feeling the fire of protective instinct ignite within me. "You don't have to go through this alone, you know that."

"I didn't want to worry you. You've got so much going on with the bakery and Max. I didn't want to add to your stress." Her guilt was palpable, but it only stoked the flames of my frustration.

"Worrying about you is my stress! You're my best friend! I'm here for you, always. I'll help you figure this out." I squeezed her hand, a silent promise.

The front door creaked open, and I turned to see Chris walk in, his demeanor casual, as if nothing was amiss. "Hey, babe! I thought I heard your voice," he called out, his gaze falling on me. A flicker of surprise crossed his features, quickly replaced by a charming smile that felt forced.

"Chris, what are you doing here?" Elara's voice quivered, and I could see the tension tighten in her shoulders.

"I just wanted to see how you were doing. Thought we could grab dinner." He took a step closer, but there was an edge to his smile that sent a chill racing down my spine.

"I'm not hungry right now," Elara said, her tone sharp. "Maybe you should leave."

His expression shifted, and I could feel the air grow heavy. "Come on, Elara. Don't be like that. You know I care about you."

"Caring isn't yelling, Chris," I interjected, my protective instincts flaring. "If you care about her, you'll respect her space."

He turned his gaze to me, and I felt a challenge simmering in the air. "And who are you to tell me how to treat my girlfriend?"

The atmosphere crackled with tension, and Elara's eyes darted between us, panic etched on her face. "Guys, please! This isn't helping!"

"Maybe you should just let your friend leave, Elara," Chris said, his voice low, almost menacing. "She clearly doesn't understand our relationship."

Something primal stirred within me, the urge to defend my friend battling against the logic that told me to tread carefully. "You don't get to talk to her like that," I shot back, my heart racing. "You don't get to intimidate her in her own home."

"Intimidate?" His laugh was humorless, and I felt my skin crawl. "I'm just trying to make sure she knows her place. You know how women can be—"

"Women?" I interrupted, my voice rising. "What an archaic way to think! Elara isn't a possession to be owned; she's a person with her own thoughts and feelings."

"Enough!" Elara's voice cut through the tension, and both Chris and I froze, caught in her fierce gaze. "You need to leave, Chris. This isn't working for me anymore."

For a heartbeat, time suspended, and I could see the fury ripple across his face. "You're making a mistake, Elara," he said, his tone dangerously soft. "You'll regret this."

And just like that, he turned on his heel, storming out the door and slamming it behind him, leaving a haunting silence in his wake. Elara and I stood there, our hearts pounding in the aftermath of his words, the weight of what had just transpired settling over us like a heavy fog.

I drew in a shaky breath, anger and fear intertwining within me. "Are you okay?" I asked, stepping closer, needing to bridge the distance between us.

"I will be," she whispered, her voice trembling. "But what if I'm not?"

The uncertainty lingered, a reminder of the world outside this haven we'd built together. The fragility of her situation loomed large, and I knew that as long as we drew breath, we would face whatever storms lay ahead together. But for now, the storm had passed, leaving a sense of vulnerability in its wake. And as I sat there, enveloped in the warmth of our friendship, I realized that sometimes love and fear walked hand in hand, and the fight was far from over.

Elara stood there, the weight of Chris's departure still clinging to the air like an unwelcome guest. I reached for her again, pulling her into a hug that felt both protective and reassuring. The warmth of her body against mine was a reminder that we were in this together, whatever "this" had become. "You did the right thing, you know," I whispered, my voice muffled against her hair. "You deserve so much better than that."

She sighed, her breath hitching in my embrace. "I just don't know how to handle this. It's all so overwhelming." Her voice cracked, and I could sense the layers of fear beneath her calm exterior. "What if he comes back? What if he doesn't let me go?"

"Then we'll deal with that together," I replied fiercely, pulling back to look her in the eyes. "You're not alone in this. I promise." The fire in my chest flared again, a mix of anger and protectiveness. Chris had crossed a line, and I wouldn't let him loom over Elara like a dark cloud.

"Okay," she said softly, a flicker of determination sparking in her gaze. "I just need a plan. I can't keep living in fear."

"Let's start by locking down the boundaries," I suggested, my mind racing through a list of practical steps we could take. "We can alert your neighbors, maybe even the landlord. He can't just waltz back in here whenever he feels like it."

"Good idea," she nodded, her voice steadier. "And I can change the locks."

I couldn't help but smile at her resilience. "There we go! The Elara I know and love is coming back. She's in there, buried under the chaos, but we'll dig her out."

We spent the next hour devising a plan, my heart swelling with pride at her determination. The more we talked, the more empowered she seemed. We crafted a list of neighbors to trust, discussed ways to document any further incidents, and mapped out a strategy for talking to her boss about the work-related issues she'd been facing because of Chris.

"I can't believe I didn't reach out sooner," she said, the hint of a smile playing on her lips as we settled on the couch with cups of tea. The steam curled upward, dancing in the soft light of her living room, creating an illusion of warmth amidst the cold reality of our conversation. "It's just... I didn't want to drag you into my mess."

"This is not a mess; this is life," I replied, raising my cup as if toasting to our shared resilience. "And life can be messy sometimes, but I'd rather be covered in flour and icing than walk through it alone."

THE TASTE OF AMBITION

Her laughter filled the space between us, a delightful sound that washed away the remnants of tension. "You make it sound so simple."

"Only because you're the one doing the hard work," I said, nudging her playfully. "I'm just here to cheer you on and make sure you have cupcakes to celebrate every victory."

As we chatted, the atmosphere shifted, the air around us warming with shared stories and laughter. For a moment, I could almost forget the storm brewing outside—until a sharp knock on the door jolted me back to reality.

"Who could that be?" Elara's expression turned wary, her earlier bravado fading in an instant.

"Stay behind me," I instructed, my protective instincts kicking in. "I'll check it out."

Peeking through the peephole, my heart sank. "It's Chris."

"What?" Elara gasped, her hands gripping the edge of the couch as though it might anchor her to the ground. "What does he want?"

"I have no idea," I murmured, my mind racing. "But whatever it is, it can't be good."

"Don't open the door," she insisted, her voice firm despite the fear swimming in her eyes.

"I won't." I took a step back, my heart pounding in my chest. "What do you want to do?"

"I... I don't know." She glanced at the door, then back at me, her face a mixture of fear and determination. "What if he tries to force his way in?"

I thought quickly, my gaze darting around the room. "We need to call the police. It's better to be safe than sorry."

"Good idea." She scrambled for her phone, but the knock came again, this time harder, more insistent.

"Cleo! I know you're in there. Open up!" His voice was too calm, too smooth, and it sent chills racing down my spine.

"No," I whispered, gripping Elara's arm. "Stay quiet. Don't say a word."

"I just want to talk! Come on, Elara! You can't hide forever!" His voice dripped with that same charm that had once drawn her in, but now it felt like a noose tightening around her.

"Call now," I urged, my voice barely above a whisper.

Elara's fingers fumbled over the screen, her expression a mix of panic and resolve. Just as she began dialing, a loud bang echoed through the apartment, making us jump.

"Let's not make this harder than it has to be!" Chris shouted, his voice laced with frustration. "I just want to talk!"

"Talk?" I scoffed, my heart racing. "That's not what it sounds like."

"Cleo, please," Elara said, her eyes pleading. "What if he gets angry? What if he tries to break the door down?"

"Then we'll deal with that when it happens," I replied, taking a deep breath to steady my racing heart. "We're not giving him the power to intimidate us."

Another bang reverberated through the door, and I winced, fear clawing at my throat. "Elara, did you call yet?"

"I'm trying! It's ringing!"

"Cleo!" Chris's voice was now laced with desperation, and I felt a pang of fear in my chest. "You don't want to do this. Just let me in! We can work this out!"

"No! You've crossed a line!" I shouted back, my voice rising. "You don't get to bully your way in here!"

With every bang against the door, I could feel the tension in the room tighten, like a bowstring pulled to its limit. The phone call was still ringing, and I prayed someone would answer before it became too late.

"Cleo, what if he breaks it down?" Elara's voice was a whisper now, fear palpable in her eyes.

"We won't let him. Just stay behind me," I reassured, though the tremor in my own voice betrayed my bravado.

The banging intensified, the door rattling in its frame, and I felt the weight of the world pressing down on us. In that moment, I realized that no amount of frosting or cupcakes could shield us from this storm. And just as I turned to grab my phone, a deafening crack echoed through the air, sending shards of fear slicing through the fragile atmosphere.

The door began to splinter, the darkness outside spilling in like a menacing tide.

Chapter 10: The Crumbling Facade

The door creaked open, and Elara's fragile smile barely illuminated the room as she stood in the dim light of her cluttered apartment. I stepped inside, the air thick with an unsettling mix of vanilla and anxiety. The remnants of her wedding plans were scattered like confetti—brittle invitations, a stack of unwritten vows resting atop a coffee table layered with bridal magazines, and a single white rose wilting in a mason jar. The sight squeezed my heart, a reminder of the fairy tale that had begun to unravel at the seams.

"Elara," I said softly, my voice barely rising above the soft hum of the ceiling fan. She looked at me with those wide, hazel eyes, the sparkle dulled by an all-consuming worry. "What happened?"

"I just got off the phone with the venue," she murmured, her voice cracking like fragile glass. "They said if I can't make a payment by the end of the week, they'll give my date to someone else. I can't believe this is happening. I thought I had everything figured out."

I stepped further into the apartment, feeling the weight of her disappointment hanging in the air. "We'll figure this out," I said, forcing a smile. The lie tasted bitter, but I hoped my resolve would bolster her spirits. "I can bake a cake, a small one, just for you and Max. Something to symbolize hope, you know? It can be a sweet reminder of what's ahead."

Elara let out a shaky laugh, a fragile sound that barely registered as joy. "A cake? Do you think that will help? I feel like everything is falling apart, and a cake is just...well, it's just sugar."

"Sometimes sugar is all you need to turn a situation around," I replied, a flicker of my old humor breaking through the heaviness. "And besides, it'll be a beautiful cake—one worthy of your fairy tale, even if it's only a small chapter right now."

Elara sighed, the weight of her anxiety pulling her shoulders down. "I don't know if it'll even matter," she said, the hint of desperation coloring her words. "What if I can't pay? What if the wedding just...doesn't happen?"

"Let's take this one step at a time," I urged, trying to guide her thoughts away from the edge. "How much do you need?"

Her gaze fell to the floor, a myriad of emotions flickering across her face—fear, shame, and, beneath it all, a deep well of longing for the dream that felt so close yet impossibly distant. "Three thousand," she whispered, her voice almost lost in the silence of the room.

I blinked, the number crashing against my chest like a wave. "Three thousand? That's...a lot. Do you have any family who could help?"

She shook her head, her dark curls bouncing defiantly. "My family can barely afford their own bills, let alone help with a wedding. Besides, I don't want to burden them."

In that moment, the conflicting emotions within me swirled like a tempest. I wanted to dive in and rescue her, to extend my hand and pull her out of the murky waters. But the unresolved tension with Max simmered just beneath the surface, a reminder of our last encounter, when anger and confusion had tangled our words like a poorly knit scarf.

"Maybe I can help," I said, my heart racing. "I could sell a few things—my old cake stands, the ones I've never used. They could bring in some cash. It won't be three thousand, but every little bit counts, right?"

Elara looked at me, her expression softening just a fraction. "You don't have to do that. You're already doing so much."

"Please. I want to," I insisted, my voice firm. "We'll get through this together. You don't have to go through it alone."

As I turned to leave for a moment, the weight of my decision pressed heavily on my chest. The sound of my heels echoed against the hardwood floor, a steady beat in the anxious silence. I could feel Elara's eyes on me, searching for something in the depths of my resolve, perhaps a glimmer of reassurance.

Before I stepped outside, I glanced back. "And if the cake doesn't work, we'll think of something else," I added, forcing a laugh. "Maybe we can sell some of those bridal magazines. They look expensive."

Elara chuckled lightly, her laughter a small but welcome flicker of light in the room. "I'm sure there's a collector somewhere who would pay a fortune for those. They're practically vintage."

"Exactly! And vintage is trendy right now. Who wouldn't want a piece of wedding history?"

The corner of her mouth turned up, and I felt a rush of relief. We shared a moment of levity, suspended between the chaos of her impending nuptials and the comfort of our friendship. It was the kind of moment that reminded me of why I cared so deeply for her, why I'd moved heaven and earth to support her dreams—even when the shadow of my own troubles loomed ominously on the horizon.

"Let's make a list," she said, her eyes glimmering with determination now. "A list of everything we can sell. Maybe we can get creative about this."

I nodded, buoyed by her sudden resolve. "And I'll start on that cake tonight. Chocolate, right?"

"Of course," she replied, her voice lifting. "It's the only flavor that makes sense in times like these."

"Then it's settled," I declared, my heart swelling with a mix of affection and apprehension. "We're going to make this happen. Together."

As we stood amidst the remnants of her dreams, a spark ignited between us—fueled by friendship, hope, and the unyielding belief that even the crumbling facade of a wedding plan could still hold the promise of something beautiful.

The scent of chocolate filled my kitchen as I carefully mixed the batter, each swirl of my whisk infusing a bit of love and determination into the cake. It was a small, bittersweet distraction from the chaos of Elara's life, but it felt monumental in its own way. Each fold of the rich mixture reminded me that even in times of despair, there was sweetness to be found, even if it was only temporary. I imagined the look on Elara's face when she tasted it, a tiny flicker of joy amid the larger storm swirling around her.

As I slid the cake into the oven, I let out a deep breath, the kind that felt like it could unravel the tension knotted in my shoulders. I glanced at the clock; it was late afternoon, and the warm light filtering through my window cast gentle shadows across the countertops. I couldn't help but feel a pang of guilt creeping in. I should have been doing more—finding a way to raise the money, hustling for a side job, anything that could ease her burden. Yet here I was, baking. But sometimes, I told myself, a little sweetness could go a long way.

While the cake baked, my mind wandered to Max. His absence felt like an uninvited guest, lurking just outside my thoughts. We had fought the last time we spoke, the argument simmering into a cold silence that neither of us seemed willing to thaw. I missed him more than I cared to admit, yet the memory of his frustrated expression when I'd mentioned Elara's wedding plans tugged at my heart. It was as if our worlds had collided in a dissonant symphony, neither of us able to harmonize with the other.

The timer buzzed, breaking my reverie, and I rushed to the oven, the heat radiating out like a warm embrace. I carefully pulled out the cake, its surface perfectly domed and cracked slightly, like the surface of an ancient desert, but I couldn't help but smile at the triumph. It was going to be beautiful, even if it was a modest size, a small token against the weight of Elara's worries. I allowed it to cool on the rack, watching as the steam curled into the air like a dancer twirling in slow motion.

My phone buzzed on the counter, jolting me from my thoughts. It was a message from Elara: "Can we talk? I have something on my mind." I felt a shiver of anxiety race down my spine. What could she possibly have to say? I wiped my hands on a kitchen towel, grabbed my phone, and texted back: "Sure, I'm just baking your cake! Can I bring it over?"

Her response came quickly: "Yes! Please!"

With a mix of anticipation and trepidation bubbling in my chest, I decided to take the cake to her, fully frosted and decorated, a symbol of our friendship, resilience, and maybe, just maybe, a bit of hope. I envisioned her face lighting up at the sight of it, but I couldn't shake the sense that something heavier was lingering in the air.

I carefully layered the chocolate frosting, each swirl a personal promise that I would be there for her, no matter the outcome of her wedding plans. After adding some delicate, homemade decorations—tiny sugar flowers that mirrored her original wedding theme—I slid the cake onto a sturdy plate and covered it with a glass dome. The cake felt like a fortress of sugar and dreams, yet it could just as easily crumble under the weight of reality.

The drive to Elara's apartment was filled with a mixture of nervous excitement and uncertainty, the evening light painting the streets in shades of amber and gold. As I parked outside her building, I took a moment to gather myself, reminding myself to be strong. I knocked on her door, the sound echoing in the stillness, and almost immediately, she opened it, her expression a cocktail of emotions.

"Oh, you're here!" she exclaimed, her eyes lighting up as she caught sight of the cake. "It looks amazing!"

I beamed, feeling a swell of pride. "It's just a little something to lift your spirits. I hope it helps."

She stepped aside, letting me in, but the shift in her demeanor was palpable. Something was off, lurking beneath her appreciation.

THE TASTE OF AMBITION

"I appreciate it, really. It's beautiful," she said, running her fingers along the edge of the dome, yet her smile didn't reach her eyes.

"Okay, what's really going on?" I asked, trying to pierce the veil of her forced cheerfulness. "You said you had something on your mind."

Elara sighed, the weight of the world pressing down on her as she sank into the plush couch. "I—well, I've been thinking about the wedding," she began, her voice wavering. "I know it's important to me, to us, but what if...what if it's not meant to be?"

The question hung between us like a pendulum, swinging back and forth. "Elara, don't say that. You've dreamed of this your entire life."

"But what if I'm not ready?" she replied, her gaze dropping to her hands, twisted together as if seeking solace from one another. "What if marrying Max means losing part of myself? What if—what if I'm just trying to fulfill this ideal of what a wedding should be?"

I sat beside her, the cake momentarily forgotten. "You're not just fulfilling a dream, Elara. You're creating your own reality. It's okay to have doubts, but don't let them dictate your happiness. If Max makes you happy, isn't that worth fighting for?"

Her eyes met mine, the turmoil swirling in them like a storm. "But what if I don't know what makes me happy?" she whispered, a crack in her facade. "What if I've lost myself in the process?"

"Then let's find you," I said firmly, feeling the flicker of determination reignite within me. "Let's strip back all the wedding nonsense and figure out what you really want. This cake—it's just a start. Maybe it's a reminder that life isn't always sweet, but that doesn't mean we can't make it beautiful."

As we sat there, surrounded by the remnants of unfulfilled dreams and the comforting scent of chocolate, I realized that perhaps we were both searching for clarity in the chaos of our lives. Her struggle echoed my own, a reminder that we all wrestle with our aspirations, fear of loss, and the daunting task of finding our truth. The cake, a symbol of our resolve, could be the turning point we both needed.

The warmth of the evening wrapped around us like a comforting blanket as I sat beside Elara, the uneaten cake still perched regally on the coffee table, a silent witness to our swirling emotions. Her hesitation hung in the air, palpable and heavy, as if every word she contemplated was a lead weight pulling her deeper into uncertainty.

"I just don't want to look back one day and realize I rushed into something because I thought that was what I was supposed to do," she confessed, her voice barely above a whisper. "It's like I'm stuck in this fairy tale I'm not even sure I believe in anymore."

I leaned in closer, my heart aching for her as the shadows danced across her face. "Maybe the fairy tale doesn't have to look like a Pinterest board," I said gently. "What if it's a little messy, a little imperfect? It could be something uniquely yours, something that reflects who you really are. You don't need to fit into anyone else's mold."

Elara nodded, her brow furrowing in thought, but I could see the flicker of hope in her eyes, like the first hint of dawn breaking over a dark horizon. "You're right," she replied slowly, "but how do I even start? I've planned this whole thing like it's a military operation, and now I feel lost."

"Start small," I suggested. "What's the one thing you've always dreamed of doing on your wedding day, something that feels like you?"

She bit her lip, considering my question, the tension in her shoulders easing just a fraction. "I've always wanted a small ceremony on the beach at sunset," she admitted, her voice gaining strength with each word. "Just me and Max and maybe our closest friends. No big fuss, no extravagant decorations. Just...love."

"Now we're talking," I said, my excitement bubbling over. "Why not turn your focus to that? We can create a plan that doesn't involve a hundred people and a grand venue. Just the two of you, the sound of the waves, and that gorgeous sunset."

Elara's smile widened, illuminating her face like the sun breaking through clouds. "That does sound beautiful," she mused, her fingers drumming against her knee, the rhythm of her thoughts returning. "And it would be much more manageable."

The conversation began to shift, the energy in the room changing as we plotted out a vision for her wedding that felt less like a checklist and more like an adventure. We tossed ideas back and forth, the cake forgotten for the moment as Elara's laughter filled the space between us. With each suggestion, I saw her spirit lift, the weight of her anxiety lightening, until she finally asked, "What about the venue?"

My heart sank momentarily. "We'll figure that out, too. Maybe we can find a beachside rental or something intimate enough that they'll let you book it last minute. I'll help you call around."

"I can't ask you to do that," she protested, her brow furrowed. "You have your own life to manage."

"And you're my best friend," I said, the words tumbling out before I could censor them. "I'd move mountains for you, Elara. This is important, and I want to be a part of it."

She looked at me, her expression softening, a mixture of gratitude and vulnerability shining through. "Thank you. Seriously, you don't know how much that means to me."

Just then, the doorbell rang, shattering the intimate atmosphere we'd created. We exchanged a glance, both of us startled. "Who could that be?" I wondered, my curiosity piqued.

"Maybe it's Max," Elara suggested, a note of hope dancing in her tone.

"Only one way to find out." I rose to answer the door, the nervous energy coursing through me as I grasped the handle. I opened it, and standing there, drenched in the golden hues of the setting sun, was Max.

His expression was a mixture of determination and something more vulnerable, a flicker of fear or perhaps regret. "Elara," he began, his voice low and earnest. "Can we talk?"

Elara stepped forward, her heart clearly racing at the sight of him. "Max, I—"

"No, please let me say this," he interrupted gently, his eyes locking onto hers with an intensity that sent a shiver down my spine. "I know we've had our issues. I shouldn't have reacted the way I did. I've been thinking about you, about us, and I can't let you make a decision about your wedding without me, without us really talking."

A heavy silence fell over the room, charged with unspoken words and lingering emotions. I felt like an intruder in a moment that was meant for just the two of them.

"Max, I—" Elara started, but he raised his hand, his gaze unwavering.

"I've realized something," he said, the weight of his words hanging in the air. "I don't want to lose you. I don't want you to feel like you have to conform to some idea of what a wedding should be. If you're having doubts, let's face them together."

Her breath caught, and I could see the walls she had built around her heart starting to crumble. "You mean it?" she asked, her voice trembling.

"More than anything," he replied, taking a tentative step closer, as if testing the waters. "I want us to create something that reflects who we really are—not what anyone else expects."

I could feel the air shift as a spark ignited between them, and suddenly, the moment felt electrifying. Yet I couldn't shake the feeling that this wasn't just about the wedding; there was something deeper simmering beneath the surface, a tension that had been unresolved for far too long.

"I think we can do that," Elara said softly, hope blooming in her eyes as she reached for his hand. "Together."

Just as the mood began to blossom, my phone buzzed in my pocket, an unexpected intrusion. I fished it out, glancing at the screen, only to find a message that froze me in place: "We need to talk. It's urgent. Meet me at the café."

A chill ran down my spine, and my heart raced. The sender's name flickered on the screen, pulling me back into a whirlwind of questions. I couldn't leave Elara and Max in this moment, not when they were finally on the brink of something beautiful. But the urgency of that message was like a gavel striking a bell, echoing through my mind, insisting I pay attention.

"Is everything okay?" Elara asked, noticing the change in my expression.

I hesitated, caught between two worlds—the warmth of friendship and the cold grip of whatever awaited me outside those familiar doors. "I... I'll be right back," I murmured, even as the question loomed larger: What could possibly be so urgent that it pulled me away now?

And just as I turned to leave, a shattering crash echoed from the kitchen, followed by the ominous sound of glass breaking. I spun around, heart pounding, to see the cake sliding off the table, a cascade of frosting and chocolate tumbling into chaos—a bittersweet omen of the turmoil we were all about to face.

Chapter 11: Sweet Redemption

The sun poured through the kitchen window, casting golden beams that danced across the countertop, illuminating the chaos of flour and sugar that seemed to have taken on a life of its own. I had a habit of letting my emotions spill into my baking, each ingredient representing a piece of my heart, a sprinkle of joy, a dash of hope, or the bitter taste of uncertainty. As I measured out the flour, my hands trembled slightly, not from the weight of the ingredients, but from the weight of my thoughts. Today was about Elara, my best friend, whose wedding was just days away. But even as I whisked and folded, my mind drifted back to Max, the man whose very presence made the air around me feel electric.

"Are you sure you don't want to take a break?" Elara's voice broke through my reverie, rich and warm like the aroma of vanilla wafting through the kitchen. She leaned against the doorframe, her auburn hair catching the light in soft waves, a smile dancing on her lips. Yet, there was something else—an undercurrent of worry that tugged at her expression.

"I'm fine, really. Just a few more batches of cupcakes, and I'll be done," I replied, forcing a cheerful lilt to my tone. I could see her eyes scan the cluttered counter, the empty flour sack, and the kitchen timer ticking down like a countdown to some impending doom. But the truth was, I was anything but fine. The cake batter in front of me wasn't just a delicious confection meant for a celebration; it was a reflection of my inner conflict.

Elara's wedding day was meant to be the culmination of her fairytale romance with Jason, a man as sweet as the confections I created. But beneath my sweetened facade, I felt the sting of jealousy and confusion creeping in. Max was supposed to be my friend, yet every glance we exchanged felt like a confession waiting to spill over, a promise unspoken. I couldn't be selfish; Elara needed me to be all in, to focus on her happiness. Still, the memory of our last encounter simmered beneath the surface like the chocolate ganache melting on the stovetop, rich and intoxicating.

"Let me know if you need help," she said, the softness of her voice an invitation rather than a command. "I don't want you burning out before the big day."

"Thanks, but I've got this," I assured her, attempting to redirect my spiraling thoughts. "I'll be done soon. And I promise to celebrate with you when it's all over." Her smile widened, yet the hint of sadness in her eyes remained, a gentle reminder that not everything was perfect beneath the surface.

The sound of the oven door opening and closing filled the silence between us as I slipped in the last tray of cupcakes. I took a moment to breathe, to savor the comforting aroma enveloping me. Just then, the unmistakable sound of Max's voice echoed through the hallway. "Is this the cake factory or a bake sale? I swear I can smell chocolate all the way from the parking lot!"

"Is that supposed to be a compliment or an insult?" I shouted back, the tension in my chest loosening slightly. He entered the kitchen with a confident stride, his dark hair slightly tousled, and a grin that could brighten the gloomiest day. "Because if you're here to make fun of my baking, you can just turn right around and—"

"I'm here to help, if you'll let me," he interrupted, raising his hands in mock surrender. "But I have to admit, I'd rather eat the cake than bake it."

"Ah, but you can't eat it if you don't bake it first." My voice dripped with playful sarcasm, a natural reaction to his easy charm. I wiped my hands on my apron, trying to hide the nervous flutter in my stomach. "Unless you're a wizard and can conjure it out of thin air."

"Can't blame a guy for trying," he replied, stepping closer as he surveyed the kitchen. The air between us crackled with unacknowledged tension, and for a moment, the world faded into the background.

Elara busied herself with organizing the decorations, but I could feel her eyes darting between us, a mixture of concern and curiosity etched on her features. I couldn't help but wonder what she saw when she looked at us. Did she sense the bond that had formed between Max and me, one so delicate yet vibrant that it threatened to shatter under the weight of unsaid words?

"Here," Max said, picking up a whisk and moving towards me. "Show me your technique. I promise I won't mess it up."

As he leaned over the mixing bowl, the warmth of his arm brushed against mine, sending a jolt through me that I struggled to ignore. The chaos of my heart danced alongside the rhythm of our conversation, a delightful interplay of laughter and teasing that made the kitchen feel alive. "You do realize you're not supposed to use that whisk for frosting, right?" I quipped, raising an eyebrow at him.

"Details, details," he replied with a lopsided grin. "I'm more about the final product than the process."

"Which explains your baking disasters," I shot back, a playful smirk forming on my lips. The banter felt effortless, a natural flow of words that danced between us like the flour in the air.

Yet, as the cupcakes baked and the frosting set, a heavier silence settled around us. Max leaned against the counter, his gaze drifting from the baking trays to Elara, who was now completely absorbed in arranging the wedding favors. The tension was palpable, thickening the air between us until it felt like we were standing on the edge of something monumental, waiting for the inevitable plunge.

"Is everything okay between you and Elara?" Max asked, his tone shifting from playful to serious. I could see the concern in his eyes, and I couldn't help but wonder if he felt the weight of my hidden feelings as much as I did.

"It's just... this wedding is a lot for her. I want to make everything perfect," I confessed, my voice barely above a whisper. "But sometimes, I wonder if I'm enough."

He met my gaze, the warmth of his presence wrapping around me like a favorite blanket. "You're more than enough. She wouldn't be where she is without you."

His words hung in the air, and for a moment, the world outside faded, leaving only the truth of our shared moment. The connection between us felt undeniable, yet it also felt like walking a tightrope over an abyss of uncharted emotions. I could feel my heart racing, caught in the tension of wanting to lean in closer while simultaneously fearing the fall.

Just then, Elara's laughter rang out, a bright sound that shattered the moment. "You two look like you're plotting something," she teased, her playful tone bringing us back to reality. It was a lighthearted reminder that while we danced around our feelings, life continued in its charmingly chaotic way.

Max and I exchanged a glance, a silent acknowledgment of the complexity woven between us. I took a deep breath, letting the warmth of the kitchen and the comfort of our friendship ground me. Elara needed me now, and for all the longing and turmoil bubbling beneath the surface, I couldn't let my own desires overshadow her moment of joy.

The kitchen buzzed with an energy all its own, an intoxicating blend of sweetness and tension that hung in the air like the scent of freshly baked cupcakes. I stood at the counter, watching the vibrant colors of the frosting swirl together, each hue a reflection of my swirling thoughts. Elara was bustling about, arranging flowers and decorations, her excitement palpable, yet her eyes held a hint of uncertainty that made my heart ache for her. I wished I could be as carefree as she seemed, lost in the joy of her impending nuptials, but my thoughts kept straying to Max, who had stepped into my world like a sudden flash of lightning—beautiful, electrifying, and impossible to ignore.

"Are you seriously going to frost those cupcakes with that much enthusiasm?" Elara's teasing voice broke through my reverie, a playful smirk on her face as she leaned against the doorway. "I'd almost think you were trying to distract me from my wedding prep."

"I'll have you know that enthusiasm is my secret ingredient," I shot back, a smile creeping onto my lips despite the tension that lingered in the room. "Besides, who could resist a cupcake that practically sings with joy?"

"True. But it's almost like you're trying to drown out your own feelings," she said, her gaze sharp and insightful. "What's going on with you? You're acting like someone who just ate a whole batch of sour gummies."

"I'm fine, really," I insisted, though the tremor in my voice betrayed me. The truth was like the sugar I had just poured into the mixing bowl—sweet and bitter all at once. I was caught between my loyalty to her and my undeniable attraction to Max, which felt like a deliciously dangerous secret I was not sure I was ready to share.

Elara stepped closer, her expression softening. "You know you can talk to me about anything, right? It's not just about the wedding. If something's bothering you, I want to know."

"Honestly, it's just... the whole wedding thing is so huge for you. I don't want to be a distraction." I sighed, feeling the weight of my feelings shift in the pit of my stomach. "I want you to be happy. That's all that matters right now."

Her eyes softened further, and I could see the gratitude shimmering behind them. "You're the best friend anyone could ask for. Just don't forget to take care of yourself in all this. You're important too."

Before I could respond, the door swung open, and Max strolled in like he owned the place, carrying the warmth of the sun outside with him. He had a box of supplies tucked under his arm and a disarming grin plastered across his face. "What do we have here? An impromptu baking contest?"

"More like a desperate attempt to keep everything from falling apart," I said, rolling my eyes in mock exasperation. "Your timing is impeccable as always."

"Must be my superpower," he quipped, setting the box down and reaching for a cupcake. His fingers brushed against mine, and I felt a jolt of warmth zip up my arm, igniting the familiar pull that had been growing between us. "I've come to the rescue. Tell me what you need."

"Help with everything," I said, leaning against the counter, trying to suppress the butterflies fluttering in my stomach. "Preferably without creating a culinary disaster that will haunt us for years to come."

He chuckled, a sound that sent a ripple of warmth through me. "No promises, but I'll do my best to avoid setting anything on fire. This kitchen has enough chaos without my added flair."

We dove into the task at hand, an easy rhythm forming between us as we mixed, frosted, and decorated. I felt a spark of happiness ignite, even as my heart wrestled with the gnawing tension of my feelings for him. I glanced over at Elara, who was now busy assembling the floral arrangements, her face glowing with anticipation. The moment felt so right, yet so incredibly fragile, as if the air around us was charged with the potential for something explosive.

"Hey, did I ever tell you how my sister ruined my first baking experience?" Max asked, his eyes twinkling with mischief.

I laughed, intrigued. "No, but I'm dying to hear this."

"It was my birthday, and I decided I wanted to bake my own cake. I was feeling all empowered, you know? My sister, being the overachiever she is, snuck into the kitchen and replaced all the sugar with salt. When I served it to my friends, you can imagine the reaction."

"Oh no! What happened?" I leaned closer, caught up in the hilarity of the story.

"They were so polite, bless their hearts. One of my friends took a big bite, smiled through the horror, and said, 'Wow, this has a really interesting texture!'" He threw his head back in laughter, the sound so genuine it made my heart swell.

"Did you ever speak to your sister again?" I asked, shaking my head, unable to hold back my laughter.

"Of course! I just made sure to bake with my back turned whenever she was in the room." The easy banter flowed, wrapping around us like the warm scents of butter and vanilla. I relished these moments of levity, knowing they were the antidote to the mounting tension that simmered beneath the surface.

As we frosted the final cupcake, Elara returned, surveying our handiwork. "Well, look at this! You two make quite the team." She beamed, genuine pride radiating from her. "I knew you'd find a way to pull this off."

"Only because I had a capable assistant," I said, nudging Max with my elbow. "He provided comic relief while I did all the heavy lifting."

"I'll take credit for being the muscle, thank you very much," he shot back, mock indignation in his voice. "You can't have a good cake without a strong foundation, after all."

Elara rolled her eyes with a grin. "Alright, Mr. Muscle, what's next? We need to get the cupcakes arranged for the tasting tonight."

I felt the weight of anticipation settle around us as we prepared for the evening. The wedding rehearsal dinner was looming, and the thought of everyone gathering to sample our creations made my heart race with both excitement and anxiety. "Let's make it

THE TASTE OF AMBITION

beautiful," I suggested, arranging the cupcakes like tiny masterpieces, their colorful frosting glistening under the kitchen lights.

"Just like Elara's big day," Max said softly, his gaze lingering on my face for just a heartbeat longer than necessary. My breath caught in my throat, a swirl of hope and fear coursing through me. What was happening between us? Did he feel it too?

"Speaking of which," Elara interjected, pulling me back from the precipice of my thoughts. "You two have to promise me you'll keep the focus on the wedding tonight. No more of this...whatever this is."

"Whatever this is?" I echoed, raising an eyebrow, feigning innocence. "What do you mean?"

"You know exactly what I mean." Her smile was teasing, yet the way she looked at us made my heart skip a beat. "Just promise me you won't let anything overshadow my moment, alright?"

"Promise," Max and I said in unison, our eyes locking for just a moment longer than necessary, a silent agreement forming between us.

The kitchen filled with laughter and warmth, the lingering scent of sugar sweetening the air. As we put the finishing touches on our creations, I realized that, for now, the wedding would take center stage. But deep down, I couldn't shake the feeling that the real drama was just beginning, and I was caught in a sweet web of emotions that would soon unravel in ways I could never have anticipated.

The evening unfolded like a well-scripted play, with Elara and me in our roles, every laugh and quip a carefully timed line meant to mask the turbulence churning beneath the surface. The rehearsal dinner was set to be a celebration, a festivity marked by laughter, toasts, and the promise of love. I glanced at Max, who stood just a few steps away, his presence a heady mix of comfort and confusion. With every stolen glance, I felt as if we were two actors sharing a secret, the chemistry between us palpable yet complicated.

As guests arrived, the air filled with chatter and clinking glasses, drowning out the last echoes of our private exchanges. I immersed myself in the preparations, ensuring the cupcake display was nothing short of a masterpiece. Brightly colored frosting peaked atop each little cake like whimsical hats, promising an explosion of flavor that would delight everyone. The tension I felt earlier faded into the background, replaced by a focused determination to make this night perfect for Elara.

"Do you think we should have a designated taste tester?" Max leaned against the table, a mischievous smile on his lips. "I volunteer as tribute."

"Not a chance," I shot back, crossing my arms with a playful glare. "You'd just eat everything before the guests even arrived."

He feigned innocence, raising an eyebrow. "Who, me? I would never!"

"Uh-huh. Your charm is just a cover for your cake-stealing tendencies," I replied, returning his grin. The light banter felt like a lifeline, keeping the weight of unspoken feelings at bay, if only for a moment.

As the guests mingled, Elara was a whirlwind of energy, flitting from group to group with the excitement of a bride-to-be. I watched her, heart swelling with happiness, while the nagging thought of how to navigate my own feelings for Max lingered in the corners of my mind. I had to focus on her, yet every time I caught his eye, it felt like a magnetic pull drawing me closer.

Just as I settled into the rhythm of the evening, the door swung open with a flourish, and in walked Jason, looking dashing in his tailored suit. Elara's face lit up like a candle, illuminating the dimly lit room. "You made it!" she exclaimed, rushing to him, her happiness infectious.

"I wouldn't miss this for the world," he replied, wrapping her in a warm embrace. Watching them together felt like observing a fairytale, and for a moment, I let the warmth wash over me, imagining my own happily-ever-after. But as soon as the thought crossed my mind, it slipped away, replaced by a flicker of uncertainty.

"Careful, you two," I called out, attempting to inject some humor into my own unease. "Don't forget, you have to save room for the cake!"

"Oh, I won't," Jason said, chuckling as he stepped back, his eyes sparkling with affection. "I'll be first in line for those cupcakes."

As laughter filled the air, I took a moment to breathe, stepping back from the whirlwind of festivities. The atmosphere thrummed with excitement, but as I stood in the corner, I felt the familiar presence of Max sidling up next to me.

"Enjoying the show?" he asked, nodding towards Elara and Jason, who were now engaged in an animated conversation.

"Very much. They look so happy," I replied, the sincerity of my words surprising even me. "It's nice to see everything come together for her."

"Yeah, she's really lucky," he said, his voice softening. "And so are you. You've done an incredible job tonight."

I felt warmth spread through me at his compliment, but it was quickly overshadowed by the deeper emotions that had been bubbling under the surface all evening. "It's all for her, really. I just want to make this night special," I said, my gaze flickering back to the happy couple. "I can't let my own feelings get in the way."

Max's eyes narrowed slightly, the depth of his gaze making my heart race. "Sometimes, it's okay to want something for yourself too, you know."

Before I could respond, Elara bounded over, her smile bright and contagious. "You two! Come on! I need you both for a toast!" She grabbed our hands, pulling us towards the center of the room where guests were beginning to gather around.

As the chatter settled, Elara raised her glass, her voice ringing clear. "I just want to say a few words before we dive into this amazing feast! To love, laughter, and the beautiful journey we're all on together. Thank you, everyone, for being here to celebrate with us tonight!"

Cheers erupted around the room, glasses clinking in a symphony of joy. I felt a swell of pride for Elara, yet my heart ached at the thought of what could have been, of moments I yearned to share with Max that felt just out of reach.

"Now, let's eat some cupcakes before I explode from excitement!" Elara announced, giggling. The laughter that followed was a sweet distraction, a reminder that the night was meant for celebration.

As everyone began to sample the treats, I watched the sheer delight on their faces, and for a brief moment, my worries melted away. But my gaze inevitably drifted to Max, who stood just a few feet away, his mouth curving into a grin as he bit into a cupcake.

"Not bad," he called out, voice laced with mock seriousness. "But I think it could use a pinch more salt."

I rolled my eyes dramatically. "You would suggest that, wouldn't you? Next, you'll be telling me to add pickles."

"Hey, I'm an adventurous eater!" he replied, laughter lacing his words. But just as our playful banter reached a crescendo, the door swung open again, this time revealing a figure I hadn't expected.

It was Jenna, a familiar face from our past, a whirlwind of energy and mischief that could light up any room. Her entrance was like a thunderclap, and I felt the air shift as she scanned the room, a gleam in her eye that promised chaos. "Did someone say cupcakes? I hope I'm not too late for the fun!"

Elara squealed with delight, rushing over to her. "You made it! Come on, let's get you some cupcakes!"

THE TASTE OF AMBITION

As Jenna moved closer, I could see the glint of mischief in her eyes as she zeroed in on Max. "Well, if it isn't Mr. Tall, Dark, and Delicious. I was hoping to find you here."

The tension in the room shifted, a palpable crackle of energy igniting as Jenna's presence stirred the pot of emotions simmering just below the surface. I watched in disbelief as Max's eyes widened, a look of surprise quickly replaced by intrigue.

I felt my heart race as they exchanged flirtatious banter, a playful dance that threatened to unravel the delicate balance I had been trying to maintain all night. Just as I was about to step in, my phone buzzed in my pocket, pulling my attention away.

I fished it out, the screen lighting up with an unfamiliar number. My heart thumped in my chest as I read the message, and suddenly, the world around me faded into a blur. It was a text from someone I hadn't heard from in years, someone whose presence could change everything. The kind of news that could shatter the delicate balance of this night.

"Hey, you okay?" Max's voice cut through the noise, his brow furrowed in concern.

I glanced up, my mind racing, my heart in my throat. "I... I need a moment."

As I turned away, my thoughts spiraled in different directions, uncertainty and fear clashing within me. The evening had been a tapestry of sweet moments, but now, an unexpected thread had been pulled, unraveling everything I thought I understood. I had to figure out what this message meant, but in the midst of all this celebration, I also couldn't shake the feeling that whatever was coming would change everything, threatening to pull me under into a wave of chaos I wasn't sure I could navigate.

With a heavy heart, I stepped outside for a breath of fresh air, the cool night enveloping me like a soothing balm. But as I glanced back toward the warmth of the gathering, I knew that the calm before the storm was upon us, and the true test of loyalty, love, and friendship was just beginning.

Chapter 12: Hidden Truths

The evening was awash in a soft, golden glow, fairy lights twinkling like distant stars strung lazily between the trees of Elara's backyard. The air carried the fragrant mix of freshly cut grass and the warm scent of lavender from the small garden she had nurtured with all the care of a new parent. Laughter floated through the air, accompanied by the clinking of glasses and the faint strains of a playlist that somehow managed to capture all the awkwardness of love and friendship in one smooth melody. I stood at the edge of the gathering, feeling like a reluctant spectator at a play where I was both the lead and an extra, my heart heavy with the weight of unsaid words.

Elara, radiant in a soft cream dress that billowed around her like the clouds above, moved among our friends with a grace that belied the turmoil swirling beneath her cheerful façade. Her laughter rang out, bright and infectious, yet I could see the shadows lurking behind her eyes—a fleeting look of longing every time someone mentioned the future, or the gentle clenching of her fists when she thought no one was watching. It struck me that, even in this moment of celebration, she was grappling with the inevitable truth of what lay ahead. I knew her well enough to recognize the signs, the way her smile faltered when no one else was looking, as if she were still holding back tears she didn't want to shed in front of us.

Max arrived shortly after, his presence cutting through the crowd like a lighthouse beam. There was something magnetic about him—tall, with tousled dark hair that begged to be raked through by a nervous hand, and eyes that sparkled with mischief and warmth. As he weaved his way toward me, I felt the familiar flutter in my stomach, an unwelcome reminder of the complicated feelings I had tried so hard to suppress. When he finally reached me, his smile was bright, genuine, and it was impossible to resist the way my heart responded. I couldn't help but wonder if he could see the battle raging within me.

"Hey there, you look like you could use a drink," he teased, tilting his head toward the makeshift bar table laden with colorful concoctions that seemed to promise a night of reckless abandon.

"Or a distraction," I shot back, unable to suppress a grin. "Are you here to save me from the world of party games and small talk?"

"Absolutely. I'm like the superhero of awkward gatherings," he replied, his voice playful. "What's your superpower? Eye-rolling at bad jokes?"

"Very funny," I laughed, though the sound felt strained. "Maybe I should borrow your cape when I need to dodge the questions about my love life."

He stepped closer, a spark igniting between us that made the rest of the world fade. "You're the only one who gets to dodge those questions tonight. Just be you."

Before I could reply, Elara appeared, her expression a mixture of determination and vulnerability. "Max! You have to try this new punch; it's incredible," she said, her eyes lighting up momentarily before I caught that flicker of uncertainty again. She grabbed his arm, pulling him away to join the throng, leaving me with a sudden void where our connection had just been.

I forced myself to look away, pretending to engage in the festivities. Conversations whirled around me, yet my thoughts remained anchored to Max. Was it wrong to want more than friendship with him? Was I betraying Elara's trust if I allowed myself to feel this way? Guilt twisted in my gut, each pulse reminding me of the unspoken bond between Elara and me—a bond that felt delicate, like gossamer spun in the fading light.

Hours drifted by, filled with laughter, heartfelt toasts, and the occasional sigh of someone reminiscing about a cherished memory. I caught glimpses of Elara and Max, their laughter mingling as they tossed playful banter like confetti. I wished for a moment that I could simply enjoy the sight without the knot tightening in my chest, but every glance only magnified my inner turmoil. How could I be a supportive friend when my heart tugged me in the opposite direction?

At one point, I found myself on the fringes of the party, my glass of punch half-finished and untouched, lost in a reverie of what-ifs and maybe-laters. Max caught my eye from across the yard, and in that moment, everything around us faded. The music dimmed, and the clamor of voices blurred into a distant hum. He strode toward me, determination etched into his features, and I felt my heart race with both anticipation and dread.

"Can we talk?" he asked, his voice low and earnest, cutting through the ambient noise.

"Sure," I replied, my voice barely above a whisper. I led him to a quieter corner, away from prying ears and watchful eyes. The night air was cooler here, a refreshing balm against the warm emotions swirling within me.

"What's wrong?" he asked, his brow furrowing in concern.

"Nothing, really. I just... Elara needs you tonight," I said, the words tumbling out before I could reign them in.

He stepped closer, his eyes locking onto mine, igniting a connection that sent shivers down my spine. "You know it's okay for you to have your own feelings, right? Just because she's going through something doesn't mean you have to push yours away."

His words hung in the air, charged and full of possibility, and I felt the dam I had built around my heart begin to crack. Maybe this was my moment, the chance to voice the truth I had kept locked away for far too long. But just as I opened my mouth, Elara's laughter rang out from behind us, pulling my focus back to the celebration, the bittersweetness of the moment crashing down like waves against the shore.

"I can't do this to her," I finally whispered, the weight of my loyalty pressing down on me. "Not now."

Max's expression shifted, an understanding dawning behind his eyes. "You're stronger than you think. You deserve happiness, too. Just remember that."

With those parting words, he stepped back, leaving me feeling more lost than before, my heart still tangled in the web of our unspoken desires. I turned back to the party, determined to celebrate Elara and yet acutely aware that my own story was just beginning to unfold.

As the night deepened, the moon hung low, spilling silver light over the gathering like an indulgent guest, eager to witness the festivities. Conversations ebbed and flowed around me, a steady tide of voices interspersed with bursts of laughter, but I felt like I was standing in a glass case, observing rather than participating. Elara's joy mingled with the melancholic undertones of what this celebration truly meant, creating a bittersweet melody that played on a loop in my mind.

Max returned to the crowd, his laughter infectious as he joined a group of our friends engaged in a game that involved embarrassing truths and ridiculous dares. I watched from my corner, a mix of admiration and regret gnawing at me. His ease in navigating the evening only highlighted my internal turmoil. I felt as though we were living in two separate worlds—one where he was just a friend, and another where my heart played the leading role, embroiled in a script I hadn't yet dared to write.

In an attempt to dissolve the tension building within me, I reached for a drink, hoping the tangy sweetness would distract me from the reality swirling in my mind. "Another punch?" a voice interrupted, pulling me from my reverie. I turned to see Ava, my perpetually effervescent friend, a half-full glass already in her hand.

"It's all I can think about," I admitted, forcing a laugh. "It's either that or confronting my unrequited feelings for Max, and I'd rather drown myself in fruit and sugar."

Ava raised an eyebrow, a knowing smirk dancing on her lips. "Sweetheart, I don't think there's enough punch in the world for that. You've been tiptoeing around him all night. Just tell him how you feel!"

"If only it were that easy," I sighed, the weight of her encouragement pulling at the threads of my composure. "Elara's going through enough without me complicating things. Besides, what if he doesn't feel the same? I don't want to risk what we have."

"Or maybe you're just afraid he does feel the same," she countered, her voice a gentle nudge toward the truth I was so desperately avoiding.

A chill ran down my spine, my heart racing at the thought. "That's not—"

"Isn't it? Because the way he looks at you says otherwise," she pressed, her gaze steady.

Before I could respond, Elara called out, her voice ringing like a bell above the crowd. "Hey, everyone! Can we gather around? I have something to say!"

The crowd fell quiet, curiosity weaving through the air like a tightening noose. I exchanged a glance with Ava, who shrugged, her expression unreadable. We moved closer, drawn in by the magnetic pull of Elara's presence. She stood before us, her face illuminated by the string lights, radiating a mixture of joy and vulnerability that made my chest ache.

"I just wanted to thank you all for being here," she began, her voice wavering slightly as she gathered herself. "This means so much to me, especially as I prepare for this new chapter. I couldn't have made it this far without your support."

A round of cheers erupted, and I felt a warmth blossom in my chest, yet it was tinged with the bittersweet understanding that her journey was a step toward leaving the comfort of our shared world. My mind drifted back to Max, and I wondered what he was feeling amidst the cheer. Did he understand the gravity of the moment, the invisible threads that would soon pull us all in different directions?

Elara continued, her voice a tapestry woven with emotion. "Life is about growth, and sometimes that means letting go of things we hold dear. I want you all to promise me that no matter what happens, we'll keep our connections strong, even if they change."

As her words echoed in my mind, I felt the surge of tears threatening to spill. I could see it clearly now: her bravery, her resolve. But I couldn't help but feel selfish, my heart tethered to a complicated truth that felt impossible to share.

Max stepped closer, brushing against me as he joined the crowd, and I could sense the warmth radiating from him. He leaned in, his breath warm against my ear. "Elara's right. We need to hold onto what matters, no matter where we end up."

I turned to him, struck by the earnestness in his eyes. "But what if holding on means letting go of something else?"

He smiled softly, an understanding in his gaze that made my heart stutter. "Maybe that's part of growing up. Sometimes, we have to be brave enough to risk it all for the chance at something real."

His words hung between us, thick with possibility, and I felt a rush of courage. But before I could respond, Elara's voice called me back from my thoughts, drawing my attention once more.

"Okay, let's lighten the mood! Who's up for a round of 'Never Have I Ever?'"

The crowd erupted in cheers, and I felt a wave of relief wash over me, the intensity of the moment dissipating. I joined the group, determined to shake off the heaviness that had settled over me like a storm cloud.

As we formed a circle, laughter erupted around me, each confession ranging from the ludicrous to the mildly scandalous. "Never have I ever..." was tossed around with gusto, the revelations becoming increasingly outrageous, sparking both laughter and playful groans. I watched Max as he participated, his competitive spirit shining through.

"Never have I ever gone skinny-dipping!" he declared, his eyes sparkling with mischief as several hands shot up, including mine, much to my own surprise.

"Really? You too?" he teased, raising an eyebrow.

"It was a daring phase!" I defended, heat creeping up my cheeks as everyone burst into laughter.

As the game progressed, I felt the tension in my chest loosening, the laughter drawing me out of my shell. With each passing round, I became more daring, reveling in the freedom of the moment.

Then it was Elara's turn. "Never have I ever kissed a stranger."

A ripple of gasps and giggles ran through the circle. I hesitated, caught in a wave of indecision, but to my surprise, my hand shot up, and the laughter swelled around me.

"What? You've kissed a stranger?" Max exclaimed, his eyebrows shooting up in mock disbelief.

"It was a party, okay?" I laughed, unable to suppress a grin as the group erupted into playful taunts and cheers.

"You have to tell us the story!" he urged, leaning closer as if the air between us buzzed with anticipation.

Before I could respond, Elara's voice broke through the noise, her expression shifting from playful to serious. "Okay, okay. But let's hear about the biggest secrets of the night!"

And just like that, the game took a turn, each person forced to share something they had never told anyone before. My heart raced as I pondered what I could possibly reveal, my mind swirling with unspoken truths. What would I say? Would I confess my feelings for Max? Would that be the secret that burst forth like fireworks, lighting up the night sky?

But as I glanced at Max, his expression an enticing mix of curiosity and challenge, I realized that perhaps this was my moment to take a leap. If I wanted to embrace what was growing between us, I had to face the music, and maybe, just maybe, I would be met with understanding instead of rejection.

"Never have I ever wished to kiss my best friend," I said, the words escaping my lips before I could stop them. Silence enveloped the circle, a hush of shock and curiosity as everyone turned to me, their eyes wide with anticipation.

Max stared at me, the weight of my confession hanging heavy in the air, a daring spark of realization igniting in his gaze. I felt my heart race, the world shrinking down to just him and me as the truth of the moment settled over us like a warm embrace. The unspoken tension lingered, and I knew this night, like Elara's celebration, was only the beginning of something far more profound than I had ever dared to imagine.

The moment hung in the air, taut and electric, as I stood before our circle of friends, the weight of my revelation mingling with the charged atmosphere. Max's eyes widened, surprise giving way to something deeper—a flicker of intrigue or maybe even longing. Laughter and teasing began to swell around us, but in that instant, the world faded into a soft blur, leaving just the two of us at the center of an unspoken challenge.

"Did you really just say that?" Max's voice was low, almost conspiratorial, as he leaned in closer, his presence both comforting and unsettling. The crowd buzzed with laughter and shouts of disbelief, yet I felt the entire party hinge on this moment, as though the universe conspired to draw out my truth.

"Maybe I did," I replied, heart racing, emboldened by the warm glow of the punch coursing through my veins. "What about you, Max? Care to share your deepest secret?"

His expression shifted, a hint of a smile tugging at the corners of his mouth. "That's a bold challenge. But fine. Never have I ever considered making a move on my best friend," he declared, his gaze steady on mine, the intensity of his words hanging in the air like a tantalizing promise.

The laughter around us faded into a reverent hush, and I could feel the heat rise to my cheeks. My heart raced, caught in the wild crossfire of thrill and terror. The truth was unspooling like a thread between us, delicate yet undeniable. "You think that's a secret?" I shot back, determination fueling my voice. "Because I've been wondering why you've never acted on it!"

The crowd erupted in cheers, a mix of playful shouts urging him on, but my focus was solely on him. Max seemed taken aback, his eyes narrowing as the realization of my words washed over him. "You can't just throw that out there and expect me to keep my composure," he replied, laughter in his voice, but it was laced with something deeper—a tension that promised more than mere friendship.

Elara, oblivious to the emotional maelstrom brewing in our corner, chimed in, "Guys, keep it PG! This is a celebration, not a drama club." Her playful reprimand broke the spell momentarily, yet the air between Max and me was electric, charged with possibilities that felt just out of reach.

As the game continued, I felt buoyed by the camaraderie surrounding us, but I remained acutely aware of Max's proximity. The thrill of our shared secret seemed to bubble beneath the surface, threatening to spill over. With every shared laugh and playful jab, my resolve wavered. I wanted to push through the barrier of friendship that loomed between us, but the nagging doubt whispered in my ear, reminding me of Elara's fragile state.

After several rounds, Elara decided to shift gears, urging everyone to step outside for a breath of fresh air. The night had turned cooler, a gentle breeze brushing against my skin as we gathered around a fire pit. Flames flickered and danced, casting shadows on our faces, and the scent of burning wood filled the air, creating an atmosphere that felt both magical and introspective.

"Alright, time for some real confessions," Elara announced, her tone playful yet serious. "What's the most embarrassing thing that's ever happened to you?"

A chorus of stories erupted, each tale more ludicrous than the last, filled with mishaps and missteps that had us rolling with laughter. But as I listened, I found myself growing quieter, the warmth of the fire not quite enough to thaw the tension pooling in my chest. I stole glances at Max, whose laughter rang out among our friends, yet he frequently turned to catch my eye, as if he too were trying to decipher the air between us.

When it was finally my turn, I hesitated. "Okay, um, once I mistook a stranger's drink for my own at a bar and ended up having to apologize profusely," I began, a grin spreading across my face as everyone laughed at the absurdity of it. "Turns out, he wasn't just some random guy. He was a well-known local musician. And he never let me live it down."

"Smooth," Max teased, his tone light yet his gaze still searching mine. "I don't know if that's more embarrassing or impressive."

"Definitely embarrassing," I shot back, feeling a warm flush creep up my cheeks. "What about you? What's your most embarrassing moment?"

His expression shifted, a playful glint in his eyes. "I once tripped on stage during a presentation, accidentally sending my notes flying. But instead of recovering, I just stood there, hoping to blend into the wall," he confessed, laughter bubbling from the group once more.

"Classic Max," Elara said, her laughter ringing out. "Always the charmer."

In that moment, I caught a glimpse of something deeper in his eyes, a silent understanding passing between us. The fire crackled, casting an amber glow that felt charged, alive with unspoken words. The game rolled on, but my focus drifted inward, caught in the web of uncertainty.

As the night wore on, the laughter and stories began to dwindle, leaving a comfortable silence hanging in the air. I noticed that Elara seemed lost in thought, her eyes reflecting the flickering flames, a slight frown etching her brow. I felt a tug of worry in my chest, the weight of her unspoken struggles creeping back into focus.

"Hey," I said gently, leaning toward her. "You okay?"

Elara looked up, her expression softening. "Yeah, just... thinking. About everything," she replied, her voice barely above a whisper.

"Anything in particular?"

She sighed, brushing a stray strand of hair behind her ear. "Just how things change, you know? I want to hold onto these moments but..." Her words trailed off, and I could see the shadows of her uncertainty flitting across her face.

I opened my mouth to reassure her, to tell her that no matter where life took us, our friendship would remain strong. But before I could speak, a sudden commotion erupted across the yard. A group of strangers had wandered onto the property, their voices loud and animated, seemingly unaware of the party's more intimate atmosphere.

"Who invited them?" Elara muttered, frowning as the intruders strolled into our circle, the laughter and warmth abruptly shattered. My heart sank as I realized they were not just here to socialize; they were too loud, too boisterous, their presence clashing with the cozy camaraderie we had cultivated.

Max shifted, his expression turning wary as he took in the newcomers. "Let's just ignore them," he suggested, but I could see the tension in his shoulders, the protective instinct flaring to life.

One of the strangers—a tall figure with an air of bravado—spotted us, a grin splitting his face. "Hey! We heard there was a party happening! Mind if we join?"

Before we could respond, he and his friends plopped down around the fire, their energy jarring against the remnants of our celebration.

Elara's smile faded, replaced by a look of uncertainty. "Um, actually—"

"Don't be rude! Come on, it's a party!" the newcomer interjected, waving his hand dismissively.

Max stiffened, a subtle shift in his demeanor that didn't go unnoticed by me. "This isn't really a public event," he said, his voice firm, edging on protective.

"Oh, lighten up, buddy! We're just here to have some fun!" The stranger's words dripped with a mix of challenge and arrogance, and I could feel the tension in the air thickening, the atmosphere shifting like the wind before a storm.

My pulse quickened, unease creeping in as the group continued to invade our space, laughter merging with the sounds of crackling wood and fading music. I exchanged a glance with Elara, whose expression mirrored my concern. The night, once filled with warmth and laughter, felt as if it were teetering on the brink of chaos.

"Maybe we should just move inside," I suggested, but even as the words left my mouth, I knew it wasn't just about the strangers. It was about the fragility of the connections we had built that night, and the fear that, just as easily as they had blossomed, they could unravel in an instant.

As if sensing the shift in our dynamics, Max turned to face me, his eyes searching mine for a signal. I knew then that whatever came next would change everything. Just as I opened my mouth to speak, a shout rang out from the gathering of strangers, their laughter growing louder, drowning out my thoughts.

"Let's make this party unforgettable!"

In that instant, I felt the chill of foreboding wash over me, the energy of the night spiraling out of control. Before I could react, one of the newcomers reached toward the fire, a reckless grin on his face. "How about a little excitement?"

And just like that, with a sudden flash and the horrified gasps of my friends echoing in the night, everything began to unravel.

Chapter 13: Torn Between Hearts

I poured a cup of steaming chamomile tea, the floral aroma filling my small kitchen like a warm hug, and gazed out the window. The sun was setting, casting a golden hue over the world outside, but the beauty didn't quite penetrate the melancholy that hung over me. Elara's laughter had always been the soundtrack of my life, vibrant and infectious, but now it was replaced by the beeping of hospital monitors and the whispers of worried friends. She was my best friend, my confidante, and seeing her fragile form lying on a hospital bed was like watching the vibrant colors of my world fade to gray.

Max had stepped in like a bright flare against the encroaching darkness. With his easy smile and effortless charm, he'd swept into my life, filling the gaps left by Elara's absence. Every time we brainstormed ideas for the bakery or bounced ridiculous cake themes off each other, I felt a spark that ignited something deep inside me, a thrill I hadn't experienced in ages. Yet, in the quiet moments, when laughter faded and reality settled like dust in the air, guilt gnawed at my heart. How could I allow myself to enjoy this, knowing that Elara was fighting her own battle? I felt as though I were standing on a precipice, teetering between two worlds, each one tugging at my heart in different directions.

As I stirred the tea, my phone buzzed, vibrating against the countertop. It was a message from Elara's mom, an update that made my heart race. "She's showing signs of improvement! They think she might wake up soon." Relief washed over me, mixing with the undercurrent of worry. I quickly typed back, my fingers dancing over the screen, excitement spilling into my words.

But as I pressed send, the doorbell rang, pulling me from my thoughts. I opened the door to find Max standing there, his hair tousled and a lopsided grin on his face, holding a small cake box like it was a treasure chest. "I thought you might need a pick-me-up," he said, his voice smooth like melted chocolate. "I might have tested a new recipe, and it's... well, it's something. You'll just have to try it to believe me."

I couldn't help but laugh, the sound bursting forth like a sudden breeze. "What is it this time? Chocolate? Lemon? Or something even more bizarre?"

"Fried pickle cake," he declared, his eyes glinting with mischief. "A culinary adventure, if you will."

My stomach twisted with equal parts curiosity and horror. "Are you serious?"

"Absolutely. If it doesn't kill you, it'll definitely change your perspective on life," he said, winking.

I stepped aside, allowing him to enter, and as he set the box down on the table, my heart fluttered with an odd sense of anticipation. "Alright, chef extraordinaire, let's see what culinary madness you've concocted." I lifted the lid, half-expecting the worst but unprepared for the strange, tantalizing aroma that wafted out. "This smells... interesting."

He leaned closer, his shoulder brushing against mine, sending an electric tingle down my arm. "Interesting? That's the spirit. Just remember, you asked for it."

With cautious optimism, I cut a slice and took a bite, the flavor explosion catching me off guard. "Holy moly, this is actually... amazing!" I exclaimed, savoring the sweet and salty combination. "You might be onto something, Max!"

His grin widened, satisfaction gleaming in his eyes. "I knew you'd come around. Now, what do you think we should call this masterpiece?"

"I vote for 'Dare to Dream' because if you can dream it, you can bake it," I said, chuckling.

"Perfect! It's got a ring to it. We should definitely add it to the menu." He leaned back, crossing his arms behind his head, an air of confidence surrounding him. "And now, how about a little brainstorming session? I need your artistic flair to help me with the presentation."

"Count me in," I said, my spirits lifting as we fell into a rhythm, tossing ideas back and forth, laughter mingling with the sweetness of cake. With each shared moment, the heaviness in my heart lightened a little more, and I couldn't deny the warmth that blossomed whenever he was near.

Just as we were about to dive into the wild ideas of garnishes and toppings, my phone buzzed again. This time, it was Elara. I quickly glanced at the message, and my heart stuttered in my chest. "I'm awake! I need to see you."

Max noticed my change in demeanor, his playful grin fading into concern. "What's wrong?"

I took a breath, steadying my racing heart. "Elara woke up. I have to go to her."

"Want me to drive you?" he asked, his tone shifting to something more serious, the carefree banter evaporating.

I hesitated. Elara needed me, but the thought of Max waiting outside her hospital room felt like a breach of trust. "No, I... I'll manage," I replied, though uncertainty laced my words.

"Hey," he said softly, his eyes locking onto mine. "You don't have to do everything alone. You have people who care about you, and I want to be one of them."

I opened my mouth to respond, but the words caught in my throat. My heart raced—not just from the urgency of Elara's message but also from the intensity in Max's gaze, a mix of understanding and something deeper. But the thought of leaving him in the wake of my chaos felt wrong.

"Okay, let's go," I finally said, and we stepped out into the warm evening air, the sweetness of cake lingering in the background as my heart wrestled with the twists of fate that seemed determined to keep me on my toes.

As we drove toward the hospital, the air in the car crackled with a mixture of anticipation and anxiety. The late evening light streamed through the windshield, casting a warm glow on Max's face, highlighting the way his brow furrowed in concentration. He seemed to sense my turmoil, his fingers drumming lightly on the steering wheel, the rhythm a steady heartbeat that matched the chaotic fluttering in my chest.

"What's going through that beautiful mind of yours?" he asked, stealing glances at me when he wasn't focused on the road. His voice was soft yet teasing, a blend that made it impossible for me to ignore the butterflies dancing in my stomach.

"I'm just worried about Elara. I hope she's okay," I replied, trying to keep my tone light, but the weight of my concern seeped through.

"Of course she'll be fine. She's a fighter," Max said, confidence lacing his words. "Besides, she has a best friend like you to cheer her on. She's got to feel the love radiating off you like a beacon."

I smiled, grateful for his unwavering support, yet the worry still knotted my insides. "I just wish I could take her pain away," I murmured, staring out at the passing streetlights that flickered like distant stars.

Max glanced at me, the warmth of his gaze making me feel seen in a way that made my heart race. "You're doing everything you can. You're her lifeline right now, and that means the world. Just remember, she'll be okay, and you need to take care of yourself too."

His words settled around me like a comforting blanket, momentarily quieting the voices of doubt that had been my constant companions.

When we reached the hospital, I felt an overwhelming wave of apprehension wash over me. It was as if stepping into the sterile environment of fluorescent lights and muted voices would somehow amplify my fears. I took a deep breath and turned to Max. "Are you sure you're okay waiting out here? I can't imagine you'd want to sit in a hospital all evening."

Max waved his hand dismissively, a playful smirk dancing on his lips. "Please, I've sat through enough boring meetings in my life. A hospital waiting room is practically a spa compared to that."

With a chuckle, I hopped out of the car, the cool air refreshing against my skin. As I walked through the glass doors, a wave of anxiety crashed over me, and the antiseptic scent filled my nostrils, reminding me of the fragility of life. I found myself in the waiting area, my heart pounding like a drum, each beat reminding me of Elara and the uncertainty that loomed over us.

After what felt like an eternity, I made my way to her room, my heart racing as I stepped inside. The sight of her, pale and fragile but with a hint of color returning to her cheeks, made my throat tighten. Elara lay nestled against the pillows, her dark hair a stark contrast against the crisp white linens. The monitors beeped softly, like a gentle reminder that she was still with us.

"Elara," I whispered, my voice barely breaking through the quiet hum of the machines.

Her eyes fluttered open, and for a moment, I was struck speechless. The bright blue of her irises glimmered with recognition, and a smile crept across her lips, illuminating her face like the sun breaking through clouds. "Amara," she croaked, her voice raspy but filled with warmth. "You're here."

I rushed to her side, taking her hand in mine, feeling the familiar comfort of her presence wash over me. "Of course, I'm here. I wouldn't be anywhere else."

Elara squeezed my hand, her grip strong despite her weakened state. "I've missed you. You look... different. Happier?"

I hesitated, unsure of how to navigate the truth without hurting her. "I've been keeping busy. The bakery is as chaotic as ever. You know how it is."

Her eyes narrowed slightly, an expression I knew well. "You're not telling me everything. There's someone, isn't there?"

"Uh, well..." I stammered, caught off guard.

"Max?" she guessed, her voice a teasing lilt that felt like home.

I bit my lip, a smile tugging at the corners of my mouth. "Maybe."

She raised an eyebrow, mischief sparkling in her gaze. "Oh, you definitely have to tell me more. Is he handsome? Smart? Charming? Does he make you laugh?"

"Okay, okay! Yes, he's all of those things," I admitted, my heart racing at the thought of Max. "But Elara, it's complicated. I feel like I shouldn't be enjoying anything while you're—"

"Stop right there," she interrupted, her voice firm but gentle. "I want you to be happy. You deserve it. I'll be fine. I need you to live your life, Amara, not just exist while I'm stuck in this bed."

"But what if I'm torn?" I confessed, my voice barely above a whisper. "What if I can't balance being there for you and exploring what's blossoming with Max?"

Elara's expression softened, a knowing smile gracing her lips. "Then you figure it out. Life isn't about choosing one or the other. It's about embracing all the chaos. I'll always be your number one, but you have to follow your heart, even if it leads you down unexpected paths."

Her words struck me like lightning, igniting something deep within. As I sat there, clutching her hand, I realized that Elara was right. It wasn't about sacrificing one love for another; it was about weaving them together into the fabric of my life.

"Okay," I said, a sense of resolve blooming in my chest. "You're right. I'll figure it out."

"Good. Now, tell me more about this Max," she urged, her eyes sparkling with curiosity.

As I recounted the absurdity of the fried pickle cake, our laughter mingled with the beeping of machines, creating a symphony of hope that filled the sterile room. The weight of my guilt began to lift, replaced by the warmth of friendship and the possibility of love, all intertwined in this beautiful, unpredictable journey we called life.

We talked late into the night, sharing dreams and fears, laughter and tears, all the while reminding each other that love, in all its forms, was worth fighting for. As I leaned back in the chair beside her bed, a sense of peace settled over me, allowing me to embrace the duality of my heart—a heart torn yet whole, navigating the complexities of life one moment at a time.

Elara's steady progress became my guiding star, illuminating the path ahead as I navigated the uncharted waters of my heart. Each day brought her closer to full recovery, her laughter gradually returning like a melody that filled the empty spaces in my life. Yet, even as I reveled in the moments of joy, the push and pull between my friendship with her and my budding feelings for Max loomed large.

One crisp morning, I stood behind the counter at the bakery, the familiar scents of vanilla and fresh pastries wrapping around me like a cozy blanket. The golden light filtered through the large windows, illuminating the flour-dusted countertops where I had spent countless hours crafting desserts. Max was supposed to come in for another brainstorming session, but this time, the thought of seeing him stirred something deeper within me—a mix of excitement and trepidation.

When the bell above the door jingled, I looked up, and there he was, a vision in a well-fitted plaid shirt that accentuated his frame. The sun caught the highlights in his hair, and I couldn't help but smile. "You look like you're about to take on the world," I teased, wiping my hands on my apron.

"I plan to. First order of business: conquer the ultimate pastry," he said, striding toward me with a playful gleam in his eye. "What do we have today? Is it chocolate? Because if it's not chocolate, I'm going to be very disappointed."

"Don't worry, I've got your chocolate fix right here," I replied, gesturing to the display case filled with decadent treats. "But first, I need to talk to you about Elara. I think she could really use a surprise visitor to lift her spirits."

Max leaned against the counter, his expression shifting to one of seriousness. "What did you have in mind?"

I couldn't help but notice how he was always so attuned to me, his energy aligning with mine as if we were two halves of a whole. "I thought we could bake her something special, something she's always loved. Her favorite carrot cake, maybe, with that cream cheese frosting she can't get enough of."

"Great idea! I'll bring the ingredients," he said, his enthusiasm infectious. "And we can turn it into a mini baking show right here."

As we began to gather the supplies, the banter flowed effortlessly between us. "You know, I think I should host a baking competition. You'd totally lose," I quipped, playfully nudging him with my shoulder.

"Lose? Ha! You underestimate my culinary prowess. I once baked a soufflé that could make a grown man cry," he boasted, puffing out his chest dramatically.

"Really? I'd like to see that. Was it made from the tears of your last relationship?"

"Touché. But I promise you, my soufflés are heartbreak-free," he shot back, grinning.

The laughter hung in the air like sugar in the air, sweet and intoxicating. Yet beneath the lightheartedness, I felt an undercurrent of something more profound, a shift that hinted at the deeper connection we were forging. As we worked side by side, the rhythm of our movements created a dance of sorts—his hands deftly measuring flour while I whipped the cream cheese frosting, our conversation bouncing from silly anecdotes to dreams and aspirations.

With the cake baking in the oven, the aroma began to fill the bakery, wrapping around us like a soft embrace. We settled into a corner table with our respective cups of coffee, the warmth radiating from the mugs a stark contrast to the cool breeze outside. I glanced out the window, watching the leaves twirling down from the trees, their vibrant colors dancing in the air.

"Do you ever think about where we'll be in five years?" Max asked suddenly, his gaze piercing through the playful facade.

"Five years? I'll probably be knee-deep in flour, running a successful bakery and baking oddball cakes for eccentric customers," I replied with a wink.

"Just cakes? I'd expect you to have expanded into a full-on dessert empire by then," he said, smirking. "Maybe even a cake reality show."

"Oh, I can see it now—'Amara's Amazing Confections,' where I teach people how to bake while dealing with chaos," I said, laughing at the image of myself in a brightly colored apron, juggling flaming desserts while simultaneously giving baking tips.

"Or you could be the queen of pastries in Paris. I can picture it," he said, leaning forward, his eyes sparkling. "The city, the lights, the pastries—the perfect life."

"I do love the idea of being the reigning pastry queen. But what about you? What's your five-year plan?" I asked, genuinely curious.

"Honestly? I'd love to have my own restaurant. Something laid-back, where people feel at home and can enjoy great food without the fuss," he said, his voice softening with the weight of his dream. "A place where laughter fills the air, and the food speaks for itself."

"That sounds amazing," I said, my heart swelling with admiration. "You'd make a fantastic chef. Your food would be the kind that draws people in and keeps them coming back."

"Thanks, but I'd need a partner-in-crime to make it happen. Someone who could whip up desserts to complement my dishes."

I raised an eyebrow, pretending to ponder. "Well, I might know a talented baker who could help you achieve that dream."

"Perfect! So, it's settled then. I'll be the chef, and you'll be the dessert queen," he said, grinning.

Just as the timer for the cake chimed, a loud crash echoed from outside, jolting us both from our playful banter. I rushed to the window, peering out to see a scene unfolding on the street—a commotion, with people gathering around what appeared to be a car accident. My heart raced, a pulse of adrenaline thrumming through my veins.

"Amara?" Max's voice pulled me from my thoughts, but I couldn't tear my gaze away from the chaos outside.

"We should check it out," I said, instinctively grabbing my coat. "What if someone's hurt?"

"Okay, but let's not rush in blindly," he cautioned, his hand finding mine. The warmth of his grip sent a jolt through me, grounding me for a moment. "We should call for help first."

I nodded, pulling out my phone to dial emergency services. As I reported the accident, I felt a growing unease twist in my stomach. The clamor outside grew louder, voices rising in alarm.

When I hung up, we made our way outside, the bakery's door swinging open to reveal a scene of disarray. A crowd had gathered, their faces painted with concern, and in the center of it all lay a crumpled car, its hood smoking. Panic gripped me as I scanned the faces, searching for anything familiar.

"Is everyone okay?" I called out, trying to make my way through the throng.

Suddenly, a figure stumbled from the wreckage, blood seeping from a gash on their forehead. My heart dropped as recognition dawned.

"Elara!" I screamed, rushing forward, my pulse racing.

Max was right behind me, his expression shifting to alarm. "Amara, wait—"

But it was too late. As I reached Elara, her eyes locked onto mine, filled with a mix of fear and desperation. "Amara, help me!" she cried, the world around us fading away as I plunged into the chaos, adrenaline pumping through my veins.

And in that moment, standing between the wreckage of the past and the uncertain future, I felt the threads of fate weaving tighter, the impending storm of emotions threatening to consume us all.

Chapter 14: Breaking Down Walls

The kitchen hummed with a lively energy, a symphony of flour-dusted countertops and the sweet aroma of vanilla that curled through the air. I stood amid a landscape of chaos, the remnants of failed experiments and half-finished creations littering every available surface. Cakes of various shapes and sizes loomed in the background like disgruntled sentinels, silently judging my competence. I was just days away from the showcase, and the pressure weighed heavily on my shoulders. It felt as if the world expected me to create a masterpiece, to craft edible art that would leave everyone speechless. Instead, I found myself staring blankly at the mound of fondant before me, the once-vibrant pink now seeming dull and uninspired.

Max appeared at the doorway, his silhouette framed by the late afternoon sun that spilled into the kitchen like warm honey. He leaned against the doorframe, arms crossed, an amused smirk playing on his lips. "You look like a tornado hit a bakery," he quipped, his voice light and teasing, yet somehow grounding. I managed a weak laugh, grateful for his presence.

"Just getting into the spirit of chaos," I replied, gesturing around me with a flour-dusted hand. "It's a new technique I'm trying. Call it 'Panic Pastry.'"

With a chuckle, he stepped inside, his tall frame effortlessly taking charge of the space. "Let's turn that chaos into something beautiful," he said, a hint of determination flickering in his eyes. The way he approached everything—the way he turned my scattered ingredients and wild dreams into something coherent—was nothing short of enchanting.

With a wave of his hand, he banished the mess from my mind and dove into the task at hand. "What do you need?" he asked, already unwrapping a roll of fondant with a deftness that made me question why I had ever doubted him. I marveled at his focus as he rolled the fondant out to an even thickness, the pin gliding smoothly over the surface like a boat cutting through calm waters.

"Colors," I said, my voice barely above a whisper, a sudden rush of warmth flooding through me. "I want this cake to pop. It needs to be memorable."

Max paused, looking up from his task, those playful eyes sparkling with mischief. "How about a sunset theme? The kind you'd see on a perfect summer evening. Warm oranges and pinks blending into a rich purple. It'll look stunning."

My heart danced at his suggestion, the vivid imagery painting itself across my mind. "That's brilliant," I replied, and as we began to mix colors, the atmosphere shifted, transforming the kitchen from a battleground of flour and frustration into a canvas of creativity.

As our hands worked side by side, I couldn't ignore the little electric sparks that flared each time our fingers brushed against one another. Each touch sent a thrilling shiver through me, awakening feelings I had buried deep under layers of worry and self-doubt. We bantered effortlessly, tossing flour and laughter around the room, each moment layering a new connection between us.

"Is it just me," he said, grinning while carefully shaping a rose from fondant, "or are we an unstoppable baking team?"

"Unstoppable? Maybe. But I'd say we're more like a wild rollercoaster—thrilling, unpredictable, and probably best suited for people with a strong stomach." I couldn't help but chuckle at my own joke, but there was something undeniably true about it.

With each passing hour, I felt the layers of tension in my chest slowly unfurl. The kitchen, once an intimidating fortress of self-imposed expectations, transformed into a sanctuary of creativity and laughter. But just as I was about to lean in and share the words that had been dancing on my lips—words that would confess the depth of my feelings for him—a shrill ping broke through the moment. I pulled my phone from my pocket, the screen illuminating with a message from Elara. My heart sank as I read her words, each letter feeling like a weight pressing down on my chest.

"Hey, can we talk? I've been feeling really alone lately, and I could use a friend."

I wanted to scream in frustration. The warmth and connection I shared with Max felt like a fragile bubble, one that could burst with the slightest poke. I glanced up at him, his brow furrowed slightly, sensing my sudden shift in mood.

"Everything okay?" he asked, his voice gentle, concern etching lines into his handsome features.

"Yeah, just... Elara," I replied, attempting to keep my tone light. "She's feeling a bit low and needs me to be there."

Max's expression shifted, a flicker of disappointment crossing his face before he masked it with a smile. "You should definitely go," he said, his voice steady. "She sounds like she really needs you right now."

I nodded, the battle between my heart and my mind raging within me. I wanted to stay, to explore this newfound connection with him, but my loyalty to Elara was a pull I couldn't ignore. "Thanks," I said softly, the weight of my decision hanging in the air like the sweet scent of vanilla.

"Let's finish up this cake together first," he suggested, picking up the spatula with an exaggerated flourish. "Then you can go save the day."

The softness of his tone wrapped around me like a comforting blanket, yet the tension in the room remained, like an unfinished puzzle with a missing piece. As we continued to work side by side, I felt the bond between us solidify, and I knew that this moment, no matter how fleeting, was something I would carry with me, tucked away like a cherished memory—a bittersweet reminder of what could have been.

I hurriedly wiped my hands on a kitchen towel, the remnants of flour clinging to my fingertips like the anxiety that refused to leave my side. Max continued to work beside me, his focus unwavering as he meticulously decorated the cake. The way he moved was fluid, almost artistic, and I couldn't help but admire how he transformed my once chaotic sanctuary into something beautiful and organized. He caught my eye and flashed a grin, the corners of his mouth curving with a warmth that melted the tension coiling in my chest.

"Okay, Miss Cake Wizard," he said, tilting his head like a puppy awaiting a treat. "What's next on our agenda? You're the maestro here, and I'm just your loyal assistant. I promise not to break any more eggs. Today."

I chuckled, the sound bubbling up from deep within me, as if the lightness in his demeanor was contagious. "Let's make some sugar flowers. If we want this cake to steal the show, it needs some flair. You up for a challenge?"

Max raised an eyebrow, a mock-serious expression overtaking his playful demeanor. "I was born for challenges. Just yesterday, I successfully navigated a minefield of Lego bricks without losing a limb." He picked up a piping bag filled with vibrant green icing, shaking it like a sword. "What do you need me to do? Battle some sugar? Slay the fondant dragon?"

"Just try not to turn them into abstract art," I teased, the warmth flooding back into my cheeks. "Let's keep them looking like flowers and not the aftermath of a toddler's tantrum."

As we settled into the rhythm of our task, the kitchen was filled with the sounds of laughter and the occasional playful jab. I watched as he carefully shaped petals, his tongue peeking out in concentration, a sight that was both adorable and utterly distracting. I felt a flutter of something inside me, a mix of admiration and an undeniable attraction that I was struggling to navigate.

"Tell me about Elara," Max said, breaking the comfortable silence that had settled between us like a warm blanket. "She sounds like she's really leaning on you right now."

I hesitated, my heart twisting at the thought of my friend feeling lonely. "Yeah, she's been going through a rough patch. Her work has been overwhelming, and she's feeling isolated. I just don't want her to feel like she's alone in this."

"Got it," he said, his expression softening as he molded a delicate petal. "Friendship is important. Especially when the world starts to feel too big to handle."

My heart ached at the truth of his words. I had always been the steady rock in Elara's life, the one she could rely on when things got tough. I had taken pride in that role, but it was also exhausting. Sometimes, it felt like I was the only one holding her up, and I wished for just a moment to lean on someone else.

Max's gaze met mine, and a moment of understanding passed between us. "You're a good friend," he added, his voice sincere. "But don't forget about yourself in the process."

A rush of warmth enveloped me, mixed with a pang of frustration. "It's hard not to get lost in someone else's chaos, you know? But it's also hard to let someone else in when you're so busy holding everything together."

His brow furrowed, a hint of concern evident in his expression. "You're not a superhero, you know. It's okay to take a step back sometimes. You deserve to be happy too."

"I know," I replied, feeling the weight of his words pressing down on me. "But what if I don't know how to let myself be happy? What if I mess it all up?"

"Then you mess it up," he said simply, a playful glint in his eye. "And then you fix it. It's part of being human."

I snorted, half-laughing and half-sighing, his wisdom catching me off guard. "A very insightful human, I must say."

We shared a laugh, the tension easing slightly as we returned to our tasks. But as I reached for the fondant to create the next layer of decoration, the fleeting joy of our conversation lingered in the air. I wanted to delve deeper into this connection, to explore what was bubbling just below the surface, but I felt the familiar tug of responsibility pulling me back.

As we decorated the cake with delicate flowers, the doorbell rang, echoing through the kitchen and pulling me from my thoughts. I exchanged a glance with Max, his brow quirked in curiosity. "Is that a delivery or a dramatic twist in the story?" he asked, a grin lighting up his face.

"Only one way to find out," I replied, a mix of excitement and dread bubbling inside me.

I hurried to the door, hoping it would be nothing more than a simple package. But as I opened it, I was met with a sight that knocked the breath from my lungs—Elara stood on my doorstep, her eyes red-rimmed and glistening, a silent plea etched on her face.

"Hey," I said softly, instinctively wrapping my arms around her as she stepped inside, pulling her into a comforting embrace. "What's going on? You look like you've been through the wringer."

"I just needed to see you," she admitted, her voice trembling. "I didn't know who else to turn to."

Max stepped into the room behind me, his expression shifting from light-hearted to concerned in an instant. I felt a pang of guilt wash over me, my heart torn between my friend and the undeniable chemistry sparking with Max. "We were in the middle of—"

"I know, I know," Elara interrupted, her hands gripping my arms as she searched my eyes. "I didn't mean to interrupt, but I just felt so lost. I really need you right now."

Max's presence in the room seemed to fade as I focused entirely on Elara, her vulnerability pulling me in like a moth to a flame. "Of course, I'm here for you," I promised, my heart aching for her pain.

THE TASTE OF AMBITION

I turned back to Max, who stood at the edge of the kitchen, a supportive smile playing on his lips, but his eyes revealed an understanding that made my heart twist. "Do you mind giving us a moment?"

"Not at all," he replied, stepping back with an easy grace, his presence leaving a void I couldn't ignore.

As he disappeared into the next room, I realized I had once again chosen to put my feelings on hold. The familiar blend of loyalty and longing tangled within me like the ribbons of fondant strewn across the counter. As Elara leaned into me, seeking comfort, I couldn't shake the nagging thought that some connections were meant to be explored, while others were simply threads that would fray with time. The moment hung in the air, heavy with unspoken words and missed opportunities, and I could only wonder if I would ever find the courage to embrace the chaos of my own desires.

Elara clung to me, her breath hitching with emotion as I enveloped her in a hug, the familiar weight of her worry pressing down on my chest. "I'm so glad you're here," I murmured, my voice barely above a whisper, unsure if I was comforting her or myself. She nodded, her forehead resting against my shoulder, a silent affirmation of her gratitude.

"I just needed you," she said, pulling back to look me in the eye. "Everything feels so heavy right now. Work is a mess, and I can't seem to shake this feeling of loneliness. I thought I could manage it on my own, but..." Her words trailed off, and a fresh wave of guilt washed over me. I had been so wrapped up in my own world that I had failed to see the depths of her struggle.

"Why didn't you say something sooner?" I asked, brushing a strand of hair behind her ear. "You know you can always talk to me."

"I didn't want to be a burden," she replied, her voice soft and shaky. "I didn't want to pull you into my storm."

I opened my mouth to reassure her, but the truth was a punch to my gut. "You could never be a burden to me. You're my best friend." The words slipped out, but the weight of them settled heavily in the air.

Just then, the unmistakable sound of a whisk clattering against a bowl caught my attention. I glanced toward the kitchen, half-expecting to see Max working quietly, but the sight that met my eyes was anything but peaceful. The kitchen counter was now an explosion of color—vivid icing smeared across surfaces and spatulas, fondant figures tumbling to the floor like soldiers in battle. Max stood at the center of the chaos, a sheepish grin plastered on his face as he surveyed the damage.

"Uh, well," he began, holding up a mismatched set of piping bags like a trophy, "I may have gotten a little too enthusiastic about the sugar flowers."

A laugh bubbled up from me, breaking the tension that had settled over Elara. "It looks like a sugar bomb went off in here."

"Hey, it's a sugar explosion of creativity!" he defended, throwing his hands up in mock surrender. "Who needs perfection when you can have pure, unadulterated joy?"

Elara's eyes sparkled with amusement, the weight on her shoulders momentarily lifting. "I can't believe you managed to create such a mess in just a few minutes," she said, her voice returning to its playful tone. "This is art. True art."

"I aim to please," he replied, bowing dramatically. "Now, if you'll excuse me, I need to salvage my masterpiece before it turns into a horror show."

As he moved to clean up, I caught his eye, and a silent understanding passed between us. He was trying to make light of the situation, and it worked. The tension that had threatened to engulf me faded like the icing smeared across the counter.

"Elara," I said, turning back to her, "why don't we make some cupcakes? They're easier to manage, and we can decorate them however we want."

Her face brightened at the suggestion, her earlier worry momentarily forgotten. "That sounds perfect! I've always wanted to try those crazy flavors you were experimenting with last week."

"Then let's get to it!" I said, a rush of energy flooding through me. "Max, you're on clean-up duty while we bake! Keep your whisking hands busy!"

He mock groaned, but I saw the laughter behind his eyes as he got to work. We moved around each other with a new sense of purpose, the kitchen buzzing with activity as we mixed, measured, and poured. With every stir of the batter, I could feel Elara's spirit lifting, and I silently hoped the cupcakes would not only satisfy our sweet tooth but also her heart.

As we whisked together cocoa powder and a splash of espresso, I turned to Elara. "What about a chocolate-hazelnut cupcake with a salted caramel drizzle? I think it would be the perfect way to cheer you up."

"Oh, that sounds heavenly," she said, her smile widening. "And maybe we could sprinkle a little sea salt on top for that extra kick!"

"Yes! I love the way you think." The banter flowed easily, and soon we were lost in a whirlwind of flour and frosting, laughter echoing through the room. For the first time in days, I felt the shadows lift, a soft glow of warmth replacing the anxiety that had clung to me like a shadow.

The sweet scent of baking cupcakes filled the kitchen, intertwining with the laughter and banter. But just as we reached for the sprinkles, a loud crash shattered the tranquility, the sound reverberating through the room like an unwelcome intruder. Max dropped a bowl, and it shattered against the floor, shards scattering like stars across the tile.

"What was that?" Elara jumped, her eyes wide as she glanced toward the source of the commotion.

"Just a minor setback," Max said, attempting to sound nonchalant, but the hint of panic in his voice betrayed him. He knelt down to start picking up the pieces, his focus unwavering as he cleared away the glass.

"Are you okay?" I asked, rushing over to help.

"Just peachy," he replied, a grin forming despite the mess. "Nothing like a little glass shrapnel to spice up a baking adventure."

Elara joined us, her demeanor shifting from playful to concerned as she surveyed the scene. "Be careful! We don't want anyone getting hurt."

"Don't worry," Max reassured her, a touch of humor lacing his words. "I'm practically a ninja when it comes to cleaning up my mistakes."

We all laughed, the tension momentarily forgotten, but as I picked up a larger piece of glass, my fingers brushed against something else hidden beneath the chaos—a small envelope, partially crumpled and stained with frosting. I froze, curiosity washing over me as I pulled it free from the debris.

"What's that?" Elara asked, her brow furrowed in confusion.

I unfolded the envelope, my heart pounding in my chest. "I don't know. It looks like..." My words trailed off as I read the name scrawled across the front.

"Who is it?" Max leaned in, curiosity piqued.

As I opened the envelope, a single piece of paper slid out, and I gasped, the air around us growing thick with tension. "It's addressed to me."

Elara's eyes widened. "From who?"

The words danced before my eyes, swirling in a whirlwind of disbelief and dread. My heart raced as I began to read, each line striking deeper than the last. "It says... I know what you did, and I won't let you get away with it."

The room fell silent, the playful atmosphere evaporating like a mist under the morning sun. Max straightened, a frown deepening on his face as he processed the words. "What does that mean?"

"I don't know," I whispered, feeling a chill creep up my spine. The lightness that had filled the kitchen moments before was gone, replaced by a palpable sense of dread that clung to me like a second skin.

Elara reached for my hand, her grip firm. "Whatever it is, you're not alone. We'll face it together."

But as I stared at the cryptic message, uncertainty clouded my thoughts. Just when I thought I had everything under control, the ground beneath me shifted, revealing cracks I hadn't seen before. The laughter, the warmth—it all felt like a distant memory now, overshadowed by the ominous words that echoed in my mind. I could feel the weight of impending chaos tightening around me, as if the universe had decided that my life needed a twist, and I was about to be plunged into a darkness I had not anticipated.

Chapter 15: The Pressure of Perfection

The sun hung low in the sky, casting a warm golden hue over the bustling event space, where the aroma of freshly baked goods mingled with the buzz of excited chatter. I stood behind my display, a concoction of delicate layers and sugary artistry, each element a testament to my dedication and late-night trials. My heart thudded in my chest, a relentless drumbeat that seemed to echo the whispered hopes and quiet anxieties swirling around me. Max was beside me, his presence a calming balm against the frenetic energy that surrounded us.

"Relax, you've got this," he said, a lopsided grin playing on his lips. His confidence was infectious, and I found myself leaning into it, if only for a moment. But as I glanced at the crowd, my stomach tightened. This was more than just a showcase; it was a chance to validate my dreams, to prove that my passion for cake design could transcend mere hobby status. The stakes felt impossibly high.

"Yeah, right. Easy for you to say," I muttered, forcing a laugh as I nervously fiddled with a small sugar flower perched delicately on the edge of my cake. Each petal, meticulously crafted, seemed to whisper the hours I'd spent perfecting them. I could almost hear them sigh in relief when I stepped back to admire the towering confection before me—three tiers of vanilla sponge, filled with raspberry cream, each layer seamlessly draped in fondant and adorned with blossoms so realistic they could almost convince a bee to land.

As I positioned the last few decorations, I caught a glimpse of Elara weaving through the throng. My heart lurched. She looked radiant, her usual understated style replaced by a flowing dress that danced with every step. But as our eyes met, I saw the flicker of something deeper in her gaze—perhaps longing, or a fleeting shadow of sadness. I swallowed hard, torn between my desire to share this moment with her and the nagging worry that my success might magnify her own disappointments.

"Should I have made the flowers pink instead of white?" I asked Max, my voice barely above a whisper. "What if she thinks it's too much?"

"Too much? Please. It's stunning," he replied, giving my shoulder a gentle squeeze. "And you know what? Elara will love it. She's always admired your work."

I nodded, but doubt clung to me like a second skin. The applause of passing attendees barely registered as I fixated on Elara's expression. Every smile from strangers felt like a taunt when my heart was anchored in worry for my friend. Would she feel diminished in the wake of my success? The thought gnawed at me, intertwining with my anticipation until I felt as if I were caught in a tug-of-war between my ambitions and my friendships.

When it was time to present my cake, a wave of energy swept through the room, and I took a deep breath, forcing myself to focus. "Hello, everyone! I'm thrilled to share my latest creation with you. This cake is not just a dessert; it represents love, celebration, and the joy of togetherness." My voice was steadier than I felt, and the crowd leaned in, intrigued.

As I unveiled the cake, the gasps of appreciation were music to my ears. The intricate sugar flowers shimmered under the ambient light, each petal reflecting the collective admiration of those who had gathered. I basked in the moment, the applause washing over me like a warm wave. Yet, in the back of my mind, I couldn't escape the feeling that this moment was bittersweet, a double-edged sword cutting through my elation.

"Wow, that's incredible!" came a voice from the front—a woman with bright blue hair and a penchant for bold fashion choices. She stepped closer, her eyes wide with awe. "How did you manage to get the sugar flowers so lifelike?"

"Thank you!" I replied, my smile genuine as I gestured to the flowers. "It took a lot of practice, but I think the secret is in the details. Each flower tells its own story."

"Can I ask you for some tips?" she continued, her enthusiasm infectious. "I'm trying to learn for my sister's wedding. This is beautiful!"

Before I could respond, a ripple of laughter erupted from the back of the room. I turned, and there was Elara, her laughter a bright, melodic sound that cut through the tension I'd been feeling. Relief flooded me as I caught her eye, her smile genuine, and something inside me eased. It was as if the world had sharpened into focus, and for a fleeting moment, all my fears seemed insignificant.

"Hey!" she called out, her voice carrying effortlessly over the chatter. "Did you really make this? It's absolutely breathtaking!"

"Yes, I did!" I exclaimed, a buoyancy lifting my spirits as I approached her. "But you know it wouldn't be possible without your encouragement over the years."

Elara stepped closer, her eyes glimmering with a mix of pride and something else I couldn't quite decipher. "You've always had the talent, and now it's shining through. You deserve every bit of this praise."

"I just hope it doesn't remind you of... well, you know," I murmured, the weight of our shared history threatening to overshadow the joy of the moment.

Her expression softened, and she shook her head, a fierce determination replacing any trace of melancholy. "No, don't you dare think that. This is your moment, and I am here to celebrate you, not wallow in my past."

Her words, laced with sincerity, lifted the heaviness in my chest. We stood there, surrounded by a sea of spectators, our friendship a sturdy anchor amidst the tumult of expectations and pressures. I realized then that it wasn't about the cake or the accolades—it was

THE TASTE OF AMBITION

about the connections we forged, the laughter we shared, and the unshakeable support that defined us.

Just as I began to relax into the moment, the room shifted, and the mood subtly changed. A newcomer, tall and impeccably dressed, strode confidently toward my display. His sharp suit and piercing gaze immediately captured attention, creating a palpable tension in the air. I could feel the collective curiosity of the crowd as he approached, and my heart raced. Who was this mysterious figure, and what did he want?

A hush fell over the room as the mysterious newcomer approached my display, his presence commanding attention like a thunderstorm looming on the horizon. The crowd seemed to hold its collective breath, and I felt the air crackle with anticipation. He had an aura of authority, sharp features framed by tousled hair that somehow managed to look effortlessly stylish, as though he'd stepped off a fashion runway. My heart raced; I couldn't decide if I was more intrigued or terrified.

"Quite the impressive spread," he said, his voice deep and smooth, each word carefully articulated as if he were tasting them. He glanced at my cake, his eyes narrowing slightly. "I must admit, I was drawn in by the artistry. You certainly know how to entice an audience."

"Thanks, I guess?" I replied, forcing a smile, unsure if he was complimenting my work or simply toying with me. "I do what I can to keep the sugar high in these trying times."

"Sugar high?" He raised an eyebrow, a playful smirk curling his lips. "Are you implying that I might be underestimating the power of pastries?"

"Only if you're planning on going the whole day without tasting any," I retorted, feeling a flicker of confidence amidst my uncertainty. "Consider this an invitation to indulge."

With a bemused expression, he leaned in closer, inspecting the sugar flowers that cascaded down the side of my cake like a vibrant waterfall. "I must say, your attention to detail is commendable. These are exquisite. Did you sculpt them all yourself?"

"Every petal, every tiny vein, hand-formed under the flickering glow of a midnight lamp and fueled by a ridiculous amount of coffee." My wit, ever my shield, slipped out with ease. "You could say they have a rather caffeinated charm."

He chuckled, the sound warm and genuine. "I can appreciate that. Though, I'd wager the charm doesn't quite match your talent. It's clear you've poured your heart into this."

His compliment lingered, wrapping around me like a soft blanket, making me forget the many eyes still glued to us. I was acutely aware of Elara standing off to the side, her brows knitted in confusion as she observed this stranger's fascination with my cake—and with me.

"Are you in the business, then?" I asked, trying to refocus my thoughts and steer the conversation back to safer waters. "Or just an enthusiastic admirer of fine pastries?"

"Something like that," he replied, his gaze still sweeping over the display. "I run a small event planning company. We specialize in making dreams come true, one celebration at a time. I suppose you could say I'm always on the lookout for talent that can help us achieve that."

I blinked, my heart momentarily stalling. "Event planning? You mean like... weddings?"

"Indeed," he replied, leaning back as if assessing the situation. "There's nothing quite like a wedding cake to embody the spirit of love, don't you think? Not to mention, they can be a pretty lucrative venture for someone with your skill set."

I felt the weight of his words settle heavily on my shoulders. This was the opportunity I had been working towards, the validation I desperately sought. But could I really dive into the world of wedding cakes? The idea seemed both thrilling and terrifying.

"Are you suggesting I should consider partnering with your company?" I asked, my voice steadier than I felt.

"Perhaps," he said, his eyes narrowing thoughtfully. "But let's not jump the gun. You're talented, no doubt, but I'd like to see how you handle feedback first. After all, the world of wedding cakes is not just about artistry; it's also about navigating client expectations, which can be rather... intense."

The words hung between us, a challenge cloaked in admiration. I felt a spark of determination ignite within me. "I thrive under pressure. It's where the magic happens."

He regarded me with a mix of surprise and intrigue. "Is that so? Well, consider me intrigued, then. Let's put that to the test."

As I absorbed his words, a rush of exhilaration coursed through me. This was not just a compliment—it was a challenge, a doorway to a new chapter. But before I could respond, Elara stepped forward, her expression shifting from concern to curiosity.

"Excuse me," she interjected, her tone light yet firm. "I couldn't help but notice the electric atmosphere. Is there an audition I wasn't aware of?"

The newcomer turned, his demeanor shifting slightly as he faced her. "Ah, you must be Elara. I've heard a lot about you from our friend here."

Elara's eyes widened, and I could see her curiosity turn into amusement. "Really? All good things, I hope?"

"Only the best," he replied smoothly. "You have quite the reputation as a support system."

Elara laughed, a bright, infectious sound that brought warmth to the moment. "Well, I do my best. But don't let that fool you. I'm also an expert in managing my own chaotic life."

The newcomer studied her for a moment, his interest clearly piqued. "Chaos can be a powerful motivator. It often reveals one's true character."

Elara raised an eyebrow, mirroring his previous expression. "And what exactly does that say about you? Or about me, for that matter?"

"Why, that's a philosophical debate for another time," he replied with a grin. "But for now, I'm interested in your friend's impressive cake skills. She's the real star of this show."

I watched as Elara leaned closer, her expression shifting from playful banter to genuine curiosity. "You really think so? I've seen her work. It's phenomenal, but you know how self-doubt can creep in, especially on a day like this."

"Yes," he replied, casting a sidelong glance at me, "but the cake speaks for itself. You have a rare talent, and I believe there are opportunities waiting for you if you're willing to seize them."

My heart raced again, excitement mingling with nerves. "What kind of opportunities are we talking about?"

"Let's just say, if you're open to it, I'd love to discuss the potential for collaboration," he said, his tone becoming serious. "I think you could elevate my events to another level. And who knows? Maybe you'll find a niche that allows you to flourish."

Elara's gaze shifted between us, her expression a blend of encouragement and a hint of protective wariness. "Just be cautious. Not all opportunities are as sweet as they seem. And sometimes, behind every cake, there's a slice of reality that can be a little... hard to swallow."

"Is that so?" he asked, amusement flickering in his eyes. "Then perhaps I should sweeten the deal even more. How about a taste of that cake for a start?"

The playful banter continued, the three of us wrapped in an invisible thread of camaraderie. I felt buoyed by their energy, an unexpected wave of hope lifting my spirits. Perhaps this was just the

THE TASTE OF AMBITION

beginning, an uncharted territory that shimmered with promise and potential. But as Elara's laughter mingled with the hum of the crowd, I couldn't shake the feeling that the pressure of this moment was just the start of something far more complicated than I could ever anticipate.

The air shimmered with excitement, the sweet scent of confections swirling around me like an intoxicating perfume. I could feel the vibrations of conversation and laughter intertwining with the melody of clinking glasses and delighted gasps. But amid the jubilant atmosphere, a current of tension ran deep, wrapping around me like a tight corset. As the newcomer and Elara bantered, I wrestled with a surge of conflicting emotions. The crowd, still captivated by the newcomer's charm, seemed to forget the cake momentarily, leaving me to ponder the precarious balance of my ambition and my friendship.

"You should really think about it, you know," Elara said, nudging me gently, her eyes bright with encouragement. "Working with him could open doors you never knew existed."

"Or lead to a cake disaster," I replied, half-joking, but the anxiety lingered. "I mean, how do I even know if he's legit? I could end up in a reality show called 'The Wedding Cake Disaster'—where dreams go to crumble."

"Just remember to keep it light," she said, her laughter spilling over the tense air like a soothing balm. "You're the artist here. This is your moment, not a performance for him to critique. Don't let him intimidate you."

I stole a glance at the newcomer. He was leaning against my display, casually picking up a delicate sugar flower as if it were a trinket from a flea market. "This is exquisite," he murmured, turning it in his fingers as though he were examining a piece of fine art.

"Are you trying to sweet-talk me into a partnership?" I shot back, a playful glimmer in my eye. "Because that might actually work."

He chuckled, a rich sound that resonated through the buzz of the crowd. "I assure you, sweet-talking isn't necessary. Your work speaks for itself. Besides, I prefer to let the desserts do the flirting."

Elara feigned a gasp. "And here I thought you were all charm and no substance! What a revelation!"

"Don't let the suit fool you," he said, his expression a mix of amusement and sincerity. "I do have a serious side. I wouldn't be in this business if I didn't care about the art of celebration. It's about capturing the essence of love and joy, isn't it? And your cakes do that beautifully."

I felt a swell of pride at his words, yet the weight of uncertainty crept back in. "But can I really handle the pressure of creating wedding cakes? What if I disappoint someone on their big day?"

"Then you learn and grow from it," he replied, his tone earnest. "Every artist faces setbacks. It's how you respond to them that defines your success. This is a chance to stretch yourself, to elevate your craft beyond what you've imagined."

Elara leaned closer, her eyes sparkling with encouragement. "You're not just a baker, you're a storyteller. Each cake is a narrative. Think about the couples who will share their most cherished moments with your creations. It's not just flour and sugar—it's part of their memories."

I nodded, their faith in me igniting a fire I didn't realize had begun to flicker. But before I could gather my thoughts, Max appeared, weaving through the crowd. "Hey, you two! Did I hear cake talk? I hope my best friend here is not letting this opportunity slip through her fingers."

"Easy for you to say," I shot back, glancing at him with mock irritation. "You're not the one facing the possibility of ruining someone's wedding day."

THE TASTE OF AMBITION

Max shrugged, an easy grin on his face. "That's the beauty of it. It's a wedding! What could possibly go wrong? Oh wait, don't answer that. Just let it be an adventure. You thrive in chaos."

I couldn't help but laugh at the truth of his words. Chaos and I had become old friends. But there was something about this moment, a glimmering possibility that made me want to step out of my comfort zone, to embrace the uncertainty rather than fear it.

"Alright," I said, taking a deep breath and steeling myself. "Let's talk. I'm willing to hear what you have in mind."

The newcomer's eyes sparkled with interest, and he straightened up, clearly pleased. "Fantastic! But first, let me get a taste of that cake. After all, what's a business deal without a little sweetness?"

As I reached for a slice, my heart raced with anticipation and nerves. The crowd was still buzzing, some lingering around my display, others moving to different booths. Yet as I handed him the slice, I felt a surge of adrenaline. This was it. I was taking a step into a world that had always seemed just out of reach.

"Here's to new beginnings," he said, raising the slice as if it were a champagne toast. I laughed and lifted my own piece in response.

"Cheers to that! And to the inevitable rise of my sugar-induced anxiety," I replied, laughter dancing in my voice.

Just then, a commotion erupted from the far end of the room, a sudden cacophony of raised voices and startled gasps. The crowd shifted like a wave, eyes darting toward the source of the disturbance. My stomach dropped as I saw a woman standing with her arms crossed, her expression a storm cloud of rage.

"What do you mean you don't have my cake?" she shouted, her voice slicing through the atmosphere.

I felt my pulse quicken. Could this be another baker? The woman's eyes, fierce and unwavering, caught mine for a fleeting moment. There was a look of desperation there, one that twisted in my gut. "I ordered it weeks ago! Do you have any idea what this means? I can't just walk down the aisle without a cake!"

The room fell silent, tension hanging thick in the air. The energy shifted from jubilant to chaotic, my heart racing as I looked between the newcomer and Elara, who wore an expression of concern.

"Maybe we should see what's going on," Elara suggested, her voice barely above a whisper.

"Maybe we should run," I replied, half-serious, half-joking, but my feet remained planted. I felt compelled to understand the unfolding drama, a gnawing instinct urging me to get involved.

As the woman's voice rose again, full of heartache and urgency, I caught the eye of the newcomer. "Do you think we should help?" I asked, the weight of the moment pulling at me.

He nodded, a sense of determination flashing across his face. "If this is about cake, then yes. We can't let someone's celebration fall apart on our watch."

Before I could respond, he stepped forward, moving toward the woman, his presence radiating calm amidst the chaos. "Excuse me, I couldn't help but overhear. Is there something we can do to help?"

But before she could reply, an unexpected figure burst through the crowd, and my heart sank as I recognized her. It was the last person I ever expected to see at an event like this—my former mentor, the one person whose opinion I had both revered and feared. "What are you doing here?" I blurted, my voice a mix of disbelief and unease.

She shot me a glance, her expression unreadable, as the room held its breath, the air thick with unspoken tension. The fragile moment hung in the balance, and I felt the ground shift beneath me. I had stepped into a realm where everything could change, and I had no idea how this would end.

Chapter 16: Unraveling Threads

The bakery was quiet, the kind of stillness that felt almost sacred, as if the world outside had decided to pause just for me. The golden light from the overhead fixtures bathed the wooden countertops in a warm glow, illuminating the floured surfaces where I had spent countless hours perfecting my craft. The gentle hum of the refrigerator provided a soothing background melody, a stark contrast to the chaos that had unfolded in my heart over the past few days.

I was elbow-deep in a fresh batch of buttercream frosting, the silky texture gliding through my fingers, when the door swung open with a soft chime. Max stepped inside, a figure silhouetted against the twilight outside, his usual easy smile replaced by an expression that sent a ripple of unease through my carefully constructed facade. The bakery had always been my sanctuary, a place where the weight of the world melted away with the scent of baking bread and sugar, but tonight, it felt more like a stage for the drama of my life to unfold.

"Hey," he said, his voice low and hesitant, as if he were testing the waters of an emotional sea we'd both been avoiding. He took a step closer, the door swinging shut behind him, sealing in the warm, comforting scents that clung to my apron.

"Hi," I replied, trying to sound casual, but my heart raced beneath the surface, a caged bird desperate to escape. I wiped my hands on a towel, the frosting leaving faint streaks across the fabric, a reminder of the mess I was trying to hide.

He leaned against the counter, crossing his arms, his gaze piercing but soft at the edges. "You've been working late a lot. Trying to outrun something?"

The way he asked felt almost intimate, like he could see right through the layers I'd draped over my thoughts. I shrugged, the gesture feeling flimsy against the weight of my internal struggle. "Just trying to keep up with orders. You know how it gets around here."

Max raised an eyebrow, unconvinced. "And how are you, really? After the showcase, I mean. I saw how hard you worked on that."

A lump formed in my throat, and I was grateful for the work in front of me, the way it kept my hands busy and my mind momentarily distracted. "It was... a relief, I guess. But there's a lot still to figure out. Elara... she's struggling."

The mention of Elara's name hung between us like a fragile thread, one that both bound us and threatened to snap. Max's face tightened slightly, a flicker of guilt passing through his eyes. "Yeah, I've noticed. She's been quiet."

"I feel like I'm stuck between two worlds," I admitted, my voice barely a whisper. "I want to help her, but I can't ignore what's happening between us."

Max took a step forward, his concern palpable. "We need to talk about this. It's not just going to go away."

I nodded, knowing he was right but dreading the implications of our conversation. "I know. But how do we even begin to untangle this? I don't want to hurt her."

He ran a hand through his hair, a gesture that had always made my heart flutter, a mix of frustration and longing. "And what about us? Are we supposed to just pretend there's nothing here?"

The air thickened with unspoken truths, and for a moment, I couldn't find my voice. The frosting began to harden on the countertop, a symbol of my own emotions solidifying into something unchangeable. "I don't know," I finally said, my voice barely above a whisper. "It feels selfish, doesn't it? Wanting something when someone else is hurting?"

"Selfishness can be part of love too," he said, a hint of mischief returning to his tone. "Even the best chocolate cake has a bit of bitterness mixed in with the sweetness. Maybe we need to embrace that contradiction."

His words hung in the air, sweet and sharp, as if they were frosting on a perfectly baked cupcake. I couldn't help but chuckle, the absurdity of it all cutting through the tension. "Is that your way of saying we're baking a mess of emotions here?"

"Something like that," he replied, a smile breaking through his serious facade. "Life's messy, and love is messier. If we don't acknowledge it, we're just ignoring the ingredients."

As the laughter faded, the silence enveloped us again, a comfortable weight between two people caught in the whirlwind of feelings. I took a breath, feeling the truth of his words settle within me. "You're right. But I just don't want to cross a line that I can't uncross."

"Lines can be redrawn," he said softly, his voice steady. "But you need to decide what you want. Do you want to keep things as they are, or are you willing to risk it for something that might be beautiful?"

His gaze held mine, a gentle challenge that stirred something deep within me. The bakery, with its flour-dusted counters and the sweet scent of vanilla lingering in the air, suddenly felt like a haven, a place where I could confront my own heart. I thought of Elara, of her struggles, and the warmth of Max's presence alongside my guilt.

The complexities of love and friendship intertwined, a tapestry woven with both joy and sorrow, a reality I had to face. The uncertainty loomed like a shadow, but perhaps it was time to start unraveling the threads instead of letting them knot tighter.

"Let's figure this out," I said, my resolve hardening like the frosting on the counter. "Together."

He nodded, a glimmer of hope in his eyes, and as we stood in that warm, fragrant bakery, a sense of purpose ignited within me. The journey ahead would be anything but easy, but perhaps it was the very challenge that made it worth taking.

The sweet aroma of freshly baked pastries enveloped me like a warm embrace, wrapping around my swirling thoughts as I focused on the task at hand. My hands moved instinctively, measuring flour, mixing, and kneading, as if the rhythmic motions could somehow smooth the jagged edges of my emotions. It was a familiar routine, a dance I had perfected, yet the music had changed. The delicate balance between my feelings for Max and my concern for Elara felt like a heavy weight pressing down on my chest, threatening to crush the joy I once found in baking.

Max lingered by the counter, watching me with an intensity that sent my heart racing. "So, what's the plan? Just keep frosting cupcakes until the world figures itself out?" His tone was light, but I could see the concern etched in the lines of his forehead.

"I could make that work," I shot back with a playful grin, trying to deflect the gravity of the conversation. "Nothing like a double chocolate ganache to drown out my existential crisis."

He chuckled, but the laughter faded quickly, replaced by a contemplative silence. "Seriously, though, I'm worried about Elara. We can't ignore her just because we have our own stuff to deal with."

His words hung heavy in the air, a reminder that while we tiptoed around our feelings, Elara was left to navigate her own storm. I sighed, leaning against the counter as I contemplated the mixture of ingredients before me. "You're right. But what do we do? Do we sit her down and confess our feelings over a slice of my famous carrot cake?"

Max's eyes sparkled with mischief. "I mean, cake does solve a lot of problems. But maybe we should approach this a bit more delicately. What if we invite her here for a chat? Keep it casual."

A sudden wave of apprehension washed over me. The thought of dragging Elara into our complicated web felt daunting, a storm

THE TASTE OF AMBITION

brewing on the horizon. "What if she feels cornered? Or worse, what if she ends up resenting us?"

"Then we deal with that when we get there," he said, his voice steady. "It's better than leaving her in the dark while we figure out our own mess."

I nodded, chewing on his words, the reality of the situation weighing heavily on me. Max was right; we couldn't simply ignore the elephant in the room—no matter how comfortable it was to pretend everything would resolve itself with a sprinkle of sugar and some clever banter.

The bell above the door jingled again, breaking the intensity of the moment. Elara stepped in, her expression a mix of weariness and forced cheerfulness, and I felt a pang of guilt. Here was the very person I was trying to protect, the one whose feelings now felt as tangled as a ball of yarn in the paws of an overzealous kitten.

"Hey, you two!" she chirped, her eyes flitting between us, searching for the source of the tension that had turned our cozy bakery into a stage for a soap opera. "What's going on? Are you planning another secret project without me?"

"Just brainstorming some new recipes," I replied quickly, my heart racing as I shot a glance at Max. "You know, the usual."

Elara raised an eyebrow, clearly unconvinced, but she moved further into the bakery, inhaling the sweet scent of vanilla and cinnamon. "It smells amazing in here! I could live in this bakery forever. What's the special today?"

"Cream-filled donuts," I said, trying to inject some enthusiasm into my voice. "Light as air and filled with dreams."

She laughed, the sound echoing in the warm space, but it didn't quite reach her eyes. "You always know how to make food sound poetic. But really, what's up? You both seem a little too serious for donuts."

Max stepped forward, hands shoved in his pockets, his casual demeanor a thin veneer over the seriousness of our situation. "We were just talking about how we haven't spent enough time together lately, you know? Just us three. I thought maybe we could have a little catch-up?"

Elara's smile faltered for a fraction of a second, a fleeting shadow that made my heart ache. "That sounds nice. I've missed our little hangouts."

As I watched her, I felt a surge of protectiveness mixed with an unsettling sense of impending change. This was the moment I had to navigate carefully, a tightrope walk where one misstep could lead to a disaster that would unravel everything we had built.

"Why don't we celebrate with a little baking session?" I suggested, a hint of enthusiasm creeping into my voice. "I could teach you both how to make those donuts. What do you think?"

Elara perked up, her eyes sparkling with interest. "I'm in! As long as I get to eat the leftovers."

We quickly fell into a comfortable rhythm, the laughter and chatter filling the space, the worries of the outside world momentarily forgotten. Flour flew as we mixed and rolled, the sweet scents weaving through the air like the threads of our friendship, binding us together even as the unspoken tension hung like a cloud above us.

While the donuts baked, we shared stories, memories spilling out like icing from an overfilled piping bag. I watched Elara, noting the moments when her laughter faltered, when her smile didn't quite reach her eyes. My heart sank with the knowledge that she was carrying more than she let on, a weight that I had been oblivious to until now.

"Remember that time we decided to make a cake for the summer fair?" Elara mused, wiping flour from her cheek with a grin. "We almost burned down my mom's kitchen!"

THE TASTE OF AMBITION

Max laughed, a rich sound that made my stomach flutter. "You mean the time we created a cake that looked like a volcano? And exploded all over the place? That was legendary."

"More like a culinary disaster," I added, chuckling as I stirred the batter. "But at least we had fun, right?"

The laughter flowed freely, and for a moment, it felt like everything was right in our world. But beneath the surface, I felt the undeniable pull of the truth waiting to be revealed, an itch that couldn't be scratched until we acknowledged the threads that wove us together and threatened to unravel.

Just as I began to relax, a loud crash echoed from the back of the bakery, snapping my focus away from our memories. My heart raced as I spun around, and the sight that met my eyes sent a jolt of adrenaline coursing through me. The shelves of sprinkles and baking supplies had toppled over, spilling their contents across the floor like a technicolor explosion.

"Not the sprinkles!" I cried, moving instinctively to grab a broom.

Elara gasped, eyes wide. "This is a disaster!"

Max, ever the quick thinker, grabbed a handful of sprinkles and tossed them into the air, his laughter ringing through the chaos. "Sprinkle party!"

And just like that, the tension dissipated into giggles as we dove into the colorful mess, the chaos of the moment overshadowing the emotional undercurrents. But as I knelt there, surrounded by laughter and mischief, I couldn't shake the feeling that this was just a brief respite—a moment before the storm we'd inevitably have to face together.

As the sprinkles rained down, a colorful cascade that momentarily obscured the tension hanging in the air, I felt a rush of adrenaline mixed with relief. It was absurdly comical—the way we all scrambled to catch the vibrant little flecks like children in a snowstorm. Max dove into the heap of baking supplies, his laughter infectious as he tossed a handful of sprinkles in the air, a mischievous grin lighting up his face.

"Is this a bakery or a circus?" Elara asked, her laughter ringing like a bell, but I could still see the underlying worry in her eyes, the shadows that flickered just out of reach.

"It's definitely a circus," I replied, my voice teasing as I pelted Max with a few stray sprinkles. "Welcome to my wild world, where the frosting is thick and the emotions are thicker."

Elara snorted, the tension in her shoulders easing as she joined in the fray. "And let's not forget the culinary disasters. This is precisely why I can't be trusted in the kitchen."

Just then, a flash of color caught my eye, and I froze. Among the chaos of scattered flour and vibrant sprinkles, a familiar envelope lay partially buried beneath a pile of discarded pastry bags. My heart sank as I bent down to retrieve it, the air around us suddenly feeling charged with an unspoken weight.

"What's that?" Max asked, stepping closer, his expression shifting from playful to curious, the lightness of our moment suspended in the air like a bubble, fragile and on the verge of bursting.

"It's...nothing," I said, trying to sound casual as I slid the envelope out from the colorful wreckage. But the return address on the front sent a jolt through me. It was from my old college, a place I had not thought about in years, yet here it was, tugging at threads of nostalgia and uncertainty.

Elara leaned over my shoulder, her brow furrowing as she read the address. "You're not still waiting for a rejection letter from that art program, are you? I thought you were over that."

"It's not a rejection letter," I replied, my voice barely above a whisper, my pulse quickening as I turned the envelope over in my hands. "I... I didn't apply. I never thought I'd hear from them again."

"What does it say?" Max asked, the weight of the moment settling heavily between us, almost palpable.

I took a deep breath, feeling the surrounding chaos fade away as I tore the envelope open, the crisp paper whispering secrets as I unfolded it. The letter was a single page, the elegant script inviting yet daunting. As I read, the room blurred around the edges, the words on the page swirling into a tempest of emotions.

"It's an invitation to exhibit my work," I said slowly, my voice trembling as I tried to process the implications. "They want to feature my pastries in a showcase. It's all very... surreal."

The room erupted in excited chatter as Elara clapped her hands together. "This is amazing! You've always had such an eye for presentation. You're finally getting recognized for your creativity!"

Max's eyes were wide, yet I could see the shadow of concern lurking behind them. "That's incredible, but... is it what you want? Are you ready for that kind of pressure?"

I hesitated, my heart racing at the prospect of being thrust back into a world I thought I had left behind. "I don't know," I admitted, my mind racing through the possibilities, both exhilarating and terrifying. "What if it's a mistake? What if I can't handle it?"

"You'll never know unless you try," Elara urged, her eyes shining with encouragement. "And I'll be there to cheer you on every step of the way."

"Yeah, me too," Max added, his tone warm and earnest, yet there was an undertone of something else—an unspoken worry that tugged at my heart.

I wanted to feel the excitement bubbling up inside me, to revel in the idea of showcasing my work, yet the swirling emotions within felt like a storm waiting to break. "It's just... everything feels so complicated right now. I want to help Elara, but what if pursuing this pulls me away from everything we've built together?"

Elara's smile faltered as she caught the implication behind my words. "I understand. You're feeling torn. But maybe this is your chance to find your own voice again. You've sacrificed so much for us."

Max stepped forward, the distance between us crackling with unspoken truths. "You deserve this, but you need to make sure you're doing it for you, not for us. You have to put yourself first sometimes."

Their words wrapped around me, pulling me in different directions as I stood there, a girl caught between loyalty and ambition. I wanted to scream and cry, to throw myself into a whirlwind of flour and frosting until everything felt right again. But the reality was stark—this was more than just a baking competition; it was an opportunity that could change everything.

Just as I wrestled with my feelings, the door swung open with a sudden gust of wind, sending a flurry of scattered sprinkles dancing through the air like confetti. A figure stepped in, silhouetted against the fading light, and my heart dropped. It was Clara, my old friend, the one person whose arrival could either bring relief or complication.

"Am I interrupting?" she called out, her voice laced with playful innocence, but the moment I met her gaze, I saw the fire of determination burning behind her eyes. "I heard there was a sprinkle disaster in progress, and I couldn't resist coming to see the chaos for myself."

Her sudden presence felt like a lightning bolt, illuminating all the tangled threads I was trying to weave together. I caught Elara's worried glance, and I knew the moment had shifted again. Clara had always had a knack for stirring the pot, and now, with her here, everything felt more precarious than before.

"Clara, we were just—" I began, but the words stuck in my throat as she stepped closer, her eyes narrowing with curiosity.

"What's going on? You look like you've seen a ghost," she said, glancing between Max and Elara. "And is that an invitation I see?"

My heart raced as I clutched the letter tightly, feeling the weight of the moment pressing down on me. "It's nothing, really. Just a silly invitation—"

"Don't downplay it," Max interrupted, his voice steady. "It's an opportunity. A huge one."

Clara's eyes sparkled with mischief. "An opportunity? Now, that's interesting. What kind of opportunity are we talking about? Because I'd hate to miss out on the good stuff."

As Clara leaned in, her curiosity sharp and unyielding, I felt the threads of my carefully constructed world begin to fray. The tension thickened, suffocating in its intensity, and I knew, at that moment, that everything was about to unravel. The question hung in the air, heavy with implication: would I risk everything to chase my dreams, or would I stay bound by the expectations of those I cared for most?

"Maybe we should all sit down and have a proper conversation," Clara suggested, her gaze unwavering as she settled into the space, a catalyst for the storm that was brewing just beneath the surface.

And with that, the air crackled with anticipation, uncertainty blooming like the sweetest frosting, and I realized that the truth was closer than I thought—ready to surface, ready to change everything.

Chapter 17: The Unraveling

Elara sat at the table in my bakery, a swirl of flour and sugar enveloping us like a comforting embrace, but there was no sweetness to the moment. The room was filled with the warm, inviting scents of vanilla and buttercream, but it felt more like a bittersweet symphony. I watched her delicate fingers tremble as she picked at a cupcake, the frosting barely touched. Her normally bright laughter was conspicuously absent, replaced by a heaviness that weighed on my chest.

"Remember when we baked those ridiculous giant cupcakes for the charity fair?" I tried to spark some joy, recalling how we'd adorned them with rainbow sprinkles and edible glitter. "You thought it would impress everyone. I'm pretty sure it just made a sticky mess all over your car."

Her lips twitched, just a hint of a smile, but it quickly faded. "Yeah, but I didn't care as long as we were laughing."

I yearned to bring back that laughter, the sound of it like music to my ears. But every time I thought I caught a glimpse of the old Elara, it slipped away, like grains of sand through my fingers. The silence hung between us, oppressive and thick. I busied myself with icing bags, squeezing them with too much pressure until the frosting oozed out in the wrong shapes.

"Why did I ever think baking would make me feel better?" she muttered, her gaze fixed on the untouched confection before her.

"Because you're magic in the kitchen," I replied, my voice buoyed by a desperate need to pull her back from the edge. "And it used to make you happy."

"It doesn't feel like it's going to again." Her voice was so quiet, almost drowned out by the whir of the mixer in the corner.

I glanced around the bakery, its shelves lined with vibrant treats—sugar cookies shaped like hearts, lemon tarts with the perfect zest, and decadent chocolate éclairs. Each one a labor of love, yet I felt a void creeping in, a silence echoing the turmoil within Elara.

The door swung open, the bell chiming a cheery tune, and in walked Max, all tousled hair and an easy grin that could light up the darkest day. His presence was a beacon, and I felt an involuntary lift in my spirits. But the moment his gaze landed on Elara, the joy in his eyes dulled.

"Hey, Elara! How are you?" He approached, his steps hesitant.

She didn't look up, merely shrugged. "I'm fine."

"Sure you are," I thought, watching him assess her like she was a puzzle with missing pieces. He turned to me, his brow furrowed with concern.

"What's going on?"

I could feel the weight of his gaze on me, a silent plea for answers. How could I explain the shifting dynamics of our friendship, the unspoken tension that had been building between us? "Just the usual cupcake therapy," I deflected, forcing a smile.

"Right. Well, I brought you both something." He reached into his backpack and pulled out a bag of flour that had clearly seen better days, with flour dusting his hands like snow. "I figured we could make a batch of cookies—your favorite, Elara."

"I don't want cookies, Max." Her voice was sharper than I expected, slicing through the air like a knife.

"Okay." He took a step back, visibly deflated. "Just trying to help."

I wished I could smooth the wrinkles between them, make the distance between Elara and Max disappear. There was a time when they had exchanged flirtatious banter over baking, their laughter mingling in the air, yet now they seemed worlds apart, caught in an emotional quagmire that I felt helpless to navigate.

"Maybe we should just..." I began, but the words caught in my throat. I couldn't finish the sentence. Maybe we should just pretend everything was fine? Maybe we should just ignore the elephant in the room? My heart felt like a tight knot, and I couldn't bear the thought of losing either of them.

"I just need some time," Elara finally admitted, her voice trembling like the frosting on her cupcake. "To... to figure things out."

I nodded, understanding the gravity of her statement. The air between us crackled with unsaid words, and I fought the impulse to reach out and pull her back. Instead, I clenched my fists, resolving to honor her wishes. If she needed distance, I would give it to her.

Max shifted awkwardly, the tension between him and Elara palpable, a tightrope walk of emotions. "I'll—uh, I'll come back later. Just text me if you want to bake, Elara. I'll be around."

He hesitated, casting a last hopeful glance at her before turning to leave, and I felt a wave of longing wash over me.

"Max, wait!" I called out, chasing him to the door. I caught him just as he reached for the handle. "Can we talk?"

His eyes met mine, a mixture of hope and uncertainty swirling within them. "Sure, what's up?"

I closed the door behind us, the quiet of the bakery wrapping around us like a blanket. "I think we both know that Elara needs more than just cookies right now."

"I want to be there for her," he said, frustration evident in his tone. "But she's shutting me out."

"Maybe she needs to process everything first," I suggested gently. "We can't rush her. Let's give her the space she needs."

Max sighed, running a hand through his hair. "It just feels wrong, you know? I hate seeing her like this."

"I do too. But pushing won't help. She'll come around when she's ready."

His expression softened, the tension in his shoulders easing just a fraction. "I hope you're right."

THE TASTE OF AMBITION

I leaned against the doorframe, the weight of uncertainty still lingering. The world outside was alive with the bustle of the street, yet inside, everything felt suspended in time. I knew the road ahead would be rocky, filled with unexpected twists and turns. But sometimes, all we could do was wait and hope, trusting that love would find its way through the darkness, even if it took a little longer than we wished.

The following days in the bakery unfolded like a cake without frosting—sweet in its simplicity, but lacking the layers of delight that once made it extraordinary. My mornings started with the hum of mixers and the sizzle of butter melting in pans, a rhythm I relied on to ground me amid the chaos of emotions swirling around Elara. But the warmth that usually filled my heart was dimmed by a shadow I couldn't shake.

Every time Elara entered the bakery, her presence seemed to drain the color from the walls. I would catch sight of her in the corner, staring out the window as if she could find solace in the world outside, her reflection caught in a glass that mirrored her pain. The sunlight could dance through the panes, but it did little to illuminate her sorrow. I poured my energy into baking, creating towering cakes and delicate pastries, but it felt like I was crafting illusions—delicious facades hiding the disarray beneath.

One afternoon, as I kneaded dough, my thoughts twisted like the strands in my hands. The doorbell jingled, and in walked a flurry of energy, a gust of fresh air that momentarily scattered the dark clouds. Olivia, my longtime friend and self-proclaimed cupcake enthusiast, entered with an enthusiastic smile and a bounce in her step.

"Hello, my favorite pastry magician!" she exclaimed, wrapping her arms around me in a tight embrace. "I can smell the sugar from down the block. What are we whipping up today?"

"Just the usual, trying to keep my sanity intact," I replied, forcing a smile that didn't quite reach my eyes. "Elara's not really in a baking mood, though."

Olivia's expression shifted from cheerful to concerned in a heartbeat. "I heard about what happened. Is she really okay?"

"Not really." I sighed, wiping flour from my hands. "I wish I could do more for her, but it feels like every time I reach out, she pulls further away."

"Maybe she just needs a distraction. You know how she is when she's in the kitchen—she loves the chaos of flour flying everywhere," Olivia suggested, her eyes sparkling with mischief. "What if we planned a surprise baking night? Just us three, like old times?"

I bit my lip, torn between wanting to help Elara and respecting her need for space. "That sounds great, but I think she might need more time to herself."

"Or maybe she needs friends to remind her she's not alone," Olivia countered, her tone gentle yet firm. "You know how we used to lose ourselves in the fun of baking. It might be just what she needs to shake off the gloom."

As I considered Olivia's words, a spark of hope flickered in my chest. Elara had always thrived on laughter and connection; maybe the comfort of familiar routines could help her find her way back. I glanced out the window where the autumn leaves swirled in hues of gold and crimson, and I could almost picture the warmth of those memories wrapping around us like a favorite blanket.

"Okay, let's do it. We'll bake up a storm," I said, determination igniting within me. "But let's keep it simple—lots of cupcakes, maybe some cookies. Nothing too extravagant."

Olivia clapped her hands, excitement radiating from her. "And we'll make her favorite frosting, the one that looks like rainbows exploded! It'll be perfect."

THE TASTE OF AMBITION

The plan felt right, a bridge to reach Elara without forcing her into anything. That evening, I sent her a text, casually inviting her to a baking night with us. I held my breath, the anticipation curling in my stomach like a pretzel. When her reply came, it was short and hesitant: Sounds fun. I'll think about it.

I watched the words linger on my screen, their weight heavy with uncertainty. But at least she didn't say no. I clung to that small victory as Olivia and I began preparing, our laughter filling the bakery as we sifted flour and mixed colors for frosting.

Later that week, as the sun dipped low in the sky, painting the horizon in shades of lavender and gold, I stood in the bakery, a cloud of excitement buzzing in the air. The night was upon us, and I had created a cozy little nook in the back, adorned with fairy lights that twinkled like stars. Olivia and I had been baking for hours, our hands dusted with flour and our aprons splattered with vibrant hues of frosting.

"Do you think she'll like it?" I asked, glancing at the table laden with an array of colorful cupcakes, each one a burst of personality.

"Of course! Who wouldn't love a cupcake that looks like a party?" Olivia grinned, her eyes glimmering with mischief. "And if not, we'll just have to eat them all ourselves."

The door creaked open, and in walked Elara, a hesitant smile creeping onto her face. She wore a cozy sweater that engulfed her, but there was something fragile about her, as if she were still finding her footing.

"What is all this?" she asked, her voice a mixture of surprise and curiosity.

"Just a little something to cheer you up," I said, gesturing to the vibrant display. "We thought we'd bring back our old baking nights. Remember those?"

Elara hesitated, her gaze flitting over the cupcakes, the flickering lights, and the warmth of the space. "I'm not sure I'm up for it..."

"C'mon! Just a few bites. It's like a hug for your taste buds," Olivia chimed in, her infectious enthusiasm wrapping around Elara like a cozy blanket.

For a moment, the silence was deafening, the weight of unspoken words hanging thick in the air. But then, slowly, Elara stepped inside, and the tension began to ebb away.

"Okay, maybe just for a little while," she relented, her lips curving into a tentative smile.

Relief washed over me as we settled into the rhythm of our baking adventure. Laughter filled the air, mixing with the sweet scents of vanilla and chocolate, and slowly, like the gradual unfurling of a flower, Elara began to let go of her sadness. We shared stories, each one a thread that stitched the frayed edges of our friendship back together, weaving warmth into the fabric of our evening.

"Remember that time we accidentally used salt instead of sugar?" Elara's laughter rang out, and I could see the flicker of her spirit reigniting, dancing in her eyes.

"And then we made that awful cake and still tried to pass it off as gourmet?" I added, my heart swelling with hope.

"I think I'm still traumatized," Elara chuckled, the sound like music.

We continued to whip up frosting and sprinkle toppings, our conversation flowing effortlessly, as if no shadows had ever lingered between us. But in the back of my mind, I couldn't shake the feeling that we were walking a tightrope, a delicate balance between healing and heartache. The warmth of Elara's laughter filled me with hope, yet I sensed that beneath her smile, layers of complexity still remained—unspoken truths and lingering fears that hung in the air, ready to unravel at the slightest misstep.

The baking session unfolded like a slow awakening, each whisk of the mixer pulling Elara closer to the surface. As the evening wore on, the laughter grew infectious, wrapping around us like the aroma of freshly baked cupcakes, thick and sweet. The fairy lights cast a warm glow, illuminating the playful chaos we created with colorful sprinkles and whimsically mismatched frosting. It felt as if the weight of the world had shifted, if only slightly, and for the first time in weeks, I believed Elara might begin to mend.

"Okay, time for the taste test," I declared, holding up a frosted cupcake that was nearly bursting with personality. "Who's brave enough to take the first bite?"

"Brave or foolish?" Elara shot back, a glint of mischief dancing in her eyes. "I might end up with frosting in my hair."

"Just like old times," I replied, my heart lifting at the sight of her playful spirit resurfacing.

"Fine, I'll be the guinea pig," she sighed dramatically, but I caught the smile creeping across her lips. As she took a tentative bite, her eyes widened, and she savored the moment with exaggerated enthusiasm.

"Holy sugar rush! This is dangerously delicious," she declared, her laughter ringing like the sweetest of chimes.

I joined in her delight, grateful for the warmth that was slowly seeping back into her demeanor. Olivia stood nearby, gleefully crafting her own creation, the kitchen an explosion of colors and flavors that mirrored our reawakening friendship.

The evening unfolded, a cascade of lighthearted banter, nostalgic stories, and renewed connections. We were three friends navigating the complex maze of laughter and lingering shadows. But beneath the surface of our merriment, I sensed an undercurrent, a delicate balance that could tip at any moment.

As the last cupcake was decorated and the final frosting swirled, I felt a prickling in my gut, a whisper that something was still amiss. Elara leaned against the counter, her smile fading slightly as she watched us.

"Thanks for this," she said, her voice quieter, more vulnerable than I had hoped. "I really needed it."

"You know we're always here for you, right?" Olivia replied, her tone sincere. "No pressure, just friendship and a ton of sugar."

"I know," Elara responded, her gaze drifting toward the window, where the night wrapped the world in a blanket of stars. "I just... it's hard to shake off everything."

"Take your time. We'll be right here, cupcakes in hand," I assured her, but even as I said it, a nagging feeling twisted in my chest. The lightheartedness of the night felt like a fragile facade, and I couldn't shake the urge to dig deeper, to unravel the layers of her pain.

"I wish I could just forget," Elara whispered, more to herself than to us.

In that moment, my heart ached for her. I wanted to pull her into my arms and tell her that everything would be okay, that the shadows would recede. But I sensed that my words might not be enough. There was something brewing beneath the surface, something we hadn't addressed.

"Why don't we take a break from baking and watch a movie?" I suggested, desperately trying to shift the mood to something lighter. "Something with plenty of popcorn and questionable plotlines?"

"Now you're speaking my language," Elara replied, her spirit flickering back to life.

As we settled onto the worn-out couch in the corner of the bakery, blankets piled around us like a fort, I glanced at Elara. She nestled into the cushions, but her fingers fidgeted with the hem of her sweater, a telltale sign of her restlessness. Olivia picked a movie that promised mindless entertainment, but I couldn't shake the feeling that beneath the popcorn and flickering screen, we were skirting around the truth.

Halfway through the film, the tension was palpable, punctuated by the sound of crunching popcorn and the distant hum of the world outside. The movie's plot thickened, but my attention drifted to Elara, who sat entranced by the screen yet lost in thought.

"Hey," I said softly, breaking the silence, "what do you really want to do right now?"

"Can't I just enjoy a stupid movie without a philosophical interrogation?" she shot back, though her tone was laced with a hint of amusement.

"Fair point, but I can't help but notice you've got that deep-in-thought look on your face. The kind that says you're plotting world domination or something."

"World domination?" she scoffed, the corner of her mouth twitching. "Please. I barely have enough energy to dominate my laundry pile."

"Look, we're here for the fun stuff, but if you need to talk..." I trailed off, letting the silence hang.

Elara shifted, her gaze flickering back to the movie. "It's just... I don't know. I feel like I'm supposed to be over this by now."

"Over what?" Olivia chimed in, her eyes sharp with concern.

"I don't want to keep dragging you guys down," Elara admitted, her voice barely above a whisper. "It feels like every time we have fun, I'm just pretending to be okay."

"No one's expecting you to be 'okay' all the time," I said, my heart aching for her. "We're your friends, and we want to help, even if that means just sitting in silence with you."

"I appreciate it," she replied, but I could see the uncertainty lurking behind her eyes. "But it's exhausting."

Just then, the bakery door swung open, a gust of wind sending a chill through the room. My heart skipped as I looked up, expecting another friend to join our gathering. Instead, a figure emerged from the shadows, silhouetted against the streetlights, a familiar shape that sent a rush of conflicting emotions coursing through me.

"Max?" I breathed, the tension in the air shifting as he stepped into the warmth of the bakery, his expression a mix of determination and hesitation.

"What are you doing here?" Elara's voice tightened, her eyes wide as she registered his presence.

"I came to talk," he said, his gaze locked onto hers, a gravity in his tone that made the air feel thicker.

Elara's breath caught in her throat, and in that moment, the comforting cocoon we had woven together began to unravel, thread by fragile thread. I glanced at Olivia, her wide eyes reflecting my own sense of disbelief. What had once felt like a moment of reconnection was suddenly teetering on the edge of chaos, and I realized that the evening we'd crafted so carefully was about to take an unexpected turn.

"Elara, we need to discuss this," Max pressed, his voice steady, but the tension crackled like static electricity.

Her expression hardened, a wall rising between them that mirrored the unspoken feelings and fears swirling in the room. The warmth of the moment evaporated, replaced by a whirlwind of unresolved emotions that threatened to engulf us all.

"Discuss what?" Elara's tone was sharp, a defensive shield that revealed how vulnerable she truly felt.

"Us," Max said, and I could see the determination in his eyes. The air hung heavy, waiting for something to break.

And then, without warning, everything shifted. A loud crash erupted from the kitchen, echoing through the bakery like a thunderclap, startling us all. My heart raced as I whipped around, dread coiling in my stomach. Whatever we had built that night was on the verge of collapsing, and the unexpected chaos looming ahead promised to shatter the fragile moment we had painstakingly constructed.

Chapter 18: Crossing Boundaries

Max stepped through the door of the bakery, and the soft chime of the bell overhead felt like a tolling reminder of the chaos that had settled in my heart over the last few weeks. Flour dust danced in the golden light filtering through the windows, and the scent of fresh cinnamon rolls enveloped us, warm and sweet, a stark contrast to the cool distance that had crept into my life. He was wearing that casual gray sweater that made his eyes pop, and for a split second, all my worries slipped away, buried under the weight of his unexpected presence.

"Hey," he said, his voice low and steady, as if he were grounding himself in the chaos that often swirled between us.

"Hey," I replied, wiping my hands on my apron, suddenly acutely aware of how flour-laden I looked. "You didn't call first. You know it's a busy morning."

"Yeah, I figured you could use a break," he replied, a teasing smile playing at the corners of his mouth. "Besides, I like my coffee served fresh, not from a pre-heated pot."

"Your timing is impeccable, then," I said, gesturing to the counter where a steaming pot of coffee awaited. "I just made a fresh batch."

As he stepped further inside, I felt the familiar flutter in my stomach, a sensation that both thrilled and terrified me. The tension between us crackled in the air, invisible yet palpable, as though we were two magnets drawn together but dangerously close to repelling. I could see it in the way his gaze lingered on me, like he was trying to decode the whirlpool of emotions swirling in my eyes.

"Let's talk," he said, the words heavy with an unspoken urgency.

I sighed, leaning against the counter, the polished wood cool against my skin. "Talk about what? You know there's not much to say when the world feels like it's falling apart."

"Maybe it's time we stopped pretending everything's okay," he said, his voice firm yet gentle, like he was coaxing a frightened animal from its hiding place.

"Okay, Max, what do you want me to say?" My voice came out sharper than intended. I was caught off guard by the vulnerability lurking beneath my bravado. The heart-to-heart we both needed felt more like an invitation to unravel the tangled mess of our feelings, and that scared me more than I cared to admit.

He stepped closer, and I could see the concern etched in the lines of his brow. "I want you to be honest. With me and with yourself. I can see the toll this whole situation with Elara has taken on you, and I can't just stand by while you're struggling."

In that moment, I could almost taste the tension between us, a heady blend of unacknowledged desires and fears. "And what about you?" I shot back, my heart racing. "What if I'm not the one you want? You don't know what you're getting into."

"Don't make this about me," he countered, his tone softening. "I'm here for you. Always have been."

The weight of his words settled over me like a comforting blanket, but underneath it lurked the reminder of my chaotic life. Elara's struggles were an ever-present shadow, creeping into every crevice of my happiness. "What if I can't be what you need?" I murmured, more to myself than to him.

"Then we figure it out together," he said simply, his gaze unwavering.

We stood there, the distance between us shrinking, like the air had shifted into something more electric. I felt a stir of hope mingled with despair. Just as I began to lose myself in his deep blue eyes, letting the worries of the world fade away, our hands brushed against each other—a soft, fleeting touch that sent a shock of warmth through me. It was as if we'd crossed an invisible line, the spark igniting something I'd been trying to ignore.

"I—" I started, but the moment stretched, heavy with possibilities. The air around us buzzed, thickening with anticipation, and I could feel the pulse of my heart in my ears. My breath quickened as I leaned in, drawn to him like a moth to a flame.

But before our lips could meet, my phone buzzed on the counter, a sudden and unwelcome reminder of reality. I glanced at the screen, and my stomach dropped—Elara's name blinked at me, a desperate call for help.

"Damn it," I muttered, snatching the phone and swiping to answer, guilt pooling in my gut like a lead weight. "Elara? Are you okay?"

Max's expression shifted, a flicker of understanding crossing his face. He stepped back, giving me space, but the warmth of his presence still clung to me like a second skin.

"I'm not okay," Elara's voice trembled through the receiver. "I don't know what to do. Everything's falling apart."

"Just breathe, okay?" I said, my heart aching for her. "I'll be there as soon as I can. We'll figure this out."

As I hung up, the reality of my fractured world crashed back down. I turned to Max, my heart heavy. "I'm sorry. I have to go."

"Of course," he said, his voice steady despite the storm brewing between us. "Just... promise me you'll take care of yourself, too."

"I will," I replied, though doubt gnawed at my insides. But as I rushed to gather my things, I knew I was leaving behind not just an unfinished conversation but a part of my heart, caught in the quiet moments we had almost shared. The bakery, once a sanctuary, suddenly felt like a cage.

As I stepped into the cool morning air, I couldn't shake the feeling that I was constantly crossing boundaries—between hope and despair, between love and fear. And yet, with Max lingering in the back of my mind, I couldn't help but wonder if, one day, I might find the courage to navigate those boundaries with him by my side.

The air outside was crisp, a brisk reminder that autumn was creeping in with its golden leaves and slightly chilly mornings. I rushed down the street, the weight of Elara's distress heavy on my shoulders. Each step felt like a tightrope walk between my responsibilities and the overwhelming desire to turn around and run back to Max. A world of uncertainty lay before me, tangled like the strands of yarn I often used to create the cozy scarves I sold in the bakery. Yet, for every thought of turning back, I felt the pull of urgency tugging me closer to my friend, her need demanding my attention like a siren's call.

Elara's apartment loomed ahead, a nondescript building nestled between two bustling cafes, its façade dull and unremarkable. But behind those walls, the storm of her struggles raged, invisible but palpable. I knocked briskly, my knuckles rapping against the door like a tattoo drummer summoning an audience. The door swung open, revealing her, a flurry of emotions painted across her face—despair mingling with hope, like clouds before a storm.

"Thank God you're here!" she exclaimed, her voice trembling as she ushered me inside. "I thought I was going to drown in my own worries."

I stepped into the small living room, the scent of burnt coffee hanging in the air, a testament to her frazzled state. "What's happened?" I asked, trying to mask the concern rippling through me.

She plopped onto the sofa, her eyes wide, hands clasped tightly in her lap. "It's my job. I'm on the chopping block, and I don't know what to do!"

"Take a deep breath," I instructed, sliding onto the couch beside her. "Start from the beginning."

Elara inhaled deeply, her shoulders relaxing just a fraction. "Okay. So, my boss called me into her office yesterday. She's been under pressure to cut costs, and I—well, I'm the newest team member. You know how that goes."

THE TASTE OF AMBITION

"Ugh, the classic case of 'let's trim the fat,'" I said, rolling my eyes. "Didn't you just start? They can't expect you to turn the ship around overnight."

Her lips quirked up momentarily before fading into a frown. "Exactly! But she didn't seem to care. It felt like I was fighting for my life in there. I tried to show her the progress I've made, but she wouldn't listen. And now, everyone's scrambling to look good. It's like being in a shark tank."

I placed a comforting hand on her knee, feeling the tension radiating from her. "What's your plan? Have you thought about what you want to do?"

She shook her head vigorously, her curls bouncing in protest. "Not really. I just don't want to be the one left holding the bag."

"Well, what if we brainstormed some ideas? You're incredible at what you do, Elara. Maybe you just need to remind them of that."

"Remind them?" she scoffed, her eyes narrowing. "I can barely remind myself to get out of bed some days."

Before I could respond, the doorbell rang, cutting through the heaviness in the air. "Who could that be?" I asked, glancing at Elara.

"God knows. Probably my landlord, wanting to discuss the rent I can't pay." She waved her hand dismissively, but I felt a rush of determination rising within me.

"I'll get it," I said, standing up and heading toward the door.

When I opened it, I was greeted by the last person I expected to see: Max. His brow furrowed, a hint of worry etched on his features as he met my gaze. "Hey, I was just passing by and thought I'd check in," he said, his voice warm and inviting.

I hesitated, torn between the warmth of his presence and the storm brewing inside Elara's apartment. "Uh, come in," I finally managed, stepping aside.

Elara looked up, her eyes widening in surprise. "Max? What are you doing here?"

"Thought I'd drop by to see how you were doing," he said, glancing between the two of us, his expression shifting from concern to curiosity. "But it looks like I walked in on something. Should I be worried?"

Elara chuckled lightly, the tension in her shoulders easing just a bit. "Only if you're afraid of a little emotional chaos."

"Sounds like my kind of party," he replied, settling onto the armrest of the couch, his gaze steady on her.

"You have impeccable timing," I said, sinking back onto the sofa. "Elara's in a bit of a crisis."

Max nodded, his expression shifting to one of seriousness. "What's going on?"

Elara sighed dramatically, her voice a mix of frustration and desperation. "I'm on the verge of losing my job, and I don't know how to save it."

"Job trouble?" Max's tone shifted, concern lining his brow. "What's happening?"

As she recounted the details, I watched the dynamic between them shift, the atmosphere thickening with an understanding I hadn't anticipated. Max was often the steady one, the anchor in turbulent waters, but here, he shared that weight with Elara, an unexpected alliance forming in the face of her dilemma.

"Have you thought about presenting a project to show your value?" he suggested, his voice low and encouraging. "Something that could demonstrate your contributions? Sometimes, a proactive approach can turn the tide."

Elara's eyes sparkled with renewed hope. "I hadn't considered that! I mean, I've been so wrapped up in my fears..."

"And who wouldn't be? You're in a tough spot," Max reassured her. "But you have skills, and if you can highlight them, it might just be what you need to convince them you belong."

"I love that idea," I chimed in, feeling the weight of my own earlier conversation with Max lighten. "What's something you're passionate about? Maybe we can brainstorm a presentation."

For the next hour, we huddled together, bouncing ideas back and forth, laughter and determination weaving through the air like the rich aroma of coffee brewing nearby. It was an unexpected trio—me, the baker turned makeshift life coach; Elara, the frantic yet brilliant employee seeking refuge; and Max, the calm strategist who somehow balanced us both.

When we finally settled on a plan, Elara's eyes sparkled with determination, and the tension that had enveloped her slowly dissipated. I felt a surge of relief wash over me, a glimmer of hope blooming in the cracks of uncertainty.

"See?" I said, nudging her playfully. "You've got this! And when you ace that presentation, you owe us both cupcakes."

Max chuckled, leaning back with an air of satisfaction. "I'd settle for just a cup of that coffee."

With that, I felt the weight of my own unvoiced emotions lift slightly. The earlier tension with Max had morphed into a camaraderie, an alliance forged in unexpected moments of vulnerability. Maybe, just maybe, I could learn to navigate the boundaries between fear and hope, and allow myself to be brave enough to reach for what I truly desired.

As we sat in Elara's cramped living room, ideas flowed freely, our laughter blending with the scents of burnt coffee and something surprisingly comforting, like a warm hug on a cold day. Max leaned forward, an animated look in his eyes as he sketched out a rough outline for Elara's presentation on a notepad I had lying around. The tension that had once filled the room had transformed into something lighter, an undercurrent of shared purpose and camaraderie.

"What if you opened with a story?" Max suggested, tapping the pen against his chin. "Something relatable, like how you almost burned down your apartment trying to make dinner last week."

Elara's laughter bubbled up, bright and infectious. "You make it sound like I'm a walking disaster!"

"Well, aren't we all a little bit? A disaster in a good way," I chimed in, winking at Max. "It adds character."

Elara feigned offense, clutching her heart dramatically. "I'll have you know that I once made a soufflé that didn't completely collapse. That counts as a success!"

Max grinned, a playful glint in his eye. "Next, you can demonstrate how that relates to your project. An unexpected rise to success?"

I couldn't help but admire how effortlessly they bounced off each other. It was as if Max had slipped into the role of her cheerleader, while I was more of a comical sidekick, providing the snacks and occasional bursts of wisdom. This dynamic was refreshing, and I relished the moment, knowing that whatever had drawn us together was weaving a stronger bond.

As we continued to plot Elara's revival, the doorbell rang again, this time more insistent. I shot a puzzled glance at Elara. "Do you expect anyone else?"

"Not that I know of," she said, a frown crossing her features.

Max stood up, the playful energy shifting back to curiosity. "Want me to get it?"

"Sure, why not? Maybe it's a surprise delivery of puppies," I quipped, and Elara snorted, shaking her head at my antics.

Max opened the door, and I caught a glimpse of his expression shifting from curiosity to surprise. The air around us thickened as a figure stepped inside—a tall woman with an air of authority that instantly commanded attention. She had striking features, sharp cheekbones, and a no-nonsense attitude that suggested she was a force to be reckoned with.

"Elara," she said, her tone crisp, cutting through the casual atmosphere we'd built. "We need to talk. Now."

Elara's face blanched, and the laughter drained from the room like water slipping through fingers. "Tara? What are you doing here?"

"Is that how you greet your boss?" Tara's eyes flicked to Max and me, her expression neutral but piercing. "Who are they?"

Elara opened her mouth to respond, but Tara cut her off. "We don't have time for pleasantries. The board is meeting in an hour, and I need you to present your project ideas. We'll discuss your position after that."

Max's brows furrowed in concern as he exchanged a glance with me. I could sense Elara's heartbeat quicken, her anxiety palpable in the room. "Wait, I thought I had more time. You can't be serious," she protested, her voice shaky.

"Oh, I'm dead serious," Tara replied, crossing her arms with a practiced ease. "You need to prove yourself today, or the board will make their decision based on what they've seen so far, and trust me, it's not enough."

Elara looked to me, her eyes wide with panic. "I wasn't ready! I thought I had time to prepare!"

Tara shrugged, her indifference cutting deep. "Time's up, Elara. Either you rise to the occasion or—" She leaned in closer, her voice a whisper, "—you sink."

I stepped forward, unable to contain myself. "You can't just drop this on her! This isn't fair."

Tara's gaze snapped to me, icy and unimpressed. "Who are you again?"

"Someone who cares about her," I shot back, feeling a spark of indignation. "She deserves a chance to shine without you breathing down her neck."

"Cute," Tara replied, not even bothering to hide her smirk. "But this isn't about you. Elara has a choice to make. It's her career at stake, and if she can't handle the pressure—"

"—then I guess I'll have to show you just how much I can handle," Elara interrupted, the fire igniting in her eyes. She squared her shoulders, taking a step forward as if she were preparing to face a charging bull. "Give me a moment, and I'll show you exactly what I can do."

"Make it quick," Tara replied, turning on her heel and marching toward the door. "The clock is ticking."

As the door slammed shut behind her, the room felt electric, a charged atmosphere lingering in the air like the tension before a storm. Elara exhaled sharply, her bravado wavering. "I can't believe she just did that. I was ready to give a presentation in a week, not an hour!"

Max's hand found hers, a gesture of reassurance that spoke volumes. "You can do this, Elara. You've got the ideas, and now you just need to pull it together. We'll help."

"I don't even have a fully formed idea yet!" she said, the weight of her anxiety pushing her toward the edge of despair.

"Not true," I countered, taking a breath to anchor myself. "You've already got a concept in mind. Let's expand on that. Remember what we talked about earlier?"

Her eyes flickered with uncertainty, but I saw a glimmer of hope in them as well. "You think I can really pull this off?"

"Absolutely," Max chimed in, his tone steady. "And we'll be right here with you, every step of the way."

Elara nodded, the fire in her eyes rekindling as she focused on the task at hand. "Okay, okay. I can do this."

THE TASTE OF AMBITION

As we gathered around the table, ideas began to flow, and I felt a surge of optimism enveloping us. The atmosphere brightened, laughter and determination mingling in a delightful blend. Elara was bouncing off us, her thoughts crystallizing into something more solid, a project born from the chaos that had threatened to consume her.

But just as she began to articulate her vision, a loud crash echoed from the kitchen, startling us all.

"What was that?" I exclaimed, leaping up from my seat.

"Stay here!" Max instructed, and I could see the protective instinct kick in as he moved toward the kitchen.

Elara and I exchanged wide-eyed glances, the mood shifting from focused determination to raw anxiety. The sound reverberated again, a metallic clang followed by an eerie silence.

"Max?" I called out, my heart racing.

Silence hung in the air, thick and foreboding, until suddenly, the lights flickered, plunging the room into darkness.

"What's happening?" Elara whispered, her voice trembling.

I felt for the wall, my fingers brushing against the cool surface as I tried to navigate the unfamiliar territory. "It must be a power outage," I said, though my voice quaked with uncertainty.

But then I heard it—a low growl, reverberating from the kitchen, followed by the unmistakable sound of shuffling footsteps.

"Max?" I called again, my voice a mere whisper now.

The growl intensified, echoing off the walls, and a rush of adrenaline surged through me, making my heart pound against my ribcage. In the pitch-black, I felt like a moth trapped in a web, each breath a frantic plea for clarity.

Suddenly, a flash of light illuminated the space for a split second, revealing a shadow lurking just beyond the doorway.

And then, just as quickly, it vanished into the darkness.

"Get back!" I shouted, pushing Elara behind me as I braced myself against the table, adrenaline coursing through my veins.

"Is that...?" she began, but the growl filled the silence once more, a chilling reminder that whatever was lurking in the shadows wasn't just a figment of our imagination.

The air crackled with tension, and just when I thought I might scream, everything went silent again, as if the darkness had swallowed the noise whole.

Max's voice cut through the stillness, sharp and commanding. "Whatever it is, we need to get out of here. Now."

But before I could move, the lights flickered back on, and my eyes locked onto the doorway where the figure loomed, unmistakable and terrifying.

The room froze, hearts racing as the truth dawned on us: we were not alone.

Chapter 19: Unmasking Truths

The park was alive with the whispers of autumn leaves, their golden hues fluttering down like confetti at a long-awaited celebration. I walked beside Elara, feeling the gentle warmth of the sun spilling over us, gilding the world in a soft glow that contrasted sharply with the weight pressing down on her shoulders. She had been quieter than usual, her laughter—a sound like wind chimes on a summer day—missing from our conversations. I stole glances at her, searching for the spark that had once ignited her eyes, only to find shadows lurking in their depths.

"Do you remember the time we came here and dared each other to climb that ridiculous tree?" I asked, nodding toward a towering oak, its branches stretching wide like welcoming arms.

A hint of a smile played on her lips, but it didn't reach her eyes. "You were convinced you could reach the top," she replied, her voice a soft echo of its usual vibrancy. "I'm pretty sure you got stuck halfway up."

"Stuck or enjoying the view from an excellent vantage point, you decide," I said, attempting to lighten the air thick with unspoken worries. "But hey, I got some great photos, didn't I?"

Her laughter, though faint, warmed the space between us. "You always have a way of turning disaster into a photo op."

We reached a bench, its weathered wood creaking under our weight as we sank into its embrace. The air carried the sweet scent of popcorn from a nearby vendor, mingling with the earthy aroma of fallen leaves. I let the silence settle for a moment, letting it grow comfortable and familiar like an old blanket. Elara gazed ahead, her focus unfocused, as if she were peering into a past that didn't quite sit right with her.

"Elara," I said, breaking the spell of stillness. "What's really going on? You can talk to me."

She drew a deep breath, her shoulders rising as if she were gathering the strength to bare her soul. "I've been feeling lost lately," she admitted, her voice barely above a whisper. "I put so much pressure on myself to be what everyone expects—successful, always happy, always together. But inside, I'm crumbling. It's exhausting trying to please everyone."

My heart ached for her. I reached out, placing my hand over hers, the warmth radiating between us a soothing balm against the chill of her fears. "You don't have to carry that weight alone. You're not just a collection of others' expectations, you know. You're so much more than that."

She looked at me, her eyes shimmering with unshed tears, the vulnerability etched on her face almost unbearable to witness. "I'm scared, Ash. Scared of losing myself in this quest to be everything to everyone. What if I can't find my way back?"

"Then we'll find a new way together," I said, my voice firm, the resolve unfurling within me like a banner in a windstorm. "Let's rediscover what makes you happy, what makes you tick. We can explore new things, take risks, or just enjoy the simple moments that make life feel alive again."

"I don't even know where to start," she confessed, biting her lip in a way that tugged at my heartstrings.

"Start with what used to excite you," I encouraged. "Remember that dance class you loved? The one where you couldn't stop smiling?"

Her brow furrowed slightly. "I don't have time for dance, Ash. I can barely keep up with my job as it is. The bills, the deadlines—it's like I'm caught in a whirlpool."

"Then let's fight the current together," I replied, my determination wrapping around us like a shield. "You can't let it swallow you whole. Let's carve out time for yourself, even if it's just a few minutes a day to do something you love."

"I don't know if I can," she sighed, but I could see a flicker of hope igniting in her eyes, a soft ember struggling against the wind.

"Of course you can," I insisted, squeezing her hand gently. "You're stronger than you realize, Elara. I see it every day, and it's time you see it too."

As we sat there, the leaves swirling around us in a dance of their own, I felt a sense of purpose emerging from the fog that had clouded my heart. Helping Elara was more than just being a friend; it was an invitation to peel back my own layers of uncertainty. In this moment, I realized that the fear of losing her had been eclipsing my longing for Max. The truth was, I was scared of my own feelings, scared of the risk involved in pursuing happiness beyond friendship.

The sun dipped lower in the sky, casting a warm glow around us. "You know," I said, a playful grin breaking through the serious conversation, "if we can survive climbing that tree, we can conquer anything."

Elara's laughter rang out, a sound that felt like spring rain, refreshing and bright. "You really think we can take on the world?"

"Absolutely. Just think of all the adventures we could have. Dance classes, art workshops, maybe even skydiving—"

"Skydiving? Are you mad?" she interjected, her laughter brightening the fading light.

"Hey, it's not just about the thrill. It's about feeling alive!"

"Right, because nothing screams 'living' like jumping out of a perfectly good plane."

"Exactly!" I shot back, a smile playing at the corners of my mouth. "You see, you're already engaging with your passions!"

She rolled her eyes, a familiar gesture that only deepened my affection for her. "Let's take it one step at a time before we launch ourselves into the sky."

I nodded, the warmth of our shared laughter lingering in the air. This moment felt pivotal, a shift in our dynamic that promised the potential for healing and growth. As Elara's shoulders relaxed, the flicker of hope blossomed into something more substantial, and I couldn't help but wonder if this journey of rediscovery might lead me to confront my own uncharted emotions for Max. For now, though, I had my best friend beside me, and together we would carve a path through the chaos, finding joy and purpose along the way.

As the sun dipped lower in the sky, draping the park in hues of crimson and gold, Elara and I remained perched on that weathered bench, cocooned in our own world, where the noise of the outside faded into a soft hum. I could sense the shift within her, a subtle loosening of the grip fear had on her heart. Her laughter, like chimes in a gentle breeze, began to punctuate our conversation, and I couldn't help but feel a rush of hope.

"Let's do something outrageous," I declared, my excitement spilling over. "Something completely outside our comfort zones."

"Like what? Dress up as superheroes and save the world?" Elara smirked, her eyes finally glinting with mischief.

"Now you're talking! We could totally pull off the dynamic duo look. You'd be Wonder Woman, and I'll be... well, I'll need to think about my superhero name." I pondered dramatically, tapping my chin. "Maybe I'll be Captain Spontaneity. I'll save the day one impromptu dance-off at a time."

"Or we could just take a pottery class. You know, like in that movie? I'll be the romantic one, and you can be my cynical sidekick." She chuckled, and for a moment, the heaviness in her eyes lifted entirely.

"Pottery? We can mold our emotions into clay. What could be more therapeutic?" I replied with mock seriousness, though a part of me was genuinely intrigued by the idea. "But I can't promise I won't throw my masterpiece at you if you laugh at my techniques."

THE TASTE OF AMBITION

"Oh, I can see it now—a classic comedy of errors, starring two hopelessly uncoordinated friends trying to channel their inner Picassos."

"Great! I'll wear an apron that says 'Messy Genius'—that'll really help the vibe," I teased, our laughter ringing through the fading light, a melody of connection amidst the chaos.

The sunlight dipped further, casting long shadows across the ground, and the park began to empty, leaving behind the echoes of laughter and the whispers of secrets shared. I turned to Elara, who was watching me with a thoughtful expression, her eyes glistening like the evening stars just beginning to peek through the twilight.

"Ash," she said slowly, her voice wavering slightly. "I want to thank you for being here, for pushing me to confront these feelings. I know it can't be easy with everything else you're juggling."

Juggling? I nearly laughed out loud. The truth was, I was teetering on a precarious edge myself, my heart divided between the fierce loyalty I felt toward Elara and the deep yearning for something more with Max. "You're worth every ounce of energy," I replied, my sincerity settling between us like a warm embrace. "And besides, I'm not exactly a poster child for balance myself. I'm currently wading through my own messy waters."

"Oh?" Her curiosity piqued, and I felt an inexplicable urge to confess my feelings for Max. "What's that about?"

I hesitated, my heart racing at the thought of revealing the complicated tangle of emotions I had kept under wraps. "It's just... there's someone I really care about, and I'm terrified of what that could mean."

"Elara," I began, but the words felt trapped, swirling like the leaves caught in the wind.

"Tell me," she urged, her expression shifting to one of concern. "You know I'm here for you too."

"I don't want to mess things up. I'm still trying to help you find your footing, and it feels selfish to bring my own desires into the mix."

"Friendship isn't about carrying burdens alone," she insisted, her voice steady, piercing through the haze of my doubts. "You can't pour from an empty cup. What's the point of helping me if you're struggling too?"

Her words hung in the air, heavy yet liberating. I took a deep breath, letting the truth flow. "Max. I like him. A lot. But I'm afraid of complicating our friendship."

"Elara," she replied, a slow smile creeping across her face, "you're allowed to like someone. It doesn't negate the support we give each other."

"Right, but what if it changes everything? What if I ruin what we have?"

"Or," she countered, her eyes sparkling, "what if it makes everything better? What if you finally embrace that happiness and take a leap of faith? You're both entitled to love without feeling like it's a betrayal."

The words struck a chord deep within me, igniting a flame I didn't realize had been flickering beneath the surface. "You really think I should just go for it?"

"Absolutely," Elara said, her confidence infectious. "We're at a point in our lives where we can't afford to hide behind our fears anymore. Not with each other."

The thought of Max brought a rush of warmth that pulsed through me like summer rain. His laughter echoed in my mind, a melody I had been missing in the chaos of life. "Okay, you're right," I admitted, a smile breaking across my face. "I'll talk to him. Just as soon as I figure out how not to sound like a babbling idiot."

"That's the spirit! Just be you. The quirky, clever, and slightly ridiculous version. Trust me; he'll love that about you."

THE TASTE OF AMBITION

The moment felt electric, a turning point that left me breathless. "What if he doesn't?" I asked, my voice dropping to a whisper.

"Then he's missing out," she replied, her gaze unwavering. "But if he does feel the same, you'll have opened the door to a whole new world, one filled with laughter and adventure."

A gust of wind rustled the leaves around us, sending a cascade of colors dancing through the air. In that moment, the heaviness began to lift, revealing a clearer horizon.

"Pottery class first, confession second?" I proposed, half-joking.

"Deal," Elara said, her laughter lighting up the dimming day. "And I promise not to throw any clay at you if you start talking about your feelings for Max in the middle of it."

With a newfound sense of clarity, I couldn't help but feel that we were on the cusp of something beautiful—a shared journey into the unknown. Life was messy, unpredictable, but as I glanced at my best friend, her determination sparking in the fading light, I knew we would face whatever lay ahead together, one imperfect moment at a time.

The next morning dawned crisp and clear, a world painted anew by the sun's golden brush. I stood at my kitchen window, the aroma of freshly brewed coffee wafting through the air, a comforting backdrop to the chaos swirling in my mind. Today was the day. I could feel it in my bones. I'd take Elara's advice, step into the light, and confront the tangled emotions I had for Max.

As I sipped my coffee, the steam curling around my fingers, I caught sight of Elara bounding up the path to my door, her dark hair billowing like a banner behind her. She looked vibrant, a whirlwind of energy that instantly lifted the weight from my shoulders. Today, we were to embark on our pottery adventure, a distraction filled with clay, laughter, and maybe a few mishaps along the way.

"Ash! You won't believe the dreams I had about pottery last night," she declared, bursting through the door like a force of nature.

"I'm convinced I'm destined to become the next Michelangelo—or at least, not the worst potter in the class."

I couldn't help but chuckle at her enthusiasm. "As long as you don't throw the clay at me, we should be fine." I grabbed my bag, feeling a mix of anticipation and anxiety swirling within me. Today was about more than just pottery; it was about making room for the emotions I'd kept tucked away.

We made our way to the studio, the sunlight bathing the streets in a warm glow. With each step, I felt the nerves fluttering in my stomach, a mix of excitement and dread. What if I did manage to confess my feelings to Max? What if everything changed, and I was left grappling with the consequences? Elara must have sensed my turmoil because she slid her arm through mine, her reassuring presence a steady anchor in the ebb and flow of my thoughts.

"Breathe, Ash. It's just clay, not a bomb," she teased, winking at me. "And if it does blow up in our faces, we'll have a great story to tell."

"Great stories are overrated if you ask me," I replied, trying to keep the mood light. "I prefer the kind where everyone leaves the room intact and unscathed."

Elara laughed, and I felt the tension ease just a little as we entered the pottery studio. The scent of wet clay enveloped us like a warm embrace, mingling with the faint aroma of paints and varnishes. The studio was bustling with activity—students at various skill levels huddled around wheels, creating their masterpieces, while the sound of laughter and conversation floated through the air.

"Look at all the talent here," I murmured, glancing around as I tried to gauge my own ability. "And then there's us, prepared to make beautiful messes."

"Embrace the mess! It's where creativity lives," Elara said, her excitement infectious. She eagerly grabbed an apron, slipping it over her head like a knight donning armor for battle. "Ready to create some clay chaos?"

I followed suit, the apron wrapping around me like a shield, and together we stepped toward the wheel. It loomed before us, both intimidating and inviting, like the precipice of a great adventure.

As we settled in, I could feel the weight of the moment creeping in. With my hands coated in cool, slick clay, I turned to Elara, who was staring at her lump of clay with a fierce concentration that made me smile. "So, how do we start this journey of artistic genius?"

"Like everything else in life, we just dive in!" she exclaimed, pressing her hands into the clay. It wobbled beneath her touch, eliciting a squeal of surprise as it flopped to one side. "Okay, maybe not that dramatically."

I laughed, watching her struggle to regain control of her creation. "This is definitely going to be a learning experience."

With our clumsy attempts, we transformed the ordinary into something wonderfully chaotic. Elara managed to shape a wonky bowl while I crafted what could only be described as an abstract sculpture—if one could call it that without laughing.

"Behold! My masterpiece!" I announced, holding up the lopsided creation like a trophy. "I call it 'A Reflection of My Inner Turmoil.'"

She burst into laughter, her eyes sparkling with joy. "A true artistic triumph! Let's call it an existential crisis in clay form!"

As the laughter faded, I found myself drifting back to the thoughts of Max, my heart tugging me in different directions. Every brush of our hands against the cool clay felt like an invitation to explore deeper connections, yet fear kept me rooted.

"Okay, confession time," I said, deciding it was now or never. "I really want to talk to Max today. Like, about us." The words tumbled out, unfiltered, the vulnerability washing over me in waves.

Elara's expression shifted to one of encouragement. "You can do this, Ash. Just be honest. That's the best way to know where you both stand."

"Easier said than done," I replied, biting my lip as a knot of anxiety formed in my stomach. "What if he doesn't feel the same? What if it ruins everything?"

"Then you adapt, just like you're doing with that clay," she said, gesturing toward my half-formed sculpture. "You reshape your expectations and create something new. That's life, Ash. You can't avoid the messiness forever."

The gravity of her words sank in, and with a newfound determination, I resolved to embrace the uncertainty. Maybe it was time to confront my feelings head-on, to see if there was a chance for something real with Max.

The class wrapped up, and as we wiped our hands clean of clay, the chatter and laughter around us faded into a soft background hum. Elara leaned closer, her eyes sparkling with mischief. "So, when are we heading to the café to summon your courage? You need your 'liquid confidence' before this conversation."

"Right. The café." My heart raced at the thought. "After all this, I might need a gallon of coffee and a side of courage."

We made our way to the quaint little café nestled on the corner of the street, its rustic charm and fragrant aroma promising comfort. The bell jingled as we entered, a familiar sound that often accompanied our lighter moments. I scanned the room for Max, hoping to find him nestled in one of the corners, lost in a book or scribbling notes in his ever-present notebook.

And there he was. My heart skipped a beat at the sight of him, hunched over a table, his brow furrowed in concentration as he scribbled furiously. The way the afternoon light danced through the window, catching the subtle curls of his hair, made my breath hitch.

He looked so engrossed in his thoughts, the world around him fading into a blur.

"Ash, breathe," Elara nudged me gently, her voice a grounding force. "You've got this. Just be yourself."

I nodded, but the churning in my stomach intensified. "Okay, I'm going in. Wish me luck."

"Not luck," she replied, her eyes twinkling. "Just be fabulous."

As I approached his table, the sound of my heart thundered in my ears. "Hey, Max," I said, my voice steady despite the whirlpool of emotions within. He looked up, his face breaking into a smile that made my heart flutter.

"Hey! I didn't expect to see you here." His warm eyes locked onto mine, making the world around us fade into insignificance.

"Yeah, just came to… you know, hang out," I said, trying to sound nonchalant while my insides did backflips. "I've actually been meaning to talk to you about something."

He raised an eyebrow, curiosity dancing in his expression. "Oh? What's on your mind?"

And just as I opened my mouth to spill my heart, a loud crash echoed from the back of the café, drawing everyone's attention. A table tipped over, sending cups and plates clattering to the floor in a chaotic symphony. My moment was interrupted, the tension in the air suddenly shifting.

"What was that?" Elara exclaimed, her gaze darting toward the commotion.

My heart sank as I turned back to Max, who looked equally bewildered. "I guess we're not the only ones in need of a little chaos today," he said, a wry smile playing on his lips, but the warmth in his eyes held something deeper.

Just as the café staff rushed to clear the scene, I couldn't shake the feeling that this was no mere accident. There was something more beneath the surface—something brewing that felt ominously familiar. I opened my mouth to speak again, to finally dive into the heart of what I wanted to say, but the weight of uncertainty loomed larger than ever, mingling with the clatter of chaos. Would I ever get the chance to reveal my feelings?

Chapter 20: The Flourish of Friendship

The sun filtered through the kitchen window, casting warm, golden beams that danced across the counters cluttered with ingredients. Flour dust hung in the air, creating a magical haze that felt almost otherworldly. I caught Elara's eye as she sifted a mountain of powdered sugar, and we both burst into laughter at the tiny white clouds that puffed up around us. Her laughter was like music—light and airy, resonating in my chest and sending ripples of warmth through my veins. It reminded me of the girl I used to know, the one whose smile could ignite a room, whose joy was as infectious as the smell of fresh-baked bread. Today, that joy was making a timid return, and I felt a surge of hope.

"Are you sure you don't want to help with the chocolate?" I teased, nudging her shoulder. The corner of her mouth quirked up, and I could see her resolve wavering, a flicker of the spirited friend I had missed so dearly.

"I'm just trying to maintain my status as 'Assistant Sifter,' thank you very much," she replied, rolling her eyes but unable to suppress the grin that threatened to spill over.

As we mixed, kneaded, and formed a delectable mess of dough and batter, I found myself absorbed in the rhythm of our culinary chaos. Each clump of flour that landed on the floor felt like a small victory, a rebellion against the chaos that had once engulfed her life. We didn't just bake; we created, and in the process, we were weaving our friendship tighter, each stir of the spatula a stitch in the fabric of our renewed bond.

With every recipe we tackled, the kitchen transformed into our sanctuary. The sweet aroma of vanilla wafted through the air, mingling with the rich, dark scent of cocoa, grounding us in the moment. It was a dance of flavors and laughter, punctuated by playful banter and the occasional flour fight that left us both shrieking and giggling.

"Okay, Miss Flour Cannon," I said, wiping a smudge of icing from my cheek, "What's next? Are we making a cake or a declaration of war?"

"I think it's both," she shot back, her eyes sparkling with mischief. "But definitely a cake. I'm thinking chocolate, with layers that are as deep as our conversation last night."

She had a knack for layering flavors and emotions with equal precision, and I found myself captivated. Perhaps that was the secret to helping her find her way back—not just coaxing her out of her shell but reminding her of the person she used to be, the one who poured her heart into everything she did.

As we let the batter rest, I leaned against the counter, savoring the moment. The sun continued to bathe us in its glow, and for a fleeting moment, everything felt perfect. But as I turned to Elara, a shadow passed over her face, and the warmth of the moment shifted. The laughter faltered, replaced by a tension that knotted in my stomach.

"Hey," I said softly, trying to catch her gaze. "What's on your mind?"

She hesitated, biting her lip as if weighing the consequences of her thoughts. "It's just... I don't want to drag you down with me. I appreciate this, truly, but I can't shake the feeling that I'm a burden."

A weight settled heavily between us, her words piercing through the joyous atmosphere we had created. "You could never be a burden to me, Elara. You're my friend. Friends lift each other up, remember?"

"But I've been so wrapped up in my own mess, and it's like I'm pulling you into my chaos. It's not fair to you."

I felt a flare of frustration bubble up, but I quelled it, choosing my words carefully. "It's not about fair or unfair. It's about us. This—" I gestured to the flour, the batter, the laughter. "This is healing for both of us. It's okay to lean on each other. That's what friends do."

The corner of her mouth twitched, a spark of hope glimmering in her eyes. "I guess that makes sense."

"More than makes sense," I countered, my heart racing as I realized just how much I meant it. I needed this as much as she did; the chaos of our lives had a way of intertwining, and in our shared struggles, I found purpose. But just as I was about to voice this revelation, the doorbell rang, a jarring interruption that startled us both.

"Who could that be?" Elara asked, her brow furrowing in confusion.

"Not a clue," I said, wiping my hands on a towel and making my way to the door. I opened it to reveal a delivery person holding a large, meticulously packaged box.

"Delivery for Elara Collins," they said, their voice cheerful.

"Uh, that's me!" she called from the kitchen, her confusion morphing into curiosity. I stepped aside to let her approach, and as she unwrapped the box, I felt an inexplicable flutter of anticipation in my stomach.

Inside lay a beautifully crafted cake stand adorned with intricate floral designs, the craftsmanship exquisite. A small card nestled among the packing peanuts caught my eye, and I glanced over Elara's shoulder as she read it aloud.

"To my favorite baker, keep creating magic. Love, M."

Her face fell, and in that moment, the buoyant atmosphere of our baking adventure seemed to teeter on the edge of a precipice. The name loomed large, casting an undeniable shadow over us, reminding me that while we baked to build anew, the ghosts of the past were not so easily swept away.

Elara's fingers trembled as she held the cake stand, her expression a delicate blend of disbelief and nostalgia. "M? As in Marcus?" The name hung in the air, heavy with memories that seemed to swirl like the flour we'd just spilled. The kitchen, once alive with laughter, now felt like a stage set for an unexpected drama.

"Looks like it," I replied, trying to gauge her reaction while the weight of the moment pressed down on both of us. "Do you want to talk about it?"

"No," she snapped, her voice sharper than I expected. The defiance in her tone was as immediate as it was unsettling, sending a ripple of unease through me. "I mean, yes—eventually, maybe. But not now, not while we're here, doing...this." She gestured toward the mess we had created, a chaotic symphony of eggshells, chocolate smudges, and laughter now turned silent.

The pause lingered between us, thick and palpable, until she softened. "Sorry, that was harsh. I just didn't expect... this."

"I get it. Let's keep our focus on baking, then," I said, attempting to lighten the mood. "Who knows? Maybe we'll invent a revolutionary cake that will take the world by storm. Or at least our taste buds."

She chuckled, and I felt the tension in her shoulders ease slightly. "A world-renowned cake made with love and lots of flour. What a concept."

As we returned to our task, I couldn't help but notice how her demeanor shifted back to that familiar rhythm, the cadence of our friendship reestablishing itself amid the turmoil. We worked in comfortable silence, the sounds of whisking and clinking utensils providing a backdrop to our unspoken understanding.

But every now and then, a flicker of uncertainty crossed her face, like a passing cloud dimming the sun. I wished I could help her navigate those shadows, to pull her from their grasp as we had done with our baked goods. Still, I couldn't shake the feeling that Marcus was an emotional landmine, one that could explode at any moment if we weren't careful.

"Okay, chocolate layer cake it is!" I announced, grabbing the mixing bowl and thrusting it toward her. "I dare you to add more chocolate."

"Oh, you're on," she replied, eyes narrowing playfully as she reached for the cocoa powder. The competitive spirit between us reignited, filling the kitchen with a lively energy that had been missing. The two of us began adding in everything we could think of—extra chocolate chips, a splash of vanilla, a pinch of sea salt to elevate the sweetness.

We were lost in our own world when I noticed the sun dipping lower in the sky, casting a rich, golden hue that bathed our kitchen in warmth. Just as I began to relax into the rhythm of our baking, the door swung open again, this time revealing my neighbor, Mrs. Jenkins. She stood there, hands on her hips, her silver curls bouncing with an authority only she could wield.

"Are you two holding a baking class without me?" she quipped, stepping inside uninvited, as was her custom. "I'm only here to save the day with my famous blueberry pie recipe."

"Mrs. Jenkins, we didn't know you were coming!" I exclaimed, stifling laughter at her dramatic entrance.

"Oh, please. As if I wouldn't catch wind of such deliciousness wafting through the air. You two have been making quite a racket, and I refuse to be left out," she declared, her eyes sparkling with mischief.

"Elara was just about to attempt a culinary masterpiece," I chimed in, trying to steer the conversation away from the earlier tension.

"Is that so?" Mrs. Jenkins raised an eyebrow, looking from me to Elara. "Care to share? Or shall I just have to settle for my pie?"

Elara shot me a glance, a shared understanding that our little circle was about to expand. "Alright, Mrs. Jenkins, how about a trade? I'll give you a slice of our chocolate cake if you share your pie."

The older woman clapped her hands together, delighted. "You've got yourself a deal! But just so you know, I make the best blueberry pie this side of town. You might want to prepare your taste buds."

With that, Mrs. Jenkins rolled up her sleeves and dove into our baking frenzy. The kitchen soon filled with her cheerful anecdotes about past baking disasters and triumphs, each story punctuated by Elara's laughter and my own. The comfort of our trio began to soothe the undercurrents of anxiety, allowing Elara a reprieve from the weight of her thoughts.

In the midst of our flour-covered chaos, I caught a glimpse of the old Elara—the one who used to dance around the kitchen with abandon, flour on her nose and joy in her heart. Yet, the brief moment of clarity shattered as the doorbell rang again.

"Is this a bakery now?" I joked, shaking my head as I wiped my hands on a towel, half-expecting another delivery.

Elara exchanged a glance with me, her eyebrows knitting together as she approached the door. "If it's another cake stand, I might just scream."

But it wasn't. A young man stood there, awkwardly shifting his weight from one foot to the other, a familiar blue-haired band tee straining against his chest. My heart skipped a beat as I recognized him from the corner café we frequented, where he'd often been a barista with an endearing but shy smile.

"Hey, um, is Elara here?" he asked, glancing around the room nervously.

"Yes, she is!" I exclaimed, trying to inject some enthusiasm into the moment, though my heart raced at the unexpected interruption.

"Hi!" Elara called, her cheeks flushing as she stepped forward. "What brings you here?"

"I brought you something," he said, pulling out a small box from behind his back, the kind that had a logo from a local bakery, the scent of fresh pastries wafting toward us. "I thought you might like

THE TASTE OF AMBITION

a pick-me-up. You know, since you've been going through a rough time."

Her surprise was palpable, her mouth opening slightly in disbelief as she took the box from him. I felt a strange mix of emotions as I watched her face brighten. The joy was genuine, yes, but there was something else lurking beneath the surface—something I couldn't quite place.

"Wow, thank you! That's so sweet of you!" she gushed, her earlier tension evaporating in an instant.

And there it was—the moment I feared but also longed to witness, the intertwining of past and present that was rapidly reshaping her reality. I wanted to cheer her on, to revel in the new spark of life igniting in her, but I also felt a familiar pang of protectiveness, as if I were standing on the sidelines watching a fire rekindle, wondering if it would burn too bright, too fast.

As the young man stepped into the kitchen, the air crackled with possibilities, and I realized that just as Elara was on the brink of rediscovering herself, I, too, was facing an unexpected turn in our story. I could sense that this moment would shift the very foundation of our friendship, igniting a series of events that would lead us into uncharted territories where laughter mingled with uncertainty, and joy came hand in hand with lingering heartache.

The young man, with his tousled hair and sheepish smile, stepped fully into the kitchen, the scent of baked goods trailing behind him like a sweet promise. I exchanged a glance with Elara, who looked completely taken aback. "Uh, this is..." she stammered, her fingers clutching the box of pastries as if it were a lifeline.

"I'm Jake," he said, extending a hand that trembled slightly, as if unsure of how to navigate the territory of unexpected visits and delicate emotions. "I work at the café down the street. I thought you might want some treats since you've been... well, you know."

Elara's eyes sparkled with surprise and a hint of something else—curiosity, perhaps, or hope. "That's really thoughtful of you," she replied, her voice gaining strength as she accepted his gesture. "You didn't have to do that."

"Oh, but I wanted to. I figured you could use a little pick-me-up," he said, glancing at me with a grin that suggested he had no idea he'd just walked into an emotional minefield.

The warmth radiating from the small box seemed to fill the kitchen, and I felt a sudden urge to take a step back, to allow this moment to unfold between them. It was the kind of tension that buzzed in the air, ripe with possibilities. The fact that Elara was smiling again was encouraging, yet my protective instincts flared.

As she opened the box to reveal an assortment of pastries—mini tarts, flaky croissants, and what appeared to be some kind of chocolate-covered delight—her excitement was palpable. "These look incredible! I've never had anything like this from the café."

"They're new on the menu," Jake said, his cheeks flushing slightly. "I figured you might appreciate something a little special."

"Consider me officially impressed," Elara replied, her laughter light and infectious. The sound danced through the air, warming the space that had felt cold only moments ago. It was as if each pastry contained a spark of joy, igniting a flame within her.

I leaned against the counter, half-listening as Elara and Jake fell into easy conversation, their words weaving a tapestry of humor and lightness that enveloped the kitchen. "So, you're into baking?" he asked, his curiosity evident as he glanced around at our chaotic setup.

"Only when I'm trying to distract myself from emotional disasters," she joked, and the moment hung in the air with a delicate balance between vulnerability and humor.

"Hey, that's my specialty too!" he replied with a playful grin. "Nothing says 'I've got my life together' quite like a homemade chocolate cake."

THE TASTE OF AMBITION

"Or a box of pastries delivered unexpectedly," I chimed in, injecting a note of camaraderie.

"Touché," Jake said, his eyes twinkling as he returned his attention to Elara. "So, what's your favorite? I'm betting it's something exotic and beautifully complicated."

"Surprisingly, I'm a sucker for anything chocolate," she admitted, her gaze lingering on the desserts. "But don't tell my mother. She still thinks I'm a fruit tart girl."

"I can keep a secret," he promised, leaning slightly closer, and I caught the hint of a spark—a subtle electricity between them that felt both thrilling and terrifying.

The moment was intoxicating, a heady mix of laughter and flirty banter, but beneath that layer of lightness, I felt the shadow of uncertainty creeping back in. How easily things could shift. Elara had barely begun to navigate her way out of the heartache left by Marcus, and here stood a new opportunity wrapped in pastry and charm.

But just as I began to ease into the warmth of the moment, the doorbell rang again, this time echoing with an urgency that set my nerves on edge. I exchanged a look with Elara, her expression shifting from delight to confusion.

"Maybe it's another delivery?" I ventured, but my heart raced with the realization that this was a different kind of visitor—an unwanted reminder.

Elara frowned, clearly rattled. "Should I get it?"

"I'll handle it," I insisted, hoping to shield her from whatever lay on the other side of that door. "You stay here and enjoy your pastries."

As I approached the door, a chill crept over me, the lighthearted atmosphere of the kitchen fading into a palpable tension. With a deep breath, I opened the door to reveal a figure cloaked in shadow, their expression hidden beneath a hood.

"Excuse me?" I managed, the confidence I had moments before waning under the weight of uncertainty.

The figure stepped forward, and as the light caught their face, my heart dropped. "We need to talk."

The words sliced through the air, sharp and foreboding, as the figure pulled back their hood, revealing the unmistakable features of Marcus. The very person we had been tiptoeing around, the ghost of Elara's past returning with a vengeance.

"Marcus?" Elara's voice was barely a whisper, a fragile sound that held both disbelief and an echo of old pain. I turned to look at her, my heart pounding, knowing that the delicate balance we had worked so hard to rebuild was now teetering on the brink of collapse.

"What are you doing here?" she asked, her voice steadier than I expected, but I could see the flicker of anxiety in her eyes.

"I came to explain. We need to talk about what happened," he replied, and the weight of his words hung in the air like a storm cloud ready to burst.

I felt a surge of protectiveness wash over me, a fierce instinct to shield Elara from the turbulence that was about to unfold. Yet I stood rooted in place, caught between the past and the present, knowing that the course of our baking adventure—and our friendship—was about to take an unexpected turn.

Elara's hand tightened around the box of pastries, the fragile joy of the moment crumbling as she processed his presence. The kitchen, once filled with laughter and the promise of new beginnings, now pulsed with unresolved tension, a silent battle waging between the shadows of yesterday and the light of tomorrow.

And as I looked between Elara and Marcus, I realized that the sweetest creations can also bring the most bitter challenges, and our journey was only just beginning.

Chapter 21: Whispers of Change

The aroma of freshly baked bread still hung in the air, mingling with the sweet scent of chocolate and the subtle, nutty fragrance of toasted almonds. As I wiped down the counters, a sense of satisfaction washed over me, mingled with the excitement of what was to come. Our baking classes had grown into something far more than just an evening activity; they had become a cherished ritual, a gathering where laughter echoed and stories unfolded. Each week, new faces stepped into our kitchen, eager to learn the alchemy of flour and sugar, and I couldn't help but feel a swell of pride.

Max was always the life of the party. His enthusiasm was infectious, radiating warmth that enveloped everyone in the room like a well-worn blanket. He bounced around the kitchen, sharing tips and teasing the students with cheeky banter. I caught snippets of his jokes, each one delivered with a wry smile and a twinkle in his eye, igniting laughter that bounced off the walls. The way he interacted with Elara, our shyest student, was particularly endearing. They shared a peculiar rapport; she would blush under his playful jibes, her laughter tinkling like wind chimes, delicate yet vibrant.

As I watched them, a familiar knot twisted in my stomach, a mix of comfort and confusion. Max had a way of pulling people in, making them feel special, and I was no exception. The connection I felt with him was electric, yet I hesitated, my heart doing a cautious dance around the idea of risking our friendship. What if the spark I sensed between us was simply an illusion, a mirage in the desert of my hopes?

The evening air was thick with the promise of change, and as I tidied the last remnants of flour from the countertops, Max leaned against the island, arms crossed, a mischievous grin tugging at his lips. "You know, we should host a baking competition. Something to stir the pot, add a little friendly rivalry to our little community."

"Like a 'Great British Bake Off' but with more chaos?" I laughed, shaking my head. "What do you have in mind, exactly? A one-legged race while icing cupcakes?"

His laughter echoed through the kitchen, deep and rich. "Maybe a little less legwork, but definitely a challenge. Picture it: a dessert-off, complete with judging, a trophy, and maybe a few witty banter battles. We could crown a 'Baking Champion' of the class."

His passion was palpable, igniting a spark of excitement in me. I imagined the decorations, the jubilant atmosphere, the community coming together to cheer on their friends. "You might be onto something," I replied, feeling the warmth of inspiration swirl in my chest. "But we'd need a theme. Something that really gets everyone fired up."

"Springtime flavors," he suggested, his eyes lighting up with the thought. "Lemon, lavender, strawberries. It's the season of renewal and all that."

I nodded, envisioning the colors, the vibrant hues of pinks and yellows splashed across tables. "Okay, I'm in. But you'll have to help me plan this thing."

"Absolutely. I'll take the lead on organizing, but you'll have to promise to judge fairly, even if I bake the best lemon tart of your life."

"Fairness is my middle name," I teased, knowing full well that his charm could sway anyone to see his creation as the best.

We bounced ideas back and forth, laughter punctuating our conversation like sprinkles on a cupcake. The more we planned, the more I felt the weight of hesitation lift. This competition could be a way to connect not only with our growing community but with Elara too. She needed a push to step out of her shell, and the prospect of a friendly rivalry might just do the trick.

As I prepared to close up for the night, a flutter of nerves danced in my stomach. The competition was a bold move, but change had a way of rippling through life, stirring things up in unexpected ways.

That thought lingered, leaving a bittersweet taste as I locked the door behind us.

Over the next few days, the air crackled with anticipation. Word of the baking competition spread like wildfire, igniting excitement in our students and even drawing in some curious onlookers from the neighborhood. The kitchen buzzed with energy during our classes, the chatter infused with playful rivalry as everyone began crafting their perfect recipes. I caught glimpses of Elara working diligently, her concentration evident as she measured ingredients with precision. It warmed my heart to see her emerging from her shell, laughter escaping her lips more freely with every passing day.

Max and I made an excellent team, dividing responsibilities and ensuring everything ran smoothly. But there was an undercurrent of tension that I couldn't quite place. Each time I caught Max's gaze lingering on me, a spark ignited, sending my heart into a wild tango.

One evening, as we prepped for the final class before the competition, he handed me a whisk, the warmth of his fingers brushing against mine. "You know," he said, a teasing lilt to his voice, "this competition isn't just about baking. It's about creating memories. And you, my dear, are one of my favorite memories."

I felt my breath hitch, a thousand unsaid words swirling between us. The air hung heavy with possibilities, like the moments before a storm. Just as I opened my mouth to respond, the door swung open, and Elara rushed in, breathless, her eyes sparkling with excitement.

"Sorry I'm late! I was testing out my recipe," she announced, a grin splitting her face. "And you're going to love it! Lemon-lavender cupcakes, but with a surprise filling."

In an instant, the tension shattered, replaced by the bright enthusiasm radiating from her. I exchanged a quick glance with Max, and in that fleeting moment, I sensed a silent agreement: this was our moment to shine.

As we dove back into the preparations, the evening unfurled like the petals of a blooming flower, each laugh, each shared recipe, deepening our connection to one another and to the community we had built. The air was filled with the promise of change, each stirring of the whisk and each sprinkle of flour a step toward something beautiful and unexpected.

The day of the baking competition dawned bright and crisp, sunlight streaming through the kitchen windows like liquid gold, illuminating the counters where flour had settled in fine layers, reminiscent of fresh snow. The air buzzed with excitement and the sweet anticipation of the delectable creations that would soon emerge. I stood in front of the mirror, adjusting my apron, my reflection a blend of nerves and determination. Today wasn't just about baking; it was about community, connection, and perhaps a chance to clear the fog that had settled around my feelings for Max.

As I made my way to the kitchen, the sound of laughter greeted me, wrapping around me like a warm hug. Our little community had gathered, an eclectic mix of bakers and spectators, their faces bright with enthusiasm. Max was already there, organizing the tables with an eye for detail, his hands deftly arranging colorful cupcake liners like a painter preparing a canvas. He caught sight of me and flashed a smile that sent a thrill through my heart, and I felt the butterflies awaken in my stomach, ready to flutter.

"Just in time! The crowd is gathering, and I could use your expert eye for aesthetics," he said, gesturing to the haphazardly arranged judging table. "What do you think? Should I swap the red napkins for something more… spring-like?"

I stepped closer, inspecting the setup. "How about a pale yellow? It would really pop against the colors of the baked goods."

"Yellow it is! You're a genius, you know that?" He grinned, the kind of smile that felt like a secret shared just between us.

THE TASTE OF AMBITION

"Flattery will get you everywhere, Max." I chuckled, my heart racing as we shared a moment that felt suspended in time. It was that kind of spark that made the world around us fade, leaving just the two of us and the electric tension simmering in the air.

As we decorated, Elara arrived, her energy buzzing like the sugar-infused air. She wore a vibrant apron, her cheeks flushed with excitement. "I'm ready to win this thing!" she declared, brandishing a tray of her lemon-lavender cupcakes, their golden tops peeking through the frosting like cheerful little suns. "I even made a secret filling."

Max and I exchanged amused glances, both equally intrigued and impressed. "What's the secret?" he asked, leaning closer as if her cupcakes were a prized treasure.

Elara grinned, a mischievous glint in her eye. "If I told you, it wouldn't be a secret anymore, would it?"

The atmosphere pulsed with playful competition, each participant eager to unveil their creations and stake their claim as the champion. Laughter bubbled up around us, mingling with the clinking of bowls and the sound of mixers whirring. My heart swelled at the sight of our community coming together, a tapestry of flavors and personalities woven into something beautiful.

With the competition officially underway, the participants scattered across the kitchen, their focused expressions revealing a mix of determination and sheer joy. I moved through the space, checking in on everyone, offering encouragement and advice when needed. It felt wonderful to see Elara stepping confidently into her role, sharing her knowledge with others, her laughter ringing out like music.

As the time ticked down, the air thickened with anticipation, the sweet aroma of baked goods mingling with the fragrant spring air wafting in through the open windows. I could see Max across the kitchen, chatting with a group of enthusiastic bakers, his laughter infectious. He caught my eye, raised an eyebrow, and tilted his head toward the dessert table, silently challenging me to try to guess his creation.

I approached him, playful defiance in my stride. "I'm going to guess... a chocolate cake with caramel drizzle?"

"Close! But I'd like to think it's much more unique than that." He leaned in, lowering his voice conspiratorially. "It's a lemon-lavender cake, infused with a touch of Earl Grey. A nod to the theme, don't you think?"

"Very sophisticated," I remarked, fighting the urge to lean in closer, to breathe in his warmth. "But it better be good; I'm a tough judge."

"Oh, I'll bring my A-game." His smile was a little too cocky, and I couldn't help but return it, feeling my cheeks heat. There was something electric about these moments, a spark that made everything else fall away.

As the countdown began, I stood beside Elara at the judging table, our hearts racing in unison. The energy crackled around us, an amalgamation of friendly rivalry and genuine excitement. Each baker stepped forward, presenting their creations with pride. Elara's cupcakes were met with enthusiastic applause, their delicate sweetness delighting the crowd.

The judging was intense, and the air thickened with anticipation as we took bites, the flavors exploding on our tongues. "Okay, but seriously, I think I'm going to need a nap after this," I joked, wiping crumbs from my lips.

"Only if I can nap beside you," Max quipped, his eyes sparkling with mischief. "But I promise to share my snacks."

"Only if you promise not to steal my dessert," I shot back, laughing.

As the last creations were tasted, the moment arrived to announce the winner. My heart raced, my palms clammy as I glanced at Elara. She stood beside me, her breath caught in her throat, a

THE TASTE OF AMBITION

mixture of hope and nervousness etched across her face. "Do you think I have a chance?" she whispered, her eyes wide.

"Absolutely. You put your heart into those cupcakes," I reassured her, squeezing her hand. "No matter what, you should be proud."

Max approached, holding a clipboard, his expression comically serious. "After much deliberation, and a few taste-testing disasters, I present to you the winners of our first community baking competition!"

The room fell silent, anticipation hanging in the air like a piñata waiting to be broken. "In third place, with her exquisite strawberry tart, we have Clara!"

Clara beamed, the crowd erupting into applause, the warm spirit of camaraderie wrapping around us like a familiar blanket.

"In second place, for her creative twist on a classic, we have Lila with her orange-infused scones!"

Elara clapped enthusiastically, her cheers mixing with those around her, the energy infectious.

"And finally, in first place, taking home the crown, we have... Elara with her incredible lemon-lavender cupcakes!"

The room exploded with applause, and I felt a rush of pride for her, my heart swelling as she squealed in delight, her eyes shimmering with happy tears. Max stepped forward, presenting her with a handmade trophy adorned with tiny cupcake charms.

"I knew you had it in you," I said, wrapping my arms around her in a jubilant hug. "You were amazing!"

As Elara basked in the glow of her triumph, I caught Max's eye again, our shared smile lingering in the air, thick with unspoken possibilities. The competition had woven a deeper connection not only among our participants but also between Max and me. I could feel the world shifting around us, the whispers of change growing louder, and I knew this was just the beginning of something wonderfully unpredictable.

Elara's joy radiated like the golden glow of freshly baked cupcakes as she clutched her trophy, her laughter ringing through the kitchen, a melodic sound that resonated with everyone present. The applause faded into a warm buzz of conversation, and I felt a swell of happiness for her, mixed with an unfamiliar twinge of longing as I glanced at Max. His eyes sparkled with pride, and that flutter in my stomach grew stronger, a delightful mix of anticipation and uncertainty.

"Okay, cupcake champion, what's your victory plan?" I asked, nudging Elara playfully. "Are you going to take over the baking world or just bask in the glow of your glory for now?"

"Oh, definitely a world takeover," she replied, her eyes dancing with excitement. "But first, I need to learn how to make that lemon-lavender cake. Max, you better be prepared for an intense apprenticeship."

Max chuckled, leaning against the counter, arms crossed, the very picture of relaxed confidence. "As long as you promise to bake some of those cupcakes for me, I'll consider myself your willing mentor."

"Deal! Just don't get too comfortable, because I'm aiming for a rematch next time," she retorted, her competitive spirit shining through.

I watched them, a smile tugging at my lips. Their banter was effortless, a dance of words that spoke of friendship and budding connections. Yet, the knowledge that I stood between them, hovering on the brink of something deeper with Max, made my heart race with conflicting emotions. Was I ready to step forward, to blur the lines of our friendship?

The kitchen slowly emptied, the laughter echoing off the walls, leaving behind the sweet remnants of celebration. As the last of the guests trickled out, I busied myself with the cleanup, avoiding the heavy weight of the unspoken words hanging in the air.

"Do you need a hand?" Max asked, appearing beside me, his presence warm and reassuring.

I turned to face him, my heart racing at the proximity. "I've got it covered. You should bask in Elara's glory. She's the star of the show tonight."

"Sure, but I'm also a little curious about your thoughts on the competition. What did you think?"

"Honestly? It was more than I expected. Everyone put so much heart into their creations. And Elara... she really shone tonight."

"Yeah, she did. It's great to see her come out of her shell." He paused, leaning casually against the counter, his eyes searching mine. "But what about you? You seem a bit distant tonight."

My breath caught in my throat. "Distant? I thought I was just cleaning up."

"Cleaning up can't be that much of a distraction," he teased, the corner of his mouth quirking up. "You're a fantastic baker, and I know there's more to you than just the cleanup crew."

I felt the heat rush to my cheeks, the playful banter tipping on the edge of something more serious. "I'm just... processing everything, I guess. The competition was a success, and I'm thrilled for Elara."

"Processing, huh?" He took a step closer, the air between us crackling with an energy I couldn't ignore. "You know, sometimes it's good to share what's on your mind. I'm here for it."

"I don't want to complicate things," I replied, my voice barely above a whisper. "We've built something nice, and I don't want to ruin it."

His gaze held mine, steady and warm. "You're not going to ruin anything by being honest. I promise."

My heart pounded, each beat a reminder of the line I was teetering on. Just as I opened my mouth to respond, the sound of a loud crash echoed from the back of the kitchen. The two of us whipped around, adrenaline rushing through me, my heart racing as I stepped toward the noise.

"Did you hear that?" I asked, my voice edged with concern.

Max nodded, his brow furrowing. "Yeah, let's check it out."

We moved cautiously toward the source of the sound, the dim light casting long shadows across the floor. The back room was a maze of storage boxes and baking supplies, and as we rounded the corner, the sight that greeted us made my breath hitch.

One of the shelves had collapsed, sending bags of flour and boxes of sprinkles tumbling to the ground in a chaotic explosion. In the midst of the mess, a figure hunched down, frantically trying to gather the scattered contents, their movements frantic.

"Elara?" I exclaimed, recognizing her. "What happened?"

Her head snapped up, flour dusting her hair like a powdered wig, eyes wide with embarrassment. "I just wanted to grab some extra decorations for the cupcakes!" she exclaimed, a sheepish grin breaking through the chaos. "I didn't mean to knock over the whole shelf!"

"Looks like you've created a baking war zone," Max quipped, stepping forward to help her. "We should have a new competition category: best clean-up technique."

Elara laughed, her tension easing as she joined us in gathering the mess. "I think I'm disqualified for that one."

As we worked together, I felt the heaviness from earlier lift, replaced by the warm camaraderie that had blossomed throughout the evening. Yet, beneath the laughter, a lingering tension pulsed between Max and me, a current that threatened to spill over at any moment.

Just as I turned to toss a box of sprinkles into a nearby trash bag, the lights flickered. For a brief moment, the world was plunged into darkness, the only sound the rustle of flour bags and our breaths. The power quickly returned, but as the lights flickered back to life, an uneasy chill slithered through the room.

"Did anyone else feel that?" I asked, glancing between Max and Elara, who looked just as puzzled.

"What do you mean?" Max asked, his expression shifting from playful to serious.

"It just... felt like something was off. Like an omen."

"An omen?" Elara teased, but I could see the unease in her eyes. "You're not about to suggest a ghost in the kitchen, are you?"

"Don't joke about that! This place is old enough to have a ghost or two," I replied, trying to inject some levity but feeling a twinge of dread creeping in.

Suddenly, the lights flickered again, this time accompanied by an eerie, low hum that seemed to vibrate through the walls. The noise grew louder, echoing around us, and my heart raced as I instinctively stepped closer to Max.

"What is that?" Elara whispered, her bravado evaporating.

"I don't know, but it doesn't sound good," Max replied, his eyes narrowing, scanning the dark corners of the room.

As we huddled together, the humming reached a fever pitch, vibrating through the floor, sending a shiver up my spine. Just then, a shadow flickered across the wall, and I caught a glimpse of something—or someone—slipping through the back door.

My heart thundered in my chest. "Did you see that?" I breathed, panic rising in my throat.

Max's jaw tightened, his expression turning serious. "We should check it out."

"Are you crazy? It could be anything! Or anyone!" Elara exclaimed, her voice laced with fear.

"Exactly," Max replied, determination lacing his tone. "And we can't just ignore it. Let's find out what's going on."

With hearts racing, we approached the door, the tension thick in the air, the anticipation of what lay ahead pulling us in like a siren's call. As I reached for the handle, a single thought echoed in my mind: whatever was out there might change everything we thought we knew.

Chapter 22: Rising Tensions

The scent of fresh paint mingled with the lingering aroma of coffee, filling the studio as I carefully added the final strokes to my mural. Each brush movement was a dance, vibrant colors intertwining in a chaotic yet harmonious array, reflecting the inner turmoil that churned within me. The competition loomed like a storm cloud on the horizon, and with each passing day, the excitement felt more like a double-edged sword. I was fully aware that this mural was my chance to shine, yet each stroke of my brush reminded me of the complex web of emotions binding me to Max and Elara.

Max had become my anchor in this whirlwind. His enthusiasm was infectious, igniting a fire within me I hadn't realized had gone dormant. We had spent countless evenings sketching ideas, brainstorming concepts, and sharing laughter that echoed off the walls like music. He had a knack for transforming the mundane into the extraordinary, and it was easy to lose myself in those moments. But as the competition approached, a gnawing guilt settled in the pit of my stomach, growing heavier with every passing hour I spent with him. Elara's trust felt like a fragile glass ornament, beautiful yet precarious, and I could feel it trembling in the balance.

The evening air was thick with anticipation as I set down my brush and wiped my hands on a paint-streaked rag, the remnants of my work decorating my fingers like a badge of honor. Max was nearby, his brows furrowed in concentration as he mixed colors, his tongue peeking out ever so slightly from the corner of his mouth—a quirk that made my heart flutter. "What do you think?" he asked, lifting a brush towards me, splattered with shades of blue and gold.

"It's brilliant," I replied, my voice slightly breathless. "But are you sure about the gold? It might overwhelm the blue." I stepped closer, captivated by the way he transformed the paint into something ethereal.

"Trust me," he said, a teasing grin tugging at his lips. "Gold is like a secret—it sneaks up on you and dazzles you when you least expect it."

I laughed, shaking my head, but a part of me wanted to reach out and smooth the furrow from his brow, to assure him that I trusted him more than he knew. But before I could speak, the door swung open, and Elara stepped in. The tension in the room shifted as her gaze flickered between us, her eyes narrowing ever so slightly. I could almost hear the gears in her mind turning, a mix of confusion and uncertainty.

"Hey, I didn't know you guys were here," she said, her voice betraying none of the emotions that danced behind her calm exterior. "I thought you'd be working on your mural."

"We were just about to," I replied, forcing a lightness into my tone that felt entirely misplaced. "Max was showing me his color palette."

Elara's smile didn't quite reach her eyes as she crossed her arms, leaning against the doorframe like a guardian at the gates of some hidden kingdom. "You both have such a way with colors. I'm sure it's going to turn out amazing."

Her words felt like a fragile bridge, one I desperately wanted to cross but feared would collapse under the weight of unspoken truths. Max, blissfully unaware, nodded enthusiastically. "Thanks, Elara! You know, I was thinking of adding a sunset effect—something vibrant but also calming. Like a moment of peace before a storm."

"I can see that," Elara replied, her tone flat. She took a step closer, her gaze piercing through the pretense. "Just remember, we're all in this together."

The reminder struck a chord, sending a ripple of unease through me. Together. The word echoed in my mind like a haunting refrain, taunting me with the reminder of the pact I had formed with Elara.

THE TASTE OF AMBITION

This was her vision too, and I was treading dangerously close to betraying her. I felt like a child caught with my hand in the cookie jar, the sweetness of my desire clashing with the bitterness of guilt.

As we resumed our work, I tried to focus on the mural, but my thoughts spiraled back to Max. The way he stood there, completely immersed in his craft, made the room feel smaller, warmer. I caught myself stealing glances, noting how the golden light illuminated the strands of hair that fell across his forehead, framing his features like a portrait. But every time I let myself get lost in those thoughts, a wave of guilt crashed over me, washing away any warmth and replacing it with a chill of remorse.

"Do you think we can pull this off?" I asked, breaking the silence, trying to steer the conversation away from the gnawing tension that filled the air.

Max glanced up, his eyes sparkling with confidence. "Of course! We've been preparing for this for weeks. We just need to bring our vision to life."

His enthusiasm was contagious, yet my heart ached with the weight of my secrets. It was absurd, the way my feelings for him had blossomed in the midst of this chaos, like wildflowers breaking through the concrete. But each petal that unfurled felt like a betrayal to Elara, who had believed in me and supported my passion.

"Right," I said, forcing a smile. "Let's show them what we've got."

The laughter that followed felt forced, yet it lingered in the air like a fragile melody, weaving between the notes of tension and uncertainty. I tried to push away the heaviness in my chest, focusing instead on the vibrant mural that was slowly taking shape. But as we painted, the looming shadows of our unspoken feelings and the unsteady foundation of trust threatened to crumble under the weight of unexpressed desires.

The following days morphed into a blur of color and creativity, yet my heart felt shackled by the weight of secrecy. Mornings bled into evenings, each hour filled with brushstrokes and laughter, but an undercurrent of tension pulsed just beneath the surface. The countdown to the competition had begun, and with it came an electric energy that fueled our every move. The studio buzzed with anticipation, but my thoughts often drifted back to Elara, her unwavering support now shadowed by the gnawing guilt I carried.

One afternoon, as sunlight streamed through the tall windows, illuminating the dust motes dancing in the air, I found myself alone with Max. The others had stepped out for lunch, leaving us in a haven of colors and quiet. I busied myself, arranging paint tubes and canvases, anything to distract from the intimacy that lingered in the air. Max leaned against the counter, a casual posture that belied the intensity in his gaze.

"You know," he said, breaking the silence, "I used to think that art was all about technique. But now I realize it's about the stories we tell." He gestured to the mural, his expression earnest. "What story are we telling here?"

The question hung between us, a delicate thread pulling taut. "I want it to be about hope," I replied, my voice softer than I intended. "A reminder that beauty can emerge from chaos."

Max nodded thoughtfully, and for a moment, I saw something flicker in his eyes—understanding, perhaps, or a reflection of his own hidden thoughts. "Hope, huh? That's a big word. It means different things to different people."

I glanced at him, suddenly acutely aware of the closeness between us. "What does it mean to you?"

He hesitated, a shadow passing over his features. "It means finding light in the darkest corners," he said slowly, his tone almost reverent. "But it also means confronting what scares you."

I swallowed hard, the weight of his words settling like lead in my stomach. Confronting fear was not something I had mastered, especially when it came to my growing feelings for him. "I guess we're all afraid of something," I offered, the casual tone a thin veil for the tempest brewing inside me.

"True. But sometimes, I think we're more afraid of what we could lose," he said, his voice dropping to a conspiratorial whisper. "What if we put everything on the line, and it all crumbles?"

Before I could respond, the door swung open with a flourish, and Elara walked in, her energy as bright as the sun spilling through the windows. "Guess who just snagged us lunch?" she declared, brandishing a takeout bag like a trophy. "I'm starving!"

"Perfect timing," I said, my heart racing as I fought to shake off the intimacy of the moment I had shared with Max. Elara dropped the bag on the table, her infectious enthusiasm breaking the palpable tension.

"Did you guys figure out the mural story?" she asked, her eyes sparkling with curiosity.

Max shot me a quick look, a silent conversation passing between us. "Yeah, we were just discussing the concept of hope," he said, leaning into the moment. "You know, the whole beauty-from-chaos thing."

Elara's expression shifted, a flicker of something I couldn't quite place crossing her face. "Hope is good," she said slowly. "I like it. But let's make sure it's not just a pretty picture. We need depth, right? Something that speaks to the judges."

"Always the strategist," I teased, grateful for the distraction.

Max grinned, his eyes sparkling. "What do you think? Should we throw in a dragon for good measure? Maybe a fire-breathing one to really capture their attention?"

Elara laughed, her smile lighting up the room. "That would definitely get their attention! But how about we stick to a less... fiery approach?"

As we devoured our lunch, the atmosphere lightened, the laughter bubbling like a stream in spring. But beneath the playful banter, I could still sense the threads of tension weaving through our interactions. I watched Max as he animatedly discussed our ideas, his passion igniting the air around him. I felt a pang of longing—how was it that one person could elicit such warmth and guilt simultaneously?

After lunch, as we returned to our respective tasks, I caught Max's gaze lingering on me, an unspoken question dancing in his eyes. "You okay?" he asked, his voice low enough that only I could hear.

I nodded, but the weight of the truth felt like a stone in my throat. "Just thinking," I replied, turning back to the mural, determined to bury my fears beneath layers of paint.

The days turned into a whirlwind of activity as we raced to finalize our mural. We worked late into the nights, sometimes finding ourselves alone in the studio, the quiet punctuated only by the sound of brushes swishing against canvas. Each stroke was cathartic, a release of the emotions I struggled to articulate. Yet, every moment spent with Max tugged at the strings of my conscience, a reminder of the growing divide between my heart and my loyalty.

One evening, after a particularly intense session, I found myself leaning against the counter, exhausted but exhilarated. The mural was shaping up beautifully, a tapestry of colors blending seamlessly together, each hue representing a piece of our collective souls. Max stood beside me, his energy unwavering despite the late hour.

"I think we've really captured something here," he said, stepping back to admire our work. The pride in his voice sent a thrill through me, a reminder of why I loved creating art in the first place.

"Yeah," I said softly, lost in the kaleidoscope of colors before me. "But it feels like there's something more beneath the surface."

Max turned to me, his expression serious. "Like what? What are you feeling?"

I opened my mouth, ready to voice the tangled emotions knotting my insides, but just then, the door swung open, and Elara walked in, a flush of excitement on her cheeks. "Guys, you have to see this!" she exclaimed, holding up a pamphlet. "I just got word about the venue for the competition. It's amazing!"

Her arrival felt like a lifeline, but it also reinforced the wall that was slowly rising between me and Max. I plastered on a smile, nodding along as Elara began to describe the venue, but inside, I was spiraling into a labyrinth of confusion. The competition was around the corner, and while the anticipation buzzed in the air like electricity, my heart felt like a tug-of-war between what I wanted and what was right.

As the week unfolded, the studio transformed into a sanctuary of creativity. The air was thick with the scent of acrylics and turpentine, a heady mixture that invigorated my senses while simultaneously pulling at my conscience. I had become a creature of habit, spending hours immersed in the mural, my hands stained with colors that mirrored my conflicting emotions. Each day brought us closer to the competition, yet every stroke of the brush felt like a step deeper into the labyrinth of my own heart.

The vibrancy of the mural began to reflect the chaotic symphony of my feelings, and despite the excitement buzzing around us, an undercurrent of tension simmered just beneath the surface. One evening, after a particularly grueling day, Max and I found ourselves alone in the dim light of the studio, our bodies fatigued but our spirits high. I sat cross-legged on the floor, surrounded by scattered paint tubes and brushes, while Max stood, lost in thought, his gaze fixed on the mural.

"It's really coming together," he said, breaking the silence, his voice carrying a hint of awe.

"Yeah, it feels like it's breathing," I replied, my own admiration for the piece palpable. But as I looked at him, my heart tightened.

"But there's so much pressure. What if it doesn't live up to expectations?"

Max turned to me, a playful glint in his eye. "What if it does? What if we blow their minds?"

"Or what if we set fire to the place?" I quipped back, half-serious. "Because I'm not above a dramatic exit."

He laughed, the sound rich and warm, and for a moment, the world outside faded away. "If we're going to go down in flames, let's at least do it with style."

"Isn't that the motto for life?" I countered, the ease of our banter momentarily pushing aside the weight of my internal conflict.

Suddenly, the moment shifted. Max stepped closer, his hands resting on the edge of the table where our palettes lay. "You know," he began, his tone softening, "there's something beautiful about taking risks, about putting everything on the line. Isn't that what art is all about?"

I opened my mouth to respond, but the words caught in my throat, tangled with the raw emotions swirling between us. There was a fleeting vulnerability in his gaze, a glimpse into the depths of his own fears. And for the briefest moment, I felt the barrier between us fracture.

"Art is one thing," I said, forcing a lightness into my voice, "but personal stakes? That's a different canvas altogether."

Max studied me, a mixture of curiosity and concern etched across his face. "What are you really afraid of?"

Before I could answer, Elara's voice echoed from the doorway, jolting us both. "Hey! Am I interrupting something?"

I nearly jumped, my heart racing as I turned to face her, desperately trying to mask the whirlwind of emotions swirling within me. "Just discussing our impending doom," I replied, a nervous laugh escaping my lips.

"Great! Let's add a little more chaos to the mix," she said, marching in with an air of determination. "I just spoke to the event coordinator. They're expecting a huge turnout, and we need to step up our game. No pressure, right?"

The weight of her words settled heavily in the air, pushing the intimacy of the moment with Max back into the shadows. "Sounds like a blast," I said, forcing a smile, my heart still fluttering from the electric charge we had just shared.

As the three of us began discussing logistics, I felt my thoughts drift back to the mural, the colors blending on the canvas like my feelings for both Elara and Max. How was it that I could love the thrill of creation and yet dread the possibility of losing my closest friend? My heart felt like a pendulum, swinging wildly between loyalty and longing.

Days flew by, the final touches being applied to the mural, and the studio buzzed with frenetic energy. It felt like a race against time, a desperate push towards something beautiful. But beneath the excitement, the tension between Max and me simmered, a thick fog hovering just out of reach, suffocating the air.

The night before the competition, we gathered for a final rehearsal. The studio glowed with a soft light, and the mural stood proudly against the wall, vibrant and alive. I could hardly believe we had created something so extraordinary together, but with every glance at Max, my heart twisted with uncertainty.

"Tomorrow is it," Elara said, her voice steady yet laced with excitement. "We're going to crush it!"

Max's gaze drifted towards me, a question lingering in his eyes, one that demanded to be addressed. "Are you ready?"

I hesitated, the weight of my feelings pressing down like an anchor. "I think so," I replied, but the words felt inadequate, a façade that barely skimmed the surface of my true emotions.

"Let's do a run-through," Elara suggested, clapping her hands together. "We need to nail our presentation. I'll explain our vision, and you two can focus on the mural."

As we prepared, I caught Max's gaze once more, and a silent understanding passed between us—a promise that the truth would surface, one way or another. The rehearsal unfolded, Elara speaking with confidence while I and Max maneuvered around the mural, ensuring every detail shone. But just as I was about to step back and admire our work, a sudden sound shattered the atmosphere—a loud crash echoed from outside.

"What was that?" Elara exclaimed, her eyes wide with surprise.

I exchanged a glance with Max, a flicker of concern igniting in my chest. "I'll check," I said, moving towards the door, but Max caught my arm.

"I'll go," he said, his voice firm. "Stay here."

As he stepped outside, I felt the tension coil tighter within me, my heart pounding with a mix of fear and curiosity. Elara's voice pulled me from my thoughts. "Do you think it's just some kids messing around?"

"I hope so," I replied, anxiety creeping into my tone.

Minutes passed like hours, the silence hanging heavily in the air. Just as I began to feel a sense of dread, Max reappeared, his expression grave, as if he had seen a ghost.

"What's wrong?" I asked, my voice barely above a whisper.

"There's something you need to see," he said, his voice low and urgent.

I felt my pulse quicken, a mix of apprehension and anticipation gripping me. Whatever had happened outside, I knew it wouldn't just be another simple distraction. It was something deeper, something that threatened to unravel everything we had worked for.

As I stepped outside to follow him, a chilling realization washed over me: the looming shadows of our secrets were about to collide with the vibrant colors of our creation. What awaited us outside could change everything—and as the night air wrapped around me, I knew we were on the brink of a revelation that would test our bonds in ways we could never have anticipated.

Chapter 23: The Competition Begins

The kitchen was a flurry of activity, a riot of colors and aromas that danced in the air like notes in a symphony. Flour dust motes floated lazily in the golden morning light that streamed through the bakery windows, illuminating the hustle and bustle around me. Every surface was a canvas, each mixing bowl and spatula a brush in the hands of artists, all competing for the title of baking champion. I couldn't help but inhale deeply, letting the scent of vanilla and fresh berries swirl into my lungs, a reminder of all the late nights I'd spent perfecting my own recipes in this very space.

Max moved beside me, his easy grin radiating warmth that pulled me closer even amid the chaos. He wore his usual apron, splattered with evidence of our frantic preparations—chocolate smudges and flour handprints painted a chaotic but somehow endearing picture of our teamwork. "Ready to unleash our secret weapon?" he teased, lifting an eyebrow in that playful way of his, a challenge sparkling in his hazel eyes.

"Secret weapon? You mean my double chocolate ganache tart?" I quipped back, smirking as I slid my hands into the flour-dusted pockets of my apron. "It's like a ninja in a world of amateur bakers."

"Exactly. They won't know what hit them," he laughed, leaning in closer. The world around us faded momentarily, leaving only the electric charge between us. The warmth of his presence sent butterflies fluttering wildly in my stomach, a sensation both thrilling and terrifying.

The competition was more than just a chance to show off our skills; it was a crucial opportunity to reconnect with the dreams I'd put on hold after everything that had happened with Elara. She stood a few feet away, her brow furrowed in concentration as she whipped egg whites into frothy peaks, her spirit palpable even among the fray of our fellow contestants. For all her competitive

THE TASTE OF AMBITION

edge, I could see the old spark returning to her eyes, a glimpse of the passionate baker I once knew. Yet, as I caught her gaze, I felt a tight knot form in my chest. Elara was my friend, my partner in crime, but there was no denying the currents that ran between Max and me. I could feel them tugging at my heart, mixing my feelings into a bittersweet batter.

"Just remember, no sabotaging the competition," Max said, breaking the tension as he elbowed me playfully. "You're a team player today. You've got this." His encouragement was a warm balm against my swirling thoughts, grounding me in the moment.

"I'd never dream of it," I replied, trying to keep my tone light, though the irony of my own divided loyalties gnawed at me. I was torn, pulled between the thrill of the competition and my commitment to helping Elara rediscover her passion. I turned my attention back to my tart, carefully pouring the glossy ganache into the delicate shell, watching it settle into a smooth, decadent surface that promised richness and depth.

As the clock ticked ominously down to zero, a wave of excitement swept through the bakery. The judges, a trio of local culinary celebrities, surveyed the room with an air of authoritative glee, their appetites whetted and their expressions inscrutable. I could practically feel the weight of their expectations pressing down on us as they approached our station. My heart raced as I wiped my hands on my apron, my palms clammy with anticipation.

"Let's show them what we've got," Max said, a fierce determination lighting up his face as he stepped forward to present our creation. I could see the pride shimmering in his eyes, and it filled me with a sense of belonging I hadn't realized I craved.

"Double chocolate ganache tart," he declared, his voice steady and clear, drawing the judges' attention. "It features a dark chocolate crust filled with a velvety ganache, topped with fresh raspberries and a hint of sea salt for balance."

"Sounds heavenly," one of the judges said, a woman with a mane of curly hair and an apron that seemed to shimmer. She leaned in closer, the fragrance wafting toward her like an enchanting spell. "May I?"

"Please," I encouraged, fighting back the nerves threatening to unravel my composure. The moment hung in the air, heavy with possibility.

The judge took a forkful of our creation and closed her eyes as she tasted it, a smile creeping across her lips. "This is delightful. The chocolate is rich, but the raspberries add just the right touch of brightness."

As she continued to rave about our tart, I caught a glimpse of Elara in my peripheral vision. She was plating her creation—a stunning lavender lemon mousse that seemed to defy gravity, the delicate swirls hinting at a complexity that could rival mine. My heart twisted in conflicting loyalties; I wanted her to shine, yet I yearned for victory alongside Max.

The tension simmered, a palpable undercurrent that made my skin prickle. When the judges reached her station, I felt a rush of sympathy for Elara as she smiled bravely, explaining her dish with enthusiasm. I could see the pride glowing in her cheeks, but behind it was the unmistakable edge of anxiety, the fear of being overshadowed by the competition.

"Look at us," Max whispered, nudging my shoulder gently. "We're really doing this. It's just a little baking competition, right?"

"Right," I replied, my voice barely above a whisper as I watched Elara, a fierce resolve blooming in my chest. Despite everything, I was determined to cheer her on. "We're all going to be champions today, one way or another."

The judges circled back to our station, their plates now decorated with a colorful assortment of baked goods. My heart raced as I caught snippets of their conversations, punctuated by laughter and animated gestures. The bakery buzzed with a palpable energy, an unspoken agreement among the competitors that we were all part of something bigger than ourselves. But my focus narrowed, zeroing in on the exchange happening between Elara and the judges, who leaned closer, their faces lighting up with curiosity.

"Your presentation is stunning," one of the judges remarked, gesturing to the lavender mousse with a flourish. "And the aroma—absolutely captivating. What inspired you to create this?"

Elara's cheeks flushed with a mix of pride and nervousness. "I wanted to create something that felt like spring—light, bright, and full of flavor. The lavender is from my grandmother's garden; it's a childhood memory turned dessert."

Her words struck a chord within me. I could see the depth of her passion pouring into every syllable, a reminder of why we both loved baking in the first place. My admiration for her talent swelled, mingling with the unsettling pang of competition. She had always been the heart of our little duo, and witnessing her rediscover that spark filled me with an ache that settled right in my chest.

"Do you think we should start with our next round?" Max asked, nudging me back to our station. He was a whirlwind of energy, flipping through our recipe notebook as if seeking inspiration from the universe itself. "We have to dazzle them again if we want to stay in the running."

"Absolutely. What are we thinking for the next creation?" I replied, grateful for the distraction from my spiraling thoughts. It was so easy to lose myself in the intoxicating chaos of the competition.

"How about a surprise element?" he suggested, his eyes glinting with mischief. "A twist on a classic? Maybe a raspberry chocolate pavlova?"

"Now you're speaking my language," I said, my enthusiasm igniting. "Light, airy meringue topped with tangy raspberry sauce and dark chocolate shavings? It's like a love letter to dessert."

Max grinned, the kind of smile that made everything feel possible. "Exactly! I'll handle the meringue if you promise to whip up that sauce. Deal?"

"Deal," I said, shaking his hand like we were sealing a pact of culinary warriors.

As we moved into our rhythm, our bodies danced around the kitchen, a choreography of culinary creation. The banter flowed as easily as the chocolate melted over the double boiler. "If this fails, we'll just tell them it's avant-garde," I joked, drizzling the raspberry sauce artfully over the delicate meringue.

"Or we could pass it off as a modern art piece," he quipped back, mimicking an exaggerated art critic's tone. "Ah yes, the chaos of young love represented in the delicate balance of flavors!"

"Please, we don't need a manifesto. Just the dessert," I laughed, feeling the tension ease as we whipped the pavlova into existence. The warmth of the kitchen, filled with the scents of our creations, wrapped around us like a comforting embrace.

But just as we were about to plate our masterpiece, a commotion erupted from the other side of the room. A participant had dropped their entire cake—an elaborate three-tiered creation—onto the floor. The thud echoed like a death knell, and I felt a shiver run down my spine. My heart sank for the baker, watching as despair washed over their face.

Elara, ever the fierce competitor but also a devoted friend, rushed over to offer help. "Don't worry! We can fix this. Just let's get it back up!" She knelt beside the ruins, her hands moving to salvage what she could. I watched, a mixture of admiration and concern churning within me. Here she was, genuinely caring for a fellow competitor while the stakes were high, a testament to her spirit that I had missed during our earlier misunderstandings.

Max nudged my side gently. "Look at her. She's something special, isn't she?"

His words took me by surprise, and for a moment, I hesitated. "Yeah, she is," I replied, forcing a smile that didn't quite reach my eyes. "It's hard to believe we were once inseparable."

"And you still can be," he said, the conviction in his voice making me pause. "Baking has a way of bringing people together, right? Maybe it's time to reconnect?"

I considered his words, the weight of them settling deep in my mind. Could I really bridge that gap between my past and present? My feelings for Max were blooming like the pastries we were crafting, and the thought of opening myself up to Elara again filled me with trepidation. "I want to, but it's complicated," I admitted, feeling the turmoil bubble up inside me.

"Complicated is my middle name," he replied with a wink, and I couldn't help but chuckle. "But seriously, don't let the fear of what was keep you from embracing what could be."

His sincerity grounded me, and as the judges made their rounds, I resolved to be brave. Elara finished salvaging the last remnants of her cake, her smile unwavering despite the setbacks. The camaraderie in the bakery was electric, a reminder that we were all here for the same reason: a love of baking.

When the judges finally reached our station again, I felt a thrill run through me. I presented our pavlova with a flourish. "A raspberry chocolate pavlova, a perfect blend of airy textures and bold flavors."

The judges took their first bites, their faces revealing nothing. My heart raced with anticipation. "This is fantastic," one of them finally said, a grin breaking across his face. "The balance is impeccable."

As they moved on, I allowed myself to breathe again, the tension ebbing away with each passing moment. But then I caught sight of Elara's cake, now transformed into a rustic, imperfect beauty. It was a tribute to resilience, an embodiment of her spirit. I felt a swell of pride for her, for the journey we had taken and the challenges we had faced.

Max squeezed my shoulder gently, his eyes twinkling with mischief. "Looks like the competition just got a whole lot more interesting."

I nodded, the words heavy with promise. Whatever the outcome, I knew one thing for certain: this day was more than just a contest. It was a celebration of our shared love for baking, the friendships we were forging anew, and the courage to face what lay ahead, no matter how complicated it might be.

The competition raged on like a culinary carnival, the air thick with the rich scents of caramel and spices, punctuated by bursts of laughter and the sound of whisking and chopping. I took a moment to steal a glance around the bakery, where the energy surged with every success and setback. Max stood beside me, meticulously arranging the fresh raspberries atop our pavlova, his brow furrowed in concentration.

"You're going to get lost in that raspberry mountain if you're not careful," I teased, nudging him playfully.

"Better a mountain of raspberries than a valley of despair," he shot back, a grin dancing on his lips as he finally stepped back to admire our creation. It was a masterpiece—light, fluffy, and punctuated with vibrant color. A true showstopper. "Besides, I'm more concerned about the imminent doom lurking in the shadows of that lavender mousse."

Elara's dessert had captured the judges' attention, and I could see her basking in the glow of their compliments. A pang of nostalgia struck me; she had always been the one who lit up the room, and

THE TASTE OF AMBITION

her joy was infectious. Watching her flourish reignited the spark of friendship I thought had dimmed, and I felt a bittersweet smile creeping onto my face.

"Don't underestimate her," I warned, trying to sound more serious than I felt. "That mousse is as dangerous as it is delicious."

"Just think of it this way," Max replied, adjusting his apron and leaning closer, "if you and Elara were both cooking up a storm, who do you think would get the crown?"

"Crown? More like a tarnished tiara," I laughed, rolling my eyes. "But seriously, Elara deserves this. She's had a rough patch, and if this competition brings back her fire, I'm all in."

"Spoken like a true friend," Max said, his tone shifting slightly. "But don't sell yourself short. You've got the skills to rival anyone here. Just look at this beauty." He gestured to the pavlova, his pride palpable.

A small voice in the back of my mind whispered doubts, but I pushed it aside. I wanted to believe in my worth, in the culinary journey I had taken to get here. Yet, as the judges continued to praise Elara's mousse, the ache of competition settled like a weight in my stomach. Would I have to choose between my past and my present? Between the fierce competitor and the kind friend?

The judges rounded the corner, plates in hand, and my heart raced. I stepped forward, ready to present our pavlova with all the flair I could muster. "Behold! The raspberry chocolate pavlova—an airy delight that dances between rich and refreshing," I announced, trying to match the confidence radiating from Max.

"Let's see what you've got," one of the judges said, a skeptical brow raised as he forked a piece and brought it to his lips. His eyes widened, and I nearly held my breath as he chewed thoughtfully.

"Wow," he said, eyes sparkling. "The texture is incredible! It practically melts in your mouth!"

I glanced at Max, who was practically vibrating with excitement. But before I could share the moment with him, another participant screamed across the room. "My soufflé! Someone help!" The chaos erupted like a volcano, flour flying, people shouting, and I felt a flash of panic grip my chest.

Elara was already sprinting toward the source of the chaos, her instinct to help overshadowing her competitive spirit. "What happened?" she yelled, rushing to the scene.

"A gas leak! It's ruined everything!" The young baker was on the verge of tears, his soufflé collapsing like a deflated balloon. Elara knelt beside him, her hands steadying his shaking ones. "Hey, it's okay. Let's see what we can salvage," she soothed, her voice a calming balm.

In that moment, I realized how fiercely she had fought through her own struggles, and I felt a swell of pride. Watching her bring light to someone else's darkness, I could almost see the path we could walk together again, should we dare to take it.

Max, noticing my gaze, nudged my arm gently. "You think she's found her groove back?"

"Definitely," I replied, my heart swelling with admiration for Elara's kindness. "She's always had it in her, just buried under all the noise of life."

"Looks like we might have a competition after all," he said, his eyes sparkling with mischief. "But can I get your focus back on our pavlova? The judges are almost ready to announce the winners."

"Right, right," I said, shaking myself from the reverie. The judges were approaching again, each bearing a thoughtful expression.

As they sampled each entry, I held my breath, hoping that our hard work would pay off. Finally, the lead judge cleared his throat, a dramatic pause that felt like an eternity. "It's been an incredibly close competition, filled with remarkable talent. But there can only be one winner."

THE TASTE OF AMBITION

My heart raced as I exchanged a glance with Max. "What if they choose Elara?" I whispered, the anxiety bubbling to the surface.

Max's eyes twinkled with determination. "Then we'll cheer for her, because she's still our friend."

"Yeah, but I don't want to lose this," I said, the tension tightening around my chest.

The judge continued, "After much deliberation, we are thrilled to announce that the winner of this year's baking competition is..."

The bakery fell into a heavy silence, all eyes glued to the judges. The seconds stretched on, suffocating in their intensity, until I thought I might burst from the suspense.

"...Elara Thompson!"

A roar of applause erupted, and I felt a rush of conflicting emotions—joy for Elara and the sinking realization that my dream of victory slipped away. Elara spun around, eyes wide with disbelief, her smile a radiant sunrise. She had done it, she had captured the crown.

As she rushed to the judges to accept her award, my heart swelled with pride, even as a shadow loomed over my joy. Max squeezed my hand, a comforting gesture that reminded me of the bond we were forging. "You're not alone in this. Remember that," he whispered, his voice steady against the rising tide of my emotions.

But before I could respond, a sharp crack echoed through the bakery, drawing our attention to the back door swinging open with a force that sent a shiver through the crowd. A figure stepped inside, their silhouette framed against the blinding sunlight. The energy in the room shifted, a wave of unease rippling through the crowd.

"Elara," the figure called, their voice cutting through the jubilant atmosphere. "We need to talk."

My heart raced. Who was this person, and what did they want with her? As Elara turned to face the intruder, a flicker of concern crossed her features, and the jubilant atmosphere of victory began to fray at the edges, leaving us all to wonder what storm was about to sweep through our carefully crafted world.

Chapter 24: Sweet Success, Bitter Realities

The air shimmered with warmth and a faint sweetness, a perfect companion to the chaos that was our annual baking competition. The scent of vanilla and chocolate mingled with the crisp autumn breeze, wrapping around me like a soft blanket. Laughter echoed off the walls of the old community center, where mismatched chairs clustered in small circles, each a refuge for its occupants, some sipping coffee, others indulging in leftover pastries that had just lost their battle against eager hands.

I stood just outside the doorway, caught in a moment suspended in time, watching the lively scene unfold. A plume of flour dusted the table in front of me, remnants of the frantic energy we'd poured into our creations—an explosion of colors and textures that had captivated our small town. I glanced down at my hands, still flecked with sugar and butter, and felt a twinge of pride. My cake, a three-tiered vanilla and raspberry masterpiece, had not only been a crowd-pleaser but had won the judge's praise for its flavor and flair.

Yet, beneath the revelry, a delicate tension simmered, weaving itself through the laughter and the shared toasts. Max, with his easy smile and disarming charm, had been my partner throughout this event, and his warmth felt like sunlight on my skin. But as his gaze met mine across the room, a knot of uncertainty twisted in my stomach. It was a warmth I craved but feared to touch, knowing the complexity it brought along. Elara, my best friend and confidante, stood beside me, her arms crossed, her eyes flitting between us like a startled bird.

"Hey, great job today," I said, forcing a brightness into my tone as I turned to her. "You really nailed that chocolate torte. I didn't think it was possible to make something so decadent in just one day."

Her smile was thin, stretched across a backdrop of worry. "Thanks, but you know, I think the judges were just being nice. My presentation was a disaster."

I felt a rush of sympathy; I knew how much she cared about her craft. Elara had a way of pouring her soul into every dessert, but her insecurities often clouded her brilliance. "You're being too hard on yourself. Everyone loved it. You should have seen the way they devoured it."

She rolled her eyes, but a flicker of warmth sparked in them. "Maybe they were just hungry. I've seen dogs eat worse things with more enthusiasm."

"Okay, fair point," I chuckled, nudging her shoulder playfully. "But still, your torte was practically perfect. If only you could see what I see."

"Which is?" she pressed, raising an eyebrow, a playful challenge evident in her tone.

"That you're an incredible baker with more talent than anyone else in this room. Maybe you just need to believe it, too."

Elara sighed, her expression shifting into something deeper, more vulnerable. "I don't know, Lily. I just feel stuck. Everyone else seems to have their lives figured out, and I'm here still trying to get a handle on my recipes."

The heartache in her voice struck me like a dagger. The weight of her words clung to the air, heavy and poignant. It was a reality I knew too well; the looming specter of our futures had crept into every moment we shared. "You're not alone, you know. We're all just figuring it out, one cake at a time," I replied softly, hoping to ease her distress.

She glanced at me, her brow furrowing. "And what about you? You seem to have it all going for you. The baking competition, the attention from Max…"

THE TASTE OF AMBITION

Her words stung, igniting an internal battle. Yes, the competition had turned my head with the intoxicating promise of victory, but it had also deepened my connection with Max—a connection I hadn't fully acknowledged. I couldn't let Elara's doubts shape my own reality. "Max is just a friend," I insisted, though even as I said it, I felt the weight of the unspoken truth.

"Sure, just a friend who looks at you like you're the only dessert in the room," Elara replied, her voice laced with a wry humor that masked her concern.

Before I could respond, Max approached us, a broad smile lighting up his face as if he had just walked out of the sun. "What's this? Secret gossip without me?" He leaned against the doorframe, his presence instantly shifting the energy, drawing my attention and quieting the doubts swirling in my mind.

"Just discussing the finer points of baking disasters," I replied, keeping my tone light, though my heart raced at the prospect of being alone with him.

"Disasters?" he echoed, feigning horror. "Did you say Elara's cake? Impossible!"

Elara chuckled, though her smile didn't quite reach her eyes. "You'd think so, but she's the expert at making disasters sound delicious."

Max's laughter was infectious, a balm against the undercurrents of tension. "Lily, I'm shocked! You've been keeping secrets from me. I demand to know more about this 'disaster.'"

As he leaned closer, our shoulders brushed, igniting a spark that sent a thrill racing down my spine. The warmth of his body mingled with the sweetness of the moment, and I realized just how much I cherished his presence. "Well, I can't share my secret recipe for disaster. That's classified information," I teased, trying to play it cool despite the flurry of emotions stirring inside me.

"Classified, huh?" he leaned in, an eyebrow raised. "Maybe I should bribe you with my signature chocolate chip cookies to get the recipe."

I felt the laughter bubbling up within me, brightening the room as I swatted at his arm playfully. "You think you can sweet-talk your way into my secrets? You're going to need more than cookies for that."

Max laughed, and for a moment, everything felt light and carefree. But Elara's earlier words hung in the air like an uninvited guest, reminding me of the delicate balance I was trying to maintain. The echoes of laughter, the smells of baked goods, and the warmth of connection held promise, but the threads of uncertainty loomed ever closer, waiting to unravel the tapestry of my life.

The laughter began to fade as the last few stragglers filtered out, leaving behind a trail of empty plates and a bittersweet aftertaste. The vibrant chatter of the crowd had been replaced by a soft rustling of chairs being stacked and the lingering hum of satisfied sighs. Max was still near, his energy almost crackling in the cool air as he surveyed the aftermath of our sweet victory. I felt his gaze on me, and for a moment, the chaos around us blurred into an intimate bubble. The weight of everything hung thickly, though, as I could still see Elara in my peripheral vision, her posture stiff and guarded.

"Should we start cleaning up?" I suggested, trying to break the tension like a stubborn piece of taffy that wouldn't yield to the pull.

"Only if you promise to help me taste-test the leftovers," Max replied, a playful glint in his eyes. "I can't let all this perfection go to waste. Think of the culinary tragedy that would ensue."

"Culinary tragedy?" I echoed, unable to suppress a grin. "You mean more like a glorious feast of butter and sugar that would have the entire neighborhood lining up for seconds?"

"Exactly! We have a duty, you know," he said, raising a brow with mock seriousness. "The community depends on us to uphold the sacred tradition of devouring baked goods."

As he walked toward the dessert table, I trailed behind, laughing softly. "And here I thought your only responsibility was looking ridiculously charming."

"Hey, it's a full-time job," he quipped, throwing me a wink that sent my heart racing, reminding me of the spark that ignited every time our eyes met.

Elara's voice sliced through our playful banter like a serrated knife. "You two seem cozy," she remarked, her tone laced with an edge that was hard to miss.

I turned to her, noting the way her arms were still crossed tightly over her chest. "Just celebrating the end of the competition, Elara. We did well!"

"Sure, but maybe save the celebrations for later. You know, when the competition's actually over," she said, her eyes narrowing slightly, betraying a sense of insecurity I was all too familiar with.

"Come on," I urged, stepping closer. "You were amazing today. We should be basking in the afterglow of victory together."

Her mouth twisted in a wry smile, but the warmth didn't reach her eyes. "Maybe you should do that with Max. It seems like he's more fun to celebrate with."

"Don't be ridiculous," I countered, my heart sinking as I sensed the gulf widening between us. "You know it's not like that."

The tension hung heavy, thick as frosting on a poorly baked cake. Max's presence, once a source of light, now cast a shadow over the conversation, and I felt torn, like a piece of dough stretched too thin. "Elara, it's not about him. It's about us," I insisted, my voice softer now, vulnerable.

She met my gaze, her resolve wavering for just a heartbeat. "Is it, though? Because it seems like your focus has shifted."

Before I could respond, the sound of a chair scraping against the floor broke our moment. It was Mrs. Hargrove, the town's beloved baker, stepping into the remnants of our celebration. She wore a broad smile, her apron still dusted with flour, and the sight of her made my heart lift momentarily. "What a marvelous day!" she proclaimed, her eyes sparkling like freshly whipped cream. "You all did an incredible job!"

"Thanks, Mrs. Hargrove!" I called, grateful for the distraction. "But we still have quite the mess to clean up."

"I can help," she offered, her hands already moving as if to dive into the remains of our sugary battlefield.

As the three of us began tidying up, I couldn't shake the weight of Elara's earlier words. Each scrape of my hands against the table felt more like an echo of my internal struggle than an actual chore. The room slowly transformed, the evidence of our celebration giving way to silence, yet the noise inside my head was deafening.

I caught a glimpse of Max as he helped Mrs. Hargrove organize the leftover pastries, his laughter a gentle balm against the backdrop of my turmoil. Yet, a gnawing anxiety lingered at the edges of my mind. Would our friendship survive the delicate dance of my feelings for him and Elara's insecurities?

"Can you grab that box over there?" Mrs. Hargrove asked, pointing to a stack of empty pastry boxes in the corner.

"Sure," I replied, moving toward it, but my focus was still on Max, who was now engaged in a light-hearted conversation with Elara, their laughter mingling together, and a pang of something sharp twisted in my gut.

When I returned, I found them leaning closer together, the way old friends do when sharing a secret. I pretended to focus on the pastries, but their dynamic pulled at me, a knot tightening in my chest.

"I'll take those," Max said, reaching for the box I was holding, his hand brushing against mine. A jolt of electricity surged between us, igniting an instinctive yearning I struggled to ignore. I blinked, momentarily lost in the warmth of his smile.

But Elara cleared her throat, breaking the moment. "You know, it's getting late. I should probably head out," she said, her tone lighter but laced with a current of urgency.

"Are you sure?" I asked, concern creeping into my voice. "We could grab dinner or something. Celebrate a little more?"

"I really can't," she replied, forcing a smile that didn't quite reach her eyes. "Maybe next time?"

The disappointment was palpable, but I didn't press her. I knew better than to push her when she was feeling this way. "Okay, just text me later, all right?"

As she turned to leave, I felt an ache deep within me. Max's eyes lingered on me as if he could sense the shift in the atmosphere. "Everything okay?" he asked, his voice low and genuine, concern etched into his features.

"Yeah, just... a lot going on," I replied, forcing a smile that I hoped masked the turmoil within. "But you're right. It was a good day."

"Good day, indeed," he said, his expression brightening. "You really outdid yourself with that cake. If you ever need a taste-tester again, I'm your guy."

"I'll hold you to that," I replied, a flicker of mischief igniting in my chest. "You may have to roll me out of my kitchen after a week of it, though."

"Deal!" he laughed, the sound pure and infectious. "But I refuse to let you skip the gym afterward. Can't have you rolling into town looking like a cupcake, right?"

"Hey!" I feigned indignation, throwing a playful glare his way. "Cupcakes are adorable and delicious! I take offense to that comparison!"

"Exactly! And who would want to be adorable and delicious when you can be a perfect slice of raspberry vanilla cake? That's far more impressive," he countered, grinning.

I couldn't help but laugh, a bubble of happiness bursting through the fog of worry. But the laughter faded as I watched Elara disappear into the cool evening, leaving behind the warmth of camaraderie and the uncertainty of our friendship hanging like a half-frosted cake—beautiful yet precarious.

"Guess it's just us now," Max said, breaking the silence that had settled between us like the last layer of frosting on a cake.

"Guess so," I replied, my heart racing as I met his gaze. The air between us crackled with unspoken words and possibilities, and I couldn't help but wonder if I had the courage to step into the unknown, to reach out and see if there was something more waiting for me beyond the frosting and the fondness we shared.

The lingering warmth of the late afternoon sun bathed the community center in a golden hue, softening the edges of the day as I stepped outside. The cheerful chaos of the baking competition had faded, replaced by a tranquil breeze that danced through the trees. Yet, the peaceful scene outside did little to ease the turmoil within me. I stood at the threshold, the scent of baked goods still clinging to my clothes, but all I could taste was the bitterness of unresolved feelings.

"Hey," Max said, his voice pulling me from my thoughts. He stepped out behind me, the sunlight casting a halo around his tousled hair, making him look almost ethereal. "You good?"

"Just...thinking," I replied, forcing a smile that didn't quite reach my eyes. "You know how it is. All this sweetness can be overwhelming sometimes."

THE TASTE OF AMBITION

He chuckled, and I felt the tension in my shoulders ease just a fraction. "That's the trouble with sugar. It looks so innocent, but it's a cunning little villain, isn't it?"

I laughed, but it was tinged with a hint of sorrow. "Right? One moment you're celebrating victory, and the next you're questioning everything."

Max's expression softened, and he stepped closer, closing the space between us. "You're talking about Elara, aren't you?"

"Is it that obvious?" I sighed, running a hand through my hair, a gesture of frustration that I couldn't shake. "I just wish she could see herself the way I see her. She's so talented, but her insecurities are like a weight she can't shake off."

"You're a good friend, you know that?" His sincerity was like a balm against the tension swirling inside me. "Not everyone has the strength to support someone else when they're struggling."

"I want to be there for her, but sometimes it feels like I'm being pulled in two directions," I admitted, the words spilling out before I could stop them. "With you, everything feels light and easy, but with Elara, it's like I'm stuck in a whirlwind."

Max studied me for a moment, his eyes searching mine as if trying to decode my thoughts. "Maybe you just need to find a way to balance both sides. Friendship doesn't have to mean sacrificing one for the other."

His words resonated deeply, igniting a flicker of hope within me. "You're right. I just have to figure out how to keep Elara close without pushing you away."

"Or pushing yourself away from me," he added, a playful grin lighting up his features. "You seem to forget that I'm more than happy to play the role of the supportive sidekick."

"Sidekick? I think you're more like the charming co-star," I teased, unable to resist the warmth that flooded my chest at the thought of him by my side.

"Ah, but what's a co-star without some drama?" He leaned back slightly, a smirk playing on his lips. "And it seems we're ripe for a good plot twist, wouldn't you say?"

Just as I opened my mouth to respond, the soft crunch of gravel underfoot drew my attention. Elara emerged from the parking lot, her expression unreadable, the shadows of the setting sun dancing across her features. My heart sank as I watched her approach, the weight of the previous conversation pressing down once more.

"Hey, I thought I'd find you two out here," she said, her tone light but her eyes betrayed the undercurrent of tension. "Did I interrupt something?"

"No, not at all," I replied quickly, my heart racing as I tried to gauge her mood. "We were just enjoying the post-competition vibes."

"Right," she said, crossing her arms, a barrier I was all too familiar with. "Looks like you two have your own little celebration going on."

"Not a celebration, just a debrief," Max interjected smoothly, his charm shining through as he flashed her a bright smile. "Care to join us? We were just discussing how to take our baking adventures to the next level."

Elara hesitated, and for a moment, the air hung thick with uncertainty. "I don't know if I'm in the mood for that. I think I just need some time alone."

"Are you sure?" I asked, my concern bubbling up. "We're all here for you, you know."

"I know," she replied, her voice softening just a bit. "But I need to sort through my own thoughts right now. I just feel like everything is changing, and I can't keep up."

Her vulnerability tugged at my heart, but I could feel Max's gaze shifting between us, a silent observer in our emotional tug-of-war. "Elara, if there's anything I can do—" I began, but she held up a hand.

"Honestly, I think I just need to figure things out myself. I'll talk to you later, okay?"

She turned away, and my heart plummeted. I wanted to reach out, to reassure her, but the walls she had built were too high for me to scale. The sun dipped lower in the sky, casting long shadows as she walked away, leaving me grappling with a sense of helplessness.

"Lily, I—" Max started, but I shook my head, my heart still tangled in worry.

"Let her be," I said, my voice shaky as I struggled to keep my emotions in check. "She needs space, and I respect that."

"I understand," he replied softly, the understanding in his eyes offering a momentary comfort. But even as he spoke, I could feel the distance between us widening, the space once filled with laughter and light now heavy with unspoken words.

"Maybe we should go, too," I suggested, trying to distract myself from the turmoil of emotions swirling around. "There's a bakery down the street we could check out."

"Sure, sounds good," Max replied, but the lilt in his voice felt forced. As we turned to leave, I caught one last glimpse of Elara, her figure retreating into the shadows of the parking lot, a ghost of the vibrant friend I had known.

The drive to the bakery was filled with a silence that felt both comfortable and uneasy. I stole glances at Max, who was lost in thought, his expression thoughtful yet distant. The laughter and banter that usually flowed so effortlessly between us felt stifled, overshadowed by the weight of the day.

As we pulled into the bakery's lot, the neon sign flickered invitingly, and the sweet aroma wafted through the air, wrapping around us like a comforting hug. "You sure you want to do this?" I asked, noting the hesitation in his gaze.

"Why not?" he replied, forcing a smile. "It's a good distraction."

We stepped out, the door creaking softly behind us as we entered the cozy shop, the warm light spilling over us like melted chocolate. The shelves were lined with an array of pastries, each more delectable than the last, but the vibrant atmosphere did little to lift the weight of our earlier conversations.

"See anything you like?" Max asked, glancing at me over the display case, his eyes twinkling with playful mischief.

"Everything," I admitted, my mouth watering as I scanned the sugary delights. "But I think my eyes are bigger than my stomach."

"Ah, the age-old struggle," he said, grinning as he placed a hand on the counter. "I suggest the raspberry tart. It's practically calling your name."

"Is it?" I smirked, leaning closer to the case. "Or is that just your charm working its magic?"

"Maybe a bit of both," he replied, his eyes sparkling with mischief. But just as I was about to respond, the shop door swung open, the jingle of the bell breaking our moment.

I turned to see Elara standing in the entrance, her expression a mixture of uncertainty and determination. My heart raced at the sight of her. "Lily, can we talk?" she said, her voice barely above a whisper.

Before I could respond, the air shifted dramatically, a crackle of tension sparking between us. I could feel Max's eyes on me, waiting for a cue, but the moment hung heavy with unspoken words and possibilities.

"Now?" I asked, surprised and cautious, my mind racing with the implications of this unexpected encounter.

"Yeah, I need to clear the air before we all drown in this unspoken mess," she said, stepping further into the bakery, her resolve shining through the uncertainty in her eyes.

The moment felt suspended, charged with an intensity I hadn't anticipated. I caught Max's gaze, and for a split second, everything felt uncertain, balancing on the precipice of change. As I opened my mouth to speak, Elara's next words hung in the air, heavy with promise and trepidation, ready to tip the scales of our tangled lives.

Chapter 25: A Recipe for Heartbreak

I poured the last batch of dough onto the floured counter, the soft thud echoing like a heartbeat in the dim light of the bakery. The sweet aroma of vanilla and cinnamon wrapped around me, a cocoon of comfort amid the chaos that had become my life. Every whisk and knead was a distraction, a way to carve out some sense of normalcy. The past few weeks had been a whirlwind, leaving me exhilarated yet heavy with uncertainty. The competition had ignited a fire in me, sparking a passion for baking that had lain dormant for too long. But with that spark came a conundrum I couldn't shake: my feelings for Max.

He had been my rock throughout the competition, a steady hand in the storm. His laugh had a way of making everything else fade into the background, the way a warm hug could make a chill evening feel like summer. Yet, as much as I reveled in his company, a gnawing sense of guilt had begun to take root, wrapping around my heart like a creeping vine. The name Elara danced in the back of my mind, a bittersweet reminder of the friendship I cherished and the potential heartbreak I dared not entertain.

Dinner with Max had felt like stepping into a dream. The sun had set, casting a golden hue over the city as we strolled to our favorite little Italian restaurant. The air was rich with the smell of garlic and herbs, enticing us through the door. Once seated, our banter flowed as effortlessly as the wine poured into our glasses. I found myself leaning in, laughing at his jokes, the way his eyes sparkled under the warm glow of the candles. But beneath the light-heartedness, an undercurrent pulsed with tension, one that neither of us dared to acknowledge.

As the conversation meandered from work to our latest baking exploits, I could feel the gravity of the moment pressing against my chest, a sweet pressure that mingled with the thrill of being close to him. I glanced at his hands, strong yet gentle as he gestured animatedly. I could almost envision them kneading dough, sculpting something beautiful. It was impossible not to notice how his presence enveloped me, like a warm blanket on a chilly evening. Yet, in the midst of my daydreams, I felt that familiar pang of hesitation.

"Do you think we'll ever compete again?" he asked, his voice low, almost conspiratorial. The question hung in the air, thick with meaning. I wanted to say yes, to express the burning desire to dive into another challenge with him by my side. But instead, the image of Elara popped into my mind, her laughter echoing like a haunting melody. "I don't know, maybe? It depends on what opportunities come our way," I replied, my voice faltering slightly.

Max raised an eyebrow, clearly not buying my evasiveness. "You're a natural at this. You can't just let it slip away." He leaned closer, his eyes searching mine. "You're too talented to walk away." His sincerity knocked the breath from my lungs, and for a moment, the world outside the restaurant faded. I could feel the pull between us, the unspoken words longing to break free.

And yet, the specter of Elara loomed over me, a ghost I couldn't shake. I loved her; she was my friend, my confidant. How could I allow myself to want Max without betraying her? Just as the tension reached its zenith, I felt a panic rising, choking the words I wanted to say. "I think we should focus on our future, you know?" I said instead, desperate to deflect the moment. It felt like a betrayal to both of us, and I hated that the connection between Max and me crumbled under the weight of my indecision.

The silence that followed was palpable, thickening the air between us. Max pulled back slightly, his smile fading, and my heart sank like a stone. The moment had slipped away, and I felt like I'd let it drown without even trying to save it. My thoughts raced as I searched for something, anything, to bridge the gap that had formed. "I just mean, there's so much to do. We could start experimenting with new recipes!" I exclaimed, trying to resurrect the spark of our earlier conversation. But the joy had dissipated, leaving a hollow echo in its place.

"Sure," he said, though the warmth in his voice felt strained, as if he were trying to convince himself. "New recipes are great. But what about us?"

There it was, the question that hung unspoken, lingering in the air like the scent of fresh bread. I had put it off, hoping it would go away, but it wouldn't. The longer I hesitated, the more I felt the walls closing in. I couldn't hide behind flour and frosting forever. I had to confront the feelings that had taken root, but fear gripped me like a vise.

"Max..." I began, but the name Elara slipped through my lips before I could gather my thoughts. His expression changed, a flicker of something I couldn't decipher crossing his face. The moment shattered, and I felt a profound sense of loss—a chance for honesty and vulnerability lost in the labyrinth of my own making. The tension, once electric, now felt charged with disappointment, and I couldn't help but feel that I had disappointed not just him but myself as well.

"Right," he said, leaning back, arms crossing defensively over his chest. The warmth between us had transformed into an icy chasm, and I could see the walls closing in around him. "Maybe I was just imagining things."

"No, you weren't," I protested, the words spilling out before I could rein them in. "I just... I can't. Not yet." The regret hung heavily on my tongue, bitter and metallic. What was I afraid of? Losing Elara? Losing Max? The answer danced tantalizingly out of reach as the evening slipped away, each moment a reminder of what could have been, layered in the complexities of friendship and love.

We finished our meal in relative silence, the once lively conversation now a whisper of what it had been. My heart felt as if it had been kneaded too many times, stretched thin, and torn. As we exited the restaurant, the night air was cool against my skin, but the chill I felt ran much deeper. I glanced at Max, his expression unreadable, and realized that I had not only lost my moment with him but perhaps the chance at something beautiful, something I had yearned for while wrestling with my conscience. And as we walked, the silence between us grew heavy, a recipe for heartbreak I hadn't anticipated.

The next morning, I arrived at the bakery early, the sun still a sleepy yawn on the horizon. A rich, golden light streamed through the windows, painting the walls in warm hues, and for a moment, I felt a flicker of hope. I tied my apron, the fabric familiar and comforting, and set to work. Kneading dough was my therapy; it allowed my fingers to find rhythm and my mind to wander, even as it danced around thoughts of Max and Elara.

The bell above the door jingled, pulling me from my reverie. I glanced up to see Sarah, my neighbor and sometimes sous-chef, walk in, her arms laden with grocery bags. "You look like you've seen a ghost," she teased, her voice light but laced with genuine concern. "Did you bake last night or summon something from the other side?"

"Just a little late-night baking," I said, forcing a smile. I didn't want to lay my burdens on her; she had enough on her plate with her own life. "You know how it is."

"Sure, and I also know how to see through a facade," she replied, her eyes narrowing playfully. "What happened? Spill it. Did Max finally confess his undying love for you, or are we still stuck in the 'will they, won't they' sitcom phase?"

I couldn't help but laugh, the sound brightening the air between us. "I wish it were that simple. We had dinner last night, and let's just say, I fumbled the ball." I picked up a rolling pin, tapping it lightly against the counter as I leaned in closer, sharing the details. "It was supposed to be celebratory, but I turned into a complete coward."

Her brow furrowed, and she crossed her arms. "Coward? You? You're the one who tackled a high-stakes baking competition like a boss." She paused, looking at me with a knowing smile. "This is about Elara, isn't it? You're worried about how she would feel if you and Max... well, you know."

"Exactly," I said, frustration bubbling beneath the surface. "I don't want to hurt her, but it's like my heart is caught in a blender. Every time I think about him, I feel this pull, and then... there's Elara's face, reminding me of everything we've built together."

Sarah shrugged, her expression softening. "You can't let guilt dictate your happiness. Elara is your friend, and if she truly cares about you, she'll want you to be happy, even if it means making tough choices."

"Yeah, well, easier said than done," I mumbled, tossing a handful of flour into the air, watching it settle like the chaos inside me. "I don't want to choose between them. It feels like I'm trying to walk a tightrope, and one wrong step could send everything crashing down."

As the morning slipped away, the bakery buzzed with the usual rhythm of flour and sugar. The clanging of mixing bowls and the gentle hum of the oven created a familiar backdrop that grounded me. I poured my heart into every cupcake and croissant, my hands moving as if they had a mind of their own. But no matter how hard I tried, the image of Max leaning closer, that sweet, vulnerable moment between us, haunted me.

Later that afternoon, with the sun now a golden orb in the sky, I decided I needed a break from my thoughts. I grabbed my phone, thinking a brisk walk could clear my mind. Just as I stepped outside, a familiar face caught my eye—Elara, walking toward me, her smile radiant against the backdrop of vibrant autumn leaves. She waved enthusiastically, and my heart did a little somersault in my chest.

"Hey! I was just thinking about you!" she called out, her voice bubbling with excitement. "I wanted to surprise you with a little something."

I forced a smile, but a pang of guilt twisted in my gut. "Oh? What is it?"

She reached into her bag and pulled out a beautifully wrapped box, tied with a delicate ribbon. "I saw these at the market and thought of you immediately. Open it!"

I hesitated, staring at the box, knowing that her gesture came from a place of pure kindness. The last thing I wanted was to taint this moment with my internal struggle. "You didn't have to do that, Elara."

"Nonsense! Friends bring each other treats. It's a rule." Her eyes sparkled with mischief, urging me to unwrap the gift. I finally relented, peeling back the paper to reveal a collection of exquisite spices and flavor extracts, each bottle labeled in her neat handwriting.

"Oh wow! This is amazing! Thank you!" I exclaimed, my excitement genuine. "I can't wait to experiment with these. You know I love trying new flavors."

"I thought you might like them," she replied, her enthusiasm infectious. But as we chatted about baking, my mind couldn't help but drift back to Max. How would she feel if she knew what had happened? Would she still smile at me with that same warmth if she understood the mess swirling beneath the surface?

The conversation flowed effortlessly, laughter punctuating our words as we shared anecdotes and baking tips. But I felt the unspoken tension, an invisible thread weaving itself tighter around us, threatening to snap. Just as I was about to voice my concern, Elara paused, her gaze shifting, as if sensing the shift in the air.

"Is everything okay? You seem a little... off today," she said, her brow furrowing slightly. "You've been distant lately."

My heart raced, panic flaring. "No! I'm fine. Just a little tired from work, you know how it is." I wanted to tell her everything, to open my heart and share my struggles, but the words caught in my throat, tangled with fear.

Her gaze bore into mine, searching for truth. "You know you can talk to me, right? Whatever it is, I'm here."

The sincerity in her voice squeezed my heart. I wanted to scream that I was caught in a whirlwind of emotions, torn between my desires and my loyalty. But the thought of seeing disappointment in her eyes was too much to bear. Instead, I offered a smile, though it felt more like a mask than genuine warmth.

"Really, I'm okay," I assured her, though my voice lacked conviction.

"Alright," she said slowly, but I could see the worry etched in her features. "Just remember, I'm your biggest fan. Always will be."

We parted ways shortly after, and I watched her disappear down the street, the brightness of her spirit lingering like an aftertaste of honey. As I stood there, the weight of my secret settled heavily on my chest. I was running out of time. The facade I had built was beginning to crack, and soon enough, I would have to confront the reality of my feelings for Max and the consequences of holding back.

Returning to the bakery, I poured myself into the next batch of pastries, the rhythm of my work a welcome distraction from the chaos inside my mind. The sweet scent of caramel filled the air as I worked, but even the sugar couldn't mask the bitter taste of uncertainty that lingered at the back of my throat. Every flick of my wrist, every sprinkle of flour felt like a countdown, each moment inching closer to a confrontation I couldn't avoid. The truth simmered just beneath the surface, waiting for the moment when I would have to face it, head-on, no more running.

The following day felt like I was wandering through a fog, each moment blurred and muted. I found myself in the bakery, but instead of the familiar joy of creating pastries, the routine felt like a chore. The whir of the mixer and the hiss of the oven were mere background noise, overshadowed by my tumultuous thoughts. Every whisk, every fold of dough, reminded me of the conversation with Max. My heart ached with a peculiar blend of hope and dread, swirling together like sugar and salt.

Sarah stopped by later in the afternoon, her usual vivaciousness dimmed slightly by the weight of the world hanging around us. "You know, you can't keep this up," she said, eyeing me as I expertly shaped a croissant. "You're going to bake yourself into oblivion if you don't let something out."

"I'm fine," I replied, more sharply than I intended, my hands working faster as if I could knead away the anxiety. "Really, just a little tired from the competition."

"Right, because rolling dough is the perfect remedy for a broken heart," she quipped, raising an eyebrow. "You need to talk to Max. Just be honest with him. You know what he's waiting for, right?"

I stopped, my fingers hovering over the dough, the thought of Max's hopeful gaze making my stomach churn. "What if I lose him and Elara both? What if I end up alone?" The vulnerability of my words struck me, but they hung in the air like a lifeline, and I suddenly craved honesty.

"Life is all about risks. You've got to put your heart on the line, or you'll just end up stuck in the bakery with me, rolling dough until we're both old and grey." She laughed, but I could see the sincerity in her eyes. "Besides, who says you can't have both? Max and Elara can exist in your life. You don't have to choose."

I wanted to believe her, wanted to embrace the idea of a world where love didn't come with boundaries, but fear twisted my insides like a knot. "It's not that easy, Sarah. This isn't a recipe we can tweak on a whim."

She crossed her arms, her expression softening. "You're the baker here. You know that sometimes the best flavors come from unexpected combinations. Maybe it's time to experiment a little."

With that lingering in my mind, I busied myself with trays of cookies and cinnamon rolls, but every slice of dough felt heavier than the last, burdened with the weight of unexpressed feelings. That evening, I set out for a walk, hoping the crisp autumn air would provide clarity. The streets were alive with the sounds of laughter and the rustle of fallen leaves, a stark contrast to the turmoil within me.

Just as I rounded the corner, I saw Max leaning against a lamppost, the soft glow illuminating his features. He looked both relaxed and anxious, and my heart leaped and sank at the same time. What was he doing here? I had thought I'd given him the cold shoulder just enough to keep him at bay.

"Hey," he said, pushing off the post and walking toward me. "I was hoping I'd run into you."

"Oh? Just strolling the streets, hoping for a serendipitous encounter?" I attempted to keep the tone light, but the tension simmered just beneath the surface.

"I'd like to think so. I've been thinking about what happened the other night," he replied, his voice low and earnest. The way he said it sent shivers down my spine, both exhilarating and terrifying. "We need to talk."

I wanted to bolt, to run back to the bakery where everything was predictable, but I stayed rooted to the spot. "About what?" I asked, trying to keep my voice steady, though my heart raced like a wild stallion.

"About us. About that moment we had. The one you shattered with Elara's name." He stepped closer, his eyes locking onto mine, searching for the truth I was reluctant to reveal.

"I didn't mean to bring her up," I said, my heart heavy with guilt. "It just... slipped out. It's complicated."

"Complicated how?" he pressed, frustration lacing his tone. "You care about her, I get it. But what about us, Gabrielle? What do you want?"

The question hung in the air, a lifeline thrown into the stormy sea of my emotions. I could feel the weight of it pressing down on me. I wanted to scream that I wanted him, but the fear of hurting Elara kept my lips sealed. "It's not that simple, Max. It never is."

He sighed, running a hand through his hair in that way that made my heart flutter. "Then let's figure it out together. I don't want to lose you to what-ifs and maybes."

"Maybe you should have thought of that before I became the backdrop to your life," I shot back, a mix of anger and sadness spilling from my mouth. "You're not the only one tangled up in this."

He stepped back, the hurt in his eyes like a dagger to my heart. "So, what? You're going to keep dancing around your feelings? Hide behind Elara? What if she's not the one you want?"

I faltered, his words striking a chord I hadn't wanted to acknowledge. "I can't just hurt her. You don't understand what she means to me."

"And what do I mean to you?" he shot back, his voice rising with frustration. "Am I just a passing phase? A side dish to your main course?"

I swallowed hard, feeling the heat of tears threaten to spill over. "You're not a side dish, Max. You're..." My voice cracked as I searched for the words. "You're everything. But I can't do this to her."

"Then maybe you're the one who's holding all the cards," he said softly, the tension between us shifting into something more vulnerable. "Maybe it's time to stop worrying about everyone else and start worrying about what you want."

His sincerity struck me like a bolt of lightning, illuminating the tangled web I had woven. But before I could respond, a loud commotion erupted from the corner of the street, drawing our attention. A small crowd had gathered, voices rising in a chaotic chorus.

"What the hell is going on?" I asked, momentarily distracted from the turmoil of emotions swirling between us.

Max's eyes darted toward the scene, and his expression turned serious. "Let's check it out," he said, moving toward the noise.

I followed him, heart pounding for reasons I couldn't quite articulate. As we pushed through the throng, the source of the chaos came into view. A car had crashed into the nearby storefront, glass shards glinting in the evening light. The driver staggered out, dazed but seemingly unharmed. But what caught my eye was the figure standing nearby, their face pale and eyes wide—Elara.

The sight of her there, shocked and shaken, sent a jolt of fear through me. I took a step forward, instinctively reaching out for her. "Elara!"

Max's hand found my arm, grounding me, but all I could focus on was her expression—panic etched into her features. She caught my gaze, and for a moment, the world around us faded into a blur. The weight of everything felt like a tidal wave crashing down, and I realized that no matter how much I wanted to keep my emotions contained, this moment was about to change everything.

As I moved toward her, a sense of urgency enveloped me. What was happening? Was she okay? But just as I reached out, the ground beneath me trembled, and my phone buzzed violently in my pocket. I glanced down to see an incoming message from an unknown number, the screen lighting up with words that chilled me to the bone: You have to choose. Time is running out.

THE TASTE OF AMBITION

A shiver danced down my spine as I looked back at Max, then at Elara, whose eyes were filled with a storm of emotions. I knew, in that moment, that nothing would ever be the same.

Chapter 26: The Unraveling

I stood in the bright, sunlit kitchen, a swirl of sweet vanilla and rich butter wafting around me as I spread a layer of frosting over the delicate cake. The morning light danced through the window, casting playful shadows on the countertop, but all I could focus on was the tightening knot in my stomach. Elara, her normally vibrant spirit dimmed, sat across from me, her brow furrowed as she meticulously piped tiny white roses onto a layer of chocolate ganache. The rhythmic swirls of icing she created looked effortless, yet I could sense the tension radiating from her like heat from an oven.

"Do you ever think we're just pretending?" Elara's voice cut through the silence, sharp and sudden, like the crack of a breaking egg. I glanced up, caught off guard. Her eyes, usually sparkling with mischief, now appeared clouded and heavy, the vibrant green dulled by a shadow of doubt.

"What do you mean?" I asked, though I felt the answer lurking at the edges of my mind, like a stubborn fly buzzing around a window.

"Like... all of this," she gestured vaguely at the colorful array of cakes and pastries surrounding us, the sugar flowers on the table a stark contrast to the somber mood settling over us. "It's like we're icing over the cracks, pretending everything's fine when it's not. I can see it in you, you know."

I swallowed hard, the frosting knife suddenly feeling like a weighty anchor in my hand. "Elara, I—"

"Stop," she interrupted, her voice softer now, tinged with something that felt like resignation. "I know. I know you're trying to keep things light. But there's a storm brewing underneath, and I'm scared it's going to break us apart."

The words hung between us, thick and sticky like the frosting I was trying to spread. My heart raced, thoughts crashing together like waves against a rocky shore. Here I was, so caught up in my budding

THE TASTE OF AMBITION 285

relationship with Max, his laughter still echoing in my ears, that I had failed to see the true depth of Elara's despair. She had been my confidante, my friend, the sister I had chosen, and yet I was letting her slip away as I chased my own happiness.

"I never meant to..." I began, but the truth felt inadequate, like trying to patch a hole with a mere band-aid. The truth was messy, uncomfortable, and I knew it would hurt her.

"Look, I know you and Max have something special," she said, her voice trembling slightly, and I could see the flicker of pain in her eyes. "I'm happy for you. I really am. But I can't help but feel like I'm losing you in the process."

Her honesty cut deeper than any blade, and I felt the burn of tears prickling at the corners of my eyes. I set the frosting knife down, my hands trembling as I met her gaze, searching for the right words to ease her heartache. "You're not losing me, Elara. I promise. I want to be here for you."

"Do you?" she asked, her expression a mix of vulnerability and defiance. "Because it feels like you're caught up in your own world, and I'm stuck on the outside looking in."

Her words were like a splash of cold water, awakening me to the reality of my own neglect. I could almost hear the echoes of laughter between Max and me, the way he lit up when he talked about his passions, his easy charm wrapping around me like a warm blanket. But the weight of Elara's sorrow overshadowed those moments, and I realized that I had unwittingly cast her into the shadows.

"Elara, I..." My voice wavered, the enormity of what I wanted to say nearly overwhelming. "I care about you. I've been so focused on how happy Max makes me that I didn't see you needed me too."

She looked down at her hands, the delicate piping tip dropping from her grasp and clattering onto the counter. "I'm just tired, you know? Tired of feeling like I have to compete with your happiness."

The words struck a chord in me, resonating with a truth I hadn't wanted to face. "You don't have to compete with anyone, especially not me. You are everything to me, Elara. We're a team."

She looked up then, eyes glistening with unshed tears, and I felt a rush of emotion crash over me like a tidal wave. The cakes, the frosting, the vibrant kitchen filled with the sweet scent of sugar — it all faded into the background. In that moment, nothing else mattered but the raw, tender connection we shared.

"Can we promise to be honest with each other?" I asked, the words tumbling out with a mixture of urgency and hope. "No more pretending? No more glossing over things?"

Elara nodded, a faint smile breaking through her sadness, a glimmer of light returning to her eyes. "Okay, I can work with that. But that means you can't run away when things get tough."

"I promise I won't," I vowed, the weight of my words settling heavily in the air between us. "We'll face it all together."

Just then, the oven timer dinged, a cheerful sound that cut through the tension, pulling us back into the present. I could see Elara's tension begin to lift, the corners of her mouth twitching upwards, and I felt a surge of relief. As we turned back to our cakes, the moment felt like a delicate rebirth — the layers of frosting, like the layers of our friendship, rebuilt and stronger than before.

Yet even as we returned to our sugary creations, I knew that the conversation had unraveled more than just the distance between us. It had opened a door to a truth I hadn't wanted to face, one that lingered in the corners of my heart like the scent of baked goods cooling on the rack. I was in a whirlwind of emotions, caught between my desire for Max and the unwavering bond I shared with Elara, and I couldn't help but wonder how long I could balance both without losing everything I held dear.

The soft hum of the kitchen mixer provided a rhythmic backdrop as I focused on the task at hand, each swirl of frosting becoming

THE TASTE OF AMBITION

a momentary refuge from the emotional storm brewing within me. The air was thick with sweetness, and as I carefully adorned each layer of cake, I found solace in the familiar motions, a soothing balm for my frayed nerves. Elara had retreated into silence, her earlier vulnerability replaced by an uncharacteristic reserve that hung between us like the weight of a fallen soufflé.

"I can't believe you've managed to turn that cake into a mini skyscraper," I remarked, trying to lighten the mood as I glanced at her creation—a towering confection covered in delicate petals and shimmering gold dust. "If this wedding doesn't go well, I think it'll be your fault for setting the bar too high."

She shot me a sideways glance, the corners of her mouth twitching in reluctant amusement. "Oh, please. As if I would sabotage my own baking reputation. I need people to think I'm a culinary genius, not a cake-wrecking ball."

"That's the spirit," I grinned, grateful for the flicker of light returning to her eyes, even if only briefly. "So, what's the plan? Are we going to serve it with a side of guilt, or just go all-in on the sweetness?"

Her laughter rang out, a sound I desperately craved to hear more often. "Let's go with the sweetness for now. Besides, I think my guilt needs a timeout."

As we worked side by side, I felt the familiar warmth of camaraderie return, and I focused on the layers of fondant, rolling and smoothing them over the edges of the cake. But beneath the surface of our banter lay an undercurrent of tension that refused to dissipate. My heart tugged at the thought of Max, his laughter and easy charm entwining themselves with the memories of Elara and me, filling the spaces in my mind and creating a dissonance I couldn't ignore.

Just as I thought we might find our way back to our usual rhythm, the door swung open, and a gust of cool air rushed into the kitchen, carrying with it the unmistakable scent of pine and freshly cut grass. Max stepped inside, shaking off droplets of water from the rain that had begun to fall outside. His dark hair, damp and tousled, framed his face perfectly, a sight that made my stomach flip and my heart skip.

"Am I interrupting something?" he asked, a playful smile dancing on his lips as he leaned against the doorframe, arms crossed.

"Only the delicate balance of my sanity," Elara replied, feigning exasperation but failing to suppress a grin. "But I'm sure you're used to that."

"I can't help it if I bring chaos wherever I go," he said with a wink, glancing at the layers of cake. "What's the occasion? Planning a wedding without me?"

"It's for a friend," I chimed in, my voice a bit too bright, the words tumbling out faster than I intended. "A little something special."

"Special, huh? I'd call it epic. If you ever need a taste tester, you know where to find me," he replied, stepping further into the kitchen, his presence filling the space with an infectious energy.

"Maybe you should start taking notes," Elara teased, her expression softening as she wiped her hands on a towel. "You could use a few culinary lessons."

"Oh, please. The last time I attempted to bake, the fire department showed up." Max laughed, and it resonated like a melody, weaving its way through the lingering tension. "I think I'll stick to my day job."

Elara and I exchanged amused glances, and for a moment, the weight of our earlier conversation felt lighter, as if Max's playful spirit had sprinkled a bit of magic over us. But beneath the laughter lurked a familiar unease, an awareness that the dynamics between us were shifting in ways I could barely comprehend.

THE TASTE OF AMBITION

"Hey, why don't we celebrate your culinary genius?" Max suggested suddenly, his eyes sparkling with mischief. "How about a mini cake-tasting party? Just us three? It could be a great distraction."

I felt a thrill of excitement at the idea, but it was quickly overshadowed by a pang of guilt. "Are you sure that's a good idea?" I glanced at Elara, gauging her reaction, but her expression remained neutral.

"Why not?" she said, surprising me with her willingness. "We've been working our butts off. A little celebration sounds nice."

I forced a smile, pushing down the worry that bubbled up inside me. "Alright, let's do it!" I declared, trying to summon the enthusiasm that I hoped would mask my conflicting emotions.

The atmosphere shifted, becoming buoyant with laughter and shared stories as we worked together to plate the various cakes and pastries. Max busied himself arranging them on a platter, while Elara and I put the finishing touches on our creations. As the cakes began to take shape, so did the camaraderie among us, each slice of frosting and sprinkle of decoration stitching us closer together.

But the ease in the air felt precarious, like a soufflé rising perfectly until someone jostled the table. As I caught Max's eye, I felt a rush of warmth, a spark of connection that made my heart race. But just as quickly, I was reminded of Elara, her unyielding support battling against the flicker of my desires.

"Okay, everyone ready for the grand unveiling?" Max announced theatrically, raising his arms like a ringmaster presenting a circus act. "Let's see what masterpieces we've created!"

"Prepare to be dazzled!" Elara declared with mock seriousness, stepping forward as we placed the platter in the center of the table.

"Or mildly impressed," I added, sharing a conspiratorial glance with Elara that broke the tension momentarily.

Max picked up a slice of the chocolate ganache cake, his eyes lighting up. "This looks amazing. Is this one of your creations, Elara?"

"Of course," she said, her cheeks flushing with pride. "And this is just a warm-up. The real challenge is how well you can resist it."

"Challenge accepted," he shot back, reaching for a fork. "You two might want to get your taste buds ready. I plan to demolish every last crumb."

As we dug into our creations, the flavors bursting in our mouths, laughter filled the air, buoyed by the sweetness that enveloped us. I watched as Elara relaxed, her laughter ringing out like music, and I felt a momentary sense of peace wash over me. But beneath that sweetness lurked the bittersweet reality of my growing feelings for Max and the shadow of Elara's heartbreak, creating a tension that was harder to ignore.

"So, what's the verdict?" I asked, trying to keep the atmosphere light, but a nagging feeling tugged at me, whispering that this reprieve was only temporary.

"It's delicious! You two are killing it in the kitchen," Max exclaimed, his eyes sparkling. "Maybe I should step back from the baking and let you take the reins."

"Don't get too comfortable," Elara teased, nudging him playfully. "Just because you're charming doesn't mean you can escape kitchen duty forever."

In that moment, surrounded by laughter and cakes, I felt the delicate balance shift again. I had opened a door, letting in a breeze of joy while standing on the precipice of something unresolved, something that could tip the scales at any moment. Would the whirlwind of emotions eventually tear us apart, or could we navigate this tangled web without losing everything we had built?

The remnants of our cake tasting lingered like sweet ghosts in the kitchen, the air thick with laughter and sugar, yet I couldn't shake the unsettling feeling that had settled in my chest. Max leaned against the counter, fork poised dramatically as he teased Elara about her overly ambitious decorating skills. I watched them, a smile frozen on my face, the joy in the room only amplifying my internal conflict. How could I bask in this moment of light-heartedness when I felt the shadows of unspoken truths lurking in the corners?

"Alright, Max, since you're clearly the judge of all things sweet, how about you share your thoughts on this masterpiece?" Elara asked, waving her hand over a pastel swirl of buttercream flowers that she had so painstakingly crafted.

"Masterpiece? I'd say it's more of a confectionary work of art," he replied, gesturing theatrically as if he were unveiling a statue in a gallery. "But I'm not sure if I should eat it or frame it. It's a tough call."

Elara laughed, the sound brightening the atmosphere, but beneath that laughter, I sensed the tension that threaded through our interactions. It was a tightrope walk I hadn't asked for but was all too aware of.

"Speaking of tough calls," I ventured cautiously, my heart thumping louder than the mixer whirring in the background. "I was thinking maybe we should discuss... our plans for the wedding? You know, the one we've been gearing up for?"

"Oh, right! We can't forget about that," Max said, abruptly shifting gears, his enthusiasm infectious. "I mean, we have to make sure the cake is the showstopper, right?"

"Right," I echoed, trying to keep my voice steady. The wedding, a celebration meant to bind people together, felt like a mirror reflecting my own disarray. "We need to finalize the flavors and maybe even discuss the layout."

Elara nodded, her brows knitting together in concentration, and for a moment, I saw the wheels turning in her mind, the familiar spark returning. "How about we do something unexpected? Like a surprise flavor? Something to really wow the guests."

Max's eyes lit up. "I'm all in for surprises! What do you have in mind?"

The shift in the conversation was like a breath of fresh air, but even as we brainstormed, the knot in my stomach tightened. I was glad to see Elara regain her passion, yet I knew that my growing connection with Max would soon intrude upon this moment of unity.

"What about a raspberry lemon cream?" I suggested, eager to keep the momentum going. "The tartness could be refreshing against all the heavy wedding fare."

"Perfect! It's a flavor explosion waiting to happen," Max chimed in, clearly excited. "I can already see it now: bridesmaids, groomsmen, all in a sugar-fueled frenzy!"

As laughter erupted again, I caught Elara's gaze drifting away, her smile faltering for just a second. It felt like a small crack in our fragile wall of happiness, and I couldn't help but want to reach out, to bridge the distance that still lingered despite our shared joy.

"Hey, Elara, how about we make this cake a little adventure?" I proposed, an idea blooming in my mind. "What if we host a little cake testing with our friends? We can get their reactions, see what works and what doesn't. It could be a fun night!"

"Now that sounds like a recipe for disaster," Elara replied, her eyes glinting with mischief. "But a disaster I might be willing to participate in."

"Count me in!" Max chimed, leaning closer. "I'm always up for a party."

"Alright then, it's settled! A cake-tasting adventure!" I declared, the excitement bubbling within me. Yet, as I grinned at them, the undercurrent of my unresolved feelings twisted tighter, making it hard to breathe.

THE TASTE OF AMBITION

The days slipped away like sugar through my fingers, and soon the night of our cake-testing event arrived. The kitchen was transformed into a vibrant gathering space, lights strung across the ceiling, twinkling like stars above our heads. Friends began to trickle in, laughter spilling out into the night air as they mingled and sampled our creations.

Elara and I moved in sync, serving slices and taking notes while Max flitted between guests, his charm on full display, captivating everyone with stories of his latest escapades. I caught glimpses of Elara watching him, her smile genuine yet tinged with something deeper—something she struggled to suppress. It pulled at my heartstrings, creating a conflict that felt unbearable.

"Okay, people! Time for the ultimate flavor showdown!" Max announced, dramatically brandishing a fork like a conductor wielding a baton. "Who's ready to declare a winner?"

Cheers erupted, and as the night wore on, the atmosphere thickened with excitement, punctuated by bites of cake and exuberant laughter. I poured myself into the role of hostess, trying to maintain the lightness, but my heart betrayed me, constantly glancing at Elara, then at Max.

"Let's not forget the surprise flavor!" I shouted above the chatter, clapping my hands for attention. "Who wants to try the raspberry lemon?"

"Bring it on!" someone shouted, and I began to serve slices, waiting for the reactions to spill forth.

The first bite was met with a chorus of "ooohs" and "ahhhs." My heart swelled with pride, but as I turned to Elara, her expression shifted, a flicker of something unreadable crossing her face. I felt a pang of regret, wondering if this celebration was a façade, a distraction from the truth we were all avoiding.

As the night drew on, and glasses clinked in cheers, I found myself standing with Max on the balcony, the cool night air brushing against my skin. The city glimmered below us, and I could hear the distant laughter of our friends inside, but my thoughts remained tangled.

"Isn't this incredible?" Max asked, leaning against the railing, his voice a warm, low hum. "I love how we've turned this into something special."

"Yeah," I said, forcing a smile that didn't quite reach my eyes. "It's... great."

He turned to face me, concern knitting his brow. "You okay? You seem a bit... off. Something on your mind?"

"Just thinking about everything," I admitted, my voice barely a whisper. "About the wedding, about us."

"About us?" He stepped closer, his eyes searching mine, the moment heavy with unspoken tension. "What do you mean by that?"

And just as I opened my mouth to respond, ready to lay bare the whirlwind of feelings that had been swirling within me, a loud crash erupted from inside. The sound reverberated through the air, a sickening thud followed by an abrupt silence. Panic surged in my chest, and I exchanged a wide-eyed glance with Max.

"What was that?" he asked, his expression shifting from warmth to concern.

"I don't know, but we should check," I replied, fear gripping my heart as we rushed back inside, the laughter of our friends replaced by an eerie stillness that sent chills down my spine.

As we entered the kitchen, I froze. The scene before us was chaos incarnate: a table overturned, shards of glass scattered across the floor, and amidst it all, Elara was bent over, cradling her arm, a pained expression on her face.

"Elara!" I shouted, rushing toward her, my heart pounding in my chest. Max was right beside me, and the air thickened with urgency.

"What happened?" he asked, his voice steady, though I could hear the underlying worry.

"I—I tripped," Elara stammered, trying to force a smile, but the fear in her eyes was palpable. "I didn't mean to..."

And in that moment, as I knelt beside her, the chaos swirling around us, I realized that the fragile balance I had been trying to maintain was on the verge of collapse. The choices I had made, the feelings I had buried, were all converging in this single moment, threatening to unravel everything I held dear.

"Just breathe," I urged her, my voice trembling. "We'll figure this out. You're going to be okay."

But as Elara winced and the world blurred into the background, I couldn't shake the feeling that something had shifted irrevocably, leaving us all standing at the precipice of change.

Chapter 27: The Heart's Dilemma

The aroma of fresh-baked croissants and coffee lingered in the air, wrapping around me like a comforting embrace as I finished wiping down the last of the countertops in the bakery. The late afternoon sun poured through the large windows, casting a warm glow over the rows of delicate pastries that seemed to beckon to anyone passing by. I sighed, leaning against the counter for a moment, feeling the weight of the past few days settle heavily on my shoulders.

Elara was busy in the back, her laughter ringing out occasionally like a soft chime. I had tried to be the supportive friend she needed after her breakup, stepping into the role of cheerleader as she navigated her heartache. But the more I focused on her, the more I felt the connection I shared with Max slipping through my fingers like grains of sand. I could practically hear the emotional gears grinding every time he walked through the door. His playful jabs and witty remarks had dulled, replaced by a palpable tension that left us both fumbling for words.

It was as if we were marionettes with tangled strings, each pull leading to awkward dances that neither of us wanted to perform. I glanced at the clock, its ticking a steady reminder that time was running out. Max was coming over after his shift, and while my heart fluttered at the thought, it also sank under the weight of my predicament. He had wanted to talk, to unravel the knot of feelings we'd both been trying to ignore, but I knew I was balancing on the edge of a precipice, one that could lead to a heart-wrenching fall.

Just as I set the last pastry box on the shelf, the bell above the door jingled, and in walked Max, his presence commanding attention without even trying. He was dressed casually, his jeans hugging him just right, and his hair tousled in that effortlessly charming way that always made me weak in the knees. But today, there was a storm brewing behind those hazel eyes, clouds of concern flickering across his face.

"Hey, can we talk?" His voice was low, serious.

"Sure, give me a minute to finish up." I forced a smile, hoping to mask the tumult of emotions roiling within me. I busied myself with a few last tasks, all the while feeling the weight of his gaze as it bore into my back.

Finally, I turned to face him. "What's up?"

"Let's step outside." He gestured toward the door, and my stomach flipped at the prospect of stepping into the cool evening air with him.

As we walked out, the soft breeze ruffled my hair, and the fading sunlight painted the world in hues of gold and amber. I couldn't shake the feeling that this was the moment that would change everything. We settled on the steps outside the bakery, the wooden planks creaking under our weight, as I silently willed the words to come, the conversation to flow easily like it used to.

"Things have been... off between us," he began, a frown tugging at the corners of his mouth.

"Yeah, I've noticed." I bit my lip, feeling the urge to reach out and touch him, to bridge the growing chasm. But what would that touch mean?

"I don't know what to make of it," he confessed, running a hand through his hair in that adorable way that made my heart race. "I want to be there for Elara, but it's hard when I feel like I'm losing you."

His words struck me like a lightning bolt, illuminating the truth I had been trying to deny. I opened my mouth to respond, to share my own fears and desires, but just then, Elara's voice broke through the tension like a hammer against glass.

"Hey, do you guys have any extra flour?" she called from inside the bakery, blissfully unaware of the emotional minefield we were navigating.

My stomach twisted. "Yeah, it's in the storage room!" I shouted back, my heart sinking as the moment slipped through my fingers.

Max sighed, leaning back against the steps, frustration etched across his face. "I can't do this while she's around. It's not fair to her, and it's not fair to us."

"I know." I felt a wave of guilt wash over me. Elara needed me, and I didn't want to abandon her. But the look on Max's face made me realize that by trying to help one friend, I was risking another friendship that had become equally important to me.

"I care about you, you know?" he said suddenly, his voice softening, and my heart fluttered at the raw honesty behind his words.

"I care about you too, but—"

"Don't say 'but,'" he interjected, his tone firm yet gentle. "It's not a 'but' situation. It's a 'this is hard' situation."

The tension crackled in the air, a palpable force that pulled us closer and further away at the same time. I wanted to lean in, to tell him everything, to confess that my heart was torn between being the friend Elara needed and the woman I wanted to be with him.

"But..."

Just then, the door swung open again, and Elara stepped out, her hands flour-dusted and a bright smile on her face. "What are you two doing? Planning a secret pastry operation without me?"

Max and I exchanged a glance, an unspoken understanding passing between us. The moment was gone, like a wisp of smoke dissipating in the night air. As I watched Elara bounce back inside, blissfully unaware of the storm brewing just beneath the surface, I felt the familiar pang of guilt twist in my stomach.

THE TASTE OF AMBITION

I wanted to scream, to shake the world and make them understand how complicated it all was. But for now, I settled back into my role, putting on the mask of the supportive friend, all while my heart screamed for the truth I couldn't yet voice.

The following days turned into a whirlwind of flour and fond memories, a steady rhythm that matched the pulse of my heart, caught between two compelling forces. Every morning, the sun would rise, drenching the bakery in golden hues, and I'd find myself staring at the pastry case as if it held the answers to the conundrum that haunted me. The familiar scent of cinnamon and sugar would fill the air, wrapping around me like a nostalgic hug. It was comforting, yet the presence of guilt lingered like a stubborn stain I couldn't scrub away.

Elara was both a balm and a burden. Her laughter would bounce off the walls, momentarily pushing away my worries, but the moment she needed my support, I felt the weight of the world on my shoulders. I tried to be there for her, diving into distractions that could keep her spirits high. We spent hours experimenting with new recipes, creating delicate pastries that could melt in your mouth, and sharing stories over steaming cups of coffee. Yet each smile I painted on my face felt like a masquerade, a cover for the brewing storm of emotions inside me.

One afternoon, as the sun dipped below the horizon, I found myself knee-deep in a new recipe for chocolate éclairs, my fingers dusted with cocoa powder. Elara was scrolling through her phone, her brow furrowing occasionally as she read through messages from her family. The bakery was quiet except for the occasional clink of dishes and the hum of the refrigerator, a serene oasis from the chaos of life outside.

"What do you think?" I asked, my voice a blend of hope and anxiety as I held out a perfectly piped éclair.

Elara took it, her expression shifting from concentration to delight as she took a bite. "This is incredible! You really outdid yourself this time."

"Just trying to distract you from your love life," I replied, my tone light, but my heart felt heavy.

She chuckled, but there was a shadow behind her smile. "I appreciate it, really. I don't know what I would do without you."

"You'll figure it out," I said, trying to keep my tone breezy, but the knot in my stomach twisted tighter. "You're stronger than you think."

She sighed, a mixture of frustration and acceptance. "Maybe. But it still hurts."

I opened my mouth to offer some platitude, but the words caught in my throat. What could I say? That I understood the ache of lost love while standing on the precipice of my own tangled heart? That each time I saw Max, I felt like I was drowning in an ocean of possibilities and guilt? The kitchen felt stifling as Elara's eyes darted back to her phone, scrolling through images of happy couples and wedding bells.

"Do you think I'll ever be happy again?" she asked, her voice barely above a whisper.

The question hung in the air like a thick fog, and I struggled to find the right words. "Of course, you will. You're... you," I said, offering a smile that I hoped looked genuine. "You'll find someone who sees how amazing you are. Just maybe not today."

Her smile faltered, and I could see the shadow of doubt creeping back into her eyes. "And what about you? What's going on with you and Max?"

That simple question sliced through the air, sharp and unexpected. My heart raced, the truth hanging heavily between us. I took a deep breath, deciding to sidestep the issue. "Max is just... Max. You know how he can be."

She narrowed her eyes, unimpressed. "Come on. You two were practically inseparable until all this happened. I can see it in the way you look at each other."

"I just want to focus on you right now," I deflected, hoping to redirect the conversation back to her.

Elara huffed, crossing her arms. "That's just it! You're trying to fix me while your heart is tangled in a mess of its own. Just because I'm a train wreck doesn't mean you have to be."

Before I could respond, the door swung open, and the familiar jingle of the bell announced another customer. I turned to see Max stepping in, his eyes immediately locking onto mine. My breath caught in my throat, and for a moment, the world outside melted away, leaving just the two of us suspended in time.

"Hey, you two," he greeted, his voice warm but cautious. "Smells amazing in here."

Elara grinned, her earlier gloom dissipating like mist in the sun. "Just testing out a new recipe! Want to try?"

"Absolutely," he replied, his gaze flicking to me with a mix of hope and uncertainty.

The air thickened again, the electric charge between Max and me palpable, a live wire that crackled with unspoken words. I watched as he leaned against the counter, effortlessly charming as he picked up an éclair, taking a bite with exaggerated pleasure. "This is fantastic! You really have a knack for this, you know?"

"Thanks," I mumbled, my stomach twisting. The compliment felt like both a blessing and a curse.

Elara, sensing the tension, jumped in. "Maybe you should help her in the kitchen more often, Max. You'd make a great sous chef."

I shot her a warning look, my heart racing at the implications of her words. The last thing I wanted was for Max to think of me in any capacity other than a friend right now.

"Only if it means I get to sample everything," he replied with a wink, causing my cheeks to flush.

As they bantered back and forth, my mind was a whirlwind of emotions. I tried to play the role of the supportive friend, laughing at their playful exchanges, but inside, I was a tempest of confusion and longing. Every laugh felt like a dagger, reminding me of how much I wanted to be with him, yet knowing that my loyalty to Elara weighed heavily on my heart.

Suddenly, the bakery door swung open again, and in walked a couple, hand in hand, their laughter bright and infectious. They made their way to the counter, completely oblivious to the emotional turmoil swirling around us. As they ordered a mountain of pastries, I caught Max's eye and saw something flicker in his expression—an understanding that mirrored my own turmoil.

I leaned against the counter, feeling the distance between us grow with each laugh shared by the couple. I had chosen to support Elara, but at what cost? The heart can only hold so much before it begins to crack, and in that moment, I felt the fissures spreading wide, threatening to break open into chaos. I was standing at a crossroads, and every choice I made would ripple through my life in ways I couldn't yet comprehend.

In the midst of their laughter, I felt the weight of my own silence. The world felt heavy, and yet it was full of possibilities. Would I choose to break free from the chains of guilt and embrace what my heart truly wanted? Or would I remain a loyal friend, treading lightly on the path of uncertainty? As I tried to find my footing, one thing became painfully clear: I was standing at the edge of a cliff, and the leap was going to be anything but easy.

The bakery bustled with life, but inside, I felt like a lone island, adrift in a sea of emotions. As I wiped down the counter, my thoughts swirled like the flour dust that settled in the corners of the room. Max's lingering gaze and the warmth of his laughter seemed like faint echoes of a happier time, a stark contrast to the emotional storm raging in my chest. Each day, the chatter of customers became a soundtrack to my internal struggle. I was surrounded by the sweet aroma of baked goods, yet the bitterness of indecision clung to me like a stubborn shadow.

Elara continued to put on a brave face, often breaking into spontaneous dance while she prepped for the day, her laughter infectious. I admired her resilience but also felt the weight of her heartbreak pressing down on my shoulders. Every time she grinned, a voice in the back of my mind whispered that I was betraying her by even thinking about Max, by longing for a connection that had been simmering beneath the surface.

One afternoon, while we baked together, the kitchen alive with the sound of clattering pans and sizzling batter, Elara turned to me, wiping her hands on her apron. "You know, I can't help but feel that you're hiding something from me."

My heart raced, the blood rushing to my cheeks as I fumbled with a spatula. "Hiding? What do you mean?"

She fixed me with a knowing gaze, her blue eyes piercing through my defenses. "You're a terrible liar, you know. It's written all over your face. It's not just about me anymore, is it?"

"Come on, Elara. I'm just focused on helping you get through this," I deflected, attempting a lighthearted chuckle, but it felt hollow even to my own ears.

"Look, I appreciate that you're trying to be supportive, but if there's something going on with you and Max, you need to be honest with me," she insisted, her tone softening. "You deserve to be happy too."

Her words struck a chord, sending ripples of guilt through my heart. I wanted to be honest, to scream my truth into the air, but the fear of hurting her kept my lips sealed. "We're just friends, Elara. That's all it is."

As if summoned by my inner turmoil, the door swung open, and Max strolled in, his presence immediately igniting an electric charge between us. He held a takeout coffee cup in one hand, the other stuffed into the pocket of his well-worn jeans. "Hope I'm not interrupting anything too serious," he said, flashing that easy grin that had the power to melt away my worries, if only temporarily.

Elara's gaze flicked from me to him, her expression unreadable, and I could feel the weight of her scrutiny. "Just discussing the merits of honesty in friendships," she said, her tone light but laced with something deeper.

"Sounds like a riveting conversation." Max leaned against the counter, his eyes glinting with mischief. "I'd like to hear more about that."

"Nothing to worry about," I interjected quickly, shooting Elara a look that pleaded for her to back off, even if just for a moment. "We were just talking about new recipes and how I need to experiment more with savory options."

"Savory, huh? That sounds... interesting." Max's brows arched, a playful challenge dancing in his gaze. "I'm all for it, as long as it doesn't involve anything with kale."

"Noted," I replied, allowing myself to relax, grateful for the shift in focus.

But as the conversation flowed, the moment I had with Max lingered in the air, like the sweet scent of vanilla that never fully dissipated. I could see Elara watching us closely, her brow slightly furrowed, and for a moment, I worried that the fragile thread we were balancing on might snap.

The days turned into a blur of flour and frosting, and our interactions morphed into a complicated dance. Max would often stop by the bakery, drawn in by the warmth of the oven and the warmth of my presence, while Elara remained oblivious, or perhaps she was just choosing not to see. Each smile he flashed my way felt like an electric shock, igniting something deep within me that I wasn't ready to confront.

On a particularly quiet evening, after Elara had left for the night, I found myself alone in the bakery, the soft glow of fairy lights illuminating the space in a cozy embrace. The scent of fresh-baked bread lingered in the air, wrapping around me like a comforting shawl. I leaned against the counter, my heart racing as I recalled the unspoken words between Max and me.

Just then, the door swung open, and there he was—Max, looking tousled and handsome, as if he'd just stepped out of a daydream. "I brought dinner," he announced, holding up a takeout bag, and my heart skipped a beat.

"You didn't have to do that," I replied, a smile breaking across my face despite the heaviness in my chest.

"Maybe not, but I figured we could use a little fuel to get through the rest of the week," he said, setting the bag down on the counter and pulling out two containers.

As we settled in, sharing food and laughter, the familiar ease between us began to resurface, but there was an undercurrent of tension that neither of us could ignore. I caught him watching me intently, a million unspoken thoughts dancing in his eyes, and the air thickened with possibility.

"Can I be honest?" he asked suddenly, his voice low, and I felt my breath hitch.

"Please do."

"I miss the way we used to be," he confessed, leaning closer, the warmth of his body igniting a spark that crackled between us. "It's been hard for me too, and I can't shake the feeling that there's something more here."

I felt the walls I had built around my heart begin to tremble, the urge to spill everything rushing to the surface. "I feel it too," I admitted, my voice barely above a whisper. "But with Elara... I just don't want to hurt her."

Max's expression softened, a blend of understanding and frustration. "But what about you? What about us?"

His question hung in the air, heavy with implications, and for a heartbeat, I allowed myself to imagine a world where we could embrace our feelings without guilt or hesitation. "I don't know," I said, my voice trembling. "I want to explore this, but..."

Just then, the bakery door swung open again, and Elara walked in, her face flushed with excitement. "You won't believe what I just found out!" she exclaimed, eyes sparkling like stars.

The moment shattered, and the words that had been hanging in the air slipped away like grains of sand through my fingers. As she rushed forward, her enthusiasm filled the room, but inside, I felt a sense of impending doom, a knot tightening in my stomach as I realized that whatever revelation she was about to share could change everything.

Max's gaze met mine, the question lingering unspoken between us, and my heart raced, teetering on the brink of a decision that could alter our lives forever. Elara's words floated in and out, a blur of excitement that I barely registered, but I felt the weight of the moment press down on me. I was caught in a tempest, and I couldn't help but wonder if we were all destined to be swept away.

Chapter 28: The Breaking Point

The bell above the bakery door jingled cheerfully, a stark contrast to the storm brewing inside me. The scent of freshly baked croissants mingled with the rich aroma of dark coffee, wrapping around us like a comforting embrace. Elara and Max arrived within moments of each other, their faces a blend of apprehension and determination. I had arranged this meeting with the fervor of a child planning a surprise party, but as I watched them take their seats, the air thickened with unsaid words and unexpressed emotions.

Elara's fingers fidgeted with the hem of her sweater, a plush blue that seemed to swallow her whole, as if it could shield her from the onslaught of feelings threatening to engulf us all. Max leaned back in his chair, arms crossed, a brooding presence with shadows dancing beneath his dark eyes. The flickering overhead lights caught his profile, etching the worry lines deeper across his brow. He was always the stoic one, but tonight his silence spoke louder than any declaration of love ever could.

"Thank you for coming," I said, my voice wavering slightly as I gestured to the steaming mugs of coffee before us. I had prepared everything—the pastries, the atmosphere, even my heart for what lay ahead. But words, those slippery little fish, seemed determined to elude me at this crucial moment.

"I really didn't think this was necessary," Max replied, his tone laced with the disinterest of someone who had learned to avoid conflict at all costs. "We're adults, right? Can't we just talk this out without a whole—"

"Please," Elara interrupted, her voice thin and trembling like the first crack of ice on a winter pond. "I need this, Max. I just need to know how we're all feeling." Her gaze darted between us, searching for something—reassurance, clarity, perhaps even a lifeline. It broke my heart to see her like this, vulnerable and exposed, as though she were standing on the precipice of something terrifying.

I took a deep breath, the air thick with the sweet notes of sugar and spice, and tried to gather my thoughts. "Elara, I—"

"I can't do this anymore," she blurted out, her eyes shimmering with unshed tears that threatened to spill over. "I'm tired of feeling like I'm losing you both. It's like I'm caught in this... this web of emotions, and every time I think I have it figured out, it unravels right in front of me."

Her words struck me like a thunderclap, reverberating through my chest. I had been so wrapped up in my own tangled feelings that I hadn't truly considered how my confusion was impacting her. I had become a player in a game I didn't even want to be a part of, dragging her and Max into my emotional mess.

Max shifted, the air around him crackling with tension. "You're not losing us," he said, his voice lower now, a soothing balm attempting to wrap around the fraying edges of Elara's heart. "I'm here for you, always. We can figure this out."

"It doesn't feel like that," she whispered, a confession that hung in the air like a delicate piece of glass ready to shatter. "I feel like I'm standing on a tightrope, and one misstep will send everything crashing down. I can't lose you both, and I don't know how to express this without sounding selfish."

Her raw honesty echoed through the bakery, where the soft hum of the espresso machine and the gentle rustle of pastry wrappers were mere background noise to our unfolding drama. The world outside, with its bustling streets and chaotic rhythm, felt far away, a distant memory compared to the emotional storm swirling around us.

"Look," I said, my voice steadier now, rising like a phoenix from the ashes of doubt. "None of this was planned. I didn't mean to create a rift between us, and I certainly didn't want to make you feel inadequate. I'm just as scared as you are."

Max met my gaze, and for a moment, the walls between us felt porous, as if we could share our fears without fear itself lurking in the corners. "It's okay to feel lost," he said. "Life is messy. Relationships are messy. It's part of being human."

Elara wiped away a tear that had dared to escape, a brave little soldier facing the onslaught of her fears. "But what if this mess tears us apart?" she asked, her voice barely above a whisper. "What if I end up alone?"

"No," I said firmly, leaning forward. "We can't let fear dictate our choices. We owe it to ourselves to be honest, to lay our cards on the table and see what we're really playing for."

She nodded, but uncertainty still clouded her features. "So, what do we do? How do we untangle this mess?"

I looked between them, the fire of determination igniting within me. "We start by being brave enough to face our feelings. We share what we want, what we fear, and what we hope for. Maybe we find a way to be together without the weight of expectation crushing us."

The air shifted, the tension palpable but no longer suffocating. The honesty we had been tiptoeing around began to fill the space between us, a tentative bridge formed from vulnerability and trust. It was an unsettling, beautiful thing—this connection forged in the fires of honesty, and I could feel it beginning to bind us together in a way that nothing else could.

In that moment, I realized the journey ahead wouldn't be easy, but we had taken the first steps toward rebuilding what had been fractured. The emotional toll had been immense, but perhaps—just perhaps—the breaking point was also the starting line of something beautiful.

As we sat there, the three of us woven together by threads of history and unspoken pain, the atmosphere shifted like the light filtering through the bakery windows. Golden rays spilled over the table, illuminating the pastries with a heavenly glow, yet the sweetness of the scene was laced with the bitter undertone of unresolved emotions. I could see the worry etched into Max's features, a crinkling of his brow that spoke volumes, and the tension in Elara's shoulders was so pronounced it felt as if they might snap.

"I don't want to make this more complicated than it already is," I began, my voice steadying, feeling the weight of their gazes on me like a warm blanket. "But we can't tiptoe around the truth anymore. I care about you both deeply, and I think we all need to understand where we stand."

Max huffed, a slight laugh escaping him that felt like the proverbial air being let out of a balloon. "It's a good thing I'm not prone to dramatic proclamations or anything." He rolled his eyes, but the faintest smile tugged at his lips, a reminder of the comfort we found in each other's humor amidst the turmoil.

Elara let out a small giggle, a sound so precious that I could almost taste its sweetness in the air. "Dramatic? Max, you are the king of melodrama! Remember that time you tried to bake a soufflé and ended up nearly burning down your kitchen?"

"Hey, that was one time!" He feigned offense, but the light in his eyes showed that he relished the distraction. The shared laughter crackled between us, knitting a fragile bond, reminding me that humor could still dance through our complicated reality. But the laughter faded as quickly as it came, leaving behind a heavy silence.

"Okay, so where do we go from here?" I asked, the words tumbling out before I could second-guess them. "I think we all need clarity on how we feel." The gravity of my request settled over us like a thick fog, both daunting and liberating.

Elara leaned forward, her hazel eyes shimmering with uncertainty yet determination. "I guess I should start," she said, her voice barely above a whisper. "I've always been the glue in our little trio, but lately, I feel like I'm coming apart at the seams. I can't help but feel... unwanted."

"Unwanted?" Max's voice sliced through the air, a fierce protective edge lacing his tone. "You're the one who brings us together, Elara! Without you, we'd be two ships passing in the night."

"Or crashing into each other," I added, trying to keep the mood light, but I could see that her feelings had struck a deeper chord. Elara glanced down at her hands, her fingers tracing the delicate pattern of the tablecloth like she was trying to map out her emotions.

"I know you care, but I'm scared," she confessed, her voice quaking with the weight of her vulnerability. "It's like I'm on this precarious tightrope, trying to keep us all balanced. And I don't know how much longer I can hold on if I feel like I'm losing my grip."

Max reached across the table, taking her hand in his, a gesture so simple yet profound. "You're not losing us. Not now, not ever. But we need to be honest about our feelings—what we want from each other and this tangled mess we've created."

I felt a rush of warmth at his words, an unspoken agreement settling in the air between us. "I've been trying to figure out my own feelings, too. There's a part of me that wants to shield you both from my confusion, but I've realized that's just making everything worse."

Elara wiped at her eyes, determination flaring back to life. "Let's not pretend anymore. I need to know if you two feel the same way I do. Am I just a side character in your story, or am I still the main plot?"

Max shifted uncomfortably, the flicker of uncertainty passing across his face like a shadow. "You're not just a side character, Elara. You're the heart of this story," he said, his voice sincere, almost reverent. "But I think we all need to admit that we're not just friends anymore. There's something deeper, and it's... complicated."

"Complicated is my middle name," I said with a weak laugh, but the gravity of his words hung heavily in the air. "But maybe it's time we all faced that truth. There's a reason we keep coming back to each other despite the chaos. We're drawn together like moths to a flame, and maybe we're too afraid to see where that leads."

Elara glanced between us, the embers of her hope rekindled. "So, what do we do about it? Do we explore this? Whatever 'this' is?"

The question lingered, heavy with the promise of possibilities. My heart raced at the thought, excitement mixed with the fear of what could happen next. "Maybe we start by being more honest about our feelings," I suggested, my voice barely above a whisper. "What if we try to navigate this together, as a team?"

Max nodded slowly, a contemplative look crossing his face. "I'm all in if you both are. I've always cared for you both in ways that defy friendship. Let's be real about it. We're not just friends; we're something more, and we owe it to ourselves to explore that."

Elara's breath hitched, a mix of surprise and relief washing over her. "You mean it? You're both willing to take this leap with me?"

The thought of jumping into uncharted waters stirred something wild and exhilarating within me. "Yes, let's explore this together. We owe it to ourselves to be honest about our feelings and see where this journey takes us."

Elara grinned, the light returning to her eyes, illuminating the entire bakery like the first rays of dawn breaking through the night. "Then here's to navigating the chaos together."

Max raised his mug, and I followed suit, the warmth of the moment enveloping us like a snug blanket. "To friendship, love, and everything in between," he declared, his eyes dancing with mischief.

"To the beautiful mess we're about to create," I added, laughter bubbling up as we clinked our mugs together. The uncertainty still loomed, but it felt less like an impending storm and more like a thrilling adventure on the horizon. As we began to unravel the layers of our relationships, the weight of our collective heartache began to lift, replaced with the promise of something new, something uncharted. We were no longer simply navigating a tangled web; we were embarking on a journey, a dance of hearts learning to beat in sync.

The laughter from our toast faded, leaving a comfortable silence where the weight of our unspoken fears hung thick. Outside, the world continued its frenetic pace, but in this little bakery, time felt suspended. As I looked at Elara and Max, a curious blend of hope and trepidation coursed through me, like the first sip of a strong coffee: invigorating yet unnerving.

"So, we've made a pact to explore this... whatever it is," Max said, breaking the stillness, his voice both teasing and thoughtful. "Now, does anyone have a roadmap? Because I'm notoriously bad at directions."

Elara laughed, a light, tinkling sound that sent warmth blooming in my chest. "Roadmaps are overrated. We'll wing it! The last time we planned something, we ended up burning your soufflé and creating an inferno."

"Let's not relive that glorious disaster," he replied, shaking his head with mock horror. "But you're right. We should embrace the chaos. No more playing it safe. It's time to throw caution to the wind. I mean, what's the worst that could happen? We become a romantic triangle straight out of a bad soap opera?"

I raised an eyebrow, laughter bubbling up. "And we all know how those end—usually in someone dramatically storming out, leaving a glass of red wine to splatter against the wall."

Elara feigned a gasp. "We must avoid that at all costs! I don't have the budget for a wall makeover. My landlord is already raising my rent because I decided to paint my living room flamingo pink."

"Flamingo pink? That's a bold choice," Max said, his eyes twinkling with mischief. "I would have thought you'd go for something more muted. Like 'I'm a responsible adult' beige."

Her mock glare could have melted ice. "Excuse you, but flamingo pink is a statement! A proclamation that I refuse to become a boring adult!"

"More like a cry for help," I interjected, unable to resist the playful banter. The warmth of camaraderie enveloped us, momentarily easing the tension and fear that had weighed so heavily just moments before. We may have been tangled in a web of emotions, but this levity felt like a lifeline.

But as laughter faded, I couldn't shake the lingering unease. What did this new dynamic really mean? As much as I yearned to dive headfirst into the possibilities, shadows of doubt crept into the corners of my mind. What if we shattered the fragile balance we had painstakingly built?

The moment hung heavy, and I took a deep breath, forcing myself to voice the thought that had been gnawing at me. "Okay, but seriously—what happens if this doesn't work out? What if we break each other instead of fixing things?"

Max's expression shifted, his easy smile faltering slightly. "That's a risk we'll have to take. But I don't think we're the type to go down without a fight."

"And fighting sounds exhausting," Elara added, her voice turning serious. "I'm not sure I can handle another emotional meltdown. I've already cried so much, I might as well start carrying a branded tissue box around."

"Emotional meltdowns are my specialty," I admitted with a half-smile. "But maybe we can figure this out without turning every discussion into a soap opera."

She sighed, her fingers nervously twisting the edge of the tablecloth. "Can we just agree that we'll communicate? No more hidden feelings or late-night existential crises alone in our rooms."

I nodded, a warm sense of solidarity blooming between us. "Agreed. Transparency is our new motto. We're in this together, right?"

"Right," they echoed, their voices a harmonious blend that made my heart swell with an unexpected sense of belonging.

As the tension eased, we fell into a rhythm of conversation, sharing dreams and fears, plans and wild ideas. It felt like we were unearthing buried treasures, each revelation a piece of ourselves we had kept hidden. I shared my desire to open my own bakery someday, to turn the joy I found in baking into something more substantial. Elara spoke of her ambition to write a novel that combined elements of her life's chaos into something beautiful, a love letter to the very confusion we were grappling with.

Max, with his artistic flair, described a vision of an interactive art installation that blurred the lines between reality and illusion, echoing our own tangled lives. "I want to capture the essence of connection, the chaos and the beauty of it all. Art is messy, and so are we."

With every exchange, I could feel the boundaries that had previously divided us beginning to dissolve, replaced with a sense of shared understanding. But as the conversation flowed, a nagging sensation still lingered at the back of my mind.

Just as I was about to suggest we make our plans concrete, the bell above the door chimed again, cutting through the comfortable intimacy that had settled over us. I turned to see a figure stepping inside, and my heart plummeted. It was my ex, Jonah.

His presence in the bakery was unexpected, and it felt like a storm cloud had suddenly obscured our sunny moment. Jonah's gaze swept over the room until it landed on me, a mix of surprise and something unreadable flickering across his face. The laughter died on my lips, replaced by a cold knot in my stomach.

"What are you doing here?" I managed to say, forcing my voice to stay steady.

Jonah took a step closer, and I noticed how he paused as if weighing his next words. "I was just passing by and thought I'd stop in. It's been a while."

A tension threaded through the air as I glanced at Elara and Max, their expressions shifting to concern. This was the last thing we needed right now. My heart raced, a chaotic rhythm that matched the swirl of emotions flooding through me.

"Elara, Max," I said, desperation creeping into my voice. "Can you give me a moment?"

They exchanged glances, the worry evident, but they nodded, rising from their seats. The moment they stepped away, the air thickened with uncertainty, leaving me alone with Jonah, the past rearing its ugly head just when I had begun to feel grounded in the present.

"What do you want, Jonah?" I asked, my heart pounding with a mixture of dread and the flickering remnants of affection that had never fully extinguished.

"I want to talk," he said, and as he stepped closer, I could see the tension in his jaw, the way his hands flexed at his sides. "About us."

Before I could respond, Elara's voice broke through from the other side of the bakery. "Hey, is everything okay?"

Jonah's gaze flicked toward them, and in that moment, I felt the walls of my carefully constructed world start to tilt. How could I explain this complicated mess? The new dynamics, the fragile balance we had just begun to explore, all threatened to unravel at the slightest pull.

I looked back at Jonah, the weight of his presence pressing down on me, and realized this confrontation could change everything. And just like that, my heart hung in the balance, poised on the edge of uncertainty.

Chapter 29: Rebuilding Foundations

The city pulsed with life, each beat of the evening air resonating with the laughter of strangers and the melodic chime of street musicians. I inhaled deeply, letting the scent of roasted chestnuts and the distant promise of rain weave through my senses. This place was alive, vibrant, and yet, there was an undercurrent of change rippling through me, something almost electric that felt both thrilling and terrifying.

As Max and I wandered down cobblestone streets bathed in the warm glow of street lamps, the world seemed to fade, leaving just the two of us. His hand slipped into mine, fingers intertwining effortlessly as if they had been crafted to fit together. The simple act of holding hands sent a thrill coursing through me, awakening every nerve. I caught myself stealing glances at him—his sandy hair tousled by the evening breeze, a hint of mischief sparkling in his hazel eyes. I'd always known Max had a way of lighting up a room, but tonight, he was illuminating the very corners of my heart.

"Are we really doing this?" I asked, my voice a whisper against the backdrop of the bustling streets. The question hung in the air, laden with unspoken fears and desires. It felt monumental, the shifting of our friendship, the layers being peeled away to reveal something raw and beautiful underneath.

"Why not?" Max shrugged, a playful grin dancing across his lips. "I mean, have you seen how cute we look together?" He gestured dramatically to a nearby window where a couple was enjoying a romantic dinner, their table adorned with flickering candles and laughter. "We could be that couple. Well, minus the awkward first date jitters, since we already know each other's quirks. Like your slight obsession with pineapple on pizza."

"Hey! It's a culinary masterpiece, and you know it," I retorted, unable to suppress my laughter. The sound felt like music, a bright note amidst the symphony of the night. His teasing was a balm, soothing the tender places still healing from the emotional fallout with Elara.

"But do you really think you can handle my penchant for spontaneous karaoke? I don't hold back," he replied, puffing out his chest in mock bravado, eliciting a chuckle from me.

"Only if you promise to stick to show tunes. I'm not ready for a full-on rock concert just yet," I quipped, enjoying the playful banter that flowed so naturally between us. We fell into step beside each other, our laughter echoing off the old stone buildings as we strolled past a park where families gathered for evening picnics.

As we passed a cluster of blooming cherry blossoms, their delicate petals fluttering down like soft pink snowflakes, Max paused. "Can I ask you something serious for a moment?"

The sudden shift in tone sent a ripple of tension through me. "Of course," I said, my heart pounding a little faster, a hint of apprehension creeping in.

"What do you want out of this?" he asked, his expression shifting to one of genuine curiosity. "With us. I mean, I care about you, and I want to be clear about what we're stepping into."

I looked up at him, searching his eyes for any trace of doubt or hesitation. Instead, I found sincerity that made my heart ache in the best possible way. "I want to explore this, whatever 'this' is. I want to see where it leads," I replied, my voice steady despite the storm of emotions brewing within me. "But I don't want to ruin what we have. Elara is still my friend, and I want her to be okay, too."

Max's gaze softened, and I could see the gears turning in his mind, the empathy reflected in his expression. "I get that. We can take our time, build this thing slowly. I don't want to pressure you either. But just so you know," he added with a teasing smirk, "the karaoke dream is still on the table. You can't back out now."

"Fine, but only if you promise to warm up with 'A Whole New World,'" I countered, laughter spilling from my lips again, banishing the tension that had threatened to strangle us. The night stretched before us, limitless and tantalizing, each moment crackling with the potential of what might come next.

As we continued walking, I felt a sense of hope unfurling within me, a delicate flower pushing through the cracks of uncertainty. Yet, shadows lurked at the edges of my mind. Elara's words echoed softly, reminding me that this journey was fraught with challenges, that the paths of friendship and love could intertwine in complicated ways. I wasn't just embarking on a new chapter with Max; I was also navigating the delicate balance of maintaining my friendship with Elara, who was bravely charting her own course.

We arrived at a small outdoor café, where the scent of freshly brewed coffee mingled with the sweet notes of pastries. Max pulled out a chair for me, the gesture both charming and unexpectedly intimate. "Your order's on me," he said, his smile warm and inviting.

"Only if you let me get the next one," I replied, grateful for this slice of normalcy amid the emotional upheaval of the past few days.

As I sipped my coffee, the rich flavor enveloping my senses, I found myself opening up in a way I hadn't expected. "You know, it's been a wild ride lately. I feel like I'm on a rollercoaster with all these twists and turns." I looked at him over the rim of my cup, trying to gauge his reaction.

"Yeah, life has a way of throwing us into the deep end," he said thoughtfully, the lighthearted banter giving way to deeper truths. "But maybe that's where we learn to swim."

A flicker of understanding passed between us, a silent acknowledgment that we were both ready to dive into these uncharted waters together, with all the uncertainty and excitement that entailed. As laughter and conversation ebbed and flowed around us, I could feel the weight of my past loosening its grip, allowing space for something new, something exhilarating. I smiled, letting the moment envelop me, knowing that I was ready to embrace whatever came next—hand in hand with Max, navigating this vibrant world together.

The following weeks unfolded like the petals of a blooming flower, each day revealing new colors and intricate patterns. I found myself eagerly anticipating the moments spent with Max, as our connection deepened beneath the surface, a shared secret thriving amid the hustle and bustle of city life. Each excursion became a treasure hunt, a quest for small adventures that drew us closer together. Whether we were sipping coffee on a sun-drenched terrace or getting lost in the labyrinthine alleys of the old town, every experience felt like a chapter in a story we were writing together.

One particularly glorious afternoon, we decided to visit a local art fair. The streets were alive with the buzz of creativity, an explosion of colors and textures. Artists displayed their work on makeshift easels, their hands stained with paint and their eyes gleaming with passion. I could hardly contain my excitement as we wandered through the booths, my fingers brushing against vibrant canvases that sang with emotion.

"Look at that!" I exclaimed, pointing at a bold abstract piece splattered with cerulean and gold. "It looks like a celebration of chaos."

Max leaned in closer, his brow furrowed in mock seriousness. "Or it could just be the aftermath of someone's paint fight gone wrong. You know, modern art is subjective," he teased, his eyes dancing with laughter.

I laughed, rolling my eyes at his interpretation. "Or maybe it's an expression of unfiltered joy. You know, capturing the moment of an artist's existential crisis. The paint represents... I don't know, their feelings!"

"Oh, so you're telling me that when I paint the bathroom walls a lovely shade of 'mystery gray,' I'm channeling my inner artist?" he quipped, raising an eyebrow.

"Absolutely! The bathroom is a canvas waiting for inspiration," I shot back, delighted by our banter.

We moved from booth to booth, each artwork sparking a new conversation, revealing layers of our personalities I hadn't fully appreciated before. As we stopped in front of a mesmerizing mural that depicted two intertwined figures reaching for the stars, I felt an unfamiliar flutter of vulnerability in my chest. "This one," I murmured, entranced, "it's like they're connected, yet reaching for their own dreams. I love that."

Max studied it for a moment, then turned to me, his expression softening. "Do you think we're like that? Connected but still finding our own way?"

A weight settled in the pit of my stomach at his words. The idea was beautiful, but it also felt precarious. "I hope so," I replied, my voice barely above a whisper. "But I also worry about losing ourselves in the process."

"I don't want to lose you," he said, the sincerity in his eyes grounding me. "I just want us to keep building, brick by brick, together. Whatever that looks like."

I smiled, warmth flooding through me. The weight of uncertainty shifted into a kind of hope, like light breaking through a thick fog. But as we stepped away from the mural, I couldn't shake the lingering shadow of worry. Elara's words about finding her path echoed in my mind, leaving me to wonder where that path might lead us all.

Later, as twilight wrapped the city in a soft embrace, we settled on a park bench, the sound of laughter and music wafting from a nearby festival. Max leaned back, looking relaxed, his face illuminated by the twinkling lights strung above us. "So, what's next for us?" he asked, a hint of mischief in his tone.

I grinned, loving the way his enthusiasm was infectious. "How about we sign up for a pottery class? I've always wanted to try my hand at the wheel. Just imagine, you could make something so beautiful!"

Max feigned a gasp, placing a hand over his heart. "And ruin my reputation as a rugged artist? I think not! But if it means I get to see your face covered in clay, I might be persuaded."

"Oh, I'll have you know I'm a clay Picasso in the making!" I challenged, laughter bubbling between us.

"Picasso? More like a Picasso-inspired abstract disaster," he retorted, and we both burst into laughter, our voices rising into the evening air. It felt good to be playful again, to allow ourselves to forget the complexities of our lives, if only for a moment.

As the festival unfolded around us, I caught sight of a few friends in the crowd, their faces lit up with joy. They waved at me, beckoning me over. "Hey, let's join them!" I suggested, my excitement bubbling over.

Max looked hesitant, the playfulness in his eyes replaced with something more serious. "Are you sure? I don't want to intrude on your time with them."

"Don't be silly! They'd love to meet you," I insisted, dragging him by the hand toward the group. As we approached, I could see Elara's familiar face among them, her smile bright but her eyes shadowed with unspoken thoughts. A flicker of tension rippled through me as I introduced Max, the very air feeling charged with unacknowledged emotions.

"Hey, everyone, this is Max!" I said, attempting to infuse cheer into the moment.

Elara's gaze shifted between us, and I felt a strange weight settle over the introduction. "Nice to meet you, Max," she said, her tone

THE TASTE OF AMBITION

friendly but lacking its usual warmth. I caught a subtle tightening of her lips, and a hint of concern washed over me. Was she struggling with her own feelings?

"Nice to meet you! Elara, right?" Max replied, his voice steady and inviting, effortlessly breaking the ice. I admired how he remained unfazed, engaging with the group and drawing them in with his natural charm.

The evening unfolded with laughter and stories shared over laughter, yet I could feel the tension simmering beneath the surface. Every joke, every glance exchanged between Elara and me felt charged with implications, unspoken words swirling like autumn leaves caught in a gust of wind. I wanted to confront it, to dive into the depths of our friendship, but it was as if we were all teetering on the edge of something fragile and undefined.

As the night drew on, the festival lights shimmering around us like stars, I sensed that this moment was a balancing act, and the stakes felt higher than ever. The weight of unspoken truths hung heavily, yet amidst the laughter and camaraderie, I could still feel the flicker of hope, the promise of new beginnings waiting just beyond the horizon.

The lingering tension from the festival danced at the edges of my consciousness as the days rolled into one another, each moment with Max feeling like a stolen fragment of bliss wrapped in the comfort of familiarity. We carved out our own little universe amid the chaos, our days filled with laughter and spontaneous adventures. Yet, that familiar tightness in my chest was a reminder that while we were forging ahead, shadows still lurked, especially when Elara was involved.

One crisp Saturday morning, with the sun stretching lazily over the rooftops, I found myself drawn to a quaint little café that promised the best pastries in the city. The scent of fresh croissants wafted through the door like a siren's call, wrapping around me as I stepped inside. Max had agreed to meet me there, and I could hardly contain my excitement.

I took a seat at a corner table, the sunlight streaming in through the window and casting warm pools of light around me. I ordered a chocolate croissant and an espresso, reveling in the anticipation of our usual playful banter. As I waited, I couldn't help but replay our recent moments together—each one was a thread weaving a tapestry of connection that felt as if it was meant to be.

When Max finally arrived, he walked in with an easy confidence, his hair slightly tousled and a teasing smile plastered on his face. "I'm here! I come bearing gifts," he announced dramatically, revealing a box of colorful macarons from a nearby bakery as if he were presenting a prized trophy.

"Is that what it takes to earn your affection? I hope you have more where that came from," I joked, my heart lifting at the sight of him.

"Of course, I'll just keep bringing sweets until you can't resist my charm anymore," he quipped, taking a seat across from me. "But you know, charm has its limits. I mean, you might eventually have to settle for a bag of chips if I run out of options."

"Not chips! Anything but that!" I exclaimed, clutching my heart in mock horror. "I have standards, you know."

Max chuckled, and for a brief moment, the world outside faded. We were in our own bubble, where laughter flowed freely and the complexities of life felt miles away. But as the conversation danced from topic to topic, the atmosphere shifted slightly. I caught Max glancing toward the door, his expression turning thoughtful.

"What's up?" I asked, tilting my head, my curiosity piqued.

"Just... I don't know. I have this feeling we should talk about Elara," he said, his tone shifting to something more serious.

A knot tightened in my stomach. "Do we have to? I thought we were enjoying the macarons, not dissecting my life choices."

"We are, but it's a part of this new foundation we're building, right? I want to make sure we're on the same page," he replied, his sincerity evident.

"Okay, okay," I sighed, reluctantly setting aside my playful facade. "What's bothering you?"

"I just worry about her. I want to be there for you, but I also care about her. I feel like I'm walking a tightrope here," he admitted, his vulnerability disarming me.

My heart softened. I appreciated his willingness to navigate these murky waters with honesty. "I know it's complicated. She's my friend, and I want to support her, but it's hard. I'm trying to give her space to figure things out. But then there's this nagging feeling that we might be stepping on her toes."

Max leaned back, running a hand through his hair. "Do you think she knows how we feel about each other? Or that we're... you know... getting closer?"

"I don't know," I confessed, my voice barely above a whisper. "I mean, I want to tell her, but what if she feels betrayed? I'm still trying to navigate my own feelings. The last thing I want to do is hurt her."

Max nodded, understanding etched on his face. "So maybe we should have an open conversation with her. Clear the air. It might help."

As soon as he spoke those words, a chill swept through me. The thought of laying everything bare was both liberating and terrifying. "You're right. It's just... daunting. What if it blows up in our faces?"

"Well, at least we'll have a front-row seat to the explosion," he replied, a hint of humor cutting through the tension. "But seriously, let's approach it together. She deserves to know the truth, and so do we."

As I considered his words, a surge of resolve washed over me. Perhaps it was time to confront the tangled threads of our lives rather than let them unravel in the shadows. We finished our pastries, the conversation flowing easily again as we crafted a plan to talk to Elara. The warmth of the café enveloped us, but outside, dark clouds began to gather ominously, mirroring the brewing storm within.

Later that day, we strolled through the city, the air thick with anticipation. I could feel the weight of our decision resting heavily between us. The park was filled with families enjoying the last remnants of the day, but all I could focus on was the task ahead. It felt as if we were walking toward a cliff, the ground crumbling beneath our feet, yet I couldn't turn back. I needed to confront this for both Elara and myself.

When we finally reached Elara's apartment, I hesitated at the door, my heart racing. "What if she reacts badly?" I asked, biting my lip nervously.

Max placed a reassuring hand on my shoulder. "We won't know until we try. Just remember, you're not alone in this. We're in it together."

I nodded, drawing in a shaky breath. "Okay. Let's do this."

I knocked softly, the sound echoing in the stillness. Moments later, the door swung open to reveal Elara, her expression shifting from surprise to something more guarded.

"Hey! What brings you two here?" she asked, her smile faltering just a touch.

"We need to talk," I said, my voice steady but filled with emotion. "Can we come in?"

She stepped aside, allowing us to enter, and I felt the air thicken with tension. This was the moment of truth, the precipice from which we could either leap into honesty or tumble into chaos.

As we settled into the living room, Elara's eyes darted between us, an unspoken question lingering in the air. Just as I opened my mouth to speak, the sound of a phone buzzing shattered the silence, cutting through the weight of our impending conversation. Elara's expression shifted, a flicker of concern flashing across her face as she glanced at her phone.

"Excuse me, I need to take this," she said, her voice tight as she stepped away to answer.

Max and I exchanged worried glances, our plans for honesty hanging precariously in the air. I leaned closer to Max, my heart pounding with uncertainty. We were so close to breaking the silence, yet now it felt like everything was slipping through our fingers.

Elara's voice grew faint as she spoke on the phone, her expression shifting from curiosity to alarm. My gut twisted as I tried to make out her words, but the tension was palpable. Then, abruptly, she turned back to us, her face pale.

"I need to go," she said, urgency dripping from her voice.

"Go where?" I asked, concern flooding my thoughts.

"There's been an accident," she replied, her eyes wide. "It's about my brother. I have to leave now."

My heart dropped. The ground beneath us felt unstable, and in that moment, the carefully constructed plans for honesty began to crumble. As Elara hurriedly grabbed her things, a sense of foreboding settled over me, the looming storm now feeling all too real.

"Wait!" I called out, my voice rising in desperation. "We need to talk about—"

But she was already out the door, leaving only the echo of her hurried footsteps behind, while Max and I stood frozen, caught in a whirlwind of emotions. Just when I thought we were finally ready to face the truth, life threw an unexpected curveball, leaving everything hanging in the balance. The world spun around me, and in that moment, uncertainty loomed larger than ever.

The Taste of Ambition

Georgia Hawthorne

Published by Georgia Hawthorne, 2024.

This is a work of fiction. Similarities to real people, places, or events are entirely coincidental.

THE TASTE OF AMBITION

First edition. October 9, 2024.

Copyright © 2024 Georgia Hawthorne.

ISBN: 979-8227256546

Written by Georgia Hawthorne.

Milton Keynes UK
Ingram Content Group UK Ltd.
UKHW020756231024
450026UK00001B/66